UNHOLY GROUND

A Max Steele Thriller

Bob O'Connor

Unholy Ground
Published by ICR Publishing
Atlanta, Georgia 30350

ISBN-13: 9780615845074
ISBN: 061584507X
LCCN: 2013913014
ICR Publishing, Atlanta, GA

Printed in the United States of America
2013 – First Edition

Prologue

Nate "Bull" Sullivan checked his watch again. 12:42am. Something was off. Accountants were never late, even mob dicks.

The cold inside met the chill outside and he shivered. They'd never kept him waiting before. Through his coat he touched the .357 magnum.

A yellow vapor light buzzed overhead. He looked left and right along the wet brick walkway skirting the harbor front, and pulled up his leather collar against tiny ice needles jabbing his neck. Salt wind from the Sound stung his eyes. He'd faced worse conditions late in the season as a University of Rhode Island tight end. His gloved hand squeezed the handle of the silver sided brief case.

Thirty-eight months in deep cover, damn good cover too. He'd sold it well. The upper echelon of the Bente Cartel trusted him, didn't they? He'd earned it. The members knew him. Mario Falducci, a successful stockbroker with lots of high roller clients hungry for rock cocaine. For this undercover operation, he'd become a bunny jumpin' single man who flashed money under female noses until they caught the scent. Eventually, he offered to be Bente's distributor to his circle of clients. No one in the Cartel knew him as the married father of twin boys. No one knew him as a man who compromised himself for a cause - day after day, night after night, and who carried his guilt like a sack of shit around his neck. His partner Max understood. You did it because you can't bust 'em any other way. And by God we've got their asses this time, he thought. I'll be home for Christmas, and my greatest assignment as an FBI agent will be to love my wife, play football in the snow with my boys, and tell my partner of twelve years he's the brother I never had. I've never told him.

A black sedan approached. His muscles tensed. It rolled to a stop twenty feet from him. The tinted glass hid passengers and driver. Nate let out a slow breath. The rear passenger side window lowered, showing the face of one of the Cartel's top men. An enormous hand motioned him to approach. He pushed himself from the railing, shoes crunching snow. "Ehhh Vinnie! Whatcha doin' here?"

The man extended his mitt through the window. "I was about to ask *you* the same thing, Mr. Faldato." He crushed Nate's hand.

Bull winced. "You lookin' to break bones?" Small wonder they call this guy, The Vice.

"Mr. S wants to see you."

"I'd like to." He attempted to get his fingers back. "Give him my regards. But my lady's coming and we're off to her place, know?"

"Boss says it's important. You better come." He released Nate's hand and blood rushed back to the fingers. No good on a trigger right now, even if he could get to it.

"Honest," he said. "Tell the boss Mario says another time for sure." The muzzle of a pistol appeared on the bottom of the window frame like a viper's head. "Get in Mario, or whoever you are."

Bull cursed under his breath, opened the door, and climbed in close to the business end of the Glock 9mm.

"Slide it this way." The man waved the fingers of his left hand toward the silver case.

Slipping the case in between the man's shoes and the back of the seat, Nate eyed him and said, "I'd be careful with that, if I were you." What he didn't say was that ten minutes without hand pressure on the case's handle would detonate its C4 plastic explosive lining.

The sedan pulled from the curb and accelerated. "Mind if I raise the window?" Nate asked. He could turn to the window, slip his hand to the holster and fire backward through his coat.

"Suit y'self," he said. "But first let's have your-"

Nate was already reaching inside two buttons of his coat, his mind running another scenario. He could pull the magnum from the holster and shoot a soup can-sized hole in the guy's chest ….

"Uh-uh," The Vice said, yanking Nate's arm. "Unbutton the coat and pull it away slow."

Nate slumped and opened the jacket, exposing his weapon. The Vice grabbed the gun from its holster and pocketed it. Nate yanked his coat closed and turned to the window. Wet air slapped his face. Tires hissed below. The window rose, and his heart sank.

The sedan turned right along commercial docks wide enough to park two semi-trailers. The causeway lights cast ghostlike shadows on sleeping metal cranes. They turned onto the last dock and drove deep into blackness. The driver killed the headlights. Nate stared into total darkness beyond the windows, thinking about his partner. *I'm sorry, Max. Seriously was damn good cover.*

"Get out," The Vice said.

Bull opened the door and stood. The harbor's foul breath assaulted his nose. He turned toward muted voices whispering in Italian somewhere to his left toward the dock's end. Beside him in the car's dome light, he saw The Vice settling a pair of night vision goggles onto his face. Nate slammed the back door and ran toward the lights in the distance at the dock's mouth. Blinded by darkness, his right foot tangled in something. He fell hard, rolled left and got to his feet again, pumping against the icy wind and regaining speed. Behind him, feet smacked hard and fast.

His legs churned. He could outrun that lard-ass. His left knee slammed into something hard, a bone snapped and he screamed through clenched teeth, hobbling forward. His left leg dragged, useless. From the blackness, a fleshy sledgehammer struck his face, sprawling him.

The enormous hand closed around his upper arm. "This way." Wheezing, The Vice yanked Nate all the way back. His left leg couldn't bear weight, and the pain roiled his gut. Twice he tripped and the ape man held him suspended in the air until he could get the good leg under him.

When they stopped, smoke from cigars burned his nose. A couple of yards from him, he heard a low voice speak, but seemingly not to him. "You have dishonored the Name," came a deep voice in thick Italian accent. "and I been good to you boys."

"Si, maledettamente ragione bastardi barare!" a higher pitched voice said.

"Silenzio Emil," the first one said. The next voice Nate recognized as the Cartel accountant he was supposed to meet. "Honest Mr. S., it's not how it looks."

"Yeah, we were gonna stick him with blank disks and then bring the money straight to you," the other accountant said through labored breath.

"Lies," the deep voice said. "Such respect? Lies to my face?" Silence followed for several seconds. "Pregare."

Two muzzle barrels flashed like camera bulbs. Bodies thudded to the asphalt, followed by gurgling sounds.

"And you, Mr. Mario Faldato," came the deep voice, now directed at him. "Or may I call you Detective Sullivan?"

Bull barely heard his voice. In his mind he hugged a son in each arm and told them to listen to their mother. Then he looked into her face. He stood and she rushed into his arms. He saw his partner smiling in the distance, offering a salute.

Next came the sound of metal crashing through skull bone. He felt the back of his head fly behind him, felt the white heat of a second and third herald of death slam through his chest and out his back. His body slipped away, and he was already rising toward a spectacular light, when the blast from the explosives in the briefcase sent the sedan's roof into the sky like a square rocket.

Chapter One

[26 months later]
Ecclesia Seminary
Kingstown, Rhode Island

Ecclesia Seminary is set on a rise in an otherwise flat section of Kingstown, Rhode Island. The lawns are manicured and bisected by sidewalks and accented by ancient and massive oaks. Sarah watches the wind orchestrate a frenzied dance through the library window, then turns back to her work. Finals are close. Soon. Oh God.

She looks up. Terry is seated across from her, his blonde, wavy hair tousled, his brow furrowed in concentration. She looks down, but then back up again, and watches his lips twitch. Then her eyes move to the hair curling slightly at the neck of his shirt. Her nipples harden and she glances down at her sweatshirt. But then her eyes move quickly back to Terry's neck, his ear lobes, and she feels herself moisten and her lips begin to swell, throb. She crosses and re-crosses her legs, and feels the rush course through her body.

Her eyes close. In her mind's eye, as if observing another, she sees herself standing up, moving around the table, taking Terry wordlessly by the hand and leading him into the stacks where there is nothing but old books. She backs herself into a wall of them, whispering the truth about how she feels about the man who is her best friend, yes, but who has become so much more in her heart. It's become love and she can't lock down her feelings anymore. She stares into his eyes and, tucking her hand into the front of his jeans, pulls him to her. Rises to him. Feels him swell and presses into him. Their lips crush together, tongues exploring feverishly, while she rubs herself back and forth over his swollen crotch. She has told him what she wants. He has answered.

Her eyes pop open. Her panties are wet. She can't breathe. *Sarah! For Christ's sake. You. Are in the Seminary! Library! Get. A. Hold. Of. Your. Self. SARAH!*

"What's up?" Terry said.

"What?" Sarah's eyes dart to his face, then quickly around the room.

"You just, like, said your name really loud." Cocks his head.

Shit! "I did?"

"Did." He nodded, staring. "You okay?

"Course. Why?"

"Your face is really red."

"Embarrassed," she lied. "Duh. Wouldn't you be?"

She stared at her book, but felt him studying her. She looked up.

"What?"

"We've been best friends for two years." Terry said. "I know you, and my bullshit meter's spiking. Wanna tell me what's really goin' on?"

"Nope," Sarah said, looking back at the book. *I'm really red? And I'm probably soaked through my jeans. I'm going to kill myself.*

"Sure?"

"Yep." *Don't even look at the man.*

"Whatever it is, must be important."

You have no clue.

"If I were you-"

"Just let me study, will ya," Sarah said.

"Whoa, fuzzy bunny turns Tasmanian."

"Leave me alone." *Love me Terry.*

"Sure thing. I gotta wrap it up early anyway."

Her head shot up. "I was gonna spring for beer and a slice later."

Shaking his head, "No can do buddy."

"What's up?"

"I got somethin' … um …. It's nothin' really."

"My bullshit meter's spiking," Sarah said, mocking him.

"Yeah, well, what's good for the goose…" He smiled, packing books into his backpack.

"Have fun." Sarah returned her stare to the book.

"Wouldn't call it that … exactly." Shouldered his backpack. "See ya round the cemetery, um, seminary, IQ."

"You said you'd stop calling me IQ," Sarah said.

"I think it's a compliment." Terry said. "To me, it says you're smart."

"You said they call me that because I'm the Ice Queen."

"Another compliment for me." He smiled. "My best friend is the hottest looking woman in the seminary. AND the most untouchable." He stuck out his chest. "Makes me special."

"You're special, " Sarah said, "and it's not a compliment. Get lost."

He waved over his shoulder and disappeared through the door.

She could feel them coming. As soon as Terry was out of sight, Sarah shot to her feet and raced for the bathroom, hot tears streaming from her eyes.

Kingstown, Rhode Island (That same time)

Morning had come without daylight. A violent rain burst from swollen clouds overhead, sounding like fireworks. Vinnie hadn't slept after that. Ten hours and no let up later, sheets of water formed a thick pall over the brown grass separating the lanes leading to and from Roslyn International Airport.

"I can't decide," Emil said from the back of the Rolls, pressing a stubby index finger in his bottom lip with great drama. "Put two in her cunt and one in her head, or slice a wide smile across her throat and watch her bleed out?" He banged ash from his gold-plated crack pipe, dropped more rock in the bowl and returned the pipe to his mouth. His size five shoe rested on his knee as he pulled the Glock 9mm from the shoulder holster. "And should this be a public execution or a private affair?" He threaded the suppressor onto the blue steel barrel.

I ain't dyin' for you today, you little shit. You got that? Vinnie wanted to say it, and then rip the chauffeur's hat from his head, throw it out the window and put these wheels in park. His shoulders slumped behind the wheel and he squinted through the windshield. The sky was as black as his mood. Even with headlights on, he couldn't see more than a few feet ahead. The highway drains had backed up, bilging brown water onto the landscape. Ponds formed between the northbound and the southbound lanes and neared road level. Traffic clotted as large green signs announced the airport exits. Vinnie aimed for the "Arrivals" sign.

From the back seat the high, choking voice said, "Get as close as you can to Baggage Claim."

Vinnie glanced in the rear view mirror. "Close as I can, Mr. Bente." In the back seat, a plume of gray smoke rose from the pipe and spread along the roof. "Are we handicapped today?" Vinnie reached for the rearview mirror hanger.

"Extremely," Emil said. "Get one of the spots down front and I'll limp a little. And park backward in case, you know, we hafta leave quick." Returning the Glock to its holster, he fished his pearl-handled switchblade from a pocket, twirling it in his hand. "And you, my precious Bic," he said, flicking the blade in and out.

Smoke slithered from his lips and lingered around his sunglasses. Sunglasses in the pitch black. *So much stupidity in such a small package.*

The Rolls crept into the parking garage. *No doubt entering my tomb, thanks to you J.R.* He wondered if he should call in, whether this one qualified. His eye caught a flash of chrome. His right foot mashed the brake, and the Rolls lurched forward and slightly sideways. The Dodge Ram in front had an enormous hitch attachment.

"Eh!" Emil said. "Christ, Vinnie, you crazy fuck! All we need today."

The chauffeur's face flushed. "Sorry, Mr. Bente." He could snap that punk like a twig! *Say the word, S ....*

Camera 6-PG swiveled in the Roslyn International Airport's short term parking garage. The camera operator, following instructions from his headset, zoomed in on the license plate of the black Rolls Royce backing into the closest handicap spot. Three seconds later, the camera zoomed back out to watch emerging passengers. He radioed to the lead Bureau car at the airport's exit, "Parked in the garage, sir."

"The fish are swimming into the net," Captain Max Steele said and drew an exclamation point in the fogged window of his unmarked Bureau car. He had headed this takedown operation, eating it and sleeping it, from the day it began over two years ago when his partner, operating under-cover, vanished. Steele's tweed sport coat lay against his sides, exposing a trim midsection and a holstered Glock. Fourteen years working his way through the FBI ranks taught him to avoid the vending machines in the break room. His short, age-flecked, hair spiked wildly in the humidity.

Rain slapped the front windshield. Steele's slate blue eyes squinted right and left. Both unmarkeds were in place, parallel to his and perpendicular to the airport exits. Across the lanes, he could barely see the outline of three more unmarkeds.

He spoke into his handheld. "No mistakes today, ladies and gentlemen. This one's as big as it gets." Lieutenant Bert Higgins nodded beside him and gripped the steering wheel. Steele continued, "On my signal I want all six exits sealed. Do not fire your weapons unless you are in mortal danger. I need these men alive."

Twenty-six months of surveillance and preparation since Bull's death were coming to a head today. They were about to cripple the kingpin cocaine cartel for the entire Eastern third of the United States. He raised the radio to his lips again. "All units confirm the exit lane you'll be blocking."

"Unit One, Lane 6 ...." Each of the agents in the vehicles rehearsed their assignments.

Steele spoke to the airport surveillance team through his bone microphone. "Ladies and gentlemen, you are our eyes. What we see depends upon you. Speak clearly and slowly. Double check the recording decks for fresh disks. There's enough Cartel cocaine coming off that flight to make convictions a slam dunk. But I need this whole show captured, evidence has to be flawless."

"Captain Steele, this is Ramirez in the control room." Steele recognized the voice of the Bureau's surveillance technician. "All cameras operational. My men are at their stations and ready to proceed. I'll stay to troubleshoot."

"No mistakes, Ramirez," Steele said. "We've got a score to settle."

"No mistakes, sir."

Steele leaned back against the headrest and let out a breath. He glanced at Lieutenant Higgins in the driver's seat. It had taken all Steele's strength and resolve to take on a new partner. He hadn't been able to do it for all these years, despite orders from the brass to take on another partner. "You've been thrown into this operation at the tail end," Steele said. "You're replacing a fine agent."

"So I've heard." Bert Higgins' face looked younger than his twenty-nine years.

Steele stared at large bands of water angling down the windshield and his mind began to drift.

Late spring in Rhode Island was the perfect time for a picnic, and Nate Sullivan's back yard was the perfect spot to have it. It was also the perfect place for backyard football. The sun was warm but the humidity had yet to hit. The flowers were in bloom. The pollen was out in full force, and everyone was sneezing. Nate was busy at the grill while Max stood beside him with a cold beer. Nate's twin 10-year-old boys were tossing the football back and forth in anticipation of the big match after lunch.

"You know they're gonna whup us," Nate said, glancing at the boys.

"They always do," Max said, grinning, then growing serious. "You're going to miss them bad."

"You don't even know."

He didn't. He'd never found the kind of life that Nate had with Vanessa and the boys. All this man-on-a-mission shit.

The only silver lining was that he would never be faced with the kind of barrel Nate was looking down now. He glanced at his partner. Tears had welled in Nate's eyes. In all their years as partners, he had never seen that. Nate was one of the toughest sons of bitches he knew. He could walk through hell grinning and eating an ice cream cone. He had saved Max's six countless times. Max had returned the favor a few times as well because sometimes Nate didn't have enough fear for his own good.

"Have they set the date for your disappearance, surgeries, other stuff?" Max said.

"Yup."

Max raised an eyebrow.

"If tell, hafta kill," Nate said and smirked, wiping his eyes quickly.

Max nodded. "Miss you already."

"Shut the fuck up and drink." Nate cuffed him on the shoulder.

Max took a long pull. "Vanessa good?"

"Define good." Max studied the hot dogs, turned two, then looked back to Max and sighed. "She hates me. She loves me. She doesn't get it. She gets that I gotta do it. I am what I am and that's all that I am."

"I think that's the most words you've said at one time. Ever." Max took a step back, dodging the incoming expression of male love.

"We're gonna Trojan Horse these fucks." The look in Nate's eyes could melt bronze.

"We are."

"What kind of putz would call himself *The Shark*?" Nate grinned over the top of his beer bottle.

"One with a very small dick."

Nate snorted beer through his nose. It sizzled and spat on the grill.

"That's it," Max said. "I'm NOT eating."

"It'll burn off."

"Boys?" Vanessa said, approaching with armloads of potato salad, beans and cole slaw.

"Us?' Nate said.

"You see any other boys?"

"No Ma'am" Max said, grinning, watching one of the twins catch a deep pass.

It was brief, but the look of pure love that flicked between husband and wife both touched Max's heart, and cored it. It was everything he wanted but never found. His childless divorce from his college sweetheart and Bull's marriage to Vanessa came in the same month. As best man, Max cried hot tears of hope for Bull and his bride at the wedding, and later stinging tears of despair for himself. Now, all these years later, moments like these were reminders that there was still only rice paper over the loss and loneliness. The super cop thing was at best a distraction, a way not to feel.

Max shook himself back to the present and glanced into the next seat. New man. Bull was gone. The Cartel ripped him away from them all. Wife, sons, partner. Today was payback.

"A few hours from now," Max said, "we'll go find us a nice bottle of champagne and drink to Bull's memory."

Emil Bente opened the car door and stepped out. The leather soles of his shoes ground against the concrete floor of the parking garage and echoed against the low ceiling. He turned up the collar of his raincoat and bent to admire himself in the side mirror. Vinnie walked around the front of the car and stood in front of him with his hand outstretched.

"Back in the car for a minute," Vinnie said in a commanding tone, immediately wishing he hadn't said it that way. Emil stiffened, his eyes narrowing behind his sunglasses. The man in the chauffeur's hat towered over Emil's fat, five foot four inch frame. Vinnie's wrestler-sized arms strained the seams of the double-breasted suit, and his thick neck billowed over the starched collar of his white shirt. It was a Rottweiler facing a pug.

Easy, Vincente. Don't blow your cover. "I'm sorry, Mr. Bente," he said aloud, tipping his hat. "I get nervous around airports. Security is so tight, and cops are crawling all over the place." Vinnie felt the tension ease, slowly at first, and then in one rush.

Emil laughed too loudly. "I'm in good hands, eh?" He opened the back door and slid over to let Vinnie sit beside him. Vinnie closed the door and reached an empty palm in Emil's direction. Emil poked his fat hand into his own double-breasted suit, and came out with the Glock and extra clip. Vinnie stuffed them under the front seat, and reached out for more. From the back pants pocket came the switchblade and from the ankle a seven inch Bowie knife.

"Anything else, Mr. Bente?" His tone was better this time. "I know you don't want to attract the wrong attention in there."

Emil patted his pockets. "I feel naked without my traveling companions."

"How 'bout the .38 in the back?"

With feigned irritation, Emil parted his jacket in the back and pulled it from the concealed holster. He snatched the sunglasses from his face, the smile long gone. "Take good care of my friends, Vinnie. I may be back for them in a minute." Emil returned the glasses to his face, smacked open the opposite rear door, swaggered toward the access lanes to the terminal.

Vinnie watched him step in front of a shuttle van. The driver slammed on his brakes, his lips moving inside the van. Emil flipped his middle finger and kept walking, checking his Rolex at the curb. Vinnie checked his watch too. Ten minutes before Nina's flight touched down.

Emil disappeared through one of the glass terminal doors. Vinnie shook his head and rubbed his face. *Guy's a walking Molotov cocktail. Bravado mixed with venom, added to hate, shaken in a container filled with cocaine courage.* He reached for the cell phone and dialed the number he'd memorized before leaving Connecticut six months ago.

Two rings later a gnarled voice said, "Yes?" The scrambler made it sound like someone was speaking and gargling at the same time.

"This is 3-3-20," Vinnie said. "I need to speak with S."

"About?"

"J.R ...."

"I'll get him."

Vinnie drummed his fingers on the wet roof of the Rolls. The cell phone crackled to life.

"S," the gargling voice said, "Is this an emergency?" The tone was hard as deep ice.

Vinnie had been instructed repeatedly about cell phone procedures. Don't call unless it's an emergency. Always assume you are being intercepted. Say nothing that reveals identity or message content.

"J.R.'s real hot and real high, Mr. S, and you know what that usually means."

"How hot?"

"Serious hot."

Vinnie heard something slam. "You sure?"

"He's carrying the stiletto again, Mr. S." Vinnie squeezed his eyelids. "But I've got it for the moment." He heard an exhale in the receiver.

"And the arrival?" S. asked.

"Any minute."

"Can you see from your desk?"

"Yes. Across the lanes, 40 feet. I can be there in three seconds."

"Good. Has he figured you?"

"No sir, Mr. S." Vinnie mashed a hand on the top of his cap.

Silence followed for several seconds and Vinnie wondered if S had hung up. Finally S spoke, softly at first, and very slowly. "If he brings dishonor to the Name, you know what to do." A different silence told him the line was dead.

Vinnie flipped the cell phone closed without lowering it from his face It was seconds before he realized he wasn't breathing. He opened his mouth and pulled wet air into his lungs, then lowered his head to the hood. His hat fell to the concrete. "Great," he said. "Just fucking great."

The secure satellite phone sounded loudly in the car and both men jumped. Higgins grabbed it, his crew cut glistening with gel and sweat. Steele smiled from the passenger seat toward his new, and overly eager, young partner.

"Higgins." The Lieutenant listened, and then passed the phone. "Headquarters with a cell phone intercept from our friend in the parking garage."

Steele put the sat phone to his ear. "Steele. What've you got?" He listened, and then snapped his fingers toward Higgins. "Write this down." Bert grabbed paper and pen from the back seat as Steele repeated the message aloud.

"Nice work, Timmons." He closed the phone.

"The first number identifies the person and his rank in the family. In this case, Vincente Bontecelli, aka Vinnie The Vice, is the highest-ranking non-blood family member. So he's 3."

"Vinnie Bontecelli calling from Rhode Island," Higgins said. "And they don't know we're listening."

"We think they suspect it, but they have no idea how sophisticated our surveillance is or how easy it is to monitor their chatter." Steele looked at the pad of paper. "Sounds like they are watching J.R. pretty closely. Hell, everybody's watching him. Us. Them. And he's clueless."

Higgins looked at his writing. "And S? Who's he?"

"We're ninety percent certain it's the boss. The head of the family, the guy I was telling you about earlier. A Mr. Emil Bente. Why he goes by 'S' has been debated. We're pretty sure it comes from his nickname in Connecticut. The Shark. But there may be another reason."

"What's that?"

"Because there is more than one Emil Bente." He let the words sink.

"How's that work, Captain?"

"About five months ago there was a rift in the Cartel. We'd been watching and collecting evidence for a little over five years at that point. As elementary as they are with their codes, they are masterful at covering tracks, leaving no trail. The Bente Cartel makes people and product disappear. We planted a man as close to them as possible and slowly moved the sting operation forward. Then one day, about two years ago, he vanished. So did the two Cartel men he was dealing with. Gone without a trace." He stopped for a moment. "He was my partner, and a top agent."

Higgins nodded quietly. After a few seconds, Steele continued. "We needed to re-group and get back after them, but we were left waiting for a break. It came when J.R. and the Shark had some kind of power struggle. It was hard to piece together because all the cell phone chatter stopped. Five months ago. Just like that, as if the whole organization was gagged.

"J.R. somehow convinced Vinnie to go with him to Rhode Island to set up a whole new shop. Strangest thing we've ever seen. I can't imagine they went with the Shark's blessing."

"I'm surprised the Shark didn't make old J.R. disappear," Higgins said.

"If it were anyone else, he would have. Count on it. Nobody slaps the Shark in the face, takes his right hand man, and sets up business in a neighboring state, unless he has a serious death wish."

"But J.R. did. Got away with it too."

Max nodded. "Probably the only one who could. J.R. is not just any thug, Bert. He is the other Emil Bente. Number One and Number Two in the family are father and son. This operation is about breaking Number One's organization by taking out his top people, beginning with his son and right hand man. As soon as this rock lands in their hands, down they go."

Chapter Two

Rosalyn International Airport

"Hope you're feeling better," the lead flight attendant said to Nina Ondolopous as she exited the plane. The woman nodded, smiled uneasily, and exited the jet way.

"Poor thing threw up three times," she said to the first assistant. "Says she's pregnant."

They continued to wish departing passengers well.

Nina glanced quickly for signs pointing to Customs and Baggage Claim. Her muscular, sun bronzed legs moved freely beneath a blue flowered sundress. She slipped a breath mint into her mouth and rolled it on her tongue and followed the crowd along the terminal corridor, watching the signs. Her dark brown hair brushed her shoulders, her puffy eyes darting right and left, then over her shoulder. She clutched her large straw shoulder bag.

The sign overhead announced restrooms and she slowed. Two men in suits rushed up behind her, towing roller bags. They walked quickly, grinning. She didn't hear them until they were at her left shoulder. "Hah!" the man closest to her shouted and burst out laughing. Nina jumped, her free hand clutching her chest.

She rushed into the women's room and entered the first stall. Hunching over the shoulder bag, she closed her eyes, panting.

She heard footsteps at the restroom entrance. The clack and scuff of thick heels echoed near the sinks. Water ran for a long time, followed by the sound of tearing paper towels. Nina waited for the clacking to fade toward the exit, but instead, the heels moved down the row of stalls and entered one. She tensed as if an intruder had invaded her home. Fear gripped her mind and squeezed. She rocked back and forth, fingernails pressing into moist palms. "Stop it," she mouthed silently.

A wave of nausea wrenched her gut. Nina pulled her shoulders back and took a deep breath. Keep moving girl. Follow the plan. Only days away from the finest rehab facility money can buy. Turning the shoulder bag upright, she opened its wide mouth and pulled three red mesh grapefruit sacks onto her lap. Each held a dozen large plastic Easter eggs filled with the purest Colombian rock cocaine American dollars could buy. The night before her flight, Nina had sealed each egg at the middle with clear packing tape, filled the sacks and taped a rainbow colored piece of paper over the bag's label area that read, "Gifts for the Children." She rolled the sacks over on her lap. No leaks. She rehearsed one last time: if Customs asks, it's rock candy from the Colombian hill country. Lame, Nina.

Returning the sacks to the shoulder bag, she stood and unlocked the stall. Glancing toward the only other occupied stall, she rushed into the herd of overnight bags and strollers pressing toward Customs.

The stall door in the women's room swung open and the occupant walked rapidly behind the blue flowered sundress. Camera C-2 swiveled. Around the corner at Customs, cameras C-3, C-4 and C-5 readied for her arrival.

Long lines swelled behind Customs. She would be easy to miss. Terry Woodrow searched the faces clogging behind the Customs turnstiles. His heart pounded in his chest.

"I'll be wearing a blue flowered sundress," Nina had told him on the phone yesterday, "and no panties. Be ready for me." He heard himself groan and he pulled at the bottom of his Ecclesia Seminary sweatshirt.

He stood on his toes, craning his neck right and left, even though his six feet two inch frame gave him a clear sight line to Customs. He pressed his hands onto his corduroys one at a time. Sweat reappeared on his palms as quickly as he wiped them. The single, long-stemmed rose trembled in his hand.

"You are my eyes, people," Steele said. "Talk to me." He felt like a blind-folded skipper steering an aircraft carrier. "O-5, you got him?"

Camera operator five zoomed on the man in sunglasses and black over-coat standing outside customs. "Got him," Operator five said, staring at his screen. In the surveillance room, the bank of monitors traversed the length of the control room. Nine operators guided their cameras, panning and zooming. Ramirez paced behind them like an expectant father.

"Good," Steele said. "Stay on him. As soon as she passes the rock to him, we move in."

"O-3," camera operator three identified herself. "Subject is passing by me and heading into O-4's territory."

"Where is she in the Customs line?" Steele said.

"O-4. Almost to the table," Operator four said. "O-3 is getting the close-ups. I'm panning the big picture."

"Good," Steele said.

"You sure they know to let her pass?" Higgins asked.

"I'm sure," Steele said for the second time.

"O-6. Vinnie Bontecelli is in the archway by the access lanes, smoking. Looks like a cat about to pounce."

Steele blinked. "Is he armed?"

"Can't tell, sir."

"O-9, can you pick him up from across the lanes?" Steele asked.

The camera mounted above the terminal entrance swiveled. "Yes, but no close-ups."

"0-4," Operator four identified himself. "Subject is at the Custom's desk. Passport's out." He laughed. "This chick's nervous."

"I cannot believe she would try something this stupid," Steele said to his partner sitting next to him. "She wouldn't have made it three seconds from the jet way if we hadn't rolled out the red carpet."

Higgins nodded. "And swept it. Either she thinks we're lead heads, or she's got over-sized balls."

"Eggs," Steele said, not looking at him.

"What?"

"Eggs, not balls." The two agents smiled and the tension eased.

It would not last.

"Welcome home, Miss Ondolopous," the Customs agent said, stamping Nina's passport and handing it back to her. Nina stretched tight lips into a smile, nodded and held the passport in her hand, inching forward in the line. She was not about to put it in the shoulder bag. She peeked over the right shoulder of the person ahead of her in line, searching for his face, feeling her heart race. Nina saw the rose first. Terry held it to his nose and looked through his long blond bangs at her. She ran into his arms, finding his lips. He lifted her out of her sandals and twirled her around. Her stomach lurched, but she smiled and kissed him again, pressing against him as her feet returned to the floor.

"Let's get out of here," she said.

"I missed you so bad," Terry said, giving her the rose.

"I can see that." She smiled toward his corduroys and rubbed his stomach up and down. They moved toward Baggage Claim, hardly noticing the mash of people elbowing, crowding, and grumbling in the mad search for luggage. Smiling into each other's faces, they passed within inches of a small man wearing sunglasses and a black trench coat.

"I'd like to ram the stem of that rose down your throat!" Emil whispered. His jaw muscles flexed. He forced fat hands into empty raincoat pockets, clenching and unclenching his fists. He would kill the blonde guy quick; watch his blood spurt from a sliced throat. But he would kill Nina slow. A joyless grin slid across his face.

He stepped behind the square pillar, watching them pass toward Baggage Claim. Then he turned and marched through the far exit.

"Oh shit," Max said, "You can't be serious!" He smacked his forehead with the handheld radio. He pressed the ear bud hard, listening to the camera operators describe the scene, move by move, second by second. "I don't believe it," he said, his mouth open, his voice a higher pitch. "O-3, tell me again. O-7, you got them in Baggage Claim? O-4, stay on Bente. O-6 and O-9 stay on Bontecelli."

Camera operator three spoke. "Subject through the turnstile, jumps into the arms of the young blonde guy holding a rose. They're kissing. They head to Baggage Claim arm in arm."

"O-5, what was Bente doing while all this happened?"

"Nothing, Captain," Operator five said. "But I zoomed in and he was purple as a stroke victim."

"Bet!" Steele said.

"Yeah if I were him-" Operator five said.

"You're not him, so save it," Steele said, throwing the handheld between his feet on the floor. He cocked his head toward Lieutenant Higgins. "This is rich. Some kid with a rose just blew our sting to bits!"

"Want me to alert the team on the ground?"

"I'll do it." Steele grabbed the radio from the floor and spoke into it. "We may have to abort, but hold your positions for now." He turned to Higgins. "It may not be over yet. If Bente grabs the rock, we are back on track and we take them all down. If not …." Steele cursed again. So much work. For nothing. His mind filled with Nate's face and a memory flashed. Football in his hands, twin boys dragging from each leg, Nate fell, on purpose, two feet from the makeshift goal line in the back yard. While Max chastised and taunted his teammate, the former All-American halfback with the enormous neck, Vanessa laughed from the porch and shook her head.

Shifting in his seat, Steele felt the lump harden in his throat. *I'm trying, Bull.*

Emil Bente, Jr. sat outside on a metal bench midway between the two terminal exits and lowered his head when Nina and Terry emerged. He watched Terry leave her at the curb and cross to the temporary parking lot. Emil got up and walked along the inside edge of the sidewalk until he was behind her.

"Ain't that sweet!" he said. "He's gettin' the car for you."

Nina jumped, whirled and grabbed her stomach as he stepped closer. "Emil! What are-"

He sprang toward her, throwing his stubby index finger to her nose like a punch. Nina's head jerked, her eyes wide. "You're dead," he said through clenched teeth. "You hear me? Dead!" Emil felt a large hand on his shoulder. He spun away from Nina and stumbled into Vinnie's heaving chest.

"We have to go right now, Mr. Bente." The huge man in the chauffeur's hat nodded toward Nina and lowered his voice. "Later. We'll deal with this later."

Emil jerked his shoulder free from Vinnie's grip, turning to face Nina again. "You won't live long enough to smoke that shit in your bag." He spun and walked beside Vinnie, leaving Nina frozen at the curb.

Steele could not believe his ears.

Operator nine continued. "Do I follow Bontecelli and Bente or stay on her?"

"Did Bente grab the shoulder bag?" he asked.

"No."

"Then stay with the eggs! O-6, get Bente and Bontecelli in the garage."

"Got 'em," Operator six said.

"O-9," the operator identified herself. "The eggs haven't left the shoulder bag. Subject is still at the curb."

"And lover boy?" Steele could not contain the tone.

"No sign of him. Still getting the car I suppose."

"You don't suppose! You just describe, OK? I'll do the supposing!" Max heard his voice, too loud, too angry. "Sorry, Nine. Seeing them slip the net makes me crazy." He leaned his head against the dash.

"Understood, Captain," Operator nine said.

"O-6. Bente is putting weapons in his pockets. Bontecelli is talking. Lots of hand gestures."

"Talking Bente down," Steele said. "Six, does he look like he's getting ready to come back to the subject?"

"Not so far."

"We going to let the rock walk?" Higgins asked.

"Guess we have to," Steele said. "Maybe the hand-off is happening elsewhere." He raised the radio to his cheek. "Units One, Two and Three, I want you through the exits and staggered on the other side, ready to follow. Units Four and Five, stay with me. We'll catch up. All units: follow, but not too closely. They will be easy to lose in this rain."

Operator nine continued. "Car stopping in front of subject. It's a yellowish brown VW Rabbit. Stopped. Luggage is in. Bag with the eggs is in…. Subject is in…. Car is leaving."

Higgins shook his head. "I thought we'd be spinning handcuffs about now."

"0-6. The Rolls is leaving the garage."

"0-9. Rabbit's out of range."

Steele pressed the radio to his lips. "Easy now, Units Four and Five. Let them pass." The Rabbit inched along lane three toward the payment booth. Less than two minutes later, the Rolls joined the queue in lane three, two vehicles behind Terry and Nina.

"Let the Rolls get to the booth, then we go," Steele said into the radio. Higgins started the car. Steele turned a weary eye on him. "That's what it's been like, Higgins, for two years now. Three steps forward, two and a half back. Sometimes three and a half."

"We'll get 'em, Captain." Higgins turned the windshield wipers on high.

Steele nodded, his eyes fixed on the windshield. "For Bull."

Chapter Three

A bitter rain lashed the Rabbit from Roslyn International Airport to Nina's flat. Oil rising from the asphalt slicked the road. The highway drains backed up, bilging brown water into the median between the northbound and the southbound lanes of I-65. Traffic crawled ahead and behind. With no sunlight, Terry noticed the transition from day to night only by his watch. Useless all day, the headlights were doing a job of making the pelting drops look like cascading yellow ice. He couldn't see anything. He glanced at Nina, who continued her silent stare straight ahead.

Her olive skin, a gift from Greek ancestors, had turned rich shades of brown. His mind flashed back to Baggage Claim where she had pressed herself hard against him, whispering, "Let's hurry and get home. I want you." He had run all the way to temporary parking. But he picked up a different Nina at the terminal curb. Quiet and withdrawn, she had not said more than three sentences in the past hour.

"You sure you're okay?" Terry asked again.

"I'm fine."

"You want to stop and get some-"

"I'm fine," Nina said.

He blew out a large breath.

"I know Sarah's anxious to see you," he said. "Maybe we can grab a suds and a slice with her after Patristic Class Monday."

Nina nodded, her hands rubbing her stomach.

"You feel okay?" he asked.

"Not really."

"Jet lag?"

"I guess. Want to go home and sleep."

Um. That wasn't the plan.

For the next hour, Terry's volleys of conversation hit a brick wall like paint splashed from a bucket. Maybe she was worried about being behind in her classes. Nah. Nina seemed content to go to class, party all night, and barely pass. Maybe it was jet lag. He saw the exit into Kingstown. "Almost there."

"Great," she said without enthusiasm, adjusting the passenger side mirror.

"Hey, that's for the driver."

"You can't see anything," Nina said. "And a woman has the right to a mirror at all times." A smile flickered across her face.

"Wonder of wonders, an honest to God smile," he said.

The exit ramp emptied them into clotted traffic on Bradley Street. Terry leaned forward. He had four blocks to get into the left lane. At one lane per block without a working turn signal, it would be a challenge. He mashed the emergency flasher button and prepared for battle.

The old Nina would be teasing him. His baby poop brown Rabbit was an endless source of jokes at Ecclesia Seminary. "Looks like a bunny with the runs," one comic said. Terry was grateful for any kind of wheels. Besides, sometimes maneuvering in traffic could be a breeze. Having nothing to lose if he smashed into another vehicle, the BMW, Lexus and Mercedes owners gave him room like he was the Chief of Police.

At Fiddler, Terry turned left. The road rose steeply. Halfway up, the road turned from asphalt to dark red brick. Two hundred feet onto the brick, Terry turned right onto Elm, a long street lined with massive trees. High branches extended toward one another, giving the feel of passing through a long green tunnel. Antique street lamps with black poles and white globes punctuated the tunnel and cast soft light. A beautiful New England street, especially at twilight when the street lights first came on. Tonight, the street looked weathered and lonely.

Nina's apartment was a converted third floor of a massive white colonial. Stairs tucked between the garage and the back of the house led to a separate third floor entrance. The owner, Dr. Nettie Spruill, lived in the first two floors. Both she and her late husband, Harvey, were retired professors at Ecclesia Seminary. One year before his sudden death from a heart attack, he and Nettie renovated the home and grounds. Their passion was gardening, and elaborate beds of roses, adorned the front and sides of the house.

Harvey's death made the lead page of all the local newspapers, not because of his preeminence as a medieval historian, but because he died in front of a packed auditorium during a mock jousting session with one of the students. It had been a well-rehearsed demonstration, complete with real swords and armor. Uncannily, as the student closed for the kill and thrust the sword along Professor Spruill's heavily armored side, Harvey collapsed with a deafening clatter and lay motionless. With the bewildered student looking on, the auditorium erupted in thunderous applause. What a show. So realistic! Harvey never moved again.

That was ten years ago. Nettie collected enough life insurance to maintain the house and grounds, but she eased the financial strain by boarding a student every year on the third floor. She also befriended James Harne, retired professor of systematic theology, who shared her passion for the flowerbeds. Harvey had spared no expense planting hundreds of rose bushes, and Nettie was determined to keep them alive in his memory. She and James spent time every day weeding, pruning, and grooming.

James, who never married, who never had time for a wife during his successful teaching and publishing career, retired from Ecclesia eight years ago. Like a steam locomotive deprived of wood, James's life coasted to a lonely, devastating stop. He had always been busy, with students, with research and writing, and with endless faculty meetings. After retirement, the walls of his one bedroom flat on Cambridge Street closed in on him. A trip to the farmer's market became the highlight of the week. He went to the market every Sunday afternoon at the same time. One Sunday, while thumping watermelons to get the perfect one and sniffing cantaloupes for the unmistakable aroma of ripeness, he renewed his acquaintance with Nettie.

She made it look like a chance encounter, but in fact she had watched James for five weeks, trying to place the familiar face. On week four, it clicked. Years before, Harvey had consulted James about the best rose bushes to buy. James even stopped by one afternoon to observe the planting and to offer advice.

Nettie remembered him saying roses were a lot like women. They were beautiful at the head, but less so as one moved down the stem, a stem that got thicker with age. He went on to say that, although they insisted that they were delicate, if you dared touch one, you were likely to bleed. Moreover, he said, you could spend your entire life trying to take good care of them and never know from one year to the next if they would still be around.

Harvey had thought the remarks hilarious. Nettie had thought them chauvinistic, but something about the twinkle in James's eye stayed with her. She had remarked to Harvey later that James knew a lot about roses, but wondered if he knew much about women.

The James she renewed acquaintance with at the market was still the kind man who knew his roses, but the twinkle was gone. His dull eyes were vacant as an abandoned barn. Nettie took him on as a project, though she never told him so. It would be seventeen months of Nettie's TLC before the twinkle reappeared. Nettie counted.

Over the succeeding last handful of years, she and James had become inseparable. No one knew when James's apartment lease expired, but one day he was at 312 Elm Street for good. To inquiring neighbors, Nettie called him her gardener and reasoned aloud that, with a house this big, why not let him sleep in the back guest room? However, the guest room appeared untouched from one grandchild's visit to the next, and no one except Nettie knew exactly where James slept.

Last year, Nettie noticed another change in her twinkle-eyed gardener. James was getting confused. A few months ago, she sent him to the market. No more than ten minutes at a leisurely pace from the house, he always walked. Four hours passed and he did not return. Nettie was about to call the police and report him missing when James appeared at the kitchen door. He was pale, sweat racing in streaks down his face, his shirt sticking to his chest and back. His breath came shallow and fast. When he saw Nettie, his eyes filled. Nettie clutched him, wrapping him in her arms. He was trembling. "It's all right, darling," she whispered. "You're home. Safely home." Nettie trembled too.

About a month ago, James tried to run off the student, Nina, living on the third floor, despite having known her for months and on several occasions enjoying iced tea with her and Nettie on the garden swing. The morning he stopped her in the driveway, his face was taut, his words coming quick through clenched teeth. "Who are you and what do you want?" Nina's eyes widened, but her recovery was remarkable. "It's me, James. I live here, and I want to go to my room." He looked troubled, and not completely convinced, but he stepped aside and Nina passed. Instead of going to her apartment, Nina opened the back door, found Nettie and reported the incident. She nodded her head. "Nothing is forever," she said. "Life is loss. I learned that a long time ago. You get what you always wanted, and then you lose it piece by piece." Nettie rested her head on Nina's shoulder and sighed. "James's latest loss is his mind, poor soul."

Terry parked on the street directly in front of 312 Elm and shut off the headlights.

Nina put a trembling hand on Terry's forearm. "Maybe we should wait until tomorrow afternoon for ... you know."

Terry slumped over the steering wheel. I knew it. The thought of not holding her naked body was physically painful. "What happened? First you say you want me and now you don't."

"A lot has happened," Nina said. I need a fix!

"Like what?"

"I don't want to talk about it here," Nina said, glancing in the side mirror.

"Then let's go upstairs and talk about it."

"We'll be fresher tomorrow and we'll make wild love all afternoon."

"That sounds good," Terry said, looking at her in the soft light from the streetlamp.

"Besides, you have your Sunday duties tomorrow morning and need to rest."

"Maybe you're right," he said. "It bothers me sometimes anyway."

"What bothers you? Being with me?"

He felt her eyes scan him.

"No. When I'm sitting there in my robes listening to George Fields drone on and on about nothing."

"The Rev. Dr. George Fields?" Nina said.

"aka Boss to Seminarian Assistant, yours truly."

"He's a bore."

Terry nodded, his words accelerating. "And so I flip through my Bible and invariably I end up reading a 'Thou shalt not do anything' passage. And I start thinking about you and the night before, and about how tired I am most Sunday mornings because I couldn't leave your arms or even rest in them."

"So it's my fault?"

"No," Terry said.

"What then? You feel guilty?"

Terry's chin rested on his chest. "It's more than that. I look at the black robed man in the pulpit, and I cannot find a single thing in common with him. He's a stick-up-the-ass, prima-donna Presbyterian minister whose pomposity and politics have earned him the Senior Pastor's position of the Chapel congregation - and soon the Dean's position at Ecclesia." Terry could hear his heart above the rain pelting the Rabbit's roof.

"He's a fourth generation Presbyterian minister, like you." Nina said. Terry stiffened. "I'm sorry," she said.

28

"No, you're right, unfortunately." The son of Rev. Samuel Woodrow, the grandson of Rev. Markus Woodrow, and the great grandson of Rev. Elijah Woodrow, he was one year away from being the fourth successive Woodrow to enter the ministry.

"The family pressure began early, especially from Dad and Grandpa," Terry said, speaking to his hands. "They dogged me all through high school and college." He saw his mother's face. "It's your choice," she had said in the driveway the day he left for seminary, but it was clear by the averted eyes and clasped hands that she didn't believe it any more than he.

Terry felt his face muscles tight against his jaw, his hand squeezing the steering wheel knuckle white. "I'm nothing like George Fields," he said. "But the wheels are in motion. The conveyor belt is moving. First I get out of this cemetery – excuse me, seminary."

Nina's smile revealed her perfect teeth. "You like saying that."

"I feel dead here," Terry said. But then once I get out, the creaking, molding, oldies of the Presbytery lay hands on me. And ... poof. I'm a minister." Pain from blood forced from his hand caught his attention and he let go of the wheel.

Nina's smile flickered like a candle flame in a gust of wind, and then disappeared. "You hate thinking about it," she said. "Ever since I've known you. It follows you." She glanced over her shoulder and then took his right hand in both of hers.

"My God, Nina, you're shaking."

"I just need some sleep. " she said. "Go on."

Terry sighed. "During the week, I sit in class and wait to get out of this God-forsaken seminary. You know how it is."

"I don't dread it like you do."

"That's because it's different for you. You're not ordination track, inching toward the "minister" cage like the rest of us." He looked up to see – what? Sadness?

"And dread is a good word," Terry said. "That's how I feel sometimes about the whole dying, gasping for breath, desperately-trying-to-reinvent-itself

Church. I dread giving my life to it." He flicked his head, "Why are we talking about this now?"

"You need to get it out," Nina said.

"No I don't," he said, but he knew she was right.

"I sit in those church services, Nina, and I want to be somewhere else, anywhere else. I want to look at my watch to see how much longer I have to endure it. But I can't look at my watch. That wouldn't be spiritual." He raised his nose and feigned his best highbrow. "One doesn't dare give the impression that one is aware of the passage of time - or the drag of the service." He wadded his fist and slammed it against the steering wheel. A large dark vehicle with its headlights off turned left onto Elm and parked in the blackness between streetlights.

She stroked the back of his hand. "You feel a trap about to spring," Nina said more as a question than a statement. "You don't have to do it, Terry."

"Do what?"

"Walk into the trap. Get ordained. Become a minister."

"Yes I do," Terry said. "I'm what they call a legacy. My father and grand-father expect it. The Presbytery expects it too. They point to guys like me as living proof that their feeble, atrophied denomination will continue generation after generation." He looked at his hands. "Most of the time I can deal with it, but Sunday morning is the worst. I sit up front in my robe trying to look … God, I don't know, ministerial, whatever that means." He grabbed two fists of his blond hair. "And I realize that the trap has already snapped, and I'm the mouse pinned by the neck." He shuddered at the image. "And I can't move, Nina. I can't even look at my watch, for Christ's sake."

A hiss, soft at first, grew louder and Nina looked through fingers of water on the windshield. A car approached from the other end of Elm, its head-lights splattering fractured light into the front seat. The car splashed past and continued to the end of the street three hundred yards behind them. Nina watched it pass and then eyed it in the side mirror.

Terry leaned toward her. "And so I run … in my mind. I run and I find you and you open your arms to me."

"You find me," Nina said. *I have four lines on a mirror in the bathroom upstairs! That'll hold me.*

"Yes."

"And you want me again."

"I want you and me, us," Terry said.

"You want me right then." He heard Nina's breath quicken. *Gotta get upstairs.*

"Yes, even then, and I can't think about my duties."

"You need me." Nina shifted in the seat and leaning toward him, tucking one leg underneath the other. The dress hiked. Terry's eyes riveted to her thigh.

"Say it," Nina breathed into his ear. "Say you need me."

"I need you."

"You need me and you want me."

"Yes." Terry's heart hammered.

"You want to take me." She put his hand on the inside of her thigh. "Come upstairs for a minute."

"For a minute?" Terry watched her mouth.

"For a long minute."

He grabbed the door handle like a man snatching a fly from the air.

"Put it over there by the closet," Nina said. "I'll deal with it later." Terry propped the large blue suitcase against the wall. He shook like a dog, amazed at how wet he got in the short sprint from the street, and looked around.

"I need to use the bathroom," Nina said.

"Great, I'll go with," Terry said, smirking.

"Don't think so perv," Nina said, shutting the door and locking it.

Same apartment, one large room and a bathroom, a thick striped poncho and large sombrero draping the wall. A cluttered coat rack listed in the corner. A leather bomber jacket and a dark gray backpack hung from two of the rungs, a leopard patterned bra from the third. Terry liked that one.

Nina returned, sniffing, and began pulling the window shades around the room. The tricky one was always the window above the headboard. She kicked off her sandals and stood on the bed, walking unsteadily across the mattress.

"I could tackle you right now," he said.

She whirled and took a long step toward him. "Don't you dare!" The straw shoulder bag bounced and toppled mouth-first from the end of the bed. Terry jumped to catch it, and missed. Three sacks of eggs, a magazine and a hairbrush spilled onto the round rag carpet. Nina lunged for the bag and landed halfway off the mattress. She stretched toward the sacks, but Terry grabbed the one nearest him.

"What's this?"

"I'll get them," Nina said, sliding the rest of the way off the bed.

"Presents for the Children," he read. Nina put the other two sacks into her shoulder bag and reached for the one in Terry's hands. He jerked the bag out of reach and smiled. "What children?"

"I found rock candy made by the Colombian mountain people."

"Rock candy? Don't I get some?" He turned the red fishnet bag over in his hands and the plastic eggs rattled. When he looked up, Nina's stare was hot stone.

"It's for Easter," she said, her hand outstretched.

"Oh, so on Easter I get some?"

"Damnit Terry. It's not for you."

"Don't be so touchy!" Terry placed the bag into her outstretched hands and quickly withdrew his fingers.

"It's for the children." Nina returned the third sack to the shoulder bag and walked to the closet. She set the bag in the closet and closed the door.

"But you don't have children." He saw her flinch. Her eyes flamed and he knew he had pushed the game too far.

"It's for the married students' children, okay? Now can we talk about something else?"

"I'm sorry. I was just playing with you." He walked to her and propped himself on the closet door with his right arm. He nuzzled her shoulder. "I'm a jerk."

"You are." She punched him softly in the stomach. He kissed her neck and felt her relax. Their lips found each other.

"Let's go to bed," he said in a low whisper.

"You mustn't stay long, lover. You need to concentrate tomorrow. Isn't it the bread and wine thing this Sunday?"

He jerked his head back. "The bread and wine thing? I've never heard Holy Communion described that way, even by you Low Church nondenominationals. It's the Body of Christ, for God's sake." Instantly, he regretted saying it. He felt his face burn.

"I don't have the right church words, is all, " Nina said. "Tease me and you'll wreck the mood."

"Sorry."

She leaned into him. "Still, you mustn't stay too long Terry."

"Shouldn't be too bad tomorrow," he said into her hair, "even though it's Palm Sunday." He didn't want to think about it. "George is preaching. I'm only reading Scripture and setting the Communion table." He pressed himself against her and stroked her waist and side. They shuffled backward together to the end of the bed and fell in a tangle of arms and legs.

Nina rolled him onto his back and propped herself over him. Her hair fell like curtains on either side of his face. "Tonight the body of Nina," she whispered. "Tomorrow the Body of Christ." She ground down hard onto him while lifting the dress over her head, revealing a perfectly bronzed and completely naked body. Terry heard an animal roar erupt from his chest, and he rolled her off him onto the bed, and leapt to his feet. He was out of his clothes in two seconds, and sprang onto her, and into her. They grunted and bit and licked. Finally, Nina arched her back, bit her lip and nearly squeezed Terry out. She screamed, and then he was back in, growling like a werewolf until he collapsed onto her breasts, spent and panting.

Chapter Four

Ecclesia Seminary
Residence of the Assistant Dean

The Study was Reverend George Fields's sanctuary from people who annoyed him, and most people annoyed him. Two years ago, he took the telephone out. Calls were coming at all hours of the day and night. Staff and faculty wanted the Assistant Dean's input about this administrative matter and that trustee decision. Usually the caller's purpose was to cover their butts and could have waited for normal office hours.

Most nights George kept the study door closed, since Hilary Fields topped his "Most Annoying" list. His first year of marriage to her was heaven. The last nineteen had been hell. Tonight he left the door open, listening, and waiting.

He heard the faint ringing of the kitchen phone downstairs. Jerking himself from the wooden swivel chair, he caught his balance on the large oak desk and hurried barefoot toward the sound. Halfway down the hall, the ringing stopped and he returned to the study door. Hearing his wife's heavy footsteps on the stairs, he stepped backward into the study and tiptoed to his desk. Hilary appeared in the doorway. "It's your boyfriend." She glared at him with fists on wide hips.

"I asked you not to say that again."

"What am I supposed to think, George? He calls almost every night, and you grab your jacket and rush to his house."

"He's my friend."

"I used to be your friend, and I've been a good friend. Wife too."

"Yes you have," George said. "We wouldn't be where we are today if it hadn't been for your political and ecclesiastical savvy." He was sick of stroking her bloated ego.

"Quite so," Hilary said, tipping her nose. It reminded George of a ship's prow.

"Now see here George, you stay over there for hours on end doing God knows what with each other. You come home exhausted, shower and pass out."

He felt his face flush. "Can I go to the phone, or are we going to rehearse these dance steps one more time?" Not wanting any more questions, he brushed past her in the doorway and padded toward the stairs.

"It gives me no pleasure, believe me," Hilary said to his back. He didn't believe it. "George Fields, you would do well to remember that I don't share. If I'm not enough for you, then you jolly well better go without. We've come too far and waited too long for your appointment as Ecclesia's Dean to have you – literally – screw it up. You will not wreck this opportunity, for yourself or for me."

At the top of the stairs, he called over his shoulder, "For the last time, Hilary, I'm not sleeping with Lawrence. Jesus, let me answer my phone call."

"And for God's sake wear a condom!"

Downstairs at the far end of the house, he pushed through the swinging kitchen doors, reached for the receiver on the counter, and tried to shake off Hilary's bile. "Brother Lawrence. How's the fine friar this evening?" George imagined his chubby friend lounging on his brown cushioned couch in front of the stone fireplace, his rotund stomach rising and falling at eye level.

"I'm waiting for you honey," Brother Lawrence said.

"Stop that." They laughed.

"You're not my type anyway," Brother Lawrence said. "I don't go for boys."

"You don't go for girls either," George said.

"That's why I raise sheep."

"You are a sick man, Lawrence."

"Don't knock it 'til you've tried it."

"Thanks, I'll pass." George felt his lips twisting.

"Nina's back," Lawrence said.

"How'd you learn that?"

"I have friends in high places."

"I thought she wasn't due until next week, George said. "Ash Wednesday, wasn't it?"

"Thought so, but she is back."

George smiled. "We've missed her."

"We have indeed."

George was certain HE had missed Nina more than Lawrence. "Things will be a little easier from now on. What time is it?"

"Nine-thirty," Lawrence said.

"If I get the signal and can get some tonight when I lock the Chapel, I'll come over. If not, it will have to be tomorrow after church."

"I'll be waiting," he said.

George replaced the receiver and reached into the liquor cabinet. Bourbon splashed on the kitchen counter as he poured his glass full. His hands trembled. He stood at the sink and waited.

"I said get closer," Emil said through the blanket of thick smoke filling the back compartment of the Rolls.

"Yes sir, Mr. Bente." Vinnie pulled away from the curb on Elm Street with the headlights off, hoping to avoid hitting one of the parked cars. The Rolls crept forward a hundred feet and returned to the curb in the blackness between two street lamps. They were less than a hundred and fifty feet from 312 Elm. In the rear view mirror, he glanced at the young man through the torrid haze and his mind flashed to the night the kid was born. From the womb, Emil had been smaller and paler than most of his family, attracting a name from his older sisters that would stalk him the rest of his life. Runt.

Every day, in one way or another, the boy screamed for respect. He seldom got it. His insistence that Vinnie call him "Mr. Bente" started after the two arrived in Rhode Island to set up shop. He demanded that his new clients do the same. Vinnie was still getting used to saying it. At first, it made him smile. Not anymore.

Both men watched the windows of Nina's flat. All of the shades were pulled except one.

"I was the good guy, and this is how she repays me." Emil said. He coughed hard and tapped his crack pipe into the metal urn. "First I give her a dime a week. Give it to her. Then she says she needs two dimes a week to share with her seminary friends. So I give her two dimes." It was the second time through this conversation.

Vinnie turned in the front seat and peered at Emil through the darkness and smoke. "You were the good guy, Mr. Bente."

"You got that right. Never saw any money for it after we got back from Vegas. But do I pinch her sweet cheeks over it? Never."

"Never, Mr. Bente."

"Never. Then she has to have her space, her own place, for appearances she says. The seminary princess can't be seen with the likes of me."

He pointed a stubby finger toward Nina's windows. "Do you know who's paying for that little whorehouse up there?"

"You are, Mr. Bente."

Emil nodded. Vinnie heard a click and strained to see Emil's outline through the smoke. The sharp point of the switchblade squeaked against the glass, and Vinnie's eyes fixed on the large blade. Emil moved it in small circles and stared toward Nina's flat.

"Ungrateful slut," Emil said. "Look at that." Vinnie spun around and stared through the rain soaked windshield at the apartment. Two shadows moved and disappeared when the light went out. "I'll kill them both." Emil said.

"I wouldn't go up there, Mr. Bente," Vinnie said.

Emil leaned forward, the switchblade still in his hand. "I wouldn't be offering unwelcome advice, if I were you." His eyes glowed hot in the dim light, and Vinnie wondered if Emil would turn his rage on him.

"You're right, Mr. Bente. I'm sorry."

The sound of an approaching car interrupted them. It moved slowly toward them from behind. Both men stared out the back window, the black tint making it difficult to see. From the side mirror, Vinnie saw the headlights.

"I don't like it," Vinnie said barely above a whisper. "Too slow."

When Vinnie saw the silhouette of a rack of lights atop the vehicle, his heart skipped.

"Cops," Emil said.

"I see them," Vinnie said. "Disappear." Emil lunged to the floor. Vinnie lay across the front seat below the window line. He waited, hearing the car close. A second later, the patrol car was beside them, and a second after that directly in front of them. The sound grew fainter, fading to a quiet sizzle. He sat up.

"Jesus," Emil said.

"Seen enough, Mr. Bente? We should go." The rain had slowed, and the hammering on the roof softened to a steady tap. He heard Emil get off the floor and return to the back seat.

"We ain't goin' anywhere until somebody pays. In blood."

Vinnie winced. "I know you're upset, Mr. Bente, but – "

"Upset? Upset?" Emil pointed toward the dark windows of Nina's flat, his voice rising to a squeak. He shook the switchblade toward the apartment. "That guy's up there doin' my wife!"

Terry had rolled away from Nina on the bed. She moved closer to Terry and touched his cheek, pressing her naked body against him. "What's wrong?" she said. "Wasn't I good enough for you?"

"You've got to be kidding. You're the sexiest thing on legs." He stared at the wall.

"But you always turn away from me. After.... Afterward."

When Terry didn't respond, Nina said, "You scare me when you're quiet."

"I don't know. I'm sorry."

"Feels like you're far away, like you've already left," Nina said. She stared at the back of his head in the darkness. "I'm trying to understand, Terry."

"I am too," Terry said. *For God's sake, Terry, you ought to want more than her body. You're such a dick.* Seconds and silence filled the room.

"You want children?" Nina asked.

"Someday."

"Someday after I've agreed to become the Reverend Terry Woodrow's dutiful wife?"

He sighed. "I wouldn't want you trapped too. Besides, I know you can't have kids." Terry remembered the night Nina told him through tears of a botched abortion three years ago that left her sterile.

"Apparently I can."

Terry's heart stopped. "You're not pregnant!" he said, sitting bolt upright.

"Apparently I am."

"You sure?"

"I flunked an EPT in Columbia."

Terry wanted to scream, "Get rid of it!" His lips didn't move. He wanted to say, "I'll pay for the abortion." He was silent. He wanted to whisper, "I don't love you." He didn't.

Nina broke the silence, sitting up but not looking at him. "Don't worry. I won't say anything to the Presbytery. Your ordination is safe. But you'll have to pay. I was thinking five thousand."

"Dollars?" Terry eyes bulged. "Where am I going to get that kind of money?"

"That's your problem." Her voice was different, suddenly hard and cold.

Terry dressed in the dark without another word and left. He was shaking before the night's chill worked through his clothes. Rain on his face mixed with the tears. He got in his car and drove away.

A hundred and fifty feet behind him, a switchblade twirled silently in a small, fat hand.

At 10:55 pm George Fields's beeper vibrated against his side. He slapped it to eye level and pushed the button. No number, only the word, "Call." He hurried from the kitchen to the master bathroom and brushed his teeth, looking at his face in the mirror. Ever since his 50th birthday four years ago, the wrinkles had come to stay, and they had brought friends. Extra skin sagged beneath his chin. He stood straight, lifting his jaw and forcing some of the jowl to disappear. Not too bad for an old guy. He remembered the kisses from her young lips on his neck and his pulse raced. "Call."

George found shoes in the walk-in closet and carried them to the end of the bed. Hilary was propped with pillows at the opposite corner reading. She wore the gray sweat suit to bed, again. Her short-cropped, blond hair lay flat against her scalp, revealing gray roots. George noticed that the hair growing out matched her sweats, but he didn't dare make the observation aloud.

He turned his back to her and sat on the bed, working the laces loose on his left shoe.

"Guess I'd better lock the Chapel."

Hilary glanced up from her book and looked over dark rimmed half glasses. "You're going to get wet," she said. And how!

He smiled. "I've got some last minute details to attend to, palms to put out. I'll try not to wake you when I get back."

"Thank you," she said.

His shoes laced, George returned to the kitchen.

The brownstone sat several hundred yards behind the main quadrangle and left of the Chapel, having housed several distinguished Assistant Deans in the past centuries. It was a mammoth structure, much more than Hilary and George needed or used. It was a long walk from the bedroom, but it afforded lots of telephone privacy. George dialed, glancing over his shoulder and walking to the corner of the kitchen furthest from the swinging doors.

"Hi baby," George said when she answered.

"Hello lover."

"You know where to find me," George said. "I'll be waiting."

"I have presents for you."

"You are the only present I need."

"Say you need me," Nina said.

"I need you, Nina. I'm going to kiss you all over. And then –"

"Show me, lover. I'll be there in ten minutes."

George's heart beat hard against his shirt as he replaced the receiver. He grabbed his raincoat, slipped out the kitchen door into the night, and paused to let his eyes adjust. Some nights were darker than others, and tonight was darkest.

There were no lights in back of the seminary. Usually, he carried a flashlight, but tonight in his haste, he forgot it. He walked carefully along his driveway to the fire lane.

He locked the Chapel several nights a week. The other nights his assistant, Terry Woodrow, locked up. The fire lane curved in a tight horseshoe around both sides and the back of Ecclesia, turning upward at the left edge of the Chapel and upward again at the right edge of the administration building. A straight section of lane connected the bottom of the horse-shoe with Spelkin Lane, running past George's driveway beneath the faculty parking lot.

The Chapel's white spire was invisible without moonlight and so were George's feet beneath him. He found the stone stairs rising between the Chapel and the administration building and he climbed them to the side entrance. The latch was cold to the touch, but it opened easily. Inside, George hurried to the main entrance at the front and locked it.

He flashed on the lights for an instant to ensure that no student had fallen asleep in the sanctuary, as had once happened. The student locked inside woke at 3 am and opened the alarmed doors to leave. The entire campus went into a spin. Lights flashed, sirens screamed, police and fire trucks came, and an angry Dean had scolded George about being more careful. After that, he always checked.

He flicked the lights off and hurried down the stone steps to the grotto beneath the sanctuary. It was a small round room with a few wooden chairs and hardcover Bibles. On the east wall a simple wooden cross hung two feet above a thin table with votive candles. Tonight there were none to blow out and total blackness enveloped him as he closed the door. George removed his raincoat, then his shoes and socks, and then his pants and underwear. He felt for one of the wooden chairs. With a large breath he sat and waited.

Moments later, he heard the grotto door handle turn. A figure slipped in and closed the door, putting something on a chair behind him to his right. George's shirt stuck to his chest and his breath came rapid and short. A familiar hand touched his shoulder. He heard footsteps move in front of him and felt bare skin brushing his thighs. The light fabric of the sundress pressed against his nose as Nina straddled him and kissed her way down to his lips. He tasted cocaine on her tongue and smelled it on her breath. She'd been sampling their supply. With one motion, the sundress was no longer between them. "I've been waiting for this," she said as she knelt before him and slowly pushed his knees apart.

George's breath came deep and hard. Nina was still straddling him backward on the chair, rhythmically rising and falling onto him. "I wanted to thank you properly for sending me on the mission trip," she whispered.

"You're doing just fine," he gasped, his chest heaving. He closed his arms around her waist and pressed himself into her again, nuzzling her breasts. With a shudder, it was over. She kissed the thinning gray hair on top of his head, wondering why older men made love so differently from younger men. She wanted to ask him, but thought it might lead to questions she didn't want to answer.

"And now for your next present." Nina stood, sweeping the sundress from the floor over the top of her head. She lit two candles. The flames glowed bright above the red wax and the room gradually brightened. George found his clothes and dressed while she grabbed the shoulder bag and pulled a chair in front of him. They sat so their knees touched. Carefully, as if handling a baby, she took the grapefruit sacks one by one from the shoulder bag and placed them on his lap.

"Mission accomplished," she said smiling. "Thirty-six orbs of raw pleasure."

George's eyes were as wide as his grin. "And for you, no more sneaking south beyond the railroad tracks for our supply."

"I will not miss that," she said. Her mind flashed to Emil and her stomach tightened. "But I've missed our nightly rendezvous at Lawrence's. You two are going to love this stuff."

"Any trouble?" he asked.

Nina hesitated. How much should she tell him? If she told him about the airport and Emil, he would find out about her affair with Terry and maybe even about the marriage to Emil. George could be a rattler if provoked. At the very least, he would find a way to ruin Terry's career, and one of her sources of income would dry up. Still, shouldn't he know about the danger that Emil might seek revenge? Maybe he knew already. She had been buying rock from Emil for over a year with their money, and George was no stranger to Emil's temper.

"Does Emil know you're back?" he asked as if hearing her thoughts. Nina's eyes met his. She hoped he couldn't read them.

"Probably. You know Emil," she said, nauseous again.

"I do. We need to be careful, all three of us."

"It's late and we should get home."

She took his left hand in hers. Her fingers toyed with the wedding ring shining in the candlelight. She looked up.

George watched her. "I don't love her. You know that."

"I know." Nina returned his hand to the grapefruit sacks on his lap. "You two are each other's ticket to the top spot in this place."

"Hilary wants it more than I."

"You want it too."

"I want you," he said, reaching for her.

She brushed his hands back. "You just had me."

"I want you again."

Now. She needed to hit him with it now. Her heart beat fast in her chest. Follow the plan. She hesitated. Maybe tomorrow. Her heart slowed. "George, will you keep the eggs for me, for us I mean?"

"Sure, I ... I guess, but where?" She could see he had not thought about it.

"Put them in your trunk or something, or leave them here somewhere safe, and tomorrow get them to Lawrence's house."

"You don't want any of it, for emergencies?"

She smiled. "Leave me one egg and take the rest.

"Okay." He opened one of the sacks and put an egg into her shoulder bag. "You go first and I'll clean up a little," George said, gathering her into his arms. "I'll take good care of you," he said, growing serious. "The more power I get, the more you'll have at your disposal."

Nina's eyes watched him. "And then if Hilary gets sick…."

"Mysteriously," he said.

"Of course. Mysteriously …"

He let go of her, spread his arms wide and laughed. "Then all this will be yours."

"Is that a proposal?

"What, for marriage? I hardly think that's in the cards, Nina."

She returned his smile with a stare that grew colder by the sentence. "So I'm good enough for you in the dark, but not in the light. Your harlot in the shadows. Is that it?"

"I would have said 'mistress,' not 'harlot.'"

"The difference being…?" Nina felt her cheeks burn.

"It's the only offer on the table," George said. "Look Nina, sweetheart, how did we get talking about this?"

"What if I don't want it?"

"Want what?"

"The only offer on the table," she said, mimicking him.

"You do."

"Perhaps." She looked away, her stomach queasy and shaking.

"You need to get some sleep, and so do I."

"So your harlot is dismissed?"

"It's not like that."

She turned to the door. *Now, Nina. Do it now.* Her hand stopped on the handle, and she turned back. "There is one other thing before I go," she said, hearing the change in her voice. "Just one little problem." She paused, feeling George's eyes on her face. "I'm pregnant with your baby." His mouth dropped open, the candle flame licking the rim of his lips and the side of his face. She felt his heat from across the room. Her body said run, run away, but instead she glared at George, determined to see her plan through.

"What are you talking about?" George was on his feet, snorting like a bull. His eyes narrowed and he started toward her. "You're lying."

"Stay back. You're scaring me."

"You're scaring me," he said. "Tell me you're kidding, lying, anything." He grabbed her arm. She shook herself free.

"I'm not kidding, and I am not lying."

"Get rid of it," he said and reached for her again.

"Don't touch me." She backed against the door, out of reach. "I'm carrying your baby, and I'm not getting rid of it. Didn't you say a minute ago that you would take good care of me?"

"I won't let you ruin everything." He panted as if he had run the hundred-yard dash.

"I won't, George, but it's going to cost you."

"Didn't take you long to get to the heart of the matter." He glowered at her.

"Nor you two minutes ago," Nina said. "Twenty-five thousand dollars. You have a week."

She opened the grotto door and stopped. "You pay, and I keep quiet. You don't, I won't." She felt her lips curl. "I wonder what the Trustees would think about the Assistant Dean smoking crack with one of the students and getting her pregnant in the grotto." She closed the door halfway and peered around it. "Oh, and don't get cute with the eggs. You can't afford to get on my bad side."

"I stand corrected," he said. "You are a harlot, the worst kind of whore for hire. But you'll never get away with it." Nina heard the words but also saw the defeat in his eyes. She turned and closed the grotto door, climbing the stone steps to the dark belly of the Chapel.

George listened as the back Chapel door opened and closed. He blew out the candles and stood in the darkness. The grotto walls closed toward him. His ears filled with the sound of a loud, guttural roar. Fool. He felt fresh beads of sweat break from his forehead and race down his cheeks. Pregnant.

George felt for the grapefruit sacks in the chair beside his leg and clutched them against his damp chest. He turned in the darkness toward the door. Where could he put this rock?

Opening the grotto door, he climbed the steps in the dark, his body feeling two hundred pounds heavier than it had an hour ago when he raced down the grotto steps. He had been younger then. And dumber.

At the top of the stairs, he angled across the carpeted Chancel, passing before the altar without a nod and entering the Sacristy. In the narrow, windowless room, wood cabinets stained a rich mahogany rose from chin level to the ceiling. They were full of altar supplies. Boxes of beeswax candles, communion wafers, jugs of sweet wine, and several sizes of clear glass cruets with ornate metal stoppers.

A linoleum counter ran beneath the cabinets with a sink at the far right end. It sat atop five wide, shallow drawers stacked to the floor. In the four lowest drawers, George kept his liturgical garments. There were stoles for every season: red for Pentecost, white for Easter, purple for Advent and Lent, and Green for ordinary Sundays in between. There were also matching, gold laced chasubles for each season. They looked more like ponchos for sissies than something one would wear to consecrate bread and wine, but George liked dressing up.

The top drawer held matches, safety pins, combs, breath mints and accumulated clutter from people who never threw anything away. And duct tape! He grabbed the heavy gray roll and slid it onto his wrist. He returned to the Chancel and got to work.

Minutes later, George stepped through, closed and locked the side Chapel door. It was still raining. He felt for the metal railing and followed it down the brick steps. At the bottom of the stairway, his foot splashed onto the fire lane. Drainage had never been good, but it was not bad enough to justify having someone come in, tear up the asphalt and regrade it. He walked left along the back of the administration building and up the connecting lane to his driveway.

Turning at the mouth of his driveway, he remembered the conversation with Hilary. He shook his head, winding around a hundred yards of tall, perfectly manicured hedges to the garage. Stupid woman thinks I'm gay! Tonight, for the first time in his life, he wished she were right.

Seconds after George's garage closed behind him, a dark vehicle inched along the fire lane without headlights toward the Chapel, having returned from a brief stop in Ecclesia's student parking lot.

Chapter Five

The silence was loud in his ears. He'd been driving around and around the same block, her block. Any solitude was shattered by the sound of Nina's voice echoing in his head. In the past six months, he had heard her laugh, heard her cry, heard her shout, whisper, and scream. But until tonight, he'd never heard her cold, or hard. Tonight in the darkness of her apartment, Terry sat naked with a complete stranger.

He turned left onto Fiddler, again, and the Rabbit complained up the steep hill toward Elm. When he turned right, his breath caught in his throat. Pulling away from the curb a hundred and fifty yards ahead was a car he knew well - Nina's blue Mustang. He had slowed, kept his distance, and followed it to the seminary.

From a moonless sky, the rain fell black behind the Ecclesia Chapel. Terry turned off the headlights. The lane behind it seemed longer when you couldn't see. Surely, it would curve soon and head up along the left side of the Chapel. His long blond hair hung loose about his face. He ran long fingers through it. Nina liked it longer, so he let it grow. His boss didn't like it. At all. It was "inconsistent with the image of the chapel staff," Reverend George Fields wrote in Terry's latest performance review. Terry extended his middle finger toward the back of the chapel. The rear bumper of Nina's navy blue Mustang loomed directly in front of him, and he stomped the brake, stopping within an inch of it.

He blew out his breath, put the Rabbit in reverse and stepped gently on the accelerator. He heard the thud and felt the car jerk to an immediate stop. "What the –" He pushed his door open and leaped out. The grass at the curb was wet mush and his shoes sank to the laces. He staggered, catching himself against the side of the car. The air was black and thick. He felt his way to the rear, leaning over the trunk. His fingers felt his wet bumper pressed tight against another, much larger bumper. Close to his right ear, he heard a strange click. Immediately, light flashed in his eyes and white fire exploded in his head, flaming bright, and then growing dimmer and dimmer, as if a stadium light had just blown out.

Terry's body slid to the ground. Vinnie wiped the butt of his Glock 9mm and returned it to the holster inside his coat.

"You … idiot! You shoulda let me cut him!" Emil said, glaring through his goggles in the darkness, his switchblade still raised menacingly.

"Sorry, Mr. Bente." Vinnie adjusted his goggles and peered at the rumpled body in the soggy grass.

"I was about to give him a smile from left ear to right." Vinnie heard the click as the blade returned inside the pearl handle. Another click and it was back. In and out, in and out. Vinnie smirked in the darkness. Probably made the runt feel like a real gangster!

"After we get Nina, Mr. Bente, you can carve this turkey. For now, let's park him in his car in the lot up there, come back, wait for Nina to come out, and take the rock. You make back some lost profits-"

"I'm likin' it."

Vinnie nodded. "We deal with her, nice and clean-like, far away from here. And then we come back and give this punk here a one way to the bay."

"Genius."

"Help me get him into the back seat," Vinnie said.

"I'll get his feet."

Vinnie grabbed Terry under the shoulders. "I'll follow in the Rolls, you park, and we'll come back."

"And how 'bout I give our rose bud here a little something to help him sleep until we get back." Emil disappeared while Vinnie arranged Terry's body across the Rabbit's back seat. He returned with a smile so large that Vinnie saw his crooked teeth, looking green through the goggles several feet away. In Emil's hand was a three-inch long syringe.

"He will wake up from this, won't he Mr. Bente?"

Emil crouched over Terry's body with the syringe tight in his fist. He slammed it into Terry's neck, pressing his thumb against the plunger until the syringe was empty. "He'll wake up alright. I want him to feel everything I'm going to do to him." He left the syringe stabbed in Terry's neck, closed the back door and climbed into the driver's seat.

Lieutenant Higgins pulled his eye from the black rubber cup. "They're wearing night vision goggles. How about that!" He adjusted the settings on the night vision monocular. In the back of the Ecclesia faculty lot, he and Captain Steele sat covered with camouflage netting among thick trees.

Thirty feet above the pavement below, they had a clear view of the fire lane behind the Chapel. The embankment was steep and muddy to the lane. An array of gear beneath black tarps surrounded them.

"No shock," Steele said. "You think we're the ones with technology?"

"Suppose not."

"But it is surprising sometimes to see them whip out gear like that. When I started with the Bureau, we spent all our time and energy running down guys with no brains and even less technology. It's a whole different deal now." He glanced at Higgins, smiling grimly. "Meet the new mob."

Higgins put his eye into the rubber cup again and watched the brown Rabbit crawl to a stop behind the blue Mustang. The black Rolls shadowed him twenty yards behind in the darkness. "I wonder if that kid even knows they're there." He passed the monocular.

"Who'd you say he was?" Steele asked, peering down the embankment toward the three automobiles.

"Rabbit's registered to Terrance Woodrow. California plates. Twenty-four, Caucasian, six feet two, a hundred and eighty-five pounds." Higgins paused. "Probably a full-time seminarian, and part-time lover of Bente's wife."

Steele scowled at his young partner and returned to the scope. "Wait, he's getting out."

"Woodrow?"

"Yep," he said, zooming the lens. "Kid's hunched over his car feeling his way to the rear. Looks like he's night blind."

"Night like this, anyone without NV is gonna be."

Steele continued softly. "He's headed straight for them! Ah!" He winced.

"What?" Higgins squinted down the embankment.

"Bente was right behind the kid with a blade when Bontecelli stepped across and gun-butted Woodrow over the head. Down like a ragdoll."

"Kill him, you think?"

"Can't tell."

"Gotta help him."

"Can't."

"Captain, you can't be serious!"

"We just got the net over them again," Steele whispered. "Radio paramedics to standby. Possible cerebral hemorrhage or spinal injury, but tell them to wait for word from me."

"Yes sir." Higgins picked up the portable radio and spoke quietly into it.

"Okay, they've got the kid in the back of the Rabbit." Steele paused. "Ahhh!" he said in a loud whisper.

Higgins stopped. Rain tapped on the leaves overhead.

"Bente just stabbed him in the neck," Steele said.

"Then he is dead."

Steele gave a quick head shake. "Not a knife, maybe a syringe. Maybe doping him."

"Or a lethal injection," Higgins said. "We learned a lot about that at the Academy. The bad guys are beginning to trade in their guns for needles. Take somebody out without a sound."

Steele shook his head slightly, not taking his eye from the night scope. "Not Bente's style. He prefers blades and blood." He took a deep breath. "We won't know for sure until after we seal the net."

Higgins spoke quietly into the radio again. He pressed an ear with his finger and listened, then whispered to Steele. "Units One and Two are in position with the locals at the top of the hill, southern mouth of the fire lane. Units Three and Four have joined two squad cars on top at the northern mouth. Unit Five will coordinate the rescue vehicles and bring them in from Spelkin Lane."

"Good." Steele adjusted the zoom on the scope again. "Now we need a little lady with a lot of rock to hand it to her husband." He paused. "Then we can get the kid some help."

"Hope it's not too late."

"They're rolling," Captain Steele cursed and slammed his hand on his wet thigh. "Bente is in the kid's car, and Bontecelli is following in the Rolls."

"Where's the girl?"

"No clue," Steele said.

"Do I instruct the units to follow or stay put?" He held the radio to his lips.

"We stick with the plan," Steele said. "We stay with the rock."

"If we do, the kid could die," Higgins said.

"Maybe."

"Maybe?" Higgins eyes were wide. "How we gonna explain Woodrow's death if it comes out we could have prevented it?" He leaned toward his Captain. "Look, let me radio the units to stop the cars, haul Bente and Bontecelli downtown, charge them with possession of a controlled substance, assault with a deadly weapon and as many other weapons charges as we can come up with, ... and we get Woodrow to the hospital."

"And they'll be back on the street in the morning, their entire operation will go underground, and we'll lose at least two years' worth of work."

Steele spit the words like an AK-47. "We are not-" He stabbed a trembling finger toward Higgins. "You got me?"

"I understand alright," Higgins said hotly. "I'm just not sure I feel good putting my butt in the same frying pan as yours - sir!" They glared and breathed.

"Thanks partner," Steele said. "Now shut up. That's an order."

Chapter Six

Nina closed the Chapel door from the inside and turned the lock, making it sound to George as if she had left. She moved silently to the last pew and laid down. The thick foam of the velvet covered pad ran the length and cradled her head. "O God, I need to talk with you," she whispered. She felt the tear slip from the corner of her eye.

Shoes on the stone steps leading from the grotto echoed across the ceiling, then rustling and the soft banging of drawers. Then, from the front of the chapel she heard footsteps. The side door rattled open in the distance and shut again. She heard George turn the key.

In that instant, the pew felt like her coffin, and she saw herself waiting at the back of the church to be wheeled forward. The lid was closed and she couldn't breathe. Nina drew a quick breath and opened her eyes. The white ceiling of the chapel felt close, and for a split second she thought it might be the white satin-lined lid. Her heart thumped in her ears and the back of her sun dress felt moist. She looked left and touched the wooden back of the pew beside her. She saw the silhouette of the pew Bible and rubbed her arms. They were clammy and cold. "O God I need to talk and there's only you," she whispered. "I need to confess. I know it's an evil plan, but it's working. A thousand dollars a week will pay for a good rehab center, and I can get clean again." The whispered words came in a gush mixed with sobs. "And I won't pray for a miscarriage anymore. I promise." She rolled off the pew and landed hard face down on the floor. "It's such a mess," she cried. "I mean, it's all coming together but I'm coming apart." Images flashed in her mind. She had to tell, had to get it out. "George was easy, you know? I knew what he wanted. Poor guy. Married to … her. His pain killers were cocaine and sex. I gave him both." Her tears puddled around her forehead on the floor.

"Terry was a prince, and a problem. I think he wants a pretty little minister's wife. Not me. Sorry, I'm just being honest."

"And then Emil … was a mistake. I met him across the railroad tracks in the cemetery. He was so small and squat, I laughed the first time I met him. But he was generous with his rock. The price for my bag of cocaine always fell after his pants dropped. He was easy to please. I pocketed the extra cash I didn't have to spend and never told George or Lawrence about the discount. But I shouldn't have married him."

Nina closed and opened her eyes slowly, flashing back to the night. The coke was top grade, the air in the Rolls dense with smoke. Vinnie was ordered to take his walk, and Emil was sweating on top of her. Nina saw her chance: all the cocaine she wanted. She pushed Emil up from her chest by the shoulders. The gold chains hanging from his flabby chest rattled near her lips. "Let's get hitched," she said, "in Vegas. We catch the red-eye tonight and marry in the morning." She ran her tongue around the outside of her lips.

"Are you serious?" Emil said, peering at her through slits. She could see he was flattered.

"Let's go, honey," she said. "We've already consummated this thing. I want to be Mrs. Emil Bente." She cocked her head as she spoke the title and grinned.

He fell hard. "Well, baby, that is exactly who you will be in a matter of hours." Emil thought they should consummate the future marriage again, for good measure.

"Are you sure, Mr. Bente?" Vinnie said when he returned from his walk.

"Fuck ya," Emil said, smiling. "Take a look at those legs. How'd you like to have them puppies wrapped around your waist every night?" Vinnie grunted and slid behind the wheel. Emil relieved himself on a barrier wall, climbed in the back and they drove to the airport.

She shook off the memory, and continued in a whisper, "So I came back from Vegas a married woman, but nobody else knew. After I married Emil, I got my rock for free but still charged George and Lawrence full freight, and I never told Emil about the income. Nobody at the Seminary knew I was married."

"Emil didn't like the arrangement one bit, wanting the world to know that I was 'Mrs. Bente.' He wanted me with him, by his side, his trophy wife. But I stayed in my room at Nettie's during the week and kept my maiden name. Except on my driver's license. I was so paranoid about somebody seeing that." She tried to wipe her nose without lifting her head. "I know I'm rambling, but I am such a lying messed up addict and I am so sorry. Can you please, please forgive me?"

The silence had gone on too long, and Steele knew it. "Ever fished with a net, Lieutenant?" he asked the hunched Higgins beneath the camouflage next to him.

"You mean like the ones you let out the back of a boat?" Lieutenant Higgins watched the side of his face. One of Steele's eyes was closed; he pressed the other into the night vision monocular.

"Nah," Steele said. "As a kid growing up in Florida, my buddies and I used to sit on the big jetty rocks and watch the old guys fish. They'd wade out thigh deep, their arms draped full of net. Weights hung every foot or so from the edges, and the whole thing hooked to their waist. They would throw as far as they could, which wasn't very far, straight out in front of them. And then they would wait. And we would wait."

"For what?"

"For the weights along the edges to hit bottom and settle the net on every side of those fish."

"And then they hauled in their catch." Higgins said with satisfaction.

"Not yet."

"What were they waiting for?"

"The moment." Steele paused, watching the fire lane through the scope, but seeing in his head the brown wrinkled skin of his favorite fisherman. His hair was charcoal gray with pewter sun highlights. His legs were boney and taut, his chest sunken and littered with patches of white hair that stuck like dry sea moss through the net in his arms. Steele continued,

"Only one old salt wasn't too proud or too preoccupied to talk with us kids. He told us once, 'What makes this kind of fishin' sport is to wait for the moment.' I remember like it was yesterday. 'There is a moment,' the old man said with sun reflecting in his eyes, 'when the fish realizes the last gap is gone and he's trapped. And he struggles like hell to find a way out, and you struggle like hell to gather the net and drag it ashore. And in that moment, if you are smarter and faster than that fish, then you eat.'"

Higgins grunted. "A salty sage."

"Lieutenant," Steele said, "we are back at step one, throwing the net. Get on the radio and make sure everyone's in place and ready to go on my signal. After that, get that spotlight hooked up and positioned."

"Then we wait for the moment."

Steele nodded, never taking his eye from the monocular. "As soon as Mrs. Bente hits that fire lane and makes the handoff, we're going to drag us some big fish to shore!"

Chapter Seven

After a time, Nina pulled herself up from the floor and made her way to the side door. This time when she opened it, she stepped through it into the night. Without a jacket, the chilled rain drops stung the back of her neck as she struggled with the door lock. Finally, her key turned. Nina folded her shoulder bag in half to keep out the rain, tucking it under her arm. She turned and grabbed for the railing, navigating the steps leading to the fire lane by feel. It wasn't usually this black and thick. The school needed a light back here. Still, tonight she was glad for the lack of light. At the bottom of the steps, a gust of wet wind slapped her and she shivered, stepping gingerly onto the fire lane and heading in the direction of her car, though she couldn't see it.

"Hello Mrs. Bente."

She knew the voice well, and it landed in her ears with the force of a mortar shell. Before she could react, Nina felt the crush of a large hand on her arm. It jerked her forward and she lost her footing. Her hip slammed into a large metal object.

"Vinnie, you're hurting me!"

"Someone wants to see you." Holding her firmly against the side of the Rolls, he opened the back door. Nina struggled to breathe. In one fluid and violent move, Vinnie thrust her inside and slammed the door.

Just then, a bright light splashed across the rain-streaked windows of the Rolls and the side of Vinnie's face. A voice boomed from the distance and bounced from the wet asphalt into his face. "FBI. Lay your weapons on the ground. Bontecelli – weapons on the ground, then kneel. In the car, come out with your hands showing."

Vinnie barely heard the last sentence. He yanked his body around the back of the car and dove for the driver's side door handle. The huge light beam snapped wildly, first right, then left, then down. Vinnie tore the door open and leapt behind the wheel. The Rolls roared to life and Vinnie deftly maneuvered it past Nina's Mustang. His eyes flicked briefly to the rear view mirror. Like a camera, his eyes took in Emil's squat frame lurched forward against the window. Nina was smashed against the opposite door, her hands pushing away from him.

Vinnie stomped the accelerator and yanked on the headlights. The Rolls careened along the fire lane behind the Chapel. Blue, red and white lights flashed brighter and brighter against the buildings and the trees. The Rolls turned sharply at the left edge of the Chapel, fishtailing around the corner. The air exploded with siren screams, and light glared from two sets of headlights and two racks of flicking colored lights dead ahead. Other headlights followed behind. Vinnie's eyes were wide, his mouth open. Emil cursed from the back seat.

The lane was steep and narrow. No time and no room for a U-turn. "Hang on!" Vinnie said. He slammed on the brakes, skidded to a halt, jammed the Rolls in reverse and smashed the accelerator to the floor, racing backward toward the curve at the back of the Chapel.

The headlights in front of him were larger and the screaming sirens louder. One hand on the steering wheel, the other holding his body in a backward twist, Vinnie raced toward the corner of the building. The steering wheel spun and the car followed. The back end of the Rolls whipped around the corner and for an instant, the back window filled with a close-up of the back chapel wall. Vinnie slammed on the brakes and the front tires spun around like the crack of a bullwhip.

Before the car could even right itself, Vinnie went from reverse to drive, and the back tires spun forward. Nina screamed in the back, and Vinnie heard the loud whack of Emil's fist against her face. "This is your fault!" Emil screamed, and Vinnie heard more thuds of fist against flesh.

The bright light from the spotlight on the hillside shone in Vinnie's eyes, blinding him. Around the edges of the light, more blue and red flashes and he heard the cry of sirens and engines and rubber skidding on wet asphalt coming from the opposite direction.

Nina's screams were becoming moans. His eyes shot to the rear view mirror. Two cars ablaze with flashing light rounded the corner. They were trapped. He was not about to go to jail with the punk he carried in the back seat, but there were only two ways out of here and both were choked with cops.

Before he could think, Vinnie looked straight ahead. No Road. Nothing but a steep drop off. He floored it. The front tires slammed against the curb and then bounced up and over the embankment. Gone in an instant was the bright light. Gone were the blue and red flashes. The Rolls sailed through the black curtain of darkness, tires bouncing and sliding out of control down the steep embankment. "One tree and we're dead!" he said to the windshield. Wet sod and mud flew in every direction. The car fished sideways and threatened to roll. Emil cursed again from the back seat.

Vinnie looked left down the hill. Elm Street rushed at them from below. His eyes shot right. Four headlights like two sets of eyes with flashing brows leapt up and over the embankment toward them, following. The front and rear tires of the Rolls slammed against the base of the hill. The thick trunk of an Elm tree filled the windshield in front of him and he heard an animal sound coming from his mouth.

The Rolls slipped past the trunk by inches and skidded across the sidewalk onto Elm Street. A white Oldsmobile parked on the opposite side of Elm served as backstop, keeping the Rolls from flipping. Black slammed into white, crushing the Oldsmobile's right side and shattering the front windshield. An instant after impact, Vinnie righted himself in the seat and stomped the accelerator. "Your fault, whore!" Emil said from the back. Vinnie heard more thuds of flesh against bone.

The wounded Rolls raced toward Fiddler. The first of the police cars crashed against the Oldsmobile backstop behind them. Ignoring the stop sign, Vinnie swung right onto Fiddler directly into the path of a truck charging down the steep hill toward Bradley Street. With no time to react, Vinnie braced for impact. At the last moment, the truck jerked right, missing the Rolls but clipping a parked car and fishtailing sideways across the road. Ignoring the stop sign, the lead squad car rounded the corner onto Fiddler and slammed into the side of the truck. The squad car behind it skidded left in a vain attempt to avoid the lead car. Its back end slid in a wide right arc and smashed into the lead patrol car's trunk and back fender, crushing the words painted there, "To serve and to protect."

"Hoooeee!" Vinnie said as the Rolls topped the hill and dropped out of sight on the other side.

"Now! Now! Now!" Lieutenant Higgins' voice screamed from the paramedic's radio. In the top lot, the paramedics screeched the ambulance to a halt next to Terry Woodrow's car and jumped out. With fingers covered by latex gloves, the lead paramedic reached his hand back and twisted the volume control on the portable radio hooked to his waist. Then he flung open the back door and knelt over the victim. "Jesse," he called over his shoulder. "Get me some light in here." Behind him, two paramedics unloaded a four wheeled stretcher from the back of the ambulance. Jesse trotted to the front of the ambulance and returned with a wide beamed flashlight. She opened the back door on the opposite side of the Rabbit and shined the light on Terry's motionless body. In three years as a paramedic, she had seen a lot of wild stuff, but never someone with a large syringe jammed into his neck.

"Is he still with us?" she asked.

"I'm getting a steady pulse," he said. His right arm ached from holding himself over Terry's body. "Let's get some vitals to call in. And get the back board. He may have a spinal injury."

The sirens, lights and commotion below brought students and staff pouring from Ecclesia's buildings. The action in the fire lane below was over so fast that most missed it. Jesse felt the stares. "Looks like we're attracting attention."

"You want me to kill the flashers?" the other paramedic called from the stretcher.

"Good idea," Jesse said. "I'll start an IV."

The lead paramedic shook his head. "We'll do it on the way in. I don't know what we're dealing with or how much time we have."

"Back board's coming with the stretcher," Jesse said. She kept the light trained on Terry's neck, his pale skin, his limp face. Blood dripped from the corner of his mouth. "What are you going to do with that?" Jesse nodded toward the syringe. An angry bruise encircled it.

"Me? Nothing. That is too close to … all kinds of stuff. Let the ER Docs handle it."

They braced Terry's head and slid the backboard beneath him. Keeping his body level, they lifted him to the height of the stretcher and laid him on it. Then they began strapping him down to keep him from slipping when they loaded him in the ambulance. Two of the four wide red straps were in place and tight when Jesse saw movement from the corner of her eye. She turned to see a thin blonde woman crest the top of the stairs to the lot and sprint toward the ambulance. Jesse walked toward her, hand up and arm outstretched.

"God! What happened?" the young woman asked, stopping in front of Jesse and peering around her. Her chest heaved, her eyes darting between the open doors of Terry's Rabbit and the back of the ambulance. "Oh my God!" The young woman bent over as if shot in the stomach.

"I'm sorry miss," Jesse said, "You'll have to stay back."

"Oh God! Is that Terry? He's not dead, is he?"

"He's not dead," Jesse said.

"Is he OK? Is he hurt? What happened? Who would-"

"I'm sorry, and you are…?" Jesse asked.

"I'm … I'm Sarah Woodrow," she lied, speaking quickly and still catching her breath. "Terry's sister."

Jesse eyed her warily, then glanced over the thin woman's shoulder and saw more than a dozen people racing toward the top of the stairs. She turned and looked behind her in time to see the other paramedics load the stretch into the ambulance.

Turning to face Sarah again, she sighed, "Alright, you can come with us, but only you." Jesse hitched her thumb over her shoulder, "Hurry. Climb in the back there with him." Sarah ran to the back of the ambulance. It was in gear before the next person reached the top of the stairs.

Steele and Higgins had watched in stunned silence as the Rolls leaped over the embankment and skidded toward Elm Street. Higgins let go of the spotlight and it snapped upward at a forty-five degree angle. Steele tucked the monocular under his arm, and both men clawed down the hill and ran to their unmarked car in the faculty lot. Higgins put it into a U-turn and aimed for the exit while Steele shouted into the radio. "Units Three and Four take the fire lane to Spelkin and back One and Two up on Elm." Units One and Two were already airborne behind the two squad cars. "Lose them and you lose your badges!"

Higgins turned right out of the faculty lot and sped down Spelkin, skidding around the corner onto Elm Street, lightly tapping a parked car on the left side of the street. The windshield wipers flicked rain left and right. Ahead, the scene coming into focus confirmed Steele's worst fears. Stationary bouquets of lights swirled and flashed close together – white, blue, then red. Then he saw the twisted metal of the two squad cars. The other two squad cars were redirecting traffic on Fiddler. Nothing else moved.

Hands welded to the steering wheel, Higgins slowed to a crawl as they approached. Steele bent and covered his face in his hands. His right hand still held the radio. He pressed it against his forehead and closed his eyes. It was not happening again. He would open his eyes, sit up in bed and find the whole thing a terrible nightmare.

"How did this happen, Higgins? That net was tight!" He opened his eyes. The flashing lights hurt his eyes. Through the wet blur of the windshield and the frantic slapping of the wipers, he saw a middle aged uniformed officer walk toward them with his hands waist high, his palms outstretched in exasperation. Higgins and Steele pulled alongside him, lowering the passenger side window.

"I'm sorry Captain," Chief Timothy Parker said. "I was right behind them."

"No time for that now, Chief," Steele said, mustering composure. "Your precinct is to be commended for your assistance. Things happen."

Parker nodded, looking away.

Steele remembered how excited Parker had been to assist, how he went on and on about his one-time dream of joining the Bureau, how he jumped at the chance to play FBI.

He heard Higgins swear in the seat next to him.

"We've got a Global Positioning System tracker on the Rolls, so we know where they are," Steele said.

"How can we assist?" Parker asked.

"Get this mess cleaned up. And call dispatch. I need replacement units right away." He heard a thud and glanced at Higgins, whose forehead rested on the steering wheel. "And tell them to scramble the helicopter."

"The helicopter is in Wayland," Parker said.

"I don't care if it's in Bolivia, Chief. Have it here as fast as possible."

"Yes sir." Parker ran toward his crumpled squad car.

Steele whirled to face Higgins. "What?"

Bert Higgins lifted his head like an iron ball. "The GPS monitor is back on the hill … next to the spotlight." He braced for the explosion.

Steele lifted the radio and slammed it against the dash. "In this rain?"

"Yes sir, I dropped everything and ran for the car and – "

"You left electronic gear, our only means of tracking Bente and the eggs – "

"Yes sir."

"In the mud!" Steele said, shaking.

"Not sure sir."

Steele glowered at him and popped the radio to his lips. "Parker, have the new units meet us at the Ecclesia faculty lot in twenty minutes."

The radio hissed. For a moment Steele wondered if he had broken it, until Parker's voice boomed, "Ten four, Captain. We'll have the units rolling to the rendezvous point within ten minutes and have them to you in twenty-five, thirty." Higgins struggled to turn the car around with parked cars on both sides of the street.

"Sooner if possible. This is a hostage situation."

"Roger that."

Steele wondered if a gangster's wife in a gangster's car actually constituted a hostage situation. The radio crackled again.

"Negative on the chopper, Captain. It's in Wayland for repairs."

"Of course it is," Steele said without punching the talk button. He pressed talk. "Copy that."

Higgins pulled into the faculty lot and steered for the far corner. "How'd you get a GPS on that Rolls anyway Cap?"

"Long story for another time."

"Think Nina Bente's still alive, Cap?" Higgins asked.

"You're a real bleeding heart, Higgins," Steele said. "First it's Woodrow's health. Now it's Mrs. Bente's." He snorted. "Need to toughen you up."

"Tough guys don't care about people?" Higgins asked. Steele glared at him. The kid had a sharp edge to him too. He admired that. Also annoyed the shit out of him.

"I wondered about Mrs. Bente's chances, that's all," Higgins said.

"Honestly?" Steele looked at him. "That GPS is her only hope."

Higgins stopped the vehicle at the far corner and stared at the windshield.

"I know." He stared straight ahead.

"Forget it," Steele said. "Things happen fast out here. You're doing fine."

Higgins jumped from the vehicle and ran to the edge of the pavement. He slid through the mud down the steep embankment to the spot light. It still blazed into the night sky, the rain looking like snow in the beam. He found the GPS monitor right where he had dropped it. The lights atop it were still blinking. He tucked it under his jacket and disconnected the spot from the battery. The hillside went black.

With one arm clutching the GPS against his stomach, he clawed with his other arm toward the faculty lot. Twice he slipped, slamming his face into the mix of leaves and mud, but sprang back up and kept climbing. At the top, he grabbed the curb and flung himself over, careful not to smack the GPS against the ground. Wiping mud from his hands, he passed the monitor through the window to his partner. Then he stripped off his jacket and used it like a washcloth to clean mud from his chest and thighs. The curb directed a thick stream of rainwater to the storm drain, and he used it as a sink, rinsing the jacket and stomping mud from his shoes.

Glancing into the car, he saw the smile on Steele's face. He threw his jacket over the embankment, opened the driver's side door and eased his frame behind the wheel.

Steele stared at the GPS screen. "We've got 'em," he said, still smiling at the blinking dot on the LCD screen. Then he glanced at Higgins. "You look like shit."

"I'm feeling much better."

"Soon as those units arrive, we'll track our fish and throw the net again."

"Spoken like a true fisherman," Higgins said, wiping a hand through his wet crew cut. "Just one more cast, one more throw of the net…."

Steele nodded.

The crowd gathering at the top of the stairs watched lights and sirens atop the ambulance spring to life as the rescue vehicle screamed away.

At the bottom of the steps in his slippers and housecoat stood George Fields. The sound of sirens met him as he stepped from the shower. After they faded, he peeked from the bedroom window, but the Assistant Dean's residence was so far back from the fire lane that he couldn't tell what was happening.

When he walked to the end of the driveway into the fire lane, he saw students running for the upper lot and lights from the ambulance reflecting from the tree branches above them. He thought he should go investigate, ask questions. He should introduce himself to the police and answer questions.

George returned to the darkness of his driveway. *Questions! He would ask none. He would answer none.*

Chapter Eight

Sarah tried to go with Terry through the Emergency Room's swinging double doors when they pulled him from the back of the ambulance, but a man in green scrubs told her to wait until they stabilized him. She wondered how many other people in the waiting room had gotten the same line.

The emergency room at Memorial was packed. Sarah knew from her hospital chaplain internship last summer that Saturday nights were the worst. The waiting room was lined on three sides with heavy plastic bucket chairs. The front wall offered a drinking fountain, a soda machine and a fire extinguisher. Several feet above the soda machine the suspended television droned. A sitcom punctuated the din of the waiting room with canned laughter.

Sarah scanned for available seats. There were two. One was next to a large woman holding on her lap a little girl with sweat-soaked hair. The child hacked and barked. The woman's eyes were locked on the television. The other seat was next to a bearded man in his late thirties with tattoos climbing his neck on both sides. He pressed a cloth against his left arm. Blood dripped from his elbow into a bucket. Sarah decided to stand.

She glared at her watch. They ought to give the emergency waiting room and the back emergency medical area different time zones. Out here, time slowed and what happened behind those metal doors seemed to take hours longer than folks out here thought it should.

But behind the metal doors in the belly of the Emergency Room's treatment area, time raced headlong from one crisis to another. Doctors, nurses and staff rushed from one set of curtains dividing beds to another. Trained not to run, they fought the urge constantly, because there were too many needs and not enough time or hands to meet them. Forced to prioritize, they treated the sickest and most injured people first. People in pain but not in danger of death waited, often for hours, despite medical personnel working at a frenzied pace.

Two different time zones. Sarah had experienced them both, but that didn't help her wait tonight.

She wondered if she should call someone. But who? Should she worry Terry's parents thousands of miles away in California? What could she tell them? She didn't know anything. Surely, the Dean should know about an assault in the seminary parking lot, but it was the middle of the night. She sighed. Then there was the Assistant Dean. Terry worked for him. Shouldn't he know that Terry would not be there for the service?

Nausea struck her gut as she remembered the unfinished sermon she was working on when she heard the sirens and rushed outside. Preaching at First Presbyterian on the Square on Palm Sunday was frightening enough, with over a thousand people expected for the two services. But unprepared, without a written sermon? Adrenaline shot through her body, and she felt like a Christmas tree with the lights plugged in. There was no way she could get out of it, too late for the Senior Minister to prepare.

The tiny hospital chapel around the corner flashed in her mind. She spun on her heel and ran down the hallway. She knew that chapel well. Having prayed with one patient after another throughout the day, Sarah knew their pain and the fear that came with every soft knock on the door. That summer, alone in the chapel at the end of the day, she had knelt and prayed aloud for each patient by name. By faith, she had asked God to comfort them and to restore them to health in body, mind and spirit. Sometimes afterward, looking at her watch as she got into her car, she had found she had been in there for hours.

Sarah stopped for a moment at the chapel door to catch her breath, and then entered. The small room with warm dark wood walls smelled of candle wax and old books. She lit two votive candles and the walls glowed. "God," she said, dropping to her knees on the red carpet. "Terry needs your help. So do I." For the next several minutes, Sarah poured her heart out. She apologized for the lie she told the paramedics about being Terry's sister. She prayed for Terry, for the doctors, nurses and staff, and for all the ministers preparing to lead worship and preach in a few hours. She also prayed for the people who assaulted Terry, whoever they were, that the Lord's mercy and love would flood them and that they would come to know Him. She felt His presence and the peace that always came with it.

"I don't know what to do, but I know I can trust you. Please be with Terry. You know how I feel…" Sarah choked and tears rolled down her face. She nodded, acknowledging that He knew all about it. "And if tomorrow I have to stand before your people without a written sermon, give me the words to speak and the confidence to rise above my fear. Thank you, Lord, for all that you have already done in my life and for all you are going to do. I love you so much!" More tears dropped onto the carpet. "Amen."

Sarah patted her pockets. Finding no cell phone, she rose and went to find a telephone. A bank of three payphones hung bolted to the wall next to the restrooms. Sarah combed through the phone book hanging from a clip beneath the center phone. She found Reverend Jeremy Tittle's home telephone number and dialed.

"Hello?" The voice was airy and hoarse.

"Dean Tittle, this is Sarah Stafford. I'm a second year seminarian, and I'm so sorry to call you at three in the morning." Sarah wiped her free hand on her shorts.

"No trouble at all, young lady," Dean Tittle cleared his throat. "One of the benefits of living alone is that there's nobody but me to disturb and I don't sleep worth a tick these days anyway." Before her death four years ago, his bride of 48 years always snuggled closer and closer to him as they slept, and he remembered calling her the land's biggest hot water bottle. Back then, he complained that she kept him from getting a sound night's sleep. Ever since she died, the bed had been too large and cold. He missed his beloved hot water bottle, ached for her most nights and never slept more than three hours.

"Terry Woodrow, another of your students, is here in the emergency room at Memorial."

"Oh dear." Jeremy swung his feet to the floor and sat on the edge of the bed. "What happened?"

"He was assaulted in the student parking lot tonight. I heard sirens and went outside to find them loading him into the back of an ambulance."

"Assaulted! Who would do such a thing?"

"No idea, sir."

"Would it help if I came?"

"Oh no, Dean Tittle. That's awesome of you to offer," Sarah said. "But I've got things covered here. I just wanted you to know. I'm going to call Reverend Fields in a minute. Terry is his assistant at the Chapel and he needs to know that Terry won't be there tomorrow."

"Good," Jeremy said. "Sounds like you have things under control. You'll make a fine minister."

"Thank you, sir."

"Let's have a prayer together." He paced the bedroom floor for a moment in silence. "Oh Lord, you are all knowing, all powerful, and endlessly loving. We cry out to you tonight for your healing touch upon our brother, Terry, who lies wounded and in pain. We ask you, Father, in Jesus' Name, to touch his body right now and heal it. We thank you in faith for his complete and speedy recovery. And I thank you, Jesus, for my sister and fellow minister of the Gospel, Sarah. Thank you that you have appointed her to this task tonight and we ask for your continued anointing to be upon her." Sarah's eyes were squeezed shut, the receiver pressed hard against her ear. She felt the familiar rush of warmth flood her body and she smiled peacefully. "In Jesus' Mighty and Holy Name we pray, Amen."

"Amen. Thank you, Dean Tittle," Sarah said.

"God bless you, Sarah. Call me tomorrow and let me know how things are going."

"I will. God bless you too."

Sarah hung up the pay phone, fished for some more change in her pockets and dialed the Assistant Dean's number. It rang repeatedly, and then a recorded message began to play. A deep voice spoke. "God be with you. You have reached the home of The Reverend George Fields and Mrs. Hillary Fields." Sarah caught herself waggling her head side to side and mimicking the pompous sounding voice. "No one is available to speak with you at this moment. If you wish to leave your name and your telephone number, we shall earnestly endeavor to speak to you at our earliest convenience. May the Holy Spirit be with us all."

The beep that followed caught Sarah off guard. "Uh, this is Sarah Stafford, third year seminarian and friend of Terry Woodrow. Terry is in the emergency room at Memorial and will not be at the Chapel service tomorrow. Thank you." She hung up the phone and flicked her fingers as if she had touched something slimy. A voice in the crowded Emergency Room waiting area reached Sarah's ears. "Miss Woodrow please." Sarah turned to see the swinging metal doors held wide by an attractive, brown-haired, woman in her early forties wearing a long white coat over green scrubs.

"Here," Sarah said, rushing toward her.

"You can come back now," the woman said. The doors closed behind them and Sarah walked quickly to keep up with her escort.

"I'm Dr. Sanchez," the woman said without offering her hand. "Your brother's a lucky man."

"Is he okay?"

"No." They continued to wind through the corridor of curtains. "But he will be. Any idea who did this?"

"No. I saw him in the library yesterday after dinner and we teased each other about being dateless on a Friday night."

"Well, somebody got him good tonight."

"But you said he was a lucky man."

Dr. Sanchez stopped in the hall. Metal utensils clanged into pans around the corner. Muted voices and rolling carts added to the swell of sounds. "He has a mild concussion and a severe headache."

"Some luck!" Sarah shook her head.

"It is," Dr. Sanchez said. "Whoever hit him on the back of the skull missed his spine by less than half an inch. Any lower and he might have been paralyzed for life."

"Thank God!" Sarah said.

"That's a good idea." Dr. Sanchez pulled the curtain back. Terry looked dead. His head was wrapped in gauze to keep the bandages in place at the back of his scalp, and his eyes were closed. "Keep your voice down when you're near him."

She took Dr. Sanchez by the elbow and eased her back into the corridor. "I have to know," she said. "The syringe."

"Jammed into his neck. The contusion around it suggests he was stabbed hard."

Sarah hunched her shoulders and winced. "So he didn't do it to himself."

"No way. Thankfully, the needle struck the fleshy part of his neck and we were able to get it out intact."

"What was in it?"

Dr. Sanchez glanced up and down the corridor. "Since you are family, I guess you can know."

Sarah stared at her mouth, waiting.

"Heroin and LSD. Enough to give him a good night's rest and some vivid dreams, but not enough to cause any long term damage beyond 24 hours."

Sarah's head reeled. "Thank you, doctor."

Dr. Sanchez nodded. "I've already told the police not to bother even trying to talk to him until morning." She chuckled. "Heaven knows what he might say." She walked away looking at the chart in her hand.

Sarah went to Terry's side. An IV bag with clear fluid hung from what looked like a stainless steel coat rack and dripped into his left hand. Sarah stroked his right forearm gently and squeezed his hand. She wanted to kiss his cheek, but did not dare touch his head. He stirred slightly. "Oh Nina," he mumbled and drifted away again.

You bastard. Sarah yanked her hand away and turned to the window.

Sleep, you elusive mistress! Jeremy Tittle turned over and fluffed his pillow again. What a young man would give for a good night of sex, this old man would give double for a good night's sleep! He sighed, his thoughts drifting to Jean. Sometimes he woke and reached for her next to him, his hand groping empty air. His best hours of rest came after crying himself back to sleep.

He and Jean had big plans for their retirement. Neither had the slightest interest in overseas travel. The vast United States captivated their interest and they were determined to explore every inch of it together. On his sixty-fifth birthday, not long after calling for the election of an Assistant Dean to succeed him, he and Jean bought a brand new motor home with all the latest navigational gadgets. A monstrous vehicle, it resembled a scaled version of a rock band's tour bus. The front was seventy-five percent windshield, and the two front bucket seats perched driver and passenger for maximum panoramic views. A ladder hung from the back, should someone braver than either Jean or Jeremy wish to climb to the roof. A tiny video camera protruded from the top center of what should have been a rear windshield. Jeremy loved this feature. Imagine navigating backward by watching a video feed from the rear of the vehicle!

Jeremy threw the covers off and lowered his bare feet to the floor. He padded to the bedroom window and parted the curtains, looking at it parked in the driveway. Has seventeen miles on it, he thought, shaking his head. A few brave folks at the seminary told him it stuck out like a sore thumb, especially because the Dean's residence sat adjacent to the front seminary entrance. But Jeremy looked at it every day and could not part with it. It reminded him of her.

They brought it home in January, 1997. In February, the specialists diagnosed Jean with terminal cancer, inoperable and very aggressive. By June, she was dead.

He lost interest in retirement after Jean died. Never spoke of it again. Tonight at the window he grimaced, certain he was a source of great irritation to George, and especially to Hilary, the epitome of an ambitious, claw-your-way-to-the-top woman. His Jean, by contrast, had been the darling of the seminary, the matron in the best sense of the word. Everyone took her death hard, everyone, that is, except Hilary Fields. She had none of Jean's grace.

Jeremy shook his head and dropped the curtains. Hilary thought the position of Dean's wife would gain her the same attention, respect and admiration Jean had gotten. It wouldn't. Jean loved people. They could feel it, and they loved her back. They admired and respected her in spite of her position, not because of it. Hilary would never understand. You cannot command love. You can only give it, and then receive it in return.

Jeremy returned to bed. He thought about Terry Woodrow. How suddenly life becomes a brittle twig, so easily snapped and left to dangle. He pulled the covers over his chest. He would call George in the morning and offer to stand in for Terry at the service.

Chapter Nine

One mile south of the railroad tracks, Vinnie parked the Rolls in the usual spot in the middle of Kingstown Cemetery. The railroad tracks ran the length of Kingstown, dividing the city both geographically and culturally into two disproportionate neighborhoods. The northern neighborhood comprised most of the city, including Ecclesia Seminary, high atop the only serious hill for fifty miles. The land was precious and high priced. With few exceptions, the lawns were deep green and carefully edged and the hedges were manicured. Down the hill and south beyond the railroad tracks, the prices and the landscape changed dramatically. The "lawns" resembled burial grounds for rusted automobiles, washing machines, and bicycles with missing parts.

The Kingstown City Council built the cemetery where land was cheap, and they kept expanding the grounds until it spanned in excess of three hundred acres. It was surrounded by a black brick wall that had been torn down and rebuilt four times during the expansions. Two wide paved roads that ran North to South and East to West connected its four entrances.

The cemetery was the final resting place for rich and poor, so the variety of grave markers differed greatly. Marble statues of riders atop muscled steeds, huge mausoleums and carved granite headstones marked the graves of the wealthy Northerners. Two-inch square painted aluminum plates, placed flush with the ground, marked the graves of less fortunate Southerners. By city ordinance, one couldn't reserve a plot, and many Northerners through the decades fought long and hard to get the ordinance changed, without success. To their horror, ornate mausoleums sat next door to graves marked with a concrete headstone no bigger than a Popsicle stick.

The latest expansion pushed the cemetery to the edge of two large trailer parks and a half-vacant strip mall built in the 70's when the City Council decided to expand its city limits and encourage subdivision growth on the South side of town by offering generous plots of land at inexpensive prices. Budding entrepreneurs pounced. The expansion plan was scrapped three years later. The City Council discovered that people with enough money to buy land in the proposed southern subdivisions were unwilling to be known as South-of-the-Tracks folk. Instead, they were willing to settle for less land and house in the more acceptable northern neighborhoods. The stores in the newly built mall were robbed so many times that two-thirds either went out of business or relocated, leaving the strip mall home to the town's drug dealers, prostitutes and free roaming, emaciated k-9s. By day, the mall resembled Main Street in a ghost town, but by night it was a busy center of underworld commerce. Seedy and dangerous, the Kingstown police rarely patrolled it, except on the rare occasion when they were called.

Emil Bente laid claim to the graveyard next door, and people wanting crack came there to buy. His office was the back of the Rolls, and he always had Vinnie park it smack in the center of the graveyard because it was furthest from listening ears or watching eyes, and because his customers could access him from every direction.

Tonight, Emil was not open for business.

"It's not safe to stay here, Mr. Bente," Vinnie said. Nina whimpered in the back, her head flat against the floor. Emil sat with his right hand in an ice-filled champagne bucket, wincing and smoking his way through a bowl of rock.

"I said, take a walk!" His high-pitched voice barked at Vinnie like a ten-week-old pit bull. "Mrs. Bente and I have some things to discuss." The words came like the hiss of a viper. He drew smoke from the pipe into his lungs, and in the bright glow Vinnie saw glassy, raging eyes.

"Tell me you won't hit her again, and I'll take a long walk." Vinnie knew a challenge like that could set Emil off, but he wasn't about to be an accessory to murder. He felt the cell phone in his jacket pocket.

"I won't." Emil repositioned his hand in the bucket. "Think I broke my hand on the bitch anyway."

"Okay." Vinnie turned to the front seat and glanced into the rear view mirror, seeing only the glow from the pipe. He stepped out and his lungs filled with freshly scrubbed air. Clouds overhead still blocked the moon but sent no more rain. Light bounced from the trailer parks into the cemetery and he was relieved to be able to see without the goggles. He walked south, away from the light toward the high wall separating the cemetery from the strip mall. He needed privacy for the call he was about to make. Darkness engulfed him the closer he got to the wall.

He opened the cell phone, the key pad glowing blue, and he hesitated. Did he really want Mr. S to give him a direct order he'd have to obey? Or should he throw the broad out, tie up Emil and drive all night to Connecticut? He could dump the runt on Daddy's doorstep and say, "He's your problem. You deal with him." Sure. That's a great way to get yourself wasted. Vinnie's neck sank into his shoulders. Either way he was fucked. The family always protected its blood. He drew a large breath and sighed against the night. He stuffed the phone in his pocket. Then he heard a woman's muffled scream behind him. He yanked the phone out again and dialed.

Emil pulled Nina to her knees in front of him, glaring at her through the darkness and the smoke. "Let's light a candle, sweetheart, like old times," he said, his voice laced with a sickeningly soft lilt. His lighter threw a long, thin flame to the wick of a candle on the retractable table next to him. Light rose from the wick and mixed with the smoke. In the light, Emil examined her face. The left eye was swollen shut, a jagged tear above her brow trickling two lines of blood over the lid. Her nose was sideways and flat against her right cheek. Her other eye was open and twitched. Blood oozed from the corner of her mouth, and her lower lip was fat and split. She steadied herself on the floor with both hands.

"We used to make love in the light from this candle, didn't we darling?" Emil's lips curled. "Tell me Nina. It was love that we made, wasn't it? Or was it something else?" The swaying woman didn't speak. Emil's smile vanished and his tone hardened. "Or did you just fuck me for the free coke?" She started to shake her head, but he grabbed her thick brown hair. "Don't lie to me!" When she cried out, his lips curled into a smile that held neither warmth nor kindness. "You fucked me for free coke, yes?" He yanked her head up, forcing her to look at him. "You married me for more free coke, yes? You sold it to your buddies and kept the money, didn't you? Then you and your palsies decided to get your own coke, but I found out, didn't I Nina?"

He spat in her face. Nina did not move. "You've had one hand in my wallet, the other hand in my coke, and your legs spread wide to everybody else. Isn't that right, slut?" Nina watched his eyes.

There was a click and Nina flinched. Emil had taken his swollen hand from the ice bucket and tightened his grip on the Bic. Its blade shimmered in the candlelight. He held it close to her throat and she stopped breathing. Then he sliced open her shoulder bag, spilling the contents onto the floor. He picked up the plastic egg that fell from the bag.

"Is this all of it?" he asked.

"Take it. It's all I have," Nina said, blubbering the words through swollen lips.

"Oh I'll take it," he said, shaking the egg in her face, "And I'll also take the rest of it. Where is it?"

"That's all I have," she mumbled, blood spilling from her mouth.

He waved the switchblade. "That's not what I asked. Maybe we should give you a little haircut until your memory improves." Grabbing a handful of her hair, he sawed through it an inch from the scalp.

"Don't!" Her open mouth revealed large gaps where several teeth had been knocked out.

"Where is it, Nina?" He grabbed another fistful of hair, cutting it off at the scalp. "Where is the rest of the rock?"

Nina wailed like a beat dog. Emil's eyes blazed.

"On second thought, I don't need your help," he said, shouting into her face. "I'll find it myself, after you're gone." Nina rocked on her knees.

Emil leaned to her left ear. "You betrayed me, Mrs. Bente.... I feel raped by my own wife.... Maybe it's time my wife knows what that feels like!"

"No Emil! Please!"

Emil shoved her backward onto the floor. The Bic sliced the front of her dress from bottom to top. "This is gonna hurt." In the minutes that followed, he inflicted as much sexual pain as he could, all the while smiling and waving the switchblade in her ruined face. At the final act of sodomic brutality, Nina screamed, her pain-filled cry muffled by the floorboard carpet.

Emil pushed her face into the floor, dressed, and flung the rear door wide. He dragged her, gasping and moaning, amongst the tombstones. "I promised Vinnie I wouldn't punch you no more," he said. "But I didn't promise nothing about kicks!" Emil kicked Nina in the stomach. She wrenched, and he kicked her in the face. She careened sideways, smashing the back of her head against a large marble tombstone. He kicked her again and again. With each kick, he whispered a word through clenched teeth.

"Bitch!" Her body convulsed. "Whore! Slut!"

Panting hard, he felt like he might pass out. Nina wasn't moving. The only sound coming from her was a faint gurgling. He spit toward her, then staggered back to the Rolls to soak his hand and wait for Vinnie's return.

After the third ring, a deep, garbled voice said, "Yes?"

"This is 3-3-20. I need S. It's an emergency." Vinnie hunched over, his chin on his chest and his back to the Rolls 200 yards away.

"I'll get him."

Vinnie glanced over his shoulder and then turned back to the phone. He waited, one ear listening for sounds in the cemetery, the other for a voice from the cell phone. He heard more screams in the distance. He leaned his weight first on one foot and then the other. He buttoned his suit coat, then unbuttoned it again. Took a slow breath. The phone crackled and he jumped.

"He says you know what to do," the same gargling voice said. Vinnie recoiled as if slapped. "You listen to me. I don't, repeat do not know what to do! Tell S we have a 212 and I have to speak with him right now."

"Call tomorrow and report."

"Did you hear what I said?" Vinnie's frustration seared into the phone, but all he heard was the silence of a line gone dead. He smacked the phone shut and hurled it against the black brick wall in front of him. He heard the chug of his breath. Surrounded by the silence of the sprawling repository of the dead, he turned and started for the car.

He found Emil in the back seat of the Rolls. Vinnie flipped on the interior light. Emil was soaking his hand in the bucket, the water the color of rose wine, his hair wet and stuck to his neck and forehead; his eyes glassy and wild; the white dress shirt spattered with blood. There was no sign of Nina. Oh shit.

"You all right, Mr. Bente?" Vinnie said. *As if I care.*

"Never better." Emil said, head cocked at an angle, a smirk on his lips.

"Where's Mrs. Bente?" Vinnie asked.

Emil pointed a stubby finger to the window. "Picking out a plot." He laughed.

Vinnie glared. "Listen to me carefully, Emil."

"Mr. Bente," Emil wagged his left index finger.

"Mr. Bente," Vinnie said. "This car is more evidence than the feds need to gas us both. Put whatever you want to take with you into that bag over there and be ready to go in two minutes." For once, Emil didn't argue. He grabbed the bag and reached for the plastic egg.

Vinnie extracted himself and went to look for Nina. He found her twenty-five feet away draped over a headstone. He put his finger to her neck and was surprised to find a pulse. Rushing back to the car he opened the trunk, smelling spilled gasoline from the emergency can strapped in the left corner. He grabbed the can, soaking the front seat as Emil emerged with the bag from the back.

"Let's put Nina in before we strike the match!" Emil said.

Vinnie wanted to tell him who his choice would be.

"Leave her right where she is," he said and brushed past. He doused the back seat and the floor, and threw the empty can into the trunk. "Go! I'll meet you at the south wall." He heard Emil's shoes tapping fast on the pavement.

Vinnie pulled his favorite Zippo from his pocket. Good-bye old friend. Stepping back five yards, he scratched the lighter, and a tall flame rose from the wick. In one motion, he threw it like a horseshoe into the back seat, turned his body and covered his head. The blast knocked him to the ground. He bounced up and ran south, glancing back long enough to see the Rolls engulfed in flames. He caught up with Emil at the south exit.

"I want a new car by tomorrow," Emil said with cocaine bravado. Light from the inferno flickered across their faces.

"First let's try to see tomorrow," Vinnie said. "Follow me and stay in the shadows." They hurried along the back side of the mall, pausing at the large dumpster to catch their breath.

"If we're lucky," Vinnie said, wheezing, "the cabby will be here tonight." A cab driver named Joe was known to come to the strip mall after his shift to smoke dope and sleep it off. Sometimes he would even get a late night customer needing to make a delivery across town. His dented yellow Caprice had become a mall fixture after dark.

Vinnie and Emil arrived at the front corner of the long building and peered around the rain gutter. The storefronts were dark, the air still, and the strip mall appeared empty. Vinnie knew it was not. He strained to see around a row of wilted azaleas and spotted the Caprice. Vinnie pointed, Emil nodded, and they sprinted the fifty yards to the driver's side back door. They were inside with the door locked before Joe could focus his eyes.

"What the-"

"Need a lift Joe," Vinnie said, smiling at the gray sandpaper face in the front seat. "And we'll pay double because it's late."

The word "double" got Joe moving. "Do I need the meter running?" he asked, glancing in the back seat.

"Not unless you want to share this hundred dollar bill with the cab company." Vinnie held it high for Joe to see in the mirror.

"Where to?" he said in his best official voice.

"The bay," Vinnie said. He could feel Emil's eyes on him, and he didn't care. The cab roared from the lot and shot south.

"Everyone understand your assignments?" Steele looked at the semi-circle of blue uniforms huddled over the unmarked's hood where the cemetery ground's blueprints had been spread. It wasn't a question. He rolled up the blueprints. "Let's go. Remember: lights, but no sirens. At the tracks, kill the lights."

The back of the Ecclesia faculty lot sparkled red, white and blue. Higgins and Steele led the procession down the hill and south on Bradley. Higgins glanced at the dash clock. 4:10.

"This time we'll have the perimeter sealed," Steele said.

Downtown Kingstown was still and all traffic lights were green as the flashing procession snaked toward the railroad tracks. Halfway through town, the blinking light on the GPS monitor disappeared and Steele cursed, slapping the handheld radio to his face. "All units. Seal the cemetery. Go. Go!"

Higgins stomped the accelerator. At the tracks, flashers died. Ahead Steele saw the sky glowing yellow and orange.

"Get Fire and Rescue here, stat," Steele said into the radio. "Scrap perimeter seal. Go straight in." He set the radio on his thigh, and then clutched it to his mouth again. "Use your spots. Bente may still be in there!" The unmarked cars splashed in and through the entrance gutters. Ahead, flames roared from the Roll's shattered windows. Thick smoke belched into the sky.

Higgins flipped on the spotlight, scanned right and left. Nothing but rows of headstones and monuments.

"We're heading west," Steele radioed, referring to himself. "Two, break north. Three, right and scan south. Four, stay with the Rolls. Five, patrol the exits." Higgins eased the vehicle past the inferno. Even from the driver's seat, he could feel the heat blast. Past the junction, his spot picked up something blue to the left. Slamming the brakes, Steele barely missed bashing his head against the dash. "What the-"

"Over there, Cap!" Higgins pointed. Steele threw the radio into Higgins' lap. "Tell the others." He grabbed the flashlight and leapt out. Higgins radioed and swung the car so the headlights shone directly on the patch of blue. As he got out, Higgins saw a wave of uniforms rushing to where Steele knelt. In the distance, wailing sirens mixed with the stench of burning rubber and paint.

Higgins started toward the crowd but a uniform running the other way caught his arm. "Captain says radio the ambulance we have a critical. Have them come in the east entrance and I'll guide them in." The officer continued running toward the east entrance. Higgins ran back to the car and raised the radio to dry lips.

Chapter Ten

Near the Bay

The Buccaneer Motel offered sixteen rooms, eight on each side of the one story barracks-looking building. Vinnie requested a room in the back. The night clerk asked for payment in advance and handed him a key to number 11. Emil had stayed in shadow by the road where the taxi had dropped them. The dark paneling and lack of windows made the tiny room even smaller. Wide-weave orange shag choked with dirt and pocked with cigarette scars covered the floor. The room smelled of stale butts and dirty socks.

From the opposite side of the room, Vinnie leveled the Glock with Emil's nose. The top of the suppressor rose higher than the front sight, but he didn't need the sight. Through the years, this piece had become an extension of his arm. "Sit." he said. Emil sat on the end of the furthest double bed from the door. Vinnie pulled the armless desk chair halfway between the door and the bed and sat backward on it. "We're overdue for a little talk, Emil."

"Mr. Bente," Emil said.

"I'm done with that 'Mr. Bente' shit as of right - fuckin' – now. You got that - Emil?" Vinnie's thumb pulled the hammer back. "I said, is that clear Emil?" Every syllable spat through his bared teeth and rang like steel pellets.

"Sure Vinnie."

"Yes, Mr. Bontecelli," Vinnie said.

Emil's chubby face flushed red and he started to stand, "What the fuckin' fuck 'ere?"

Vinnie was on his feet quicker, with the chair in his left hand, and he used the outstretched legs to push Emil back down. "Say, 'Yes Mr. Bontecelli,' or the maid's gonna wipe your splatter off that headboard."

"Take it easy, Vinnie."

"Yes, Mr. Bontecelli. Say it or die. Right. Now." The barrel was steady on the bridge of Emil's nose.

"Yes, Mr. Bontecelli."

"I like the sound of that," Vinnie said. "Now that we've had our lesson in manners, let's have your hardware. All of it. And don't get cute. Toss it on the other bed." Emil threw the Bic and the Bowie knife onto the bed. He unhooked the shoulder holster and tossed the Glock. Then he reached behind his back for the 38.

"Easy," Vinnie said. Emil unclipped the concealed holster and gun and flung them onto the bed.

"Now slide yourself back to the headboard behind you." He did as he was told, never taking his eyes from Vinnie.

"My father's going to kill you for this, your whole family."

"Daddy's not here, is he?" Vinnie snapped his fingers. "Come to think of it, let's talk about your father," he said. "It's nice to talk, wouldn't you agree Emil?"

"Sure, fine, whatever," Emil said, looking at his shoes.

The pillow to his immediate right exploded and Emil screamed. Pieces of pillow landed in his lap and his hair.

"Yes, *Mr. Bontecelli*," Vinnie said behind the curling smoke from the end of the suppressor.

"Yes, *Mr. Bontecelli*. Jesus Christ!" Emil's eyes flashed about the room like a wild animal seeing its cage for the first time.

"That's better Emil," Vinnie said, a smile mask pasted on his face. "Please don't make me remind you again. Now, what were we talking about? Oh yes, your father."

Emil sat motionless. Vinnie continued, "Your father is the one who sent me to Rhode Island with you. He let you slap his face and 'leave' to carve out a territory of your own. But he sent a babysitter." Vinnie raised his hand and wiggled his fingers.

"Liar!" Emil said. "I hired you."

"I said I would come. You paid me to come. But I never told you why I came."

Emil shook his head, but Vinnie saw a flash of recognition pass over his face. "My father should have minded his own business!" His eyes narrowed.

"Oh but he did, Emil. He minded his own business." Vinnie broke into a grin. "Just how large do you think the Shark's territory is, Junior?"

"Connecticut's his territory. Told me so himself many times. That's why I set up in Rhode Island."

"Would you believe the entire Eastern third of the United States?" The words landed like a grenade across the room.

"I don't think so!" Emil said, glaring.

"If you live through the night you can call him yourself," Vinnie said. "But the pathetic fact of the matter, Emil, is that I've been babysitting you for Daddy ever since we left Connecticut." He touched his lips. "Let me see if I can remember how he described you. Oh yes, I believe he said you were a hot-headed little runt with the emotional maturity of a seven year old."

Emil was breathing so hard, Vinnie was sure he would hyperventilate.

"But you know what, runt?" Vinnie said, spitting his words again, "I'm done with you, and I'm done with your dad."

"I'll see you dead," Emil said without conviction.

"Ah, I just don't think so." Vinnie stood, gathering the weapons from the other bed. "Here's how I see it. You got two choices. Choice is good, right

Emil? I'll give you a hint. Right about now, you say, 'Yes, Mr. Bontecelli,' and I let you live a little bit more." He cocked his head theatrically.

"Yes, Mr. Bontecelli."

Vinnie continued. "Sure, choice is good. You get to pick from one of these two choices, and then we know where we're going. Choice number one: you help me get the rest of the eggs; I take them and disappear. You're free to go home to Big Shark Daddy and hopefully grow up before you get killed.

Or choice number two: you continue with this punk attitude, and I put two in your forehead, carve you up with your own knife and ship you in several small boxes to Daddy's doorstep." Vinnie wiped his nose on his sleeve. "I think it's pretty decent of me to let you make the choice, don't you Emil?"

"Yes, Mr. Bontecelli."

Vinnie lifted his eyebrows. "Ahhhh, see how easy that was? Sure, it's decent of me to let you choose." He glared down the barrel of the Glock again. "You don't want me to make the choice."

"My father didn't send you to babysit me!" Emil said, his lip trembling.

Vinnie smiled. "Oh but he did, and I've put up with your shit ever since. I've played along with your 'I'm-a-big-shot, call-me-Mr.-Bente' shtick, and I've worked overtime to keep you from fucking us both over so bad we end up in prison or dead. I did it out of loyalty to the Shark. But no more." The smile disappeared from Vinnie's face. "Apparently, he can't be bothered with you anymore … so I'm done with the both of you."

Emil's chin rested on his chest, his unbuttoned shirt clinging wet. "I'll help you get the rock," he said.

"That's a very good choice, Emil. We'll start in the morning."

"But I ain't going back to Connecticut." He slammed his fat right fist into the remains of the pillow, then howled in pain, clutching the broken hand.

Vinnie lowered the Glock. *You are so right, runt! So right.*

Memorial Hospital Emergency

A swarm of green hospital scrubs met the ambulance at Memorial emergency. Mushroom shaped hats lay at awkward angles on each head. Two people pushed the stretcher, two more pulled from the front and one on each side prepped IVs. Agents Steele and Higgins watched the green team whisk Nina through the Emergency Room doors. A slender woman wearing a long white coat over scrubs approached, carrying a clipboard. Both men flashed their badges.

"I'm Captain Max Steele, and this is my partner, Lieutenant Bert Higgins, FBI." The woman nodded and escorted them through the doors to a small room with a coffee pot and vending machines. "It's our break room," she said. "We'll stabilize the patient and let you know what we're dealing with as soon as possible."

"Thank you, Doctor …" His eyes fell to the name tag, "Dr. Sanchez." She nodded from the door and turned to leave.

"Oh, Dr. Sanchez," Steele said, taking a step toward her. "One more thing while we've got you?" Higgins searched the cabinets behind him for a coffee filter.

"Top drawer, all the way to the right," Dr. Sanchez said over Steele's shoulder. Then her brown eyes returned to him.

"A few hours ago, you should have seen a white male, 26, blond hair, with a head wound," Steele said.

She nodded, raising top sheets on her clipboard and peering beneath. "Woodrow, Terrence. Concussion."

"That's him."

Dr. Sanchez continued to read her notes. "Neck contusion. Appears someone stabbed him with a syringe cocktail of heroin & LSD."

"Whoa!"

"He was accompanied by his sister."

"Who?" he said, not really asking. "He's a student. Family is in California."

"She's not his sister," Dr. Sanchez said, still looking at her notes. "People tell us all kinds of things to get back here." Steele nodded and she continued. "The way she looks at him, I'm guessing girlfriend."

Steele snorted and rubbed the back of his neck. "Nah. The lady we just brought in is his girlfriend." Dr. Sanchez snapped the page down and scanned. "Bente?"

"Yep."

Higgins had put too much water in the coffee maker and it overflowed. The machine popped and sizzled. He dashed for paper towels.

Dr. Sanchez glanced at Higgins and then returned to the clipboard. "My notes indicate Bente's married."

"Right again," Steele feigned a wince. "Married to the East Coast mob. That's why we're here."

"Sounds like Mrs. Bente's been rolling some dangerous dice," she said. "Woodrow too."

"You have no idea." She stared at him, but Steele fell silent.

"Well," she flipped the top page up again. "Woodrow was admitted about an hour ago. He's in Room ... 316."

"Thank you. Obviously we would like to talk to him."

"Obviously." She turned again to leave.

"Sorry, one last thing doctor."

"Yes?" She glanced over her shoulder.

"Just to be clear, Mrs. Bente doesn't have a sister, or a brother. "

She smiled. "I got it. No one gets to her."

"And please, as soon as you know anything about her condition...."

"You'll be next to know."

"Thank you, Doctor." Steele accompanied his extended hand with a warm smile. "You've been terrific."

"My pleasure Captain." Her smile showed teeth for the first time.

"Max," he said, still shaking her hand. He caught her glance at his left hand, then smile into his eyes for a moment. Then she was gone. Max Steele stared after her, a grin still pasted on his lips.

"Forgive me, Captain, but you are a hound," Higgins said, hunched over a struggling coffee maker.

"Watch and learn, my boy," Steele said, turning to the coffee pot. "Watch … and learn."

"Whatever." He laughed.

Max winced. If he only knew.

The round white table was not large enough for both men to sit. Steele eased into the other chair. He scalded his tongue with the first sip and lurched forward. He could swallow or spit. He swallowed, squinting as the hot liquid seared his throat.

"The stars in your eyes blind you to the steam in your cup?" Higgins said.

"It was worth it."

"Pretty good lookin' for an older woman." Higgins smiled over the rim of his cup.

Steele ignored him. "Let's focus. The GPS is fried. Bente and Bontecelli could be anywhere. I want two uniforms outside Room 316. I want two plain clothes in the ER parking lot, and two more inside. Tell them to bandage up and blend in."

"On it." Higgins pushed his chair back.

Steele held up a hand. "Finish your coffee, Lieutenant. It's been a long night."

"Thank you sir."

"I actually like it when you call me Cap," Steele said. "Nate's okay too… most of the time."

"Roger that."

Dr. Sanchez's face appeared in the doorway. She was winded, her eyes wide. "Captain." Her voice broke like glass into the room. "I just called for the Chaplain."

Steele cursed and turned to Higgins. "Get started. Go."

Higgins leapt from the table, finished his coffee in two large gulps and hurried from the room.

"Sit, Dr. Sanchez," Steele said.

"Can't. Let me brief you on what we have so far." She paused and looked at the clipboard.

"Go ahead."

"Bente has fluid on the brain, head swollen twice its size. Rushing her into surgery to drain the skull and relieve the pressure. Front teeth are gone; jaw fractured in several places. She has five broken ribs, one punctured lung. She's on a ventilator."

Steele squeezed his eyelids.

"Sorry, Captain, but it's worse." He opened his eyes, nodded.

Dr. Sanchez continued, "We're still determining the extent of her internal injuries, but she's vomiting blood. She's been raped and sodomized."

"Semen samples?"

"Of course. Rushed to the lab with the blood samples."

As she spoke, his mind filled again with Nina's mangled frame, blood dripping from the smashed face onto the marble headstone, more coursing down the insides of her legs. He shoved his coffee away.

"Sorry," Dr. Sanchez said, "but you wanted-"

"I did." He held up his hand. "I do." He swallowed. "Is she going to make it?"

"Unfair question. You know that. Look, a team of excellent surgeons and internists are working on her right now." Holding her clipboard with her right hand, she patted the back of his hand with the other. Her hand was moist and warm.

"One more thing you should know," she said. Her hand rested on his and her gaze held his for a moment. "She's pregnant."

His whole body jerked. "So we may be looking at a double homicide, " he said, "If she-"

"I have to go." Dr. Sanchez's voice was strong again. She righted herself and disappeared through the doorway. "Sorry, she's not the only crisis in this place."

Steele's eyes were unfocused. He pushed his chair from the table and leaned forward, resting forearms on thighs. Lowering his forehead to the table, he let his face hang over the edge. His shirt smelled foul beneath his jacket. A wave of exhaustion and nausea hit him at the belt line. The cemetery scene returned, images flashing rapid-fire. His body ached and felt twice its weight. His gut roiled and his mind raged. A whole year of busting work! *If she dies, who will testify? Shut up right now with that shit, Nate! That's a person in there. A person! But -*

"You okay, Cap?" Higgins leaned in from the doorway. The remaining coffee in the pot had scorched on the burner and the air smelled of burnt beans and body odor.

Steele lifted his head. "Peachy," he nodded without looking.

"Is Bente okay?"

"Nope."

"Alive?"

"About as much as our whole operation."

"Then she's in bad shape."

"Awful," Steele said.

Silence thickened the air.

From beyond the doorway, a vibrating metal cart passed.

Higgins spoke, "Chief Parker is posting two of his finest – his words - outside Woodrow's room. Should be in place soon. Our E.R. people are onsite."

Steele stared at the ceiling.

"Maybe you should get some rest," Higgins said.

"Not until we look in on lover boy," Steele said, rubbing his eyes. "Tell Dr. Sanchez that we'll be in Room 316 if anything happens."

"On my way."

"Meet you at the elevator."

Room 316

The morning sun peered into the hospital window, casting bright spears onto the pale blue blanket draped across two chairs. From the top edge of the blanket, Sarah watched two official looking men enter Room 316. One scanned the right wall, the bathroom, the floor and Terry's clothes in the open cabinet on the left wall. The other approached Terry. Both men's eyes were bloodshot, their suits wrinkled and mud spattered.

"Excuse me. Can I help you?" Sarah asked. Both men started. Terry jerked upright in his bed. Instantly, he saw the dazzling rose-colored elephant on the high wire explode into shards of red glass that blasted through his forehead and scalp. He clutched his head with both hands, yelping, and lowered himself to the mattress. A strong male voice to his left spoke and he turned to see the shadow of a puffy face with bags under the eyes. Everything looked blurry and pulsed. The ear on the left side of the man's head flapped slowly like a wing. The right ear spun fast like a pinwheel.

Captain Steele answered the young woman peering at him over the edge of the blanket. "I'm sorry, you are…."

"And I'm sorry, you are…." Sarah said.

Steele reached into his jacket pocket and produced a wallet with a gold badge and his photo identification card. Higgins followed suit, then re-sumed his visual scan of the room.

"Captain Steele and Lieutenant Higgins, F.B.I. And now young lady, who are you?" Sarah's eyes shifted from one agent to the other. Terry's eyes clicked toward Sarah's face like the second hand on a wall clock.

"I'm Sarah Stafford," she said through the fabric of the blanket, then lowered it to her chin and sat up in one of the chairs. "What can I do for you?"

From the bed, Terry laughed and closed his eyes. Sarah's face sat atop an ostrich neck and her nose was as red as Rudolph's. And it blinked.

"Terry thinks that's funny too," Steele said. "Downstairs you told the paramedics and Dr. Sanchez that you were Sarah Woodrow, Terry's sister."

Terry's eyes clicked toward the ceiling. One thought after the other drifted overhead in the yellow mist, each moving at a different speed, carried on magic carpets with gold tassels. He reached for the slowest one, and missed. "Oops!" he said.

"I ... well ..." The commanding tone was gone from Sarah's voice. She fell silent, looked at the blanket, felt the agent's eyes on her. "Am I in trouble?"

"I don't know, are you?" Exhausted, Steele could not conceal his irritation.

Sarah shrugged.

"Do you know Nina Bente?" Steele asked. He watched her body for a reaction.

"No."

"You sure about that?" He waited. Nothing. "A fellow classmate of yours and someone so ... involved with Mr. Woodrow?"

"I said, no" Sarah said. "And involved how?" She rose to her feet and looked into Captain Steele's eyes. "Is Terry in some kind of danger?"

At that moment, Terry sucked in a large breath of air. Porky the Pig came straight for him in the Red Barron's airplane. As he bore down on him, Porky morphed into Darth Vader. Terry covered his face and braced for impact.

"More like a world of trouble," Higgins said and received a severe look from Steele.

"Terry? What for?"

Terry's forearms were crossed in front of his face and he peeked through them at the pair of lime green anacondas coiled between his calves at the end of the bed.

"Don't let them hurt me!" he said.

Sarah's eyes iced.

"Just relax son, we're not going to hurt you," Steele said. Terry saw the words come from the mouth of the larger anaconda on the left.

"Yeah, right!" he said, and clutched his head again in pain.

"He is under investigation, Miss Stafford," Steele said. "We haven't charged him with anything yet."

"Charge!" Terry shouted, lifting the heavy sword in his hand and kicking spurs into his white stallion's side.

Steele turned to Terry, "But I do have to read you your rights, Mr. Woodrow." Terry's teeth were gritted and his lips were parted wide. He puffed and rocked, lowering his arm straight in front of him, "All for England!" Then he clutched his head and screamed in pain.

Sarah jabbed her finger to Steele's nose. "You'll do no such thing, Captain. Can't you see he's hallucinating?" Steele scrubbed fingers against the bristles on his chin.

Sarah turned toward the door. "I'm getting the nurse."

"That won't be necessary, Miss Stafford," Steele said. "Tell lover boy we'll be back this evening to read him his rights."

"Lover boy?"

"Forgive me, I meant Mr. Woodrow." He and Higgins retreated to the door.

Sarah watched them pass.

"Haieeeyyyah!" She turned back to the bed. Terry gave something he saw a vicious karate chop.

Chapter Eleven

Residence of the Assistant Dean
Ecclesia Seminary

From the kitchen, George heard Hilary's tennis shoes squeak on the hard wood living room floor. She pressed through the kitchen doors with car keys in hand. His eyes took her in from wide bottom to narrow top, and his chin did a quick, involuntary side-to-side bobble. "Lovely, darling," he said. Hilary wore her raincoat buttoned top to bottom. The gray sweat pants she slept in fell beneath the hem to bare ankles and dirt smattered tennis shoes. On her head, she wore George's dark brown bucket hat. "I'm going to get a paper," she said.

"You go for one every morning," George said, turning back to the counter. "Why don't we start getting it delivered?"

"Because I like going for my paper. Besides, I like my cup of coffee."

George glanced at the unplugged coffee maker in the far counter corner. He never touched the stuff, and Hilary never touched the coffee maker. The warranty card was still inside the pot. But she had to have the best one money could buy.

"I was hoping you'd help me this morning," he said over his shoulder, reaching for a piece of toast. "I could use a hand setting up the Chapel."

Hilary stood with hands on broad hips, sneering from beneath the rim of the bucket hat. "Why didn't you get that done last night George? You were over there long enough." She reached for the door handle. "I'll see you at the service."

"Change clothes before you come."

The door slammed and he heard her Saab roar to life. Pinching the toast between his fingers, he noticed the blinking message light atop the answering machine. The LED indicated two messages awaited him. He got early Sunday morning panic calls from the guild of elderly women who fussed over the altar linens and flowers. They called in crisis almost every Saturday, and especially on Sunday morning, and it irritated him more every year. Why bother having volunteers if they monopolize so much of your time and energy that you could have done the job yourself – twice, and better. He punched the play button and the cassette tape rewound. His butter-laden knife stopped halfway across toast when a woman's voice identified herself as Sarah Stafford.

He listened. Terry got hurt. That would explain the commotion in the parking lot last night. "Bad timing surfer boy," George called to the machine even before Sarah finished speaking. "It's Palm Sunday and you'd better be in that damned Chapel!"

The first message ended and the machine beeped. The second message began. "Yes, Reverend Fields, this is Dr. James Barton at Memorial Hospital. I'm a member of the surgical team. A patient critically injured last night requires surgery and we're trying to get authorization to perform it. We've been unable to reach her husband or next of kin and believe she is a student at Ecclesia. Her name is Nina Bente, but an Ecclesia photo identification card found by investigators identifies her as Nina Ondolopous." George pushed the pause button, then the repeat button. The answering machine clicked, the tape rewound and the machine clicked again.

The toast lay buttered side down on the floor at his feet. He staggered to the nearest chair and collapsed into it. "Yes, Reverend Fields, this is Dr. James Barton at Memorial Hospital...." The voice continued, but George no longer heard it. Nina Bente? His mind spun like tires in mud ruts. The Nina in my arms last night, and who claims to be carrying my child ... is married to that bucket of shit Bente? It couldn't be. Or had it been a trap all along? Maybe Ondolopous wasn't her real name. Maybe Emil Bente had her infiltrate Ecclesia to set him up. Maybe the sex and the cocaine were a setup to the blackmail she sprang last night! Son-of-a-bitch!

Beads of sweat broke from his hairline and raced toward his chin. Maybe she gave him the eggs last night so she could threaten to tell the police that the Assistant Dean at Ecclesia had several pounds of rock cocaine that he forced her to smuggle into the country. Extortion!

But the surgeon said she was badly injured. The police must be crawling over her like picnic ants. What if she talks? Confesses? Plea bargains in exchange for testimony about him ... throwing him to the wolves in exchange for leniency. What would Hilary do when she found out? What would the Ecclesia Board do? He would lose everything! He heard his heart beat loudly in his ears, and felt his eyes darting erratically around the kitchen.

He shifted in the chair and took a deep breath. Maybe she hadn't talked ... maybe she was unconscious ... maybe she'd die. That would be good. What am I saying? Oh shit. Maybe I can get to her before she talks, tells, maybe strike a deal, give her enough green to buy her silence. Nah. She wouldn't go away quietly, unless he hired someone to ... encourage her.

The telephone rang and George jumped, his thighs slamming into the kitchen table. He cursed. The telephone rang again. Pushing from the table, he reached for the phone on the wall. An inch from the receiver, his hand stopped. Maybe he wouldn't answer it. They could leave a message. No, they couldn't! He cursed again, seeing he had not reset the machine. The telephone sounded the third ring. George looked at his outstretched hand as if it was a foreign object. It shook and jerked. Halfway through the fourth ring, he lifted the receiver to his ear, but did not speak.

"Hello?" a familiar voice sounded through the earpiece. "George, are you there?" Jeremy Tittle, Dean of Ecclesia, said.

"Yes, Jeremy, good morning," George said, "Piece of toast in my throat."

"Quite a night last night," Jeremy said.

"Guess so. I was just listening to my messages."

"So you heard from Miss Stafford?"

"Yes. Obviously, you did too. Mugging in the top lot, she said. That's a first." He paced the length of the kitchen.

"Woodward suffered a nasty blow," Jeremy said. "I wouldn't expect your assistant in Chapel this morning." Jeremy paused. "Are you exercising right now?"

"Sorry. I'll take a break." He heard his breath chugging.

"One of the reasons I'm calling is to volunteer to stand in for Woodrow as your liturgical assistant, if you can put up with an old man."

"Absolutely! Very generous of you, Jeremy."

"My pleasure. Now listen, the other reason I'm calling is this Nina Bente woman."

"The hospital called you too?"

"They did. A surgeon by the name of …."

"Barton."

"That's him," Jeremy said. "Barton said we had a student needing emergency surgery. I thought it was going to be Woodrow, but he said it was Nina Bente. Strange. They found a charred Ecclesia ID near the body identifying her as Nina Ondolopous, one of our students. But the police claim her last name is Bente. You know her?"

"I know a Nina Ondolopous, vaguely." George snatched a paper towel from the roll and wiped his forehead.

"Same woman. Dr. Barton said the FBI-"

"FBI!" George had not intended to shout.

Silence from the other end of the phone.

"Startled me there, George," Jeremy continued, "But yes, Dr. Barton said there is some big FBI investigation underway."

"Did she say anything? I mean, did they operate?" Stay calm. For Heaven's sake!

"I assume they operated, yes."

"Who authorized it?

"I did," Jeremy said.

"You realize you could be sued if they botch it?"

"The Lord will protect me. He always has." George rolled his eyes and began pacing again.

Dean Tittle continued. "I promised Miss Stafford I'd look in on Terry Woodrow at Memorial after services today. I'll see what else I can find out about our mystery student."

"You needn't trouble yourself with hospital calls, Jeremy. I'll head over there after lunch."

"Suit yourself, but I promised Miss Stafford. Besides, rumor has it you make your assistants do all the hospital visits." Jeremy chuckled into the phone.

"Don't believe everything you hear, Dean," George said, faking a chuckle in return.

"I'm curious about this Mrs. Bente. Married, but using a different last name. Assaulted and beaten nearly to death in the graveyard across town-"

"What?"

"And pregnant."

"Pregnant." George feigned surprise.

"That's what Dr. Barton said. They're getting heart tones, so the baby is still with us, thank God."

"Oh no," he whispered aloud.

"Mmmm," Jeremy said. "Seems we have a student with secrets. Dangerous things, secrets."

George hung up without saying good-bye, his eyes fixed on the large block of wood on the counter. Twelve black handles with stainless rivets protruded in three rows. Blades of varying lengths and widths hid inside the wood block. The largest knives were in the top row.

The telephone rang again, but George made no move toward it. A second ring, then a third, a fourth, a fifth. He pulled the largest knife out, laying the flat side of the blade against his wrist.

Secrets. Some will take them to the grave.

He grabbed the knife by its blade, whirled and threw it across the room. It stuck in the wall, its thick blade quivering an inch above the toaster.

Lavish Latte's Café
Kingstown

"Three hundred dollars per cassette, Mrs. Fields," Bo Brady said. His eyes scanned the raincoat and the bucket hat from the back booth at Lavish Latte's.

"Money first, then a cassette today, and another every day for five more days." Light without sunshine slipped through the plate glass storefront. The place teemed with puff-eyed people hunched over newspapers. The air smelled of fresh ground coffee beans. Outside, someone's car alarm went off.

Hilary stood at the edge of the booth, her face flushed, glaring at the man she'd hired. Half a dozen black hairs lay slicked to his otherwise bald head.

"That's rape, Bo," she said, setting her latte on the table and sliding into the booth across from him. From the first call to Bo Brady's private investigation firm, she'd felt his ooze, even washed her hands after every phone call.

"Call it whatever you want," Bo said. "I call it business. You trade your money for my information. If I was to give you the information first, I might not get paid."

"I'm not like you."

"That's okay." He shrugged, raised the remaining half of his bagel toward her. "Want some? Garlic bagel with lox and cream cheese." The stench of fish reached her nostrils. Her lips pursed and she recoiled.

"You have the cassette?" Hilary asked.

"Right here." He tapped the right pocket of his leather jacket. "I think you'll be pleased. Your George is a very bad boy."

"Forgive me, but I don't wish to discuss it with you."

"That's okay too."

"Are you still recording?"

"Even as we speak. The gear runs midnight to midnight."

Hilary unbuttoned the top half of her raincoat and reached into the inside pocket. She felt Bo's eyes on her chest. She pulled out a white envelope and slid it across the table.

Bo took a bite of his bagel that was much too large for his mouth. His lips opened and closed around the brown and white lump, and Hilary's stomach twisted. He lifted the envelope like a napkin, broke the seal with the longest fingernail she had ever seen on a man, and took his time counting the twenty dollar bills.

"I want a receipt with your signature on it," she said.

He nodded, chewing with his mouth open. Without looking at her, he pulled a business card and an ink pen from his shirt pocket, flipped it over and wrote "Received from Hilary Fields $300." He signed and dated it. Then he pulled the cassette from his right pocket, slapped the business card on top and pushed them across the table. She grabbed them, slid to the end of the booth and stood, snatching her latte.

"A pleasure, Mrs. Fields," Bo said without smiling or looking up. "See you tomorrow morning."

Hilary stomped to the door. Outside, she spilled coffee on herself trying to get the ring of car keys from her pinky finger. She set the coffee on the roof of the car and opened the door, jumped in and slammed the door. She started the engine. Glancing behind her, she put the Saab in reverse and stamped on the accelerator. Something struck the car roof and Hilary jumped. Sand colored liquid and foam splashed down the windshield. "My latte! Damn it to Hell!" She hit the windshield wipers and sped toward the highway. It was more than a minute before the pain registered in her left hand and she realized she had been slamming it against the left door's arm rest.

She found and jammed the audio cassette into the player in the dash. After a pause, she heard through the car speakers the buzz of a telephone ringing, followed by her own voice, "Fields residence." "Mrs. Fields, this is Mr. Turner with Turner Pest Control...." Hilary remembered this call. Mid-morning yesterday. She snaked with traffic onto the eastbound ramp. Sun burned through the cloud cover and she pulled the bucket hat lower, squinting against the glare and listening. The cassette continued to repeat her conversations throughout the day. She hated the sound of her voice and considered fast forwarding, but didn't want to miss anything. She remembered Bo's comment that George had been a very bad boy and turned up the volume.

Ecclesia Chapel
Palm Sunday Service

"And so the political climate was quite remarkable at the time Jesus made the triumphal entry into Jerusalem," George droned. "The Essenes out in the Diaspora had long been disenfranchised from the political debate and were becoming increasingly separatist, and the Sadducees were applying pressure for reform upon the Pharisees."

Jeremy sat in the Assistant's chair to the right of the altar and watched the congregation as George continued in monotone. Many heads were down, eyes shut. The children fidgeted. One red-headed little boy slapped the top of the pew in front of him with his palm branch. Two other boys were sword fighting with theirs on the other side of the Nave. George should dismiss the children for the sermon. Why make them suffer with the rest of us?

Most of the eyes looking up toward George in the raised pulpit were glassy. How effective can a sermon be when the majority of the congregation counted the minutes until it was over? Jeremy's cheeks burned. George charged forward without inflection. "Of course the assertion of a monarchical privilege for a carpenter's son was an outrage to the Pharisees. His knowledge of the Scriptures, though, kept Jesus in the debate for a long time ..." The sound of plastic crashing against plastic echoed against the ceiling. Several people gasped and one man in the back awakened from sleep, sprang to his feet and shouted, "I'm awake!" He looked around sheepishly and sat back down. A chuckle rippled through the back pews. Most eyes, however, fixed upon the altar. Beneath it, two grapefruit sacks of brightly colored Easter eggs lay atop one another, and a third sack dangled from the underside of the altar. Duct tape stuck from each corner of the sacks and the label on each sack read "Presents for the Children." Jeremy looked from the altar to the pulpit. George fell silent. He had paled visibly and leaned against the side of the pulpit. Squeals and laughter erupted in the pews and several children dashed down the center aisle toward the eggs.

"Stop!" George boomed with the loudest voice Jeremy had ever heard in the Chapel. The children froze in the aisles. His eyes wild and his hand outstretched, George leaned forward. The children cowered, a few running back to their parents. Jeremy wondered if he should do something. But what? Should he get out of his chair and usher the children back to their seats? Could he think of a joke to ease the tension?

A man's voice sounding from the back of the Sanctuary popped his thoughts like a soap bubble. "Reverend Fields, I'll take those."

The chubby, smiling face behind the bellowing voice transformed looks of fear and irritation into warm smiles. Even Jeremy smiled as Brother Lawrence strolled up the center aisle.

Brother Lawrence had been on staff at Ecclesia as the Spiritual Director since 1987 and was much beloved by the congregation. He showed up from time to time on Sunday mornings. He told Jeremy some months ago that a few of the board members tried to convert him from Catholicism to Presbyterianism, but he assured them that once a Franciscan monk, always a Franciscan monk.

Dean Tittle knew Brother Lawrence when he was Larry Stiles, a young man who grew up in a violent and impoverished Detroit neighborhood. Grew up too fast, he admitted to the Search Committee, and it made him hard. Hard to get along with. Hard to control.

A group of Franciscan monks who ran a mission three blocks from his gang's flophouse rescued him from the jaws of jail. To this day, Jeremy remembers Brother Lawrence's description of himself when Brother Timothy found him. Strung out on rock cocaine, with a belly that had emptied a pint of stolen sour mash onto his Laker's shirt. He was fourteen, but Brother Timothy told him years later that the face he saw that day carried the hardness and the tragedy of a fifty year old.

"Reverend Fields," Brother Lawrence boomed, "you need to have a better hiding place than that, or these children are going to find their presents before Easter." He reached on both sides of the aisle and patted a couple of the children.

"They're too smart for us old guys, aren't you children." Several nodded as they made their way back to their parents. Chuckles rippled through the pews.

Jeremy glanced back at George, whose color was returning and who had relaxed his grip on the pulpit rail. Jeremy watched him mop his face with a handkerchief.

Brother Lawrence bent over in his brown, floor length robe and reached under the altar. He pulled the dangling bag free from the underside, gathered the other two sacks into his arms and turned to face the congregation. "Okay kids, I'm going to take these presents with me and over this coming week I'm going to hide them really well. Next Sunday, be sure to bring your baskets because we're going to have a big Easter egg hunt and we'll have lots more eggs than these!" The congregation rumbled and the children bounced in their seats and whispered to each other. Brother Lawrence turned around and walked through the Sacristy door.

George smiled, "I guess I underestimated you children. How many of you kids think I did an awful job hiding your presents? Raise your hands." Jeremy saw lots of little arms shoot skyward. "And how many of you kids are coming back next week for the congregation's greatest Easter egg hunt ever?" Hands bounced and waved. "Good! We'll make sure Brother Lawrence is here to help us." He paused and glanced at Jeremy. "Well, I guess I've preached enough for one day. We'll talk next Sunday about the dynamics of pre-resurrection Jerusalem and its impact upon the socio-political climate of Judaism."

Thank God I'll miss that one, Jeremy thought. He listened for a few moments while George made the rest of the announcements, and then tuned him out. It had been a bizarre morning, and Jeremy felt, well, he wasn't sure quite how he felt. Perhaps times had changed and the new order of service is that there is no order. George must have staged the eggs dropping beneath the altar as a setup for next week. But announcement gimmicks should be left with the other announcements. And the sacred altar should never be used as a prop. He could feel his head shaking as he remembered the eggs crashing to the carpet.

And what a mixture of pagan and Christian symbols! Surely, someone of George's education and training knew that the egg was not in itself a Christian symbol, that it in fact played a significant role as a symbol of fertility in ancient Greek, Persian and Chinese culture. The fuzzy little chicks that hatched from eggs had more ties symbolically to fertility cults than they did to Christianity. Yet they have peeped their way into most Church Easter decorations and Sunday school activities. Then there was the Easter bunny. Rabbits, known for their incredible fertility, hopped straight from paganism into Christian Easter celebrations, despite adding nothing but confusion to the already muddied waters of Christian symbolism during this sacred holiday.

"And now, Dean Tittle will prepare the altar for Communion." Jeremy heard his name and the word "Communion," and he stood. In his mind he saw himself stopping the service, speaking about why they were here today, explaining the altar and Communion. But it was George's show. He could imagine the hornet's nest he would awaken if he interfered with the Assistant Dean's Chapel service. The Board would get involved. There would be a review. The Chapel congregation elders would issue a statement condemning the Dean's interference.

Ecclesiastical politics made him sick. He and his wife were supposed to have been thousands of miles away from it by now.

He set out the bread, poured wine into the chalice and returned to stand in front of his chair. George moved behind the altar and raised his hands to bless the bread and the wine. Jeremy stared at the floor, too ashamed of them both to participate.

Chapter Twelve

Memorial Hospital

The door opened and Sarah stepped from Terry's bathroom, wrapped in a white hospital towel. From the bed across the room, Terry watched her walk past the clothes closet to the mirror. She leaned over the sink and the undersized towel hiked. Lean, muscular legs climbed and climbed toward what promised to be a tight butt under the hem. Not an ounce of fat on her, Terry thought. Daily exercise. And no junk food. Except beer. And pizza.

Word got around Ecclesia that she had chosen to save her virginity for her wedding night, and many of the seminarians took the news hard.

Terry studied the back of her thighs, and he felt the stirring. Shouldn't think such things about your best friend. Memories ticked through his mind, distracting him momentarily. The way her eyes sparkled when she smiled, and flashed when she was irritated. The curious mixture of poise and grace. The tough-minded, disciplined, hard-driving woman. The amazing senior minister in the making.

"Good morning," Terry said, figuring he had better let her know he was awake before she dropped the towel and started getting dressed. She'd never forgive him.

Sarah whirled, makeup in both hands. "Good morning sleepy head. And speaking of," she knocked the side of her head through wet strands of blond hair. "How is the noggin?"

"Like a thick malted. Nothing's moving."

"And it's afternoon," she said.

"Pardon?"

"It's good afternoon, not good morning."

"You're kidding."

She shook her head.

"Didn't you say you were preaching today?" Terry said.

"Got back an hour ago. When we have time, I want to tell you about it. So incredible."

"I've got time."

"No you don't." He watched the smile vanish. "A lot's happened."

"I can't even begin to guess." His hand explored the bruise on the right side of his neck.

"You can't." Sarah turned away from him and bent over, snatching clothes from the floor. He got one last eyeful, a big one, and his heart pounded. *Look away Dude.* He didn't.

"I'm going to throw some clothes on," she said, grabbing the last sock. "Back in a sec." She disappeared through the bathroom door. Terry stared at the door, wishing Sarah would pick up some more clothes. Then he shook his head. *Note to self. Get head out of crotch.*

He eased himself upright and stared at his reflection in the plate glass window to his right. His hair stuck straight up through the gauze wrap. His hand found the bandage at the back of his skull. He felt around the edges of it. Sparks of pain convinced him to leave it alone.

Someone knocked, the door handle swung, and two men in suits walked to the side of the bed.

"Come in," Terry said, ticked that they already were.

"Who is it?" Sarah asked from the bathroom.

"I'm about to find out."

"Terrance Woodrow?" the taller man said.

"Yes."

The men retrieved thin wallets from inside jacket pockets and flipped them open. "I'm Captain Steele and this is Lieutenant Higgins, Federal Bureau of Investigation."

"FBI," Terry said, smiling. "Whoever did this to me must be in some serious trouble."

"We'd like to ask you a few questions."

Wow, just like TV. "Sure, and I hope you can also give me a few answers."

"If we can," Steele said. He nodded to Higgins, who disappeared through the door.

Sarah burst from the bathroom working the last button of her white blouse. "Hello, Miss Stafford," Steele said.

"You know him?" Terry's eyes searched her unsmiling face.

"They've been here before," Sarah answered, not taking her eyes from Steele.

"You were unavailable last night when we came," he said. Higgins returned with a short, wiry man carrying a large black case in one arm and a folded metal table in the other. "We'll give the stenographer a moment to set up and then we'll begin."

"Be careful, Terry," Sarah said.

"Relax," he said, leaning back. The bed was raised at a forty-five degree angle. Terry rested his head against the pillow. "These are the good guys."

"Ready," the stenographer said.

Steele began. "For the record, I'm Captain Max Steele from the Federal Bureau of Investigation, and I am here with my partner, Lieutenant Bert Higgins. Also present in the room are Mr. Terrence Woodrow and Miss Sarah Stafford." Terry grinned, looking from face to face. Sarah sunk into one of the chairs. What is her problem? He would ask, later.

"Terrance Woodrow," Steele continued, "you have the right to remain silent." Terry's face fell like a cake when the oven door slams. "Anything you say can and will be used against you in a court of law. You have the right to have an attorney present during this questioning...."

"Get a lawyer, Terry." Sarah stood. Terry held up his hand without looking at her. His heart banged in his chest and his head throbbed.

"Do you understand your rights, Mr. Woodrow?"

"Yes. What I don't understand is why I'm hearing them from you."

Steele pulled several sheets of paper from his coat pocket and unfolded them. "Mr. Woodrow, do you know a woman by the name of Nina Bente?"

"Terry, please listen to me," Sarah said, leaning over the bed rail. "Get a lawyer before you answer any of his questions."

"What for? I haven't done anything wrong. Try to relax." He wished he could relax! He turned back to Captain Steele. "No, I do not know Nina Bente," he said.

"Are you certain?" Steele asked.

"Positive."

"You do not know Nina Ondolopous Bente?"

Sarah's inhale screeched in her throat and a trembling hand flew over her mouth. Terry felt his heart flip like an engine trying to start.

"Wait a second, Captain. Let's slow down a little here. I do know Nina Ondolopous, but I do not know Nina Bente."

"Same person, Mr. Woodrow."

"Impossible." Terry swiped at a bead of sweat above his brow.

Sarah dropped to her knees on the tile floor. "Nina's married, Terry, and something's wrong-"

"Miss Stafford, please!" Steele said. "We are interrogating a suspect."

Terry jerked. *Interrogating? Suspect?*

Steele turned to Sarah. "I've let you remain, but one more outburst and I'll have you removed." Sarah doubled over onto the floor.

"Now, Mr. Woodrow—"

Terry cut him off, words coming fast from his mouth. "I thought you were taking a police report or something here. Am I a suspect, Captain Steele, because I've never in my life stolen anything since I was seven when I took that blue rubber ball from the five-and-dime. I don't even drive over the speed limit. Makes my friends nuts." Terry ignored Steele's attempt to speak. "And what's this with Nina?"

Steele's eyebrows rose. "Tell me, Mr. Woodrow, how well would you say you know Nina Bente?"

"Until two seconds ago, I would have said I know her very well." He stared at the bed, and could hear his breath loud in his ears.

"Tell me about the nature of your relationship."

"Well," Terry glanced at the agent, then back to the bed. "She came to Ecclesia in the fall and we've known each other ever since."

"That tells me the timetable, Mr. Woodrow. Tell me how you would characterize your relationship with Nina Bente. Would you say it was … distant? Casual? Intimate?" The stenographer's fingers flew over the keys.

Terry's eyes shot to the door. Could Steele know already? No one knew. Except Nina. So if he lied and said "casual," who would know the difference? If he said "intimate," then he'll have admitted not only to having sex outside of marriage, but also to adultery. Kiss ordination good-bye. But it was wrong to lie. His pastor back home called every lie a slap in Jesus' face. He had never forgotten it.

"Mr. Woodrow?"

Terry did not look at him.

"Do you want me to repeat the question?"

"I heard you." Terry took another deep breath and squeezed his eyes shut. "Intimate. My relationship with Nina was intimate." A scream erupted beneath the bed and everyone in the room jumped. Two uniformed officers burst through the door with hands on holsters.

"Sarah!" Terry said. He forgot she was still in the room. He never wanted her to know. "Oh God," he said.

Sarah wailed and rocked on the floor, and Steele motioned to the uniforms. Terry watched them escort her out. He wanted to say something, do something, explain. *But explain what? That I'm a fornicator and an adulterer? She already knew that now. What then, that I'm sorry? I wasn't sorry until I got caught!* "I hate you Woodrow!" he screamed, slamming his palm against the side of his head. I hate you. I hate your guts!" He slammed his palm again and again into his wounds, screaming in pain. Sarah's face wrenched back toward the room, her eyes swollen and red. Before she disappeared through the doorway, her eyes met his. Pain, like he'd never seen. "I wish they'd killed me," he said as nurses pushed past the officers into the room.

The nurses finished changing the dressing on Terry's head. He had not opened his eyes since the officers helped Sarah from the room. He refused the soda offered him. Steele left the room and spoke with the officers. "You send her home?" he asked.

One shook his head. "She's pretty upset. Said she wanted to pray in the Chapel."

"We got a Police Chaplain for this stuff, don't we?" the other said. "Should we call?"

"Do that," Steele said. He shook his head. "Shoulda seen it comin' in there."

"Makes you wonder whether he was sleepin' with both of them and not telling one about the other," the other officer said, snorting. They had seen it before, and plenty worse. Steele slapped them each on the shoulder and left to find Dr. Sanchez in the Emergency Room.

He found her standing a few feet from the metal entry doors studying that clipboard. His eyes scanned her down to the ankles and back up again. Nice, very. As he approached her from behind, he imagined wrapping his arms around her small waist and kissing her neck. That would get him ... slapped!

"Excuse me, Dr. Sanchez," he said, smiling at her back. "I'm looking for an update on a patient I dropped off here last night." When she turned to face him, her smile matched his, warm and wide. She shook her thick brown hair behind her shoulders, bouncing gold hoop earrings.

"I'm sorry, Captain Steele, but your patient was taken directly from the operating room to intensive care. You'll find her on the fourth floor."

"What if I wasn't really looking for her?" His eyes danced over her face. Dr. Sanchez cocked her head, glanced down, and then up again. She felt a rush of heat to her cheeks.

"What are you looking for then?" she asked.

Several things, actually. He chickened out on every clever answer. No wonder you're single, Steele! "Maybe a little coffee. And a little company."

She tucked the clipboard under her arm. "I think we can fix you up, Captain."

"I was hoping." She looked at him as they walked toward the break room.

"I guess maybe I was too."

Max felt a loud whoop rise in his throat. He coughed instead.

"I'll let you in on my secret for making a perfect cup of coffee," she said. He followed her into the break room.

"I didn't realize I was in the presence of a gourmet."

"Practice, Captain. Lots of practice." She unlocked a cabinet and extracted small bag of coffee beans and an electric grinder.

"Private stash?" he said.

"Privileges extended to those who rarely get to go home."

"So that's your secret to the perfect cup?"

"Nope." She poured coffee beans into her hands and then massaged them together slowly. "You must caress the beans."

Max stopped breathing, wishing for but one thing in this life: to be a coffee bean.

She brought them to her nose, inhaled, then dropped them into the grinder and poured the water into the top of the coffeemaker.

"So, have you been to see Mrs. Bente today?" she said.

Max had leaned against the door jamb to steady himself. "Yes," he said, crossing his hands over his fly, "You heard she made it through the night."

Dr. Sanchez shook her head no. "Once they leave us, we seldom hear about them again."

He looked at the floor, the images, smells and sounds flashing through his mind, sobering him instantly. "There were so many plastic tubes and blinking machines and pieces of tape and gauze …. It was hard to believe there was a living person in there."

"Two people," Dr. Sanchez said. "The baby's still alive. You know it's a crack baby."

"I didn't. Doctors said something about heart tone levels, but I couldn't catch much of it. They kicked me out pretty quick."

"Don't take it personally," she said. "They'd kick me out too … and I carry a badge." She flashed the hospital ID clipped to her white coat.

He laughed. "That's supposed to be my line." She handed him a steaming Styrofoam cup.

"So," he said, feeling like he was on the dance floor but couldn't hear the music. "So, what do your friends call you when you're not rushing around the ER in your white coat?"

"They call me for dinner at my favorite restaurant," she said, looking over the rim of her cup.

"Can I be your friend?"

"Why don't you call and find out."

"Feeling a little better, Mr. Woodrow?" Captain Steele asked. The stenographer rearranged his machine and sat back down behind it.

"No," Terry said. "When do I get to ask some questions?"

"Soon, Mr. Woodrow. Answer a couple more questions of mine, and I'll fill in a few blanks for you. You said that your relationship with Nina Bente was intimate. Is that right?"

"Yes, but I didn't know she was married. I know her as Nina Ondolopous, and so does the rest of the seminary."

"Was it a sexual relationship?"

"Isn't that what intimate means to you?" Terry felt heat in his face.

"Clarifying, Mr. Woodrow, for the record."

"Yes, it was a sexual relationship."

"For how long?"

"Five months, maybe more."

"And was it unprotected sex?"

"Yes. She said she couldn't have children." In his mind, he saw Nina's naked body next to his, and he heard her voice announce that she was pregnant.

He glared at Steele. "Why on earth do you want to know that?"

"Because she is pregnant, Mr. Woodrow."

"She told me last night. I assumed I was the father. But that was before I knew she was married."

Steele studied Terry's face. "So you didn't know Nina Ondolopous was married?"

"No."

"And you didn't know that in reality she could become pregnant?"

"No, I did not..."

"And you didn't know before last night that she was pregnant?"

"No."

"Well then Mr. Woodrow, what did you know about this woman other than how to take her clothes off?" Steele noticed his voice had risen.

"Easy Cap," Higgins said.

Max ignored him, "You're either lying, or you're stupid."

"Are those the only choices? How about I'm a dickhead?" Terry glared at the wall.

Silence sat like a rhino in the room for several seconds, then Terry's shoulders slumped.

"She came to Ecclesia last fall to finish a degree she started years ago. She told me she was in rehab for drugs, got herself cleaned up, and wanted to finish her degree. I admired her courage. It's not easy to climb out of such a deep hole, but she did it. We became friends."

"Good enough friends to sleep together, but not good enough friends to know much of anything about her personal life?"

"I know it sounds bad," Terry said.

"It sounds like a lie," Steele said. He watched Terry flinch. Steele continued to press. "Two seminary students who hardly know each other, in a purely sexual relationship. Doesn't seem to be the kind of thing seminarians do."

"There's a lot you don't know about seminarians," Terry said. Even he was amazed at some of the things his fellow seminarians were up to. This was tame.

"Do you use illegal drugs, Mr. Woodrow?"

"Absolutely not."

"Have you ever used illegal drugs? Cocaine, crystal meth, marijuana, anything?"

"No. Never."

"Are you saying you never used cocaine with Nina Bente?"

"I told you, she's clean."

"Is that right!"

"That's right!" Terry and Steele glared at each other.

"Then tell me, Mr. Woodrow, why you helped Nina Bente smuggle thirty-six plastic eggs filled with rock cocaine into the country last night."

"I didn't," Terry said with less conviction. His mind flashed to Nina's shoulder bag. In slow motion, he saw it fall from the bed, spilling three bags of plastic eggs. Oh! No!

"Sorry, Mr. Woodrow, but you did. We got it all on camera. You're a documented accessory."

Nina's House

Even at 76 years old, Nettie walked to the market every Sunday after church. James liked the time alone in the garden. There were weeds to pull, dead blooms to pinch, and bugs to curse. Nettie loved the open-air market on Sunday. After one o'clock, all the fresh produce brought in by local farmers went on sale. James remembered the time he rushed to her at the bottom of the porch steps. Completely out of breath, she couldn't speak for over a minute. She held above her head a dozen ears of sweet corn in a clear plastic bag. Got them for a quarter, she said, and was so excited she ran all the way home to tell him. Crazy old woman.

James leaned on his hoe. The rain swamped the garden, but he watched with satisfaction as the sun beat on the muddy ground and dried the bay leaves and tomato plants. The roses opened their petals and took in the warm rays. Watching them stretch toward the sun was an incredible experience. He could watch again and again and never tire of it. Nettie ought to see them today. He looked up Elm Street, and couldn't remember how long she had been gone. Could hardly see that far anyway.

A clatter at the back of the house bounced off the garage and rattled in his ears. He hoisted the hoe over his shoulder. It brushed against his broad-brimmed straw hat, the chinstrap tapping his bony chest as he walked to the back yard. Craning his neck as far as he could, he saw two men, one big as a linebacker and one small and chubby, halfway up the back steps.

"Whatta you want?" he said.

"Here to see Nina," the big man called from the stairs.

"Who?"

"Nina."

"There's no Nina here," James said, not sure whether that was right.

"This is Nina's apartment, old man!" the short, chubby one said. The large man climbed to the landing and knocked on the door.

James lowered his head and walked toward the front of the house. He didn't like them, not one bit. Trespassers! He angled to the front porch, leaned his hoe on one of the large white pillars, and went through the front door into the bedroom.

"There you are, sweetheart," he said, clutching the barrel of his civil war musket.

He'd have her loaded in a jiffy.

Nina's House

"You see him?" Vinnie asked.

"For the third time, no," Emil said.

With a thin metal pick in each hand, Vinnie worked the ends back and forth inside the door lock. He paused. "You watch your tone with me, kid. I ain't tellin' you again." He went back to the lock and worked his tools until it clicked and gave way. "Be quick. I want to be outta here in ninety seconds." Emil rushed through the door and headed for the closet. Vinnie flipped the mattress off the box spring, then lifted the box spring and searched the floor underneath. Emil emerged from the closet empty-handed and went for the bathroom cabinets. Vinnie pulled the cushions from the couch and easy chair. Emil lifted the toilet tank lid and peered in.

"Anything?" Vinnie said.

"Nothin'."

"Only one other place they could be then. Let's go."

Vinnie stepped over the corner of the box spring as Emil emerged from the bathroom.

"Hold it!" The voice was loud and winded. The two men stared at the straw hat draped over a rusted metal barrel that flared at the end. The thin, spotted skin on James's hands trembled, but he held the musket tight to his shoulder in the doorway.

Emil and Vinnie exchanged glances. "That thing loaded old man?" Emil said.

"Want to find out, punk?" James's voice sounded reedy coming through the brim. Vinnie could not see his eyes, and wondered if the old guy could see anything at all from under there. "We don't want any trouble, sir. Came to see Nina," Vinnie said in his most respectful voice.

"Looks like it," the straw hat said.

Vinnie took a step toward him. If he could get a little closer, he might be able to slap the barrel down and jerk it out of the old man's hands. He'd seen it done on Perry Mason once.

"Don't come any closer if you value your head."

"Sir, we're sorry for the intrusion. I guess Nina's not here," Vinnie took another step toward James, "So we'll be leaving."

The hammer smacked against the flint and Vinnie ducked. Nothing. He lunged for the barrel, slapping the unfired musket to the floor. The old man fell with it.

"It didn't go off!" Emil beamed, picking the musket from the floor.

"Careful," Vinnie said, "It still could." Emil carried it to the closet and leaned it on the wall.

"Get off my property!" James said from the floor. Vinnie stepped on him with one foot and tore the bed's top sheet into wide strips.

"Give me the Bic and I'll slice 'im and dice 'im," Emil said. Vinnie tossed a couple of cloth strips to him. "Tie him and gag him instead. We'll leave him in the bathtub."

"But he's seen our faces!"

Vinnie glared at him. "You watch too many gangster movies. By the time anyone finds him, we'll be long gone."

Emil pulled the knots tight, and Vinnie heard James's muffled screams through the gag in his mouth. He shook his head. Anything to inflict pain. Emil got off on it.

They carried James to the bathtub and lowered him into it. Vinnie saw the terror in James's eyes.

"Sorry old man," he said. "You shoulda stayed in your garden."

Vinnie closed the bathroom door and joined Emil on the landing, locking the door behind him. They hurried down the stairs and disappeared around the tall hedge.

"Where to, Vinnie baby?" Emil's voice dripped with sarcasm. He followed Vinnie through the narrow alley formed by the seven-foot hedge on one side and the neighbor's towering lilacs on the other.

The backhand was so sudden, it left Emil's eyes wide and his mouth frozen open. A small trickle of blood formed at his mouth's edge and spilled from the corner toward his chin. Vinnie rubbed the back of his right hand, red from the impact. "The next time you show disrespect," he said, poking Emil's over-sized nose with his finger, "I'm gonna smash this sucker all over your face. You got that?"

Memorial Hospital

Sarah emerged puff-eyed from the small Chapel at Memorial Hospital and headed for the bathroom to splash water on her face. She threw two fists full of soggy tissues into the trash can and looked in the mirror. Her mind flashed to this morning's church service. How can one day be both the best and the worst you have ever had? She looked at the swollen face staring back from the mirror. You are a train wreck! But she still wasn't ready to go back to her dorm. Too many people. Too many questions.

She walked out of the bathroom and pushed the elevator button, glad that it didn't come right away. She needed time to decide what to do. Terry on the third floor? Nina on the fourth? A soft bell toned and the elevator's metal doors retreated to each side. Several people crowded into the elevator behind her. An enormous woman with three children hanging on her shouted at a fourth child to hurry up and get on. Closest to the buttons, the woman glanced over her shoulder and pushed the numbers people called out. The elevator started to move. "Four," Sarah said.

At the fourth floor, Sarah followed the corridor toward Intensive Care. Halfway up the right wall near the two large metal ICU doors, a square red button read, "Press." Sarah pushed it and the doors yawned open. She wished she had brought her hospital ID from last summer. It might have gotten her back to see Nina. She walked to the semi-circular nurse's station and looked at the chalkboard scrawled top to bottom with room numbers and names. Behind her, a bank of rooms marched out of sight opposite the long, curved counter. The front wall of the rooms was clear glass, making each patient visible to the physicians and nurses. A woman in purple scrubs rose from her chair twenty feet away.

"Help you?"

Sarah continued to scan the chalkboard. "Uh yes, um, I was one of the chaplains here and I would like to see Nina Bente." She held her breath and stared at the board.

"Excuse me. You say you were one of the chaplains?"

"Yes, last summer. You've got a fellow student from the seminary here, Nina Bente, and I'd like to see her for a minute." Sarah felt the nurse scanning her. In these clothes and with these eyes, she did not look much like a chaplain.

"I'm sorry miss, but this area is restricted to immediate family and staff." Sarah looked at her. Short-cropped red hair, a chubby face, and thighs that forced her feet apart.

"I understand. Thank you." Sarah turned and searched the wall for the button that would open the doors to the hallway. They were open and closing again. She passed a silver haired man in a dark overcoat on his way in. He held a dark, expensive looking felt hat in his hands.

"Can I help you, sir?" chubby face said.

Bet he gets in! Sarah pressed the button, the doors swung wide, and she marched down the hallway toward the ICU waiting room. The doors closed behind her.

The man spoke. "I'm Reverend George Fields from Ecclesia Seminary and I'm here to see a student of ours, a Nina Bente." The nurse checked the approved list of visitors from the FBI agents, and then looked up smiling. "May I see some ID, Reverend Fields?"

"Of course," the man said, pulling an Ecclesia photo identification card from his wallet.

"Right this way, Reverend." The man followed her from the other side of the counter to Room 14.

Sarah scanned the ICU waiting room for a familiar face. Not one. A large family took up the back third of the room. Five grease-blotched pizza boxes, empty except for gnawed crusts, sat on two coffee tables pushed together. She felt her stomach clench, and decided to walk the hall, a weak substitute for her run today. The fourth floor was designed in an oval. The main hallway traversed both sides of a wide inside wall that housed, among other things, the ICU. A hallway on each end connected the two and made for an excellent walking track. On her third lap, Sarah recognized a man stepping from the elevator fifty yards ahead. "Dean Tittle,"

she called, but he walked down the hall the other way. She sped up and caught him near the ICU doors.

"Dean Tittle," she said touching his jacket at the elbow, "I'm Sarah Stafford." He smiled and shook her outstretched hand.

"Of course I recognize you Sarah," Jeremy said, though she wasn't sure he did. He paused and looked into her eyes. She felt something tender in them and her poise caved, her eyes filling with tears.

"You've had a long couple of days," he said.

"Yes sir," Sarah choked and looked away.

Jeremy Tittle took her in his arms and she sobbed into his shoulder. "There, there now. There, there." Then he looked toward the ceiling. "Touch her where it hurts, Lord. Give her your peace that passes all understanding, the kind of peace that comes despite the circumstances. Thank you Lord. In Jesus' name."

He unwrapped her from his arms.

"Thank you, Dean Tittle," she said. "I'm such a baby." She reached into her pocket and produced a tissue.

"No more than the rest of us," he said. "And besides, it's a good thing. Jesus said that unless we come to him like a little baby, we will not inherit the kingdom of God."

Sarah nodded, but couldn't get words past the knot in her throat. The ICU doors hissed, and then opened wide. The man in the dark coat passed them and walked toward the elevators. He pressed the felt hat tight and low on his forehead. Who wears a hat indoors? She watched him hurry to the elevator.

"I came to see Nina Bente," Jeremy said.

"I've been walking laps around the corridor praying for her," Sarah said. "They wouldn't let me see her."

He nodded. "They're fussy about it in ICU. You either have to be a relative, a doctor with a badge, a clergyman with a collar, or you've got to be on somebody's VIP list."

Sarah shook her head and grinned.

"Ah, that's better," Jeremy said looking the way her grandfather did when she laughed at his jokes.

"So, you two guarding the doors?" George Fields patted them on the shoulders.

"Hello George," Jeremy said. "No, talking about the pit bulls on the other side of them. You remember Sarah Stafford from Ecclesia."

"Thank you for your call," George shook her hand. Sarah nodded. "And how is our friend, Mr. Woodrow?"

"Recovering well, sir," she said and looked up the hallway at nothing.

"Splendid." George turned to Jeremy. "I was about to look in on Mrs. Bente … unless of course you want to go first. Or have you been already?"

"Not yet, but go ahead," Jeremy said, "Sarah and I are still catching up on some things." With a wave, George slapped the red button and disappeared through the massive doors.

"We were?"

Jeremy's face softened. He took her hand. "Before I came to ICU, I looked in on Terry." She stared at her hand in his and blinked back a fresh wave of tears. "Took a nasty shot to the back of the head, didn't he."

Sarah nodded, still looking down. She felt his gentle eyes.

"He didn't say much," Jeremy continued. "Stared out the window…. looked like he'd lost his best friend." Tears burst from her eyes, and she pressed herself into his shoulder again, sobbing.

"How'd you know?" she said.

"I know two broken hearts when I see them."

The ICU doors flew open and George rushed toward them, face red and fists clenched.

"Idiots!" he said.

Jeremy let go of Sarah and took George by the shoulders. "What on earth, George! Are you all right?"

"Apparently not. Apparently, I'm not here at all. Apparently, I just left!" he said, his voice trembling.

"Slow down, man. You're making no sense."

"That's because it makes no sense."

Sarah watched the two men, and felt herself backing to the opposite wall.

"I went in there," George said, "I identified myself and asked to see Nina Bente."

"Yes ...."

"And I swear to you, Jeremy, that woman looked at me like I was some kind of villainous creature, and said, 'Excuse me, but Reverend Fields has just been here and left.'"

"No! Did you show her your ID?"

"Can't believe I left the bloody thing at home." George said, speaking in quick bursts. "I told her so, and she gave me that 'liar' look. And of course by now we're drawing a crowd behind the counter – so embarrassing - and I say to her that I don't know who she let in to see Nina Bente, but by Christ I am the real Reverend George Fields."

"Good for you, George," Jeremy said. Sarah watched him steady George with his hands and follow his face with those same steady eyes.

"And then, get this! She says, 'But he is the only Reverend Fields with an ID!'"

"But how-"

"This pit bull is shredding my credibility to bits and I look like a complete idiot in front of a gallery." Sarah glowered at him. *Like there is nothing more important than what you look like. I'm not the biggest baby around here after all.*

"I'll go with you and sort that out," Jeremy said. "I've got my ID and I'll vouch for you." Jeremy hit the red button and the doors yielded. "The scarier thing is that someone is walking around with your ID."

"And wanting to get to Nina," Sarah said.

"Exactly," Jeremy said. "Sarah, come with us." Jeremy glanced at the tall man in a dark suit following them in. Sarah saw Dean Tittle staring behind her, and she looked over her shoulder.

"Captain Steele," she said.

"Hello, Miss Stafford," he said. "Feeling better?"

"Worse."

"I'm sorry." He moved toward Jeremy and George with his hand outstretched, his face cordial but not warm. Jeremy met his hand. "I'm Reverend Tittle, Dean of Ecclesia and this is my Assistant Dean, George Fields."

"Max Steele, FBI. Pleasure," he said shaking hands. "ICU paged me in the cafeteria. Perhaps they'll give us an office to talk for a few minutes." The nurse nodded and led them to a smallish room with an oval table and several swivel chairs. Steele asked her to stay a few moments.

Captain Steele began. "I'm sorry for the trouble getting in to see Mrs. Bente. That's my doing." He leaned forward. "We've got a dangerous situation here."

"Perhaps I shouldn't be here," Sarah said. "I'm just a student."

"You stay put," Jeremy said, patting her hand on the table. "You've been the lead minister from the beginning." Sarah wondered if anyone but him saw it that way.

"As long as everyone understands that what I'm about to tell you is confidential. Sharing it with anyone could compromise our investigation and put both of your student's lives in danger." Steele looked around the table. "But first let's clear up one piece of confusion, and then we can send Nurse Farlow here back to work." He smiled toward the nurse standing by the door. "Tell us, Ms. Farlow, about the visit by Reverend George Fields." George jerked, twisting in his chair.

"A gentleman came in and asked to see Nina Bente," she said. "He identified himself as Reverend George Fields. I asked for identification, and he showed me his Ecclesia photo identification card."

"Wait a minute," Jeremy said, fishing in his jacket pocket. He produced his wallet and thumbed through credit cards and wrinkled slips of paper, plucking his Ecclesia ID. "Did it look like this one?"

Ms. Farlow leaned forward and studied the card. "No. But it said Ecclesia Seminary and had his photo on it."

Captain Steele whistled.

"So my ID's probably still at home," George said. "We thought maybe someone stole it."

"Forged," Steele said.

"Was he carrying a felt hat?" Sarah asked.

"Yes, as a matter of fact," Nancy said.

"Then I saw him."

"I'll need a description from each of you before you leave today," Captain Steele said. "Ms. Farlow, thank you for your time. Please tell the staff that I want Mrs. Bente checked from head to toe right away." She left, closing the door.

"I didn't get much of a look at him," Sarah said.

"Tell us what you can, and then write it up for me later."

"Older gentleman. Silver hair slicked back. One of those people where every hair is in place. Large hooked nose." Steele stopped scribbling and his head snapped up. Sarah continued. "He passed me as I left the ICU. He carried an expensive looking felt hat, the kind with the little feather in the side of the band. Later in the hall, I remember him passing us on the way to the elevator because he pulled the hat down tight on his forehead and I thought it strange that anyone would wear a hat inside the hospital."

"Anything else?"

Sarah shook her head.

"Thank you, Miss Stafford," Steele said, running his fingers through his bristly hair. He looked like he'd been punched in the stomach.

"Who was it?" Jeremy asked.

"Not sure, but my best guess would also be my worst nightmare." Steele said. "So perhaps you can appreciate why I was being so careful about visitors."

Jeremy nodded. "You were filling us in."

"Obviously I can't tell you everything, but here's the thumbnail sketch," Steele said. "Your student, Nina Ondolopous, married the number two man in the largest crime family in the Northeast. The Bente Cartel controls the entire East Coast and is pushing west. Drugs, weapons, prostitution, gambling, identity theft. You name it, the Bente Cartel controls it.

"The number one man is Emil Bente." Sarah saw George flinch. "His nickname on the street is the Shark because he eats his competition. They just disappear." He paused, and she felt a chill trace her back. "In January, Nina married the Shark's son, also named Emil Bente."

"Of this year?" Sarah said.

Captain Steele nodded. "He's got none of his father's savvy. He's not much more than a common thug, really, too stupid to stay under Daddy's protective cover. Junior set up shop in Rhode Island. He thinks he hired the number three man, Vincente Bontecelli, away from his father to be his chauffeur and body guard. But Vinnie and the Shark stay in touch."

"How did you learn all this?" Jeremy asked.

"We've been monitoring their cell phone conversations for over a year."

"You can do that?" Jeremy asked.

"You would be stunned," Steele said. "But so far it hasn't been enough to nail them. Anyway, Bente Junior is Kingstown's main cocaine dealer. So far, he's been running small quantities, some of it to the seminary." George leapt to his feet, pacing.

"You're not serious," Jeremy said.

"I'm very serious, Dean Tittle," Captain Steele said. "Nina couriered most of it. And she's a big user."

"Who'd she bring it to at the seminary?" Jeremy said. Sarah closed her eyes. *Don't say Terry Woodrow. Don't say Terry Woodrow.*

"Does it matter, Jeremy?" George said. Sarah opened her eyes, watched George take off his jacket, noticed the sweat rings under his arms.

"It matters to me," Jeremy said.

"Unfortunately for you," Steele continued, "it didn't matter enough to us to follow her. The small stuff won't get us the convictions we need, so we stayed on Bente Junior waiting for him to screw up big." Steele paused. "And he did when he sent his wife to Colombia to pick up several pounds of crack cocaine and smuggle it into the country."

"Wait a minute," George banged the table. "I sent Nina to Colombia —"

"I know. "

"On a mission trip."

"She was on a mission all right," Steele said.

"What are you saying?"

"I'm saying, Reverend Fields, that you were used - chosen as their patsy - used to finance their smuggling operation. And today it appears they impersonated you to get to Nina Bente in ICU."

"Wonderful," George said. "I need a glass of water." He slipped from the room.

"So who brutalized Nina like this?" Jeremy asked.

"That I can't say."

"Can't or won't?"

"Let me say this, Dean Tittle. Bente Junior is as vicious as he is stupid. And he is a crack addict. Bontecelli's no boy scout either."

"Where are they now?" Sarah asked.

Steele shrugged. "They slipped us last night, disappeared with the coke. That's why we're sitting on Nina. We hope she'll recover enough to talk. In the meantime, we protect her. By tomorrow, we'll have several agents under cover up here."

"What about Terry Woodrow? We have two wounded students," Jeremy said.

Steele paused. "Yes, and you have two students who are in trouble. Mr. Woodrow was part of the drug smuggling operation. We have video of him at the airport with Nina and the drugs. He drove her and the rock cocaine to her flat on Elm Street.

Sarah jerked.

George returned, carrying a Styrofoam cup. Steele continued, "Later, he followed her to the back of the seminary. We couldn't tell if he was guarding her car or acting as lookout."

"Did you see anybody else?" George asked.

"Why do you ask?"

"Um, I'm trying to get the picture in my mind."

"No, but something wasn't right. Woodrow must have gotten sideways of Bente and Bontecelli somehow because Bontecelli hit him over the head with the butt of his pistol. Then we watched Bontecelli and Bente drive Woodrow to the top lot in his own car and leave him. They grabbed Nina as soon as she left the Chapel and things got crazy. We dropped the net and they slipped it. By the time we caught up with them, they'd torched the car, beaten and raped Nina –"

"Raped?" George's eyes were wide, his voice high and piercing.

"Why don't you sit down, George," Jeremy said.

Steele nodded. "Semen samples show that several different men raped her."

"How awful," Jeremy said, shaking his head.

"She'll be able to tell us about it when she wakes up."

A knock at the door spun everyone's head. Nancy Farlow said, "Captain, there's something you should see."

"Mrs. Bente?"

She nodded.

"Please let us come," Jeremy said, placing his hand on Captain Steele's forearm. "We want to have a quick prayer over her and then we'll be on our way."

Captain Steele hesitated, and then shrugged.

Everyone followed Nurse Farlow to the ICU. Sarah's eyes fell to Nina's midsection. Something long and thin and dark was under the sheet at the belly button. She stepped back.

"Please tell me no one's touched it," Steele said.

"No one, sir."

"Scissors!" he said.

Nurse Farlow snatched a pair of scissors. Steele lifted the edge of the top sheet and cut two inches above Nina's belly button. At the opposite edge of the bed, the scissors took a right turn and cut parallel to Nina's side for several inches. He lifted the sheet. A rosary lay serpentine across Nina's abdomen. The beads were shining black pearls with glimmering diamonds separating them, the cross of black stone with diamond studs running the length of both arms. It rose and fell mechanically with the ventilator. Large brown and purple bruises from Emil's beating blotched the skin around it.

Sarah's stomach churned and she felt a sheen form on her forehead. "Am I over thinking," she asked, "or is that rosary in the shape of an S?"

A loud crash next to her brought staff scurrying. Sarah looked down. George lay unconscious at her feet.

Chapter Thirteen

Residence of the Assistant Dean
Ecclesia Seminary

"Why doesn't she leave?" Vinnie squatted among the low branches of a fir tree and watched the Assistant Dean's house. Trees were thick from the faculty lot all the way down the hill to Elm Street, providing plenty of cover and a good view of the house and driveway. Hilary Fields's red Saab glistened in the driveway.

A large piece of rock cocaine from the plastic egg glowed in the throat of Emil's crack pipe. He leaned against a large fallen log behind Vinnie and sucked smoke into his lungs. "Soon as I finish this bowl, let's pay Mrs. Fields a visit."

"Haven't you had enough trouble for today?"

"Nope." He inhaled, choked, and bent forward hacking and spitting.

Vinnie glanced at him. Spit dangled from Emil's bottom lip. "You been more than enough trouble for one day."

"Shut up," Emil said.

Vinnie whirled to face him, his eyes darkening. "Shut up? Is that what you said to me?"

"Okay. Shut up, Mr. Bontecelli," Emil said and burst into a fit of silent, gassy laughter that rolled him off the log. He fell on his broken hand and howled in pain.

Vinnie snorted, turning to watch the house again. Sometimes he felt sorry for the kid. The Runt never had his mama, and Daddy kept his distance because he looked so much like her. Made older Emil cry. Images filled Vinnie's head of the night he and Emil, Sr. walked into the house to find Mrs. Bente gang raped and murdered. She had been seven months pregnant. Doctors saved the baby, and the runt was born. Vinnie and the Shark left the hospital that night, and by morning had tracked and killed every one of the perps. Cut their parts off and mailed 'em to their mamas. Vinnie shook the fractured scenes from his head. Gone for now, but some memories are forever.

A glint of light flashed in his eye. George's car pulled into the driveway. "Now we're getting somewhere," he said.

"What?" Emil still struggled to push to his feet with his good hand.

"Our egg thief has returned to the coop."

Emil found that comment hilarious too, but Vinnie shushed him. They watched George extract himself from his tan Cadillac, stand by the side of the car and touch a white bandage stuck to his temple. He jerked his hand away like he'd been scalded and walked into the house.

"Tell me Emil," Vinnie said, "If you were George, where would you hide thirty-five Easter eggs?"

"Up my butt!" Emil said and squealed. He staggered back to the log.

Vinnie shook his head. Must be some good crack. Sometimes that shit made him meaner than a moccasin, other times the class clown. He wouldn't have to put up with it much longer.

From the faculty parking lot, a powerful scope focused on the back section of the woods across from the Fields residence.

Still light-headed, George's vision had cleared enough to drive home. A nasty fall, but the ICU doc didn't think he had a concussion. My God, if ever he needed a clear head it was now. He needed to call Lawrence immediately. The smell of cigarette smoke hit his nose at the kitchen door and he froze. Someone probably broke in, and now held Hilary at gunpoint. He tiptoed, but was unsteady on his feet and crashed into the stainless steel trash can in front of the sink. He bounced against the swinging door. It gave way and he tumbled into the living room.

Hilary sat in his overstuffed chair smoking a cigarette and looking at him over her reading glasses.

"Hilary, thank God!" George said. "I smelled the smoke and thought we had intruders." She said nothing. He stopped and stared back at her. "What in God's name are you doing anyway? You don't smoke."

"I do now," Hilary said. She tapped cigarette ash into a teacup balanced on the chair arm.

"How nice," he said with disdain. His nose wrinkled at the smell and the sight of his portly wife, still unbathed and still in the gray sweat suit. "Missed you in Chapel this morning. Were you worshipping your coffee? Shopping for ash trays?"

"I was out."

"Do tell." He removed his jacket and headed to the hall closet.

"In fact I'm going out again." She smashed the cigarette into the bottom of the cup and stood.

"Splendid. The fresh air will do me good."

"I said I'm going out."

"I heard you," he said, eyeing her from around the closet door. "No doubt the air will be better when you do."

Her keys jangled and the kitchen door flapped. The back door slammed.

"Good," he said into the belly of the closet and made straight for the liquor cabinet. "Whiskey on the rocks, hold the rocks," he said and poured the glass half full. He took two large swallows. The alcohol burned his throat and he shuddered. He rushed into the kitchen, snapped up the phone and dialed Brother Lawrence.

Lawrence answered on the second ring. "Expecting you," he said.

"Is this my savior?" George asked and took another long pull from the glass.

"It is. I saved your wide backside this morning, my son."

"You did indeed," George smiled into the phone. "And then you stole my coke, walked out with it under your arm. Thief."

"Right again, and I'm not giving it back. You can't be trusted. Of all the stupid places to hide it!" Lawrence blew into the receiver. "You, sir, are an idiot."

"Guilty as charged."

"Hilary must not be there," Lawrence said.

"She just waddled out. Been in that foul gray sweat suit for two days. Stank as badly as her attitude."

"She's a bitch."

"That, my brother, is a fact." George poured the rest of the glass down his throat and went for a refill. "Listen, Lawrence, keep the eggs at your place. They're not safe here anymore."

"Something else happen?"

"I just came from the hospital. Brace yourself." He poured the glass half full again. "Nina's in ICU and the place is crawling with FBI."

"Oh fuck."

"No kidding. I saw her last night at the Chapel and she gave me the eggs. When she left, Bente and his gorilla grabbed her in the fire lane, took her somewhere and beat the bejesus out of her. FBI found her in the cemetery. Turns out she married Bente in January, for Christ's sake. And never said a word to me!" He took a swallow. The room felt hot. "And that's not all. At the hospital, they find out she's pregnant!"

"Is it your baby?"

George put the glass down. "Why would you say that?"

"I'm no fool, George. The way you two look at each other when we party, I know you're playing hide the weenie. When you leave there, you're not going home. Are you doing her on the altar?"

"Close," he said, "And it might be mine."

"Hey, if I had to live with Hilary, I'd look for an alternative too." He paused. "Nina going to make it?"

"God I hope not." The alcohol had loosened George's tongue. Thickened it too.

"You're not serious."

"Sure would simplify our lives, especially mine. If she wakes up and starts talking, it's over."

"You're not thinking about –"

"Off and on," George said. "This morning when I first heard about it, I figured it was either her or me … and I chose me."

"Jesus, George!"

"But, after seeing you walk out of the sanctuary with the eggs and listening to the FBI agent, I'm changing my mind. It isn't going to be me!" He fingered the gash in the wall above the toaster.

"FBI on the wrong trail?"

"It's wonderful, Lawrence. They think Emil and Nina used me to finance their smuggling operation. And they're accusing another student who picked her up at the airport. I'm an innocent victim."

"So it's a cold trail to us."

"Looks like it."

"Let's keep it that way," Lawrence said. "Now get your ass over here for a smoke."

"On my way." George hung up the phone and went upstairs to change clothes. He was putting on his shoes when he heard a knock. Halfway down the stairs, he heard it again. The kitchen door. Doesn't anyone use the front door anymore? He reached the handle and opened it with a liquor-induced grin. In an instant, it vanished and he shoved the door toward its latch. Vinnie hit the other side like a linebacker, and George went sprawling.

Chapter Fourteen

312 Elm Street

She'd gone ninety minutes. Only ninety minutes. She wanted to run up and down the street, call for James, but didn't want to leave the house in case he turned up.

In the past three hours, Nettie Spruill lost years from her life. She propped her forehead on her arms and leaned onto the kitchen table. Her chest ached and wild strands of hair fell over her fingers. Clear plastic bags with okra, string beans and sweet onions lay on the counter where she dropped them. The telephone book lay open, surrounded by a litter of paper scraps. An hour ago she called the police to report him missing, even told them he might be violent so they would put more effort into the search. Then she called every neighbor she knew, and a few she didn't.

James's favorite hoe, the one with the small face, was still propped against the pillar in front of the house. It was in his hands when she left for the market. Twice since her return, Nettie climbed the back steps to Nina's flat thinking he might be there having afternoon tea. The knuckles of her right hand were sore from knocking. Twice she returned to the house and waited in the kitchen by the back door.

God knows he could be anywhere. She should have taken him along, but he'd been so lucid lately. Nettie's arms collapsed and her nose pressed against the papers. Come home to me, James. She imagined holding him at the back door, comforting him. It's all right sweetheart; you're safe. She wanted to say it, to hold him and say it. She listened. Nothing but silence and the ticking of that cursed clock, marking time, adding to the panic.

Without him, the house was vacant, hollow like the door closing after the moving van pulls away. The garden meant nothing. Nettie felt hot drops fall from her eyes and splash onto the papers. Please come home to me, James.

A knock at the front door brought Nettie upright in the kitchen chair. She wiped her face on her dress and hurried to the living room, yanking the door wide. Two men stood on the porch.

"Mrs. Spruill?" the taller one said. "I'm Captain Steele and this is Lieutenant Higgins, with the Federal Bureau of Investigation."

Nettie opened the screen door. "Yes yes, come in." She led them to the faded green couch in the center of the room and sat with a sigh in a rocker. "Is he all right? Where is he? Did you pick him up downtown?"

"Ma'am?" Higgins said.

"James Harne, my … gardener. He's missing, I called 911, and here you are."

"I'm sorry, Mrs. Spruill," Steele said. "We're here on another matter." Nettie's face fell, her eyes narrowing, searching. Steele cleared his throat. "Nina Bente is in the hospital-"

"Who?"

"You may know her as Nina Ondolopous."

"I know Nina Ondolopous. She's my tenant, but she's out of the country."

"She returned yesterday," Higgins said. "Someone attacked her last night. She is in the Intensive Care Unit at Memorial."

"Dear God, my Nina?" Nettie's eyes filled again.

"I'm sorry to bring this news, Mrs. Spruill. Sounds like you've already got your hands full."

She nodded. Tears ran along the wrinkles in her cheeks. She wiped them with her index fingers.

"We've obtained a search warrant for the apartment," Steele said, "and we hoped you could let us in."

"Of course." She rose from the rocker. "I'll get my key." She started for the kitchen. "Follow me. We can go out the back door."

She sniffled up the back stairs, stopping at the edge of the landing and breathing heavily. She aimed the trembling key into the lock. It stuck halfway in. She wiggled it up and down, then pulled it back out and examined it. "That's odd," she said, and inserted it into the lock again. This time, the key went three quarters of the way into the lock and stopped.

"Can we help you, ma'am?" Higgins asked behind her.

"It's never given me a moment's trouble before," she said, jiggling the key. "There!" The key turned and the door opened. Steele looked into the room. He figured they wouldn't be the only ones on this Easter egg hunt.

Nettie gasped at the overturned furniture, "Nina, are you in there?" The question hung in the air.

"Nina's in the hospital Mrs. Spruill," Steele said.

"Yes, of course." She steadied herself against the open door.

"Stay here, Mrs. Spruill," Steele said. He and Higgins brushed past her, drawing their guns.

Higgins readied himself to enter the closet. Steele entered the bathroom, rushed to the man in the tub and felt for a pulse. Then he hurried back to the apartment door. "Mrs. Spruill, what is your gardener wearing today?"

She paused for a moment, "A red plaid shirt and an old pair of blue jeans, why?"

"I want you to go back to the main house and call 911 again. Tell them we need an ambulance."

"Oh!" She hurried down the steps.

Steele met Higgins in the middle of the room by the overturned box spring. "Anything?"

Higgins pointed to a civil war musket leaning against the far closet wall. "Loaded but not fired. No eggs."

"Get on the apartment phone and call the coroner's office. Also call homicide and tell them to send a team."

Higgins reached for the phone, nodding toward the bathroom. "Somebody in there?"

"Used to be. The lady's gardener, bound, gagged, and tossed in the tub. He is cold and going stiff." He walked through the door to the landing. "I'm not letting her back up here."

"Think he was actually the gardener?" Higgins asked, covering the mouthpiece.

"Not a chance. You see her face?" He hurried down the stairs and found Nettie in the kitchen, sobbing. She neglected to hang up the phone. It dangled at the end of her thin arm next to the kitchen chair.

"He's dead," she said, not looking up. "He's gone."

"I'm so sorry."

"I knew it. I've been feeling it."

"Feeling what?"

"Nothing."

"Nothing," he said.

"The nothing ... of everything ... without ... him." A frightening wail rose from somewhere deep inside her. She heard it even before it reached her lips and exploded into the room. She fell sideways from the chair to the kitchen floor. Steele lunged to break her fall. She hit the floor, her knees curling into her chest. Another wail followed and then another. Steele caught movement from the corner of his eye. The box-like rescue squad vehicle backed into the driveway. He ran through the screen door, flashed his credentials and motioned the paramedics to him.

The lead paramedic spoke. "We received a call for a white male, 74, in the upstairs apartment."

Captain Steele shook his head. "He's already gone. Homicide and the coroner are on their way." He heard the faint scream of sirens in the distance, then a closer, louder wail from the kitchen. He jerked his head in Nettie's direction. "The lady who called you didn't know it, but the ambulance is for her. She's on the kitchen floor. I think she's going into shock."

Residence of the Dean
Ecclesia Seminary

Sarah turned the pages. A cool breeze blew through the screened-in porch, carrying a mockingbird's medley across Dean Tittle's back yard. "Is that really you in the grass skirt?" she asked him, laughing. Jeremy appeared in the doorway from the kitchen carrying a tray with a steaming teapot and two cups. He set it on the table between the two wicker rocking chairs.

"Afraid so," he said, leaning toward the photo album. "Our children sent Jean and me to Hawaii for our sixtieth birthdays. She and I were born two days and twenty-one hundred miles apart." Sarah smiled and turned the page.

"She was so much fun," Jeremy said, pouring green tea into each cup. "That day I remember we teased each other about our scrawny chicken legs."

"Hey, a woman doesn't want to hear that stuff about her legs."

"When you've loved someone that much, for that long, you can say almost anything."

Sarah closed the album and took her tea from the tray. She looked at Dean Tittle. Such a kind man. She was grateful to have somewhere to go besides the dorm or the hospital. He seemed to sense it, invited her over, led her through several photo albums, several hundred pictures, regaling her with stories of his and Jean's adventures. Sarah felt his love for Jean, could see it all over his face. He rocked and smiled, a far-away look settling on him.

He glanced at her. "Your turn to tell me about this young Woodrow fellow in Room 316."

Sarah felt her chest tighten. "We were friends, really close friends," she said.

"Were?"

Sarah looked into her teacup. "I don't want to cry."

"You need to talk about it. And who better to talk with than your self-appointed substitute grandfather?" He smiled at her.

"Actually, you remind me a lot of him."

"I'm honored."

"Terry and I were best friends. We told each other everything, even some really personal stuff. He said he trusted me, and I said the same thing." She traced the history of their relationship without welling up until it came to Terry's relationship with Nina. Tears dripped onto her white blouse. "He never told me about it. Not a word. I only knew her because all three of us studied at the public library downtown. Sometimes you just have to get away from the seminary. A couple of times Terry invited her to join us for a slice of pizza and a beer afterward. They acted like, you know, just acquaintances." She dabbed her eye with the napkin. "Then Terry lands in Memorial with a baseball sized knot on his head and heroin in his veins. And the FBI interrogates him, and I learn he's not only in a love relationship with Nina, who is married, but that he's been having sex with her and she's pregnant. It could be his baby." She stood from the rocker and stepped to the screened window.

"Heard something about that," Jeremy nodded, studying the back of her head. "When I went to see him. The nurse requested a sample."

"Blood?"

"No."

"Oh God."

"Let's leave it to the doctors."

Sarah blinked and then continued through the screen. "And to make matters worse, she's a crack addict and he's probably been doing drugs with her." Sarah paused, turning to face Dean Tittle, her breathe coming hard. "I don't know what hurts more: that Terry's been doing all this, or that he's been lying to me by his silence all this time."

"Both," Jeremy said, "they both hurt. It's so far from what you wanted, expected."

"Exactly," she said, returning to her rocker.

"And you wonder how a friend could do this to you, to himself? He's wrecking everything." Sarah nodded and Jeremy continued softly, "You wonder if maybe you were never friends, and maybe it was all a lie. And you never want to speak to him again because you trusted him and he violated that trust and you're not sure you could ever trust him again." He looked into her tear-filled eyes. "But you also can't bear the thought of not seeing or speaking to him again."

Sarah's eyes widened. "How did you - Are you a mind reader or something?"

"Maybe I understand a little better than most," he said. "I know you can't turn love off like a spigot or pull some magic plug and drain your heart of it, no matter how badly someone hurts you." They rocked in silence.

"Got time for a story?" he said.

"Of course." Sarah watched the far-away look descend on his face again.

"In 1970, Jean and I celebrated our thirty-seventh year of life and our fifteenth year of marriage. In October of that year, Jean went to Massachusetts for a weeklong Christian conference on spirituality. I took vacation time to care for the children. When she returned, Jean told me she'd had a marvelous time and went into elaborate detail about the speakers and the topics. Less than eight weeks and two missed periods later, Jean returned hysterical from the doctor. She was pregnant. The reason for the hysteria was because she got pregnant exactly one year and three months after my vasectomy.

"Oh no," Sarah whispered.

"Oh yes," Dean Tittle said. "We sent the kids to the neighbors and then we sat down. Jean told me she met a man at the conference. Like her, he was married and in the ministry. They knew it was wrong every time they were in each other's arms, but they made love for the entire week."

"What did you do?" Sarah asked.

"You mean after I broke my knuckle on the wall, and screamed and said things I shouldn't have?" He rose from the rocker. "Be right back." Jeremy returned with a framed family photo. He pointed, "These are my children. See the youngest one? You notice he doesn't look like the others and certainly not a thing like me?" Sarah nodded. Jeremy returned to his rocker.

"What did I do, Sarah?" He smiled. "I loved that child. From the day I knew about him, I loved that boy, not like he was my own, but because he was my own. When I married Jean, the two of us became one flesh, so any child of her flesh was a child of my flesh. And as for Jean? I loved her too, more than the day before she told me and no less the day after. Reject her? No. Push her away, refuse to speak to her for a time? No. Make her pay? No. Let her suffer a while? No. Expect her to make it up to me?"

He paused. "Look at me Sarah." His eyes locked with hers. "When God created me, I became this perfectly imperfect, but no less miraculous, gift to the world. That means that I'm loving and I'm hateful; I'm smart and I'm dumb, I'm selfish and I'm selfless. I am both light and shadow, and God wants me to bless all of that. Likewise, God wants me to bless all of that in Jean, and not to judge her when her shadow side showed up. Likewise with you and everyone else. I chose not to make Jean wrong, but instead to look for the blessing in her shadow behavior. And the blessing is obvious - just look at our precious son."

Sarah didn't know how long she held his gaze. She stood without a word, walked through the house and out the front door.

Chapter Fifteen

Residence of the Assistant Dean
Ecclesia Seminary

George Fields screamed all the way to the living room. Vinnie dragged him by the hair like a pup who had just crapped on the Persian rug. Now he held the sweat-and-whisky-soaked Assistant Dean by the throat in his overstuffed leather chair. "Maybe you don't know how bad Emil here wants to cut you, Fields," Vinnie said. "I'll ask you again. Where are the eggs?"

Emil grinned from across the room. "Maybe they're in here," he said. He held the three foot tall porcelain Chinese urn over his head, shook it, and pretended to listen for rattling inside. Then he smashed it at his feet on the living room floor. George yelped when the 200-year-old urn shattered.

"Maybe they're in here!" Emil shouted, kicking his foot through the beveled glass in the six-foot tall antique china cabinet. Thick, leaded glass and thin china shattered to the bottom and sprayed onto the hard wood floor. Emil stepped to the back of the china cabinet and pushed it to the floor. George's eyes were wet as he choked and heaved air past Vinnie's fingers.

"You know, Emil, I don't think George wants to tell us where those eggs are," Vinnie said. "Maybe he's waiting to give us a tour of the house."

"Maybe," Emil called from inside the hall closet. The wooden coat rod cracked and tore from the interior walls. Vinnie released George's throat and yanked him from the chair. The left side of his face ached where the back door hit him. He'd probably lost half his hair from the kitchen to the living room. Vinnie pushed him toward the stairs. Emil followed, poking George in the back with the jagged coat rod. For the first time in years, George wished Hilary would come home.

In the master bedroom, Vinnie shoved him backward onto the bed. "You'll save us a lot of time, and yourself a lot of blood, by telling us where the eggs are."

"I told you the eggs aren't here."

"Then where are they?" Vinnie bared yellow teeth in George's face.

"I don't have them."

Emil grabbed a bedside lamp with his left hand and hurled it into the mirror above the walnut dresser. He seemed more interested in breaking things than in finding the cocaine.

Vinnie called to him. "Emil, it seems our friend George here still ain't interested in helping us."

"So it seems!" Emil said, breaking one of the hand-carved spires off the end of the four poster bed. He grabbed the thin end below the spindle. It looked like a baseball bat. He raised it over George, who screeched like an barn owl. Instead of bringing the post down, Emil swung it horizontally over George in a vicious tennis forehand. It swooshed three inches above George's nose and struck the other post at the foot of the bed with an enormous, echoing crack. Splinters flew like grenade shards toward the bathroom and walk-in closet.

"I-I don't have them, I tell you!" George said.

"But you know where they are, don't you Reverend?" Vinnie spoke the title with great sarcasm. Wide-eyed and silent, chest heaving, George watched Vinnie shake his head. Emil tore another post from the bed frame like an ear of corn from its stalk. Vinnie reached into his pants pocket and produced Emil's switchblade. The blade itself, all six inches of double-edged, razor-sharp steel still rested within the belly of the handle. Vinnie raised the riveted pearl handle and examined each side. George pushed himself toward the middle of the bed away from Vinnie. When

Emil caught sight of his Bic, he stopped, watching it move in Vinnie's hand like a lover watching his beloved undress.

"I didn't want it to come to this, George, honest I didn't," Vinnie said. "I've seen what our friend Emil does with the blade inside this handle." He faked a shudder. "But you're not helping us, and I'm thinking, why not give it to him." Emil rounded the end of the bed, leaning forward.

"Let me," Emil said. He sounded like a child wanting to push the elevator button.

George thought this might be a good time to pray, but he doubted it would do any good. It never had before.

"This is sorta your last chance," Vinnie said. There was a click, then a flash. The blade fired like a bullet from the handle and stood gleaming at attention.

"Lemme cut him," Emil said, with the eyes of a starved animal.

Vinnie cocked his head, raised his eyebrows, and looked at George. "Your move."

"Okay, I'll tell you!" George choked the words, and wiped his forehead on the comforter. "But you have to promise not to let that maniac cut me!" He pointed a trembling finger toward Emil.

Vinnie nodded. George looked at him, then at Emil, then back to him. "Brother Lawrence has the eggs." He sagged and laid his head back on the bed.

Vinnie continued to stare at the switchblade in his hand. "All of them?"

"All but the one Nina has."

"Had!" Emil said.

"Like you were planning to leave me out of it?" Emil said. "You were happy to smoke my stuff, until you got the genius idea to go get your own. Cut me out of the equation, was that the plan?"

"Bad idea, George," Vinnie said.

"Ask Nina how bad an idea it was," Emil said, grinning.

George closed his eyes. He wanted them to be gone. He heard Vinnie's voice in his ear. "Looks like we're all going for a little ride in that fine Cadillac of yours."

George's eyes popped open and he sat up. "You got what you came for. Now leave."

Vinnie shook his head, "You both caused us a lot of trouble, George. We don't want no more, so you're with us until we disappear." Vinnie paused and clicked the switchblade. The blade retreated into the throat of the handle. "But before we do, you need to understand how upset we are with you."

He tossed the Bic to Emil and George's heart slammed against the inside of his rib cage. He sucked an enormous breath of air through his open mouth.

"Cut him," Vinnie said.

George screamed. Horror thundered like a thousand hooves in his head. He heard the mechanical click in Emil's hand, "You promised!" He buried his face in his hands.

Vinnie laughed, "I lied. Now I'm like you."

Vinnie moved to Emil's side and leaned toward him. "I'm lettin' you have some fun, but we still need this sorry piece of squirrel shit until the rock's in our hands. Here's how I want you to do it." Vinnie leaned into Emil's ear, whispered, and Emil's face glowed. He twirled the switchblade over and over in his hand.

"Hold him," Emil said.

Ecclesia Seminary

Sarah walked until her legs ached, despite her well-toned muscles. From her first week at Ecclesia, she discovered its beauty and solitude. Trees thick with age and top heavy dotted the quadrangle. Wide sidewalks traced the perimeter and formed a massive X within the ring. Benches, birds and a light breeze made it a perfect place to walk and think.

Sarah dropped onto a solid teak bench halfway down a row of elms. Squirrels chattered on both sides of a trunk next to her and raced its girth. It was hard to tell whether they were fighting or mating. Leaping like gymnasts sideways from the tree on the right, they bounded behind her to the tree left of the bench. They sped around and around the trunk, their claws crunching and scratching into the bark.

Sarah smiled. Why doesn't she let him catch her? Or maybe she is the pursuer. Why is he running from her? The chase stopped with one squirrel four feet higher than the other on the opposite side of the trunk, tails flicking against their backs. Terry told her once, sitting on this very bench, that when squirrels flicked their tails, it meant they were angry. So we've got two males scuffling over a female! Or maybe … it was two females fighting over a male! Did squirrels do that too?

Nina. Would the two of us chase each other around the tree for Terry? We certainly wouldn't admit it. Sarah made a face and stood. Every woman she knew proclaimed she didn't have to compete - wouldn't lower herself. But, women competed. With other women, with men, around and around the tree, tails flicking. She was no different.

Sarah started toward the Chapel. She felt her head shaking side to side. The longer she lived and the further she got, the less sense any of it made. Life. Passion. Accomplishment. Was Solomon right? In the end is it all vanity? And someday will I be hidden beneath the cloaks of vanity I have desired, fought for, achieved? The Reverend Sarah Stafford, wearing a flowing velvet robe. But would she be wearing that robe to reveal the strength of her character, or to hide her character defects? Would she be an adorned, ornate shell, have the title but not the godliness, the position but lacking the spiritual substance to hold it?

She shuddered at the recollection of looking into her soul an hour ago when Dean Tittle held up the mirror. What she saw hurt, deep. In that mirror, she saw the real Sarah - critical, pious, selfish.

She reached the Chapel doors and pulled. They were locked. She walked around to the side doors - also locked. She knocked, to no avail. Her heart cried for some time in the grotto to pray. She would go to the Fields house and ask to borrow the key. She hesitated. Terry always gave her his key. And she didn't like George Fields, speaking of chancel prancers. She turned back towards her dormitory but then stopped and hurried to the back steps toward George and Hilary Fields's house. *Lord, I will not run from your mirror this time!*

In the woods across from the Assistant Dean's house, a gloved hand took the caps off the scope and rested it on a tripod with a level built into its side. The steady hand focused the lens and waited for the next command.

"Five straight lines. Make them the same length," Vinnie said, holding George's head in a flesh vise with his hands.

"Shh! I want to savor every scream," Emil said. He pulled the tip of the blade at a forty-five degree angle toward George's eyebrow. George shrieked and blood spattered onto Vinnie's hands and the bed. By the time Emil made the fifth and final cut, Vinnie could not see George's forehead for the bubbling red pool.

Emil watched drops of blood form on the tip of the blade and fall onto the comforter. He wiped each side of the blade on George's shorts, causing another squeal from the bed. "Relax," he said. "Your nuts are safe, for now."

"Get a washcloth from the bathroom Emil," Vinnie said. "Let's admire your craftsmanship." Emil returned with a white monogrammed bath towel. He pressed it to George's forehead and pulled across the length of his brow. Shadows lengthened from the windows, but there was still enough light to see the oozing red outline of a pentagram in the center of George's forehead.

"Try preachin' with that scar, Reverend," Vinnie said.

"What have you done to me?" George wailed.

"Find out soon enough." Vinnie grabbed him by the arm. "Hold the towel to your head. It's time to go."

Emil looked up to see Vinnie's hand outstretched toward the Bic. For a brief moment, their eyes met and a violent current passed between them. Vinnie read the I-ought-to-bury-this-blade-in-your-eye look, and returned a give-it-back-or-die-right-here look. With a click, the blade was gone and Emil slapped it into Vinnie's hand.

"Get the car keys from his pants," Vinnie said, pocketing the switchblade. Emil fished them out and yanked George into the hall. Unsteady on his feet and blind with the towel in front of his face, George caught his shoulder on one of the thick portrait frames hanging along the narrow hallway. It crashed to the floor. He screamed. Emil laughed. George missed the top stair and thudded against the back of Vinnie's shoulder, then righted himself with the rail.

At the back door, Vinnie jangled the keys. "Nothing like a Sunday evening drive, eh Reverend?" As he reached for the door handle, a loud knock came from the other side. He jerked back, grabbed George with one hand and his Glock with the other and all three walked backward to the swinging kitchen door. "Whoever it is, get rid of them," he whispered to Emil. Another knock. Vinnie backed George through the door into the living room.

As soon as the swinging door closed, Emil lunged for the butcher block on the counter. He grabbed a large kitchen knife and slid it down the back of his pants. The second knife he pulled from the block was a little larger than a steak knife, but with a wide blade. He stuck it in his sock beneath his right pant leg. Then he smiled and opened the door. "Can I help you?" he said to the young woman standing on the threshold.

Sarah stood open-mouthed, her request already starting to spill from her lips. She didn't recognize the short, squat man with the over-sized hooknose and braided gold chest chains. She felt him scan her body from top to bottom and back.

"I-I was hoping to speak with Reverend Fields," she said.

"Come on in, sweetheart," the man said, still smiling. Sweetheart? Sarah felt a surge of fear stab her chest. She stepped through the door into the middle of the kitchen, hearing the door close behind her. Before she could turn to face him, she felt the short man's hot breath on the back of her neck and cold steel against the front of her throat. A high-pitched scream flew from her lips. Her breath came in short gasps. "You got a car, sweetheart?" he said into her ear.

"Yes."

"Here?"

"No. In the lot." Sarah was on her tiptoes trying to retreat from the knife edge.

The swinging door between the kitchen and the living room burst open and Vinnie raged into the kitchen, dragging George behind him. "I told you to get rid of her!" He eyed Emil and then the ten-inch kitchen knife in his hand. "Put that down!"

"I don't think so, Vinnie." Emil spit the big man's first name.

Vinnie leveled the Glock at Emil's head. "Put it down, Bente."

Bente? Sarah felt the room spin. Emil jerked his head behind Sarah's and peered at Vinnie from behind her ear. "Way I see it, you ain't gettin' me without killin' her and I don't think you're up to it. So I reckon I got me a taxi outta here." He backed Sarah into the corner by the door. "Why don't you be a good boy and drive Missy and me to her car."

Sarah watched the pistol trained in her direction. It looked puny in the man's huge hand. His face was red and his whole body shook. George cried into the blood-soaked towel. The man cursed and lowered the gun, yanking George toward the back door. He peered out for a moment, then marched George to the Cadillac and shoved him into the back seat. Still holding Sarah close, Emil rounded the back fender, easing them both into the back seat next to George. Vinnie jammed the key into the ignition and slammed the front door.

The windshield exploded. Thousands of tiny glass cubes sprayed across the front seat. Sarah screamed. Then the driver's side window shattered.

Vinnie howled and flattened across the front seat. The engine started and gears clanked. Emil shouted, "Who the hell?" He slid low in the back seat and peered toward the woods. George's toweled head was between his legs. The Cadillac raced backward. Righting himself behind the wheel, Vinnie tore backward down the driveway and skidded into the fire lane. He slammed the Cadillac into drive and stomped the accelerator. The nose lifted with a roar and they shot past the woods onto Spelkin Lane.

"Jesus Vinnie, you shot?" Emil said.

"Don't think so, but I oughtta be!" He glanced at the driver's side door. "You?" Cubes of safety glass lifted in the wind and peppered the inside of the car.

"Nah, but I jerked so hard when that second shot came that I damn near sliced Missy's throat." Sarah lowered her chin and looked down. Her white blouse was streaked with blood and hot pain throbbed on the right side of her neck. "How 'bout we call a truce and work together again," he said, shouting through the wind. "Then we can both get out of this town."

Vinnie nodded without looking back. Emil lowered the knife from Sarah's throat and tossed it into the front seat. With trembling fingers, Sarah felt her throat. It was warm and sticky. She pulled a red hand away.

"Nothin' but a scratch, sweetheart." His breath reminded her of septic tank back up. "I cut you for real, you gonna know it." He put his hand on her bare knee and she slapped it away. "You and me, we gonna party later." She shuddered and turned toward George. Emil continued in her ear. "You ever smoke crack? I got the best in the world. You'll like it. We'll party, just the two of us. You'll get into my crack and I'll get into yours." He wiggled his tongue toward her.

"I'd rather die."

"Ooohh, that'll work too. My second most favorite pastime."

Vinnie barked at George for directions to Brother Lawrence's house. Every few seconds he glanced into the rear view mirror. With no glass to stop it, the wind howled and whistled. George lowered the towel and Sarah stared in horror at his forehead. "I'm an artist too," Emil called into her ear, pointing toward George and chuckling. Sarah leaned forward and wretched. Emil jerked his legs away from her.

"Stay on Bradley to Route 60; go left on 60 for nine miles," George said. "Bingham is a small road on the right. He's at the end of it."

In April, the time between dusk and dark is about three minutes. Vinnie flipped on the headlights and glanced in the rear view mirror again. "We're being followed." He shot past Route 60 and pressed the accelerator.

Emil's head snapped around and he stared hard at the blackness behind them. "You see something?"

Vinnie shook his head. "I can feel it. In all my years, I've never been wrong."

Memorial Hospital

"You're wasting our time, Mr. Woodrow," Lieutenant Higgins said to the man sitting in the hospital bed.

Captain Steele nodded. "And in the meantime, somebody is getting away with your rock."

"Told you it's not my rock," Terry said, looking through the window at the darkness. "I don't use it. I don't sell it."

"You just smuggle it," Higgins said.

Terry rolled his eyes. "Why would I smuggle it if I don't use it or sell it?"

"Maybe you smuggle it and sell it to someone who sells it on the street."

"I don't."

"And we're supposed to take your word for it, is that it?" Steele said.

Terry shrugged. "Whatever."

"Whatever?" Steele walked around the end of the bed and leaned toward Terry's face. "Listen Woodrow. The people you're dicking with didn't go to the same prep school as you. And they sure as hell don't live by your rules."

"I resent that."

"Whatever," Higgins said, mocking him.

Steele continued. "They went to street school and they live by street rules. It's not even survival of the fittest, my man. It's survival of the sickest. You following me here?" He glared at Terry.

Higgins chimed in. "They grew up in crime families and they live by their rules." He leaned in close to Terry. "Let me be specific. By their rules, you play poke-poke with the wife of a crime boss, you're dead. Simple as that. Strike three. Forget strikes one and two." He paused and let it sink in, then continued.

"Here's another one. You mess with their product or disrupt their supply chain, you die. Disappear. Become part of the great harbor fish tank in the harbor. End of discussion."

Steele weighed in again. "Add to it that you are in police custody and able to finger them. If they think there's even a remote possibility you could give us information to compromise their operation or ID, you die. Iced from within the cage. You getting this?"

Terry looked into Steele's eyes for several seconds. Then Steele lowered his voice.

"We know they've been in the hospital already since you and Nina got here. Those two officers outside your door will do their best to keep you alive, but plenty of murders happen with armed guards standing outside the door. These are really bad people, Mr. Woodrow, and they are really good at what they do."

Terry leaned his head back on the pillow and put his forearm over his eyes. Steele watched all the quills fall from the porcupine. "I'm so scared," Terry said in a whisper. "I'm scared of you. I'm scared of them. I'm scared of what might happen. I'm scared about what it's going to mean for my future." He sighed, "And I don't have anything to tell you. Honest I don't." He gave Captain Steele a pained glance.

"Mr. Woodrow-"

"Terry."

"Terry," Steele said. "We're not trying to scare you. We are trying to level with you. And we are trying to gather enough to get these guys, before you or anyone else gets hurt. So what say we figure out together what we do know?"

Terry nodded.

"Okay," Steele said, "you say you went to the airport to pick up Nina Bente because she called you from Columbia and asked. You knew her as Nina Ondolopous."

"Right."

"But you didn't take her to the airport when she left for Columbia."

"True, but how'd you know that?"

Steele tendered a weary smile. "We have thousands of pieces of information. Like pieces of a jig saw puzzle, we don't know how they fit until people like you help us put them together." He walked to the end of the bed.

"So, you knew she was overseas, but you didn't know she intended to smuggle crack," Higgins said. "What did you think she was doing there?"

"She won a preaching prize at the Chapel last semester. She is a wonderful preacher. Knows her Bible inside out."

"I find that hard to believe."

"It's true. Nina's smart, articulate-"

"And a crack addict," Higgins said.

"And a darn good liar," Terry said. "Anyway, the prize was an all-expenses paid month overseas as a missionary preacher. She sent back text of some sermons she preached over there and they were excellent. Two got read aloud to the entire seminary."

Steele grimaced and scratched his head. "So her month is up," he paced, "and it's time to come back. She calls you to pick her up at the airport.... why didn't she call her husband?"

"There's a zillion dollar question," Terry said.

"He was at the airport, you know," Steele said.

"Are you serious?" Terry's face drained.

"Serious."

"Why am I still alive?"

"Another good question," Steele said. "We seem to be gathering buckets full. Nina saw him. They had words. Then Bente's bodyguard pulled him back to their car. You came around the corner and loaded his wife and thirty-six plastic eggs filled with Columbia's finest rock cocaine, and off you went."

Terry sat upright in the bed, his mouth agape.

"You didn't know about the eggs?" Steele asked.

Terry shook his head. "In fact, I asked about them when we got back to her apartment. One of the grapefruit sacks fell out of her shoulder bag."

"Tell me exactly what she said about them."

"She said they were filled with rock candy from mountain villagers, said they were for the married students' kids. For Easter."

"Rock candy."

"Yep. Made sense too, because she wrote on the outside of the sacks, 'Presents for the Children.' How sick is that!"

"Or how clever." Captain Steele smiled. "Worked on you."

"Worked on everybody." Terry shook his head.

Steele didn't follow him, almost let the comment pass, but something stopped him. "Everybody? Are you referring to something specific?"

Terry nodded. "Dean Tittle came in here earlier. He filled in for me at the Chapel service this morning. Said that right in the middle of Reverend Field's most boring sermon yet, two grapefruit sacks of plastic eggs fell to the floor under the altar. He said there was duct tape on the corners that came loose and when they crashed, Fields looked like somebody had shot him. But Brother Lawrence came from the back of the church, picked up the sacks and carried them out."

"All three?" Higgins asked.

"Excuse me?"

"Did Brother Lawrence take all three sacks with him?"

"I assume so, but you can ask Dean Tittle."

"Did Fields and Brother Lawrence know what was in those eggs?" Steele asked.

"Don't know. Ask them."

"An excellent idea," Steele pulled his chin. "Especially since Fields financed the missionary trip."

Terry shook his head. "Nina won that fair and square."

"Perhaps."

Chapter Sixteen

Gaslight Motel

Hilary Fields rose from the motel bed and swished to the bathroom. She avoided glancing at the large mirror covering the entire section of wall above the bathroom counter, not wanting to look until after her shower, the first in three days. She wanted her own special soap and shampoo, but the motel's tightly wrapped white slabs and tiny yellow bottles would have to do.

The water was hot and steam rose in billows. She padded to the armoire and removed the new clothes she bought last night. The colors were drab and muted, the fabric functional. Who cared anymore? She dreaded another rendezvous at the coffee shop in less than an hour. But she would go. Then she would know for sure. She grabbed the new underwear and headed in the direction of the steam.

The hot water bounced from her shoulders and head, and streamed toward her feet. Hilary felt her back muscles relax under the blast of heat. She wiped water from her eyes and searched for the soap, lathered and wondered about George. Why should she care? Did she care?

What would today's tape reveal? She didn't want to hear any more, but she had to know. She would not let him flush their lives. She'd worked too hard, earned her place, deserved their elevation. She could feel the power as if it were already hers.

Tittle would retire any day. But then, she had recycled that thought for three years. She scrubbed. The old bag was overdue for a fall and a broken hip, or the onset of some debilitating disease. She grinned and water fell over her parted lips, filling her mouth. She spit.

Or maybe his mind would rot enough for the Board to force retirement. Over the last four years, Tittle had been losing it. From the moment "Queen Jean" died, he was a lost soul, a dinghy cut adrift. It showed in his personal hygiene. He would show up for staff meetings unshaven, yellow specks of yoke stuck to his chin whiskers. His khaki trousers begged to be washed and pressed; even the wrinkles had wrinkles. There were stains in the front from trips to the refrigerator and stains in the back from trips to the bathroom. Shocks of gray hair ringed a pocked and age-spotted bald crown. Most of the time his hair was oily and clung to the folds of his neck.

Sometimes Hilary had enjoyed Jeremy's dementia for the sheer harassment it caused her arrogant and distant husband. George used to come home raging about scheduled meetings Tittle forgot about. Tittle the "no show." He resented having to organize a manhunt for the Dean. After a while, his staff knew where to look. He could be found wandering the quadrangle with his head down, brows knitted with a mixture of thought and grief, hands behind his back, belly protruding over a straining belt. He fell asleep during chapel most mornings, and during several key Board meetings. His greatest faux pax had been to snore into his lapel microphone during a sermon delivered by the visiting George Cartey, Archbishop of Canterbury. It made him the talk of the water cooler, and the local tavern.

Tittle was the barricade standing in her way, the only barricade, until now. Hilary smacked the water off and stood in the steam, dripping and trying to concentrate. No one must ever know. One slip and she would watch the whole thing collapse.

She dressed in her new garb, gathering dirty clothes into a plastic dry cleaning bag she found hanging in the closet. She threw the plastic cardkey in the bag with them. She paid cash up front for the room under the name, Mrs. Bridget Sterling. The memory flashed and she shook off a chill. She almost gave the clerk her credit card when he asked for a copy of it, "for incidentals." With her hand rummaging the bottom of her purse, she stopped, glared and announced, "There will be no incidentals." After a brief skirmish, the clerk shrugged and surrendered. There would be no incidentals.

She hurried to her rental car, a tan Ford Focus. She despised it. It was like driving a discarded beer can. But no one would expect to see her in it, and that's the way she wanted it. She started the engine. Okay - tape, house. Then she clutched her throat and laughed at the reflection in the rear view mirror.

It was a ten minute drive to the coffee shop. She made it in five. The tiny engine whined and complained. Hilary's gray-blotched hair was still wet when she emerged from the driver's side door and entered Lavish . She didn't look at him, but she knew he was there. She would make him wait until she got her latte. This morning she ordered an extra shot of espresso.

Latte in hand, Hilary walked to the last booth in the back and slid in across from the man behind the raised newspaper. "Morning, Mrs. Fields," the voice said through the paper.

"Morning, Bo. The cassette please."

Bo lowered the paper. The sunglasses were gone and large toad eyes looked across the table, the thick-jowled face unsmiling and detached, like a man who was both there and not there at the same time. "You're doing the right thing, Hilary."

"*Mrs. Fields*, if you please, and I am not interested in your opinion."

"You're doing the right thing, *Mrs. Fields*," Bo said in a low voice. "Your boy, George, is into some bad action. I'd be careful if I were you." He slid the cassette to her hands.

"Thanks for the unsolicited advice." Her voice was tense and tough.

"No problem. You know we offer protective services if you should ever need them."

So that's where this was going, Hilary thought. "I'm certain the current level of service is more than I'll need."

"I'm not," he snapped, leaning over the paper. "Listen to the cassette, lady. Then see if you still say that." Hilary pushed herself out of the booth without another word.

169

Hilary wasn't certain how long or far she drove, but the latte was long finished and she had listened to the cassette twice though. Her hands gripped the steering wheel white to the knuckle, like she was driving the edge of a cliff. Hot tears of rage fell from her eyes onto the new gray trench coat. "You arrogant, asshole..." she screamed at the windshield, "you lying ..., you stupid fucking idiot! I will never forgive you. Never!" She slammed her right palm against the steering wheel and the Focus lurched to the right. She exited the ramp onto Bradley and raged toward the seminary. She swung into the student lot high above the fire lane without slowing and slammed on the brakes, skidding within inches of a parked car. She burst from the car almost as soon as it was in park, and stood, trying to concentrate.

She removed the trench coat, opened the trunk, threw it in, slammed the trunk and locked all the doors. Then she jogged to the stairs, raced down to the fire lane, up her driveway, and burst through the back door. Passing through the kitchen door, her mouth dropped and her eyes filled. She wiped tears from both cheeks and raced for the stairs. There was no time to grieve the loss of broken and irreplaceable treasures. She gave the entire scene an emotional stiff arm and climbed to the bedroom.

She glanced at the bed frame's broken spires, and stamped her foot. But that was all the reaction she allowed herself. Follow the list. She ran to the closet and grabbed her favorite suit and blouse combination, the red one. She changed and donned the matching red heels. Hilary bagged the clothes she changed out of and ran down the stairs and out the door.

She ran in the low heels the length of the driveway and headed for the stairs to the upper lot. Keep going, she said to herself. The more sweat the better. At the top of the stairs, Hilary was dizzy and her chest heaved. Her blouse stuck to her back beneath the suit jacket and sweat streaked the make-up on her face. She opened the trunk and threw the bag of clothes in it, then slammed the trunk again and headed back to the stairs as fast as her heels would allow. Down the stairs she raced, holding the rail to avoid falling. Across the fire lane and up the driveway at a dead run.

Hilary burst through the back door again and crunched over the broken glass to the telephone. She dialed 9-1-1. When the operator answered, Hilary's breath was so labored she couldn't talk for a couple seconds. Between gasps, she said, "This is Hilary fields, Ecclesia Seminary. I'm...

having… severe chest pains. Hurry." She hung up the phone. Her high heels clacked on the kitchen floor as she did set after set of jumping jacks, waiting for the paramedics to arrive.

Home of Dr. Maria Sanchez

Maria heard the doorbell and sprayed one extra shot of perfume onto the cleavage of her breasts and adjusted the plunge of her black dress. *Oh God.* She felt the hot moistness soak into her panties, and she raced to the door.

She found Max grinning on the door step with a bottle of wine in one hand and a bouquet of stargazer lilies in the other.

"I'm sorry sir, but the party is tomorrow evening," she said.

"Then I recommend we start one of our own," Max said, crossing the threshold in two strides and pressing his lips against hers. Maria heard the moan and knew it had come from the deepest place within her, felt her arms wrap at the back of his neck, felt her tongue thrust into his mouth. Max backed her slowly until he could kick the door closed behind him, his tongue flicking and thrusting and rolling with hers. He felt her heat, heard her breath coming hard through her nose, wanted to close around her, wished his hands weren't full of wine and flowers, felt his manhood harden against his boxers.

Then they were dropping to the oriental rug, slowly, gently, until they lay pressed against each other and his hands… at last… were free.

Memorial Hospital

"Excuse me Doctor, but can you give me something for this smile? Seems to have stuck right here." Captain Steele touched his hand to his heart.

He had sent Higgins for information about Brother Lawrence – current address, background, criminal record, whatever he could find. Then he had hurried to the Emergency Room.

Dr. Sanchez smiled, her face turned away from him. "I never diagnose smiles on duty." She pretended to study the notes on her clipboard.

He stepped close behind her and whispered. "I hardly slept a wink after I left you."

"Insomnia?"

"Your perfume. I smelled it all night."

"I'm sorry."

"Really?" Max said.

"No." The urge to fold into his arms, right there in the Emergency Room corridor, was so strong that Dr. Sanchez started walking before something intoxicating and highly inappropriate happened.

He followed her toward the break room. "They say aroma therapy is good."

"Relaxing they say," she said over her shoulder, moving to the coffee pot.

"Not for me," he said, closing the gap between them. "My heart pounded all night."

"So did mine." She stopped at the sink, embarrassed by her honesty. She should keep him guessing more. But whenever her eyes met his, she felt the rush between them. How much had she revealed last night? Could he tell that the sound of his voice loosed butterflies in her stomach?

She heard the door close and latch behind her, and whirled in time for two strong and familiar arms to wrap around her. "Max, we can't. This is a busy place."

"One kiss and I'll open the door again."

She threw her lips against his and their mouths opened. She felt him press against her, all of him. Electric shocks raced back and forth between them and she felt him swell against her. She pulled away. "If we get caught, I'll never hear the end of it."

He kissed her neck, and her breath came in bursts, like she had run the hundred yard dash. She could tell she was as excited as he, felt it, and wondered if it showed through her blouse. She pushed away and buttoned her lab coat, steadying herself on the sink. Max crossed the room and opened the door. Emergency Room sounds rushed them like a cold ocean wave. He sat in one of the chairs and pulled himself to the table until he could calm down.

Dr. Sanchez struggled to get her professional face back. "So, you bring me any more victims this morning?" She poured water into the top of the coffee maker and it began to gurgle and hiss into the pot below. A wisp of steam rose from the belly of the machine and vanished into the ceiling.

He smiled and shook his head. "What's the status of the two I brought you yesterday afternoon?"

"One's in the morgue."

"Of course. You didn't by any chance get a peek at the cause of death?"

"I knew you would ask, so I made a point to copy it on the last page here." She flipped the papers on her clipboard. "James Harnes, 74, Caucasian, 5'10", 165. COD: CVA, Cerebral Vascular Accident."

"What's that?"

"Stroke."

"Those dirt bags scared him to death." He pursed his lips. "What about Mrs. Spruill?"

"I've got a note on her, too. Nettie Spruill, 73, Caucasian, 5'6", 120. Condition: guarded. They admitted her for observation overnight. I saw a notation that the Psych nurse was contacted. They'll start meds and see if she stabilizes. If she does, they'll send her home either today or tomorrow. If she doesn't …"

"If she strokes out, too?"

Maria nodded. "Or refuses to eat. Or stops taking all her medications. Or finds some other way to avoid having to keep living. If she shows signs of that– different story entirely." She paused, seeing painful images from years of medical practice, feeling the pain again. "Sometimes when you get ready to sign their discharge papers, you get the feeling you're signing their death warrant."

"Going home to die?" Steele said. "You must see it a lot."

"I do. I call it 'subtle suicide.' It's prevalent among the elderly and the severely depressed."

"Those are two very different groups of people."

"They are, and they aren't. The one thing they share is a loss of will to live. With the severely depressed, it's most often the result of hopelessness that things will ever get any better. With the elderly, it's often that life is difficult – everything is difficult- but the one thing that makes it worth struggling on is the chance to share a little more life with their spouse. When the spouse dies, the struggle doesn't seem worth it anymore."

"These two weren't married."

"Does it look like it mattered to her whether she wore his ring and carried his name?"

"No." He took the steaming cup of coffee from her soft, slender hands, and he set it before him.

"But he mattered to her," Maria said. "I saw it in her eyes, all over her body in fact."

"I hate this part of the work," he said, pulling the thin red plastic stick around the Styrofoam rim. The non-dairy creamer spun in tiny powder islands, unwilling to relent and blend. "I don't mind hauling the bad guys in here shot up, bleeding, traumatized, even dead. They chose their pain and deserve what they get." His voice was hard, clinical. "But these cases really get to me."

His voice softened. She studied his face as he studied the vanishing white islands in his cup. "It's the innocent who have suffering thrust upon them. I think about James Stafford and the terror he must have felt with his hands, feet and mouth duct taped, gasping for breath through his nose, wondering if he would be found, then feeling something burst in his head or neck or wherever the heck it bursts, and then the sudden panic of not being able to breathe or see or think." He shuddered. "No one should have to die alone, not like that, and not because of some wretched excuse for a human being who doesn't even know his name."

Dr. Sanchez covered his hand with hers, and then returned to her coffee cup. "And then there's the suffering of the one left behind."

He looked into her eyes. "Exactly. Look at Nettie Spruill. In a moment of barbaric cruelty, someone stole her reason for living and shattered her life. She asks why and is met with the great silent shrug. It makes no sense to her, and no one can explain it. The religious try, and sometimes I wish they wouldn't. They tell the Nettie's of this world that it is God's will. Terrific. Now she has a double crisis." He shook his head. "It will never make sense, because it is senseless. She will struggle to make peace with it for the rest of her life." He took a long drink of coffee.

Dr. Sanchez stared at her hands. "Life is difficult, sometimes cruel, sometimes unfair, and always brittle. A chip gets knocked off here, a chunk there, and sometimes the whole thing shatters before our eyes. None of us escapes it entirely." A long and pregnant pause rested in the room.

Max pushed back from the table, his eyebrows raised. "Well. Glad we solved that problem." He gestured in a wide circle with his arms. "What problem shall we tackle next? World hunger?"

Maria laughed. "I've got to get back out there." She rose from the table and touched his shoulder as she passed behind him to the door. He smiled and reached for her hand.

"May I call you tonight, Doctor? I suspect my condition will be dire by then." He smiled up toward her face.

She smiled back. "You can call, Captain, but my social calendar stays pretty full. I can't guarantee I'll be available." That was better, girl.

"I'll call every ten minutes, have flowers delivered every half hour, and chocolates every hour."

"Then I won't answer the phone for at least three hours." She disappeared around the corner.

Captain Steele poured himself another cup of coffee and flipped open his cell phone. He tapped the speed dial number for Higgins. After the second ring, he heard the familiar voice.

"Higgins here."

"Steele here," he said, mocking.

"Hi Cap. Got the locals mobilized."

"Good. First precinct?"

"Yes sir."

"Ask them for the forensics report from Nina Bente's flat, and have them send a team with escorts to the Fieldses' residence."

"Already done, Captain. Just got off the phone with Chief Parker. Thanked me again and again for letting them work with us."

"The one who always wanted to be an FBI agent?"

"That's the one."

Steele smiled. If he only knew. "You didn't tell him we've done everything we could to leave them out of our investigation?"

"And break his heart?" He could tell Higgins enjoyed his assignment. "How's your surveillance going?"

"What surveillance?" Steele asked.

"Thought you were watching one of the ER doctors over there."

"Just doing my job."

"Bet."

"You and your team flushing the little foxes from their holes?"

"You bet. Seems Brother Lawrence has quite a past."

"Oh?"

"And a big secret. I talked with the head skirt at Mercy Mission in Detroit. The good friar remembered Larry Stiles. That's his given name. Seems Larry grew up in a neighborhood on the fringe of the Detroit city limits. Like lots of kids in that slum, he was ripe for drugs and for gang banging."

"He join one?"

"Yep. Drugs, guns, territory wars. He was right in the thick of it before he hit puberty. The monks got him cleaned, he got religion, got a calling, entered the novitiate, and at the age of 25 started wearing one of those long brown robes with a rope belt."

"Kicked the habit, donned a habit, and joined a different gang," Steele laughed.

"Something like that." Higgins paused and Steele heard papers shuffling. "Yep. He became part of the God-squad on the Detroit streets, the head friar said."

"You keep referring to the guy you talked with as the skirt and the head friar. Why don't you use his name?"

"I thought it'd help you concentrate, Cap," Higgins said.

"You lost me."

"I was afraid every time I used his name, I'd lose you!" He chuckled.

"Keep going, Lieutenant."

"It's Pickle, sir."

"Friar Pickle?" Steele laughed. "Bet he couldn't wait to dump that last name!"

There was a pause on the other end. "That's not his last name."

"Oh Christ, don't tell me it's his first name!"

"Afraid so. I knew I would lose you. I just got my team here working again. Lost them for twenty minutes."

Steele laughed, "Please don't tell me his last name is "Jar" or "Relish.""

"Worse. It's Poaker."

Captain Steele loosed a blast of laughter that echoed off the break room walls. "Father Pickle Poaker," he squeaked and roared again. "I can't breathe. His mother ought to be spanked!"

"Arrested," Higgins said and pulled the phone from his ear as another blast of laughter squawked through the speaker.

Steele wiped tears from his eyes. "I'll call you back." He slapped the phone closed and went for a paper towel. Poor guy. Probably got tortured on the playground. Pickle Poaker's pecker…. He convulsed again, fresh tears shooting from the smile wrinkles around his eyes. He had to stop thinking about it, had to call Higgins back. He leaned on the sink. His face hurt. His chest hurt. He tilted the handle on the water faucet to cold and shoved cupped hands into the stream. After the third palm of water to his face, he heard a knock behind him. He slapped the paper towel to his eyes and turned around. By the clinical look on Dr. Sanchez's face, he could tell that something happened.

"Thought you should know, we got another one in here from the seminary."

The laughter was gone in an instant. "What is it this time?" "Who - this time?"

Dr. Sanchez looked at her clipboard. "Hilary Fields, 54, Caucasian, haven't gotten height and weight yet, complaining of severe chest pains."

That's Reverend Field's wife. He's Assistant Dean," he said. "Met him in ICU yesterday. Higgins and I have a few questions we'd like to ask him." He motioned behind her. "Is the wife having a heart attack?"

"They're hooking her to an EKG machine. Once they run a strip, we'll know more. But she's soaked in sweat."

"Not a good sign I guess."

"No."

"Can I ask her a few questions?"

She held up her hand, "Give us a chance to see what we're dealing with."

He nodded. "I've got more to discuss with Higgins anyway. Okay if I hang out here until you come back with more details?"

She nodded. "But don't leave the room with that." She pointed to his cell phone on the table.

"Whatever you say, Maria," he said.

"You should practice that phrase." She smiled over her shoulder and was gone.

Max grinned toward the empty doorway. He threw the paper towel in the wastebasket and picked up his cell phone. A few moments later, he dialed Higgins.

"I'm back," Steele said.

"That was a fast recovery, faster than my team. Impressed."

"Don't be. I got a bucket of ice down my back."

Higgins waited.

"Two minutes ago, the Assistant Dean's wife arrived in the back of an ambulance with chest pains."

"Fields?"

"Right. George's wife. Go figure."

"If we wait at Memorial long enough, maybe they'll all come to us."

"We wait long enough, they might all arrive in body bags." He tapped his empty Styrofoam cup on the table. "That Bente was born in hell and brought it to earth with him."

"We'll get him, Cap."

"Wish I shared your optimism," Steele said. "He should have been an easy catch. He's stupid. He's impulsive. He's reckless. But he's slipped a damn tight net, twice."

"Third time's a charm."

"Finish telling me about Brother Lawrence, and don't mention the head friar's name again." He chuckled.

"Wasn't planning to. Seems Stiles - Brother Lawrence – worked the Detroit streets with the other monks for eight years, when he was discharged."

"Discharged? Did he use that word?"

"He did, Higgins said. "But then he got tight-lipped, all of a sudden. Said the file was confidential. I tried to get the details, but he wouldn't budge."

"The Church and its religious orders are the most notorious of the secret societies."

"I never thought of them as secret societies."

"They're not supposed to be," Steele said. "But they function like them. Secrets are shared in the confessional, and they go unspoken to the hearer's grave."

"Is that Christian?"

"Ask a theologian at the seminary. All I know is that it keeps in the dark, stuff that ought to be brought into the light."

"Like here," Higgins said.

"Like here. The head skirt is keeping information from us that could be vital to our investigation."

"Could we subpoena it?"

"We could try," Steele answered, "but history suggests we'll never get it."

"That's illegal."

"And immoral. But that's the church," Steele said.

"So, Brother Lawrence left the Mission under suspicious circumstances, and we'll have to ask him about it ourselves," Higgins said.

"Can't wait," Steele said. "'So Brother Lawrence,' I'll say to him, 'Got yourself in a real pickle there, didn't you.'"

"Stop right there," Higgins said.

Steele couldn't suppress the laugh. "So tell me what his connection is to the seminary."

"Came to the seminary straight from the Mission and been there ever since. Job title is Spiritual Director. Lives alone on a farm several miles out of town. Raises sheep. That's about all I know."

"Got the address?"

"Right here."

"How about a drive in the country later on? I'd like to ask Brother Lawrence how it is that an ex-crack addict walked out of the seminary chapel with three dozen plastic eggs full of Colombian rock." He paced the break room. "In the meantime, I'm waiting to ask Mrs. Fields a few questions, if the docs will let me."

"Oh they'll let you, Cap. I hear you've got an inside track."

"Stop right there," he said, smiling. He didn't mind being teased and Higgins seemed to know it. "What can you tell me about Reverend and Mrs. Fields?"

"Some of this stuff you already know. Reverend Fields is Assistant Dean of the seminary. He's next in line for the Dean's position once Dean Jeremy Tittle retires. Fields is a church ladder climber and it's rumored that he and Hilary are upset they aren't already Commander-and-Mrs.-in-Chief. Tittle was supposed to retire four years ago, but he changed his mind. My sources aren't sure why, but they speculated that after his wife died he didn't have much else to do."

"Or to live for, maybe. Maria and I talked about that this morning."

"Oh, so it's Maria, not Dr. Sanchez."

"Lieutenant…." He heard Higgins chuckle.

"Anyway, I learned the Dean's position is not filled by search process or vote of the Board, but by simple accession of the Assistant Dean. The Assistant Dean is an elected position, and it is understood by all that the Assistant they choose today would become tomorrow's Dean. George was chosen five years ago, when Tittle was sixty-five and ripe for retirement. Ever since, he's waited for the acting Dean to step aside, both he and his ambitious wife, Hilary. Their mutual ambition was the glue to hold together an otherwise empty marriage."

"How, where, do you get details like this?" Steele continued to be amazed by the information Higgins could unearth.

"It's a gift."

"And you pay your sources handsomely with government funds."

"Perhaps."

"Go on."

"In addition to being Assistant Dean, Reverend Fields is also in charge of the chapel services and the chapel congregation. Terry Woodrow is his assistant and student intern. Now, Hilary Fields. You'll love this. It comes from a reliable source who's known her most of her life. Hilary was the daughter of a hard driving executive with the largest oil conglomerate in Texas. She was raised in the country clubs of Houston and competed for status with the other rising Texas debutantes. She was schooled at Sweetmount College. It's the school of choice for social climbers.

"Hilary met George on a blind date, something no debutante would have considered normally. But her new, best and only friend at Sweetmount pressured her into it. The friend – let's call her Isabelle-"

"Let's call her your source," Steele said, "and she calls you her cash cow."

Higgins continued without missing a syllable. "Isabelle was seeing a guy from West Point, a real catch likely to vault her in the unofficial social ratings. He had a friend, a fellow swimmer on the team. Hilary went on the date with visions of Speedos and ratings dancing in her head. She found George slightly above average in looks with a boyish face and bristles of jet black hair. But she liked the muscular swimmer's body and felt as much of it as she could through his shirt as they danced. She never made it home that night and George experienced a rite of passage he had never made.

"Hilary was thrilled to hear of George's plans to go to law school when he graduated. She wished his parents had been as enthusiastic. He was raised in a strict religious environment by a father who was a third generation ordained Presbyterian minister. No dancing, drinking, or card playing. And no dating. George fled to West Point like a caged animal who found the door ajar. As strict as West Point was, it was the land of liberty compared to the strictures of home.

"When, at the last moment he headed to seminary, she broke the engagement. Pastors didn't make any money, didn't live in nice homes in nice neighborhoods and couldn't afford membership fees to the local country club.

"Nevertheless, Hilary changed her mind, married him two months before graduation, convinced she could bring him to his senses before it was too late. She failed, and had driven poor George to the top of the church ladders with cattle prods ever since."

"Higgins, you are the best sleuth I've ever met."

"Thank you, sir."

"Sounds like no ugly skeletons in the Fields closet. No drugs. No prison time."

"None that I found."

"So what was he doing with the eggs?" He sensed a presence behind him and turned to the smiling face of Dr. Sanchez. "Gotta go, Higgins. Meet me here with a couple of sandwiches as soon as you can." He snapped the cell phone closed.

"Mrs. Fields' strip is normal, but she's complaining like she's got a lit corncob pipe lodged in her anal cavity."

"Anal cavity? Do all doctors talk like that?"

"Worse."

"From the briefing Higgins gave me, I think the complaining is normal behavior."

"We can't find anything wrong with her medically," Dr. Sanchez said, "but emotionally she's distraught. And with good reason. It sounds from her ranting that someone tore her house to pieces."

"Hers too?"

"Hmmm?"

"Nina Bente's place was trashed, too. I wonder if we'll find George's stiff body among the wreckage of the Fieldses' residence."

"Mrs. Fields said she didn't find anyone there when she got home. Sounds like she has no idea where her husband is."

"Good work, Maria. We may have to promote you to Assistant Detective."

She grinned and shook her head. "I only snoop for the cute detectives."

Captain Steele returned the grin. "Think they'll admit her?"

"Likely. I heard the cardiologist scheduling an echocardiogram first thing tomorrow morning."

"Good. Wanna know where to find her."

"I hope you'll be able to talk with her soon."

"Hope?"

Dr. Sanchez leaned in the door frame, "I'm sorry, Max, but when I mentioned the possibility to her, she flew into a rage. At this point she refuses to see you. But let me work with her a bit." She left without another word.

He leaned back in the chair and looked at the ceiling and asked the empty room, "What are you hiding, Mrs. Fields?"

Chapter Seventeen

Lago-Mar Motel

The argument between blue jays outside the motel window escalated to a screaming brawl, and Sarah knew she wouldn't sleep anymore. She had hardly closed her eyes all night. Her head pounded and her right foot had fallen asleep beneath her. The air reeked of stale smoke from Bente's pipe and heavy grease from delivered pizzas. The smell brought vivid images of last evening - Emil sucking lungs of putrid smelling smoke from the pipe and then passing it to the eager hands of Ecclesia's Assistant Dean, for God's sake!

Images flashed in her mind of George Fields inhaling crack cocaine smoke, choking, laughing, his eyes glazing, inhaling more, sharing with the same man who had carved a pentagram into his forehead. Last night George hadn't seemed to care. And he hadn't cared that one of his students was across the room watching him do drugs with a gangster!

She remembered listening to their comparisons between this uncut Colombian cocaine and the stuff they obviously had been smoking together before, stuff that had come from domestic suppliers. She couldn't believe it. They were regular crack buddies.

Once the initial shock had worn off, the worry had set in. She wondered why Reverend Fields didn't mind Sarah seeing him do all this, hearing him say all this. Surely he didn't think she would keep it to herself when she got back to Ecclesia! Surely he knew she would notify the authorities and

Dean Tittle. She remembered the chill when reality slapped her face. She wasn't going back to Ecclesia. Not ever. She was going to God.

Sarah had chosen to sleep on the floor wedged in a sitting position in the far back corner of the motel room. A camel colored blanket covered her. It was old and thin and covered with what her Mom called age pills, tight pellets of fuzz. When her eyes weren't scanning the room, she counted pellets.

Emil Bente had approached her once, late, with that leer in his eyes, but the larger man had backhanded him to the bed with loud threats. Otherwise the big man ignored her, except to tell her and George to call him "Mr. V." and Bente "Mr. B" from now on. Not long after that, she heard snoring on the double bed across the room where Bente had crawled, and she had relaxed. A little.

Vinnie ordered George to stop whining and to go to sleep on the double bed next to Bente. He took the other double bed closest to her. She wasn't afraid of him until he pulled an ominous looking pistol from his underarm and went to sleep with it in his hand. The barrel was pointing right at her head. What if it went off in the middle of the night? She watched it for hours, prayed it would not spit its messenger of death, as she listened to the obnoxious trio of snores from the three men. Several times sleep called to her amid the din, but fear overpowered it.

Finally she slept. She hadn't given herself permission to doze, didn't know the moment it happened, but she awoke now to the blue-winged conflict outside. The only movement in the room was the rising and falling of rib cages from the bed covers. Her stomach growled and she needed to use the bathroom, but the barrel at the end of Vinnie's arm still issued its silent threat. She tried not to move.

A few minutes later she heard him sneeze violently, and he sat straight up in bed. His gray hair flew in every direction. He raised the gun to his head, gave it a brief what-the-heck-is-this look, and then scratched with the other hand.

"Mr. V?" Sarah spoke softly. Vinnie lowered the gun to the mattress and squinted toward Sarah's head poking from the blanket. "I'd like to use the bathroom."

Vinnie waved her toward it with the pistol. "Getcha a shower while you're in there, before these boys take all the hot water." He sneezed again and wiped his nose with the bed sheet. Sarah rose, still clutching the blanket around her even though she was fully clothed.

"That hurt?" he asked, pointing with his free hand to the dried blood scab on her neck. She lied and shook her head. "It might start stingin' and bleedin' again when the water hits it."

Great. She dragged the blanket with her to the bathroom door, letting it drop as she opened it and locked herself in.

She sat on the toilet and listened. Heavy footsteps. A grunt, then a yelp that sounded like Bente's voice. Then Vinnie's voice. "I'm going to pick us out a car from the grocery lot up the street. If that girl in there tells me you messed with her while I was gone, I'll ice you right here. I swear I will."

"I gotta headache," Bente's voice groaned. Sarah heard footsteps, a door opening and closing quietly. She breathed heavily, not realizing she had been holding it. Only one thought looped her mind. She was going to stay in this bathroom until Vinnie got back.

The shower warmed her, even her feet eventually. The spray felt like needles against her back. She checked for blood gathering at the drain but didn't see any. She washed her entire body three times, but still felt unclean. She could not scrub off the images, the memories. The terrifying hours of whistling wind and dropping temperatures, the bone chill caused more by terror than by wind. Bente's whispers. Bente's hands. Bente's terrible breath, sometimes mercifully swept from her by blasts of wind and sometimes hurled toward her when the wind changed. George's tears. George's whimpers. George's blood. The road racing toward them in the headlights. Two state welcome signs. The long waits hiding in rest areas. Vinnie watching every vehicle exiting behind them. Bente's inane chatter. His thick gold chains lying heavy against that scrawny chest. His obsession with the rock cocaine in his pocket. The pizza she couldn't swallow.

Sarah shook her drooped head in the spray. Her teeth felt hairy in her mouth and she scrubbed them with the washcloth. She wondered if Vinnie had returned.

Vinnie picked George's Cadillac as clean as he could in the dawn's semi-darkness, and he deposited the two plastic bags of "evidence" into the dumpster behind the grocery store. There was no time to remove the plates. Besides, there was no screwdriver. Emil's switchblade was the only tool, and not much of one. Vinnie lowered the dumpster lid as quietly as possible. He smelled his underarm when he raised the lid and the stink overpowered the smells rising from the trash. His legs felt heavy. Sleep had granted little rest and even less refreshment.

Who was following them? It nagged him. Cops were clumsy. He could usually spot them. Maybe they'd gotten better over the years. It had been many flips of the calendar since he'd had to shake a tail.

Vinnie eyed the array of employee vehicles lining the store's back wall. Slim pickings. There wasn't a designer car among them. Guess it made sense. What would the owner of a Rolls be doing pulling night shift at a grocery store? The vehicle at the end of the row, the one parked nearly sideways five yards from the rest of the herd, caught his interest. He walked toward it, glancing behind him several times. A Mustang. Black convertible, mag wheels. Not one of the new, weak ones. This baby was a restored '83, when they still put those rubber-melting V-8s under the hood. Simpler electronics too, a snap to hot wire.

Vinnie fished the Bic from his pocket, and the cloth above the driver's door yielded. The inside lock knob rose with the pressure of his index and middle fingers. The door swung wide before him.

Vinnie grabbed a fistful of wires from beneath the steering wheel and sliced wires with the switchblade like a pro. In less than sixty seconds, a satisfied smile filled his face. The Mustang's engine sparked to life, and he was heading for the exit. He hadn't done that since he was 19 years old. Still have the touch!

Seconds later he whipped the Mustang into the motel lot and pulled it around the back. A large hill with dense, wheat-like weeds blanketing its face rose steeply from the back of the narrow lot. A few large trees and a dozen saplings rose from the weeds at sharp angles parallel to the slope. Vinnie sprang from the black bucket seat and went to collect his passengers. He stepped quickly to the door and opened it. The only sounds he heard were his own breath and the muffled hiss of the shower head. He studied the double bed nearest him. Neither man had moved since he left. He had expected them to be showered and dressed by now. Women take such long showers.

"Sarah, get out of there. It's time to go," he said.

George started, sat up, and blinked at Vinnie like a cow being milked. "Get up gentlemen," Vinnie shouted, "I want to be through that door and on our way in less than ten minutes."

George's hand tentatively explored the wound on his forehead. Emil didn't move. Vinnie stepped from the end of the bed to Emil's side and towered over him. The genetic mutant had fallen back asleep! He considered picking him up and throwing him over the end of the bed, but then he'd have to listen to the cursing and whining.

Better idea. He turned to the sink next to the bathroom door and unwrapped a plastic cup from its protective sheath. He ran the water cold for a few seconds, then filled the cup and dumped it on Emil's face. Emil screamed like a cat that had just had its tail crushed in the door. He sprang from the bed spewing a string of obscenities. Vinnie was leaning on the wall laughing so hard that his breath came in labored spurts.

Emil's arms were out from his sides and he was hunched in the middle of the room. He looked like a waterlogged cormorant trying to dry out. Vinnie tossed him a hand towel.

"You fucking …." Emil said, catching the towel against his chest with the good hand. He had slept in his clothes and cold water dripped from his face and blotched the front of his shirt.

"Serves you right. I been doin' all the dirty work pinching a car, and instead of getting these two ready to go," Vinnie gestured with his hand, " you fall back asleep."

"I've got to pee," George said, pacing the room.

"Sarah's in there," Vinnie said. Then he turned to the bathroom door again. "Come on, Sarah, for Christ's sake! How long's it take to wash your skinny little butt?" That made Emil laugh, and cough. Vinnie was still high from his Mustang conquest. The weariness had left him and he could feel himself smiling. The water continued its monotonous hiss from inside the bathroom.

Slowly, the smile faded from Vinnie's face. Then it disappeared. He returned to the bathroom door. "Sarah, you all right in there?" He knew she had locked the door. Vinnie had heard the lock snap when she first went in. He tried the handle anyway. It turned!

"Sarah, if you don't say somethin' in five seconds, I'm coming in after you!" He listened hard. Nothing but the hiss of water. "One," he shouted. "Two." George stopped pacing. "Three... four... five!" Vinnie pushed the door open and was met immediately with a blast of steam. He pulled his head back and waved the cloud away. He stepped into the bathroom. Empty. He jerked the door and looked behind it - nothing.

"That does it Emil!" he said from inside the bathroom. "You're dead! You hear me? Dead!" He slapped the shower handle and the hissing stopped. Vinnie sprang from the bathroom and lunged for Emil, grabbing him by the throat. "I'm gonna carve you up with your own knife!"

Emil choked. "Jesus, Vinnie -"

George gasped. "She knows too much!"

"She's gone Emil, and you let her get away!" Vinnie's yellow teeth were bared less than two inches from Emil's nose. He brought the blade to Emil's red, trembling cheek, resting the tip just below Emil's right eye and pressed.

"Oh God," George said. Vinnie glanced across the room to see him, wide-eyed and trembling, watching his own urine soak down both pant legs.

Vinnie turned back to Emil. A pencil-thin stream of blood inched down Emil's cheek to his chin, where a drop was forming and growing larger. Eventually, it let go and splashed onto his shirt. Vinnie pulled the switchblade away and with a click, retired the blade to its pearl handle.

Emil put his hand to his cheek, but otherwise didn't move. Vinnie glowered at him. "We'll continue this later!" He looked around the darkened room. "Get your shit and let's find her! Now!"

"She could be anywhere," Emil said.

"No she couldn't." Both George and Emil looked at Vinnie's outstretched arm and index finger. "Not without those!"

They saw Sarah's white tennis shoes in the corner of the room. Emil began to grin.

"Maybe I'm still going to be the Assistant Dean after all," George said.

Emil's grin broadened. "She's probably tip-toeing her way up the side of the road, flapping her arms." He gestured wildly.

"Get in the car. Every second wasted makes it harder to grab her," Vinnie said. George bent to pick up Sarah's shoes.

"Leave 'em," Vinnie said. "She's barefoot from now on, so she won't try this again." Less than two minutes later, they were through the door and headed for the Mustang. Vinnie wedged his massive frame behind the wheel. Emil shoved George in the back seat with wise cracks about peeing his pants. As the engine roared to life, Emil dropped into the passenger seat. Vinnie jerked the Mustang in reverse and shot to the street.

Sarah waited. Listened. She had prayed she wouldn't panic. She hadn't. She had prayed her legs would stop cramping. They did. She had prayed she would be invisible to them. She was. She was still praying there were no spiders under here.

The space beneath the bed was so small that the hard wood of the box spring pressed against her breast bone. Every movement was painful. The silence became a high-pitched hum in her ears. She wasn't sure how long they had been gone so she waited longer, listening and not moving. Finally, she inched herself to the right. A little more. A little more. There! Sarah reached behind her head and strained toward the cord. A little more. Her fingers closed around it, and she pulled gently, first forward toward her waist, and then down. The motel telephone fell to the floor between the two double beds. It landed next to her right hand, even with her chest. The receiver fell closer to her than the base. She lifted it, and with three upraised fingers, awkwardly returned it to its cradle.

Dialing was going to be the toughest because no way was she coming out from beneath the bed. Vinnie, Bente and George might come back. She paused and thanked God silently that she was still alive. She thanked Him for all the help He was giving her. She asked for help dialing. She even asked for perfect recall of her long distance calling card number. Instantly, the number glowed clearly in her mind, and she almost shouted. She thanked Him with tears and lifted the receiver. She set it on the carpet, pulled it as close as possible to her ear, and heard the quiet buzz of a dial tone. Then she stretched her arm toward the keypad on the base and rolled her hand over.

Sarah couldn't see the keys, but her fingers knew from memory which squares corresponded to each number. She pressed 8 for an outside line, hoping this one was like most motel phones. Sometimes it was 9. The dial tone burped, paused, and then buzzed a stronger dial tone. She smiled, ignoring the pain that snaked up the left side of her neck. She dialed the access number slowly and listened hard for the prompts. Finally she dialed the number that she had called so many times before. After the third ring, she heard a voice.

"Terry Woodrow."

Sarah's fingers gripped the receiver and pulled it to her lips. She whispered as loudly as she dared. "Terry!" Silence on the other end. "Terry, it's Sarah."

"Oh my gosh, Sarah," he said. "I almost hung up."

"Glad you didn't. "

"I wasn't sure I'd ever hear from you again. Listen Sarah, I..."

"Terry, shut up and listen!"

"I know you're..."

"Listen with your ears, not your mouth!"

"Okay! What's wrong with your voice?"

"Terry, I'm in trouble, and may have to hang up fast. If I do, keep your cell phone on and I'll call you back when I can."

"Are you okay?"

"No."

"Are you hurt?"

"Not much, yet." Sarah's voice cracked.

"Where are you?"

"I don't know." She started to cry softly. "Terry, I'm so scared. I'm in a motel room in another state. I'm under the bed and they just left to look for me."

"Who's they?"

"Nina's husband and a huge guy named Vinnie and George Fields. They grabbed me and held a knife to my throat and the car windows exploded and somebody was shooting at us."

"Whoa, slow down. I want all the details but not right now. The longer you stay on the phone the more danger you might be in. I'm coming to get you and you can tell me all about it on the ride home."

"But you have two policemen outside your door. They'll never let you leave." She was squeaking the words quietly through the tears, wishing. She'd lost it as soon as she heard his voice. Her nose was running onto the carpet and she was suddenly as embarrassed as she would have been had Terry seen it.

"Do you want me to tell them, or call 9-1-1?"

"I don't trust them, Terry." Sarah throat closed and she choked. "I can't tell the good guys from the bad guys, and I don't trust them. I only trust you."

"Ironic, isn't it" Terry said and blew out his breath.

"For one thing, they're making you out to be some monster."

Maybe they're right," Terry said.

"Stop it," Sarah sniffed.

"I'll find a way out of here and I'll come get you. I promise."

"But you don't know where I am!" She sobbed into the receiver.

"I'll find you, honey. Just hang on and stay put."

"Okay," she snorted and a shot of fear blasted through her chest. Had she been too loud? She listened with one ear to the receiver and with the other to the room. Terry's voice was strong and comforting.

"Can you tell me the name of the motel you're in?" Sarah hadn't thought of that.

"No. Wait. Maybe. Hang on." Sarah dropped the receiver and reached for the base of the telephone. Slowly she tipped it up and held it on its side. The logo was green and white. She lowered the base again and picked up the receiver. "The Lago-Mar motel."

"Did you see an address?"

"No." She was grateful that he was being patient with her, thinking for her.

"Okay, how about an area code?"

"Hold on." Sarah dropped the receiver and tilted the base again. Halfway between the indentations of the receiver cradle, behind a thin strip of clear plastic, was not only the area code, but the whole motel telephone number. Why hadn't she thought of that? She stared hard at the number and repeated it over and over in her mind before she set the base back down and picked up the receiver. She recited the number for Terry, twice so he could write it down.

"I'll know exactly where you are two minutes after we hang up, and I'll be there as fast as the tires will take me."

"You have to get out first." Sarah tried to swallow the knot in her throat. "What if you can't? What if -"

"God loves you so much, Sarah. He'll get me out."

Sarah could feel her back muscles relax a little. Her chest was sore against the box spring, but a trickle of peace began to flow. "Use my car. Remember where the hide-a-key is?"

"Good thinking. It's in a lot better shape."

"And if anyone goes looking for you they won't recognize the car."

"You're so smart."

"No I'm not. I can't even think." A tear fell over her nose and trickled all the way to her ear.

"I can't call you without the motel knowing someone's still in the room. Can you try to call me in say, an hour and a half?"

"I'll try, if I'm still here."

"Don't leave unless you have to."

"I won't." Suddenly the quiet hung like a wet towel between them. The call was approaching an end. What was said next would – what? Sarah wanted to say something. It was right on her lips. She wanted Terry to say something – first, to be the first. Slowly, she pulled the receiver from her ear and returned it to its cradle.

Terry snapped the cell phone closed and fell back against the angled bed. The back of his head slapped hard against the mattress and an arrow of pain shot through to his forehead. The bandage was off, but the stitches hadn't been removed and the lump was still the size of a golf ball. He breathed through the pain. Slowly, it subsided and he was able to think. He needed a plan. A good one. A God one.

He'd been avoiding the conversation for a day and a half. Now suddenly it couldn't wait another second. Terry got off the bed, got down on his hands and knees on the cold hospital tile, and then laid flat with his face pressed against the floor. The tears came before any words. Lots of tears, rushing from a crack in his heart.

He felt God's nearness, and that caused a whole new wave of tears. Grateful tears. Terry started thanking God for not giving up on him, for keeping His promise never to leave him or forsake him, no matter how bad he screwed up. Terry had no idea how long he was on the floor. He didn't notice when the tears stopped and the words began to flow, or when the words stopped and the thanks began. But he knew the exact moment the heaviness left his heart and mind. He felt like he was floating. He was free.

Someone knocked from the other side of the door and Terry heard the door open.

"You all right man?" A young man about Terry's height and build walked toward him, carrying a peach colored tray. He was wearing tan colored scrubs and black rubber soled shoes.

Terry looked up from the floor. "I am now, thanks. Just having a talk with the Man." The words were out of his mouth before he even thought about his audience. He found annoying these "Bless God, Praise the Lord, Hallelujah" people, the ones who said it every other second to the cashier in the grocery store, the teller at the bank, and anyone else they happened upon. What a put off for non-Christians and Christians alike. He tried not to be like them.

"Mmmm. One of those talks, huh?" the man said knowingly. Terry looked in the man's eyes standing over him and saw that they were shining. Terry had pushed himself to his hands and knees and was getting up slowly. The man set the tray down on the rolling bedside table and helped Terry up.

"Afraid so."

"Why afraid so?" the man asked gently. "Perfect love cast out all fear. He said so. And He loves you perfectly."

"It's amazing," Terry grinned. "I feel so much better."

"Ready to start again?" His eyes were still shining. Terry knew that, whoever this guy was, he knew God.

"I am."

"Brought you some food." The man pointed to the tray.

"You in a big hurry?" Terry asked.

The man shook his head. "You were my last stop. You need something?"

Terry leaned against the bed and motioned the man into the chair next to it. "You know Him pretty well, don't you," Terry said, pointing his index finger straight up. He knew the answer before he spoke a word.

"Intimately," the man said, smiling.

"I need His help."

"He knows that."

"And I may need yours." Terry paused before continuing, struck by whatever was radiating from the man seated in front of him. He could feel it press into his chest.

"I think I need three things," Terry said. "One, I just need you to listen. I've got a whale of a problem. Someone I love is in danger." Terry explained as thoroughly and as briefly as he could. The man nodded in silence. "Second, I need you to pray with me for a miracle." He explained his need to get to Sarah, but first to get past the officers outside the door. "Third, I need your clothes."

The man didn't flinch. He didn't even blink. He stood without a word, laid his hands on Terry's head, and began to pray. Terry felt electric shocks fire through his head and course down his body. Wave after wave. He felt his body trembling forcefully, but his mind was calm and peaceful. The next thing he knew, Terry was back on the floor, uncertain what had happened to him, but knowing it was good. He didn't want to move. Suddenly there was no hurry. He felt the presence of God so strongly, he was certain he would open his eyes and find himself lying at God's feet.

When Terry finally opened his eyes, the man was gone. Terry got up, wrestling feelings of disappointment. Did he leave without a word? Just like that? He looked in the bathroom to see if he had slipped in there, but it was empty. When Terry emerged from the bathroom, his eyes riveted to the bed. There, perfectly folded and laid in the center of the bed were the man's tan scrubs. Hurriedly, Terry changed into them, pocketed his cell phone, grabbed the food tray, and opened the door. The officers were seated on either side of the door. One was flipping through the newspaper, the other reading a book. Neither officer looked up as Terry passed and headed down the hall to the elevator. He hadn't expected them to.

Sarah's stomach growled, the sound hollow and distant. Then she heard another sound and she stopped breathing. It was metal scraping softly against metal. She heard the latch pop and the door creaked as it opened. Two seconds of silence were broken by low whispers in a language she didn't recognize. The deep voice was raspy, and though it was only slightly above the whispers of other voices, it spoke with authority. She heard her heart pound against the box spring. Then she heard paper crumpling amid more whispers. Then the door closed, its latch catching the hole in the jam with a metallic clunk. Sarah tried to breathe as quietly as she could. Who were they? What did they want?

She felt him before she heard the soft sounds of shoes on the carpet near the end of the bed. The raspy voice spoke softly and with a heavy accent. For all its gruffness, it was a gentle voice.

But it still struck terror in her heart.

"Are you hurt, my dear? Have they harmed you?"

Sarah's eyes darted along the sides of the bed, first one and then the other. Did he know she was under here? She didn't speak.

"I'm sure you are frightened, but try not to be," the voice said gently. "I'm here because I saw three men and a lovely young woman enter this room, and only the three men came back out." The steps on the carpet had stopped. "I know you are alive, because they rushed off to look for you." She heard him chuckle softly.

"It would be better if you remain under the bed, my dear. So much less complicated. But if you are hurt, just stick your hand out to the telephone. That will be our little signal, and I'll have a doctor here immediately. I'll sit here on the other bed and wait for your signal."

Sarah saw one shoe and then another come into view at the end of the bed to her right. Expensive shoes with tassels. Not a mark on them. She heard him sit on the other double bed. He was still speaking softly to her. "I have three daughters, all older than you. They are the joy of my heart. Their mother would be so proud." He paused. "I'm sure your father is proud of you too, my dear." She heard the rustling of paper again.

"No signal. That is good news," the voice continued softly. "I wanted to make sure you were unharmed and to leave you a few things if I may." Sarah watched the shoes. They twisted. Then something dark dropped to the floor. It was dark and round.... with feathers. The hat! The man in the ICU! An elderly hand reached for the hat and snatched it up quickly. Then a large paper sack with a colored Burger King logo lowered slowly in between the beds and rested noisily against the side of the bed. The smell of eggs and ham and melted cheese reached her nose. She heard the man place something else behind the bag. Then the shoes moved again. Sarah's mind was reeling.

"I'll go now, my dear. I'm glad you're safe. Grow old. Get married. Be happy. And delight your parents with many grandbabies." She heard the door open, and men whispering in a foreign tongue. Then it closed again and there was silence. And the smell of breakfast.

Sarah listened and didn't move for a full minute. She was so hungry, she had to force herself to count the full sixty seconds before she grabbed the bag and pulled it open. In it was enough food for three people. Orange juice, hash browns, scrambled eggs, pancakes, sausage links, cinnamon buns. Milk! How in the world was she going to drink anything under this bed? She felt along the bottom of the bag until her fingers touched it. A straw! Bless him. He had thought of everything.

Sarah pulled everything under the bed. Behind the bag she saw something dark and sparkling. Instantly she knew what it was. She had never held a rosary before, didn't even know how to use one. But now, rubbing the solid cross between her fingers, it was filled with meaning. She thanked the Lord for His protection, and for His provision. Then, she ate more greasy food than she would in a month, and loved it.

When she pushed the last sausage link into her mouth, Sarah reached for the napkins. She chewed more slowly and turned them over in her hand.

There were a dozen or so napkins folded in half and held closed by a large rubber band. Getting them open with one hand while flat on her back proved a real chore. The rubber band clung stubbornly to the outside napkin. She couldn't roll it off or pick it off. Finally, she peeled the outer napkin like a banana and the rubber band rolled away easily. The other napkins dropped open on the carpet, revealing something hidden inside. She blinked. Twice. Counting as she went, she picked from the center of the napkins fifteen one thousand dollar bills.

And a note. "Apologies, my dear, for everything."

Chapter Eighteen

Memorial Hospital

"Unacceptable, gentlemen!" Chief Parker paced in front of the two goat-eyed police officers while Captain Steele looked on. Parker's face was red and his eyebrows pushed downward toward each other at the bridge of his nose. "You see this?" He pointed dramatically at his buttocks. "That's half of what I had an hour ago. The FBI chewed the rest of it off, thanks to you."

Steele said, "I didn't rip you that badly, did I?"

"Sir, we can't explain it," the senior officer said to Parker's back as he paced. "One of us was here, in front of this door at all times, and most of the time both of us were here."

"I swear if you're lying to me, I'll have both your badges."

"Sir, I've served with you for ten years. You know me better than my own dad. You know I'm not lying."

"That's what has got me so upset. I told these agents that you two were the finest officers I had."

"Sir," the other officer spoke, "Woodrow did not come through that door."

"Then what'd he do, evaporate into the ceiling vent?" Chief Parker asked. "The nurses tell me all of his clothes are still in the room. Explain that."

"That's just it, sir. We can't."

"I ought to bust you both," Chief Parker said, not looking at them. "But my problem is I believe you. So we've got an escaped suspect, possibly naked, and no explanation for how it happened. This is not going to look good on anybody's resume."

"We'll find him Chief," the senior officer said.

"That's what I told Captain Steele here." He stared into both sets of eyes. "I promised him that we would find Terry Woodrow and return him to that room unharmed. Don't let me down." He pointed down the hospital hall like a man sending his beagles for the rabbit. The two officers hurried to the elevator without another word.

Terry Woodrow pulled the cord that ran above the bus windows and a soft tone chimed in the front near the driver. As the bus slowed, Terry sprang from his seat. He was through the parting back doors before they were fully opened. He ran full speed up the long hill to Ecclesia's top lot. His long blond hair curled in the sweat on his forehead and the back of his neck. The air was unusually thick and hot for May, and Terry's lungs ached for oxygen. He stood at the far end of the parking lot, his chest heaving and the tan scrubs sticking to his back and chest.

Sarah's car was easy to spot. He loved this car! He ran his fingers along the clean, white front panel of Sarah's two year old BMW. Still panting loudly, he felt for and found the metal box stuck to the inside wheel well. He slid the top open and grabbed the spare key. Seconds later, the engine sprang to life. He adjusted the seat and mirrors and checked the gas gauge. He smiled. Sarah always kept her tank full. Said it was something her Daddy had always insisted on, along with an oil change and tire rotation every three thousand miles.

Terry had never changed the oil in his car. When the red light came on, he just added a quart or two and figured eventually there'd be enough new oil in there to qualify as an oil change.

He put her sunglasses on, even though thick clouds grayed the landscape and there was no need for them. Part of the disguise. He looked at himself in the rear view mirror and laughed. The sunglasses were distinctly feminine, and he hoped nobody recognized him, especially his friends. He headed for the exit. At the street, he stopped and looked left. All clear. He glanced right. Racing up the hill toward him were four police cars with blue and red lights blazing. A surge of adrenaline went through him. Should he floor it and flee left away from them? Could he outrun them? If he was caught, he'd lose all hope of getting Sarah back safely. The patrol cars came closer. Terry sat motionless behind the wheel. Suddenly, the lead car whipped left into the fire lane and shot toward the back of the chapel. The other three followed in a blur of flashing light. Terry let out a soft whoop and turned left. Sarah, I'm on my way to you!

He pressed the accelerator carefully. He didn't want to squeal tires and draw attention to himself. At the stop sign he turned left. The road stretched before him in a wide arc.

His eyes glanced behind the sunglasses at the streets he passed. Most were shallow cul-de-sacs with one or two homes with expansive lawns. One he just passed had a small wooden bridge over what appeared at first glance to be a dry stream. A white Gazebo with hanging ferns, surrounded at ground level with bursts of reds and purples and greens. It looked like a wedding chapel he had seen once in a magazine.

Terry sighed again. But in his family, men of the cloth were always married within church walls. The ceremony would not be diluted by fresh air and the sounds of creation. Terry shook his head and stared at the street sign coming up. The yellow "No Outlet" sign glared at him.

It was the sign of his life. He had lived in a "No Outlet" world where choice was limited and where the options were tendered by someone else, something else. By tradition and by those who served it, who never questioned it. It shaped his reality. He had champed at that bit between his teeth many times, but the gravitational pull had been too great. He must carry on the tradition, not let his father down, or his grandfather. You are a Woodrow, the next pillar, following your forbears, one pillar of the church following another to prop up God's house. What crap!

Terry approached a traffic light and turned right. He loved the feel of the BMW hugging the corner and shooting over the brim of the hill. The voice in his head continued. A Woodrow should never be seen driving a car like this. Too ostentatious, too luxurious. Think of the mouths that could be fed by the money this thing cost.

A minister shouldn't want a car like this. A minister never concerned himself with things like nice houses or automobiles or clothes. It shouldn't matter that the majority of the congregation lived in beautiful homes, drove fancy cars and gave their children all the latest toys and gadgets and clothes. He was a minister and his family must live in a style beneath the poorest members of the congregation, lest people begin to talk, to murmur, to question his godliness. He remembered his mother washing four times, the new sweater he had received from his aunt one Christmas. Four times, and it was brand new! But of course it mustn't look new because people would talk, might think their pastor was getting paid a bit too much if his children wore anything but hand-me-downs. Even then he had tasted the bit in his mouth, felt its jerk. And he had wanted to run.

A familiar emotion welled deep inside. Three months ago, he had finally managed to let himself feel it, let it come and hadn't stuffed it back down, vented it to someone he trusted. His spiritual director, Brother Lawrence, had named it. Rage.

Terry braked at the light and prepared to turn left onto Bradley. Route 69 would be ahead, somewhere. He checked the rear view mirror - no one behind, no one following, no flashing lights. But Terry saw something else in the rear view mirror. Where had they come from? Two wide streams had formed, one on each side of his face. Tears.

The light turned green and Terry shot left. He wiped his cheeks with his hand between gears, tried to concentrate, but the road kept blurring. It was happening again. He felt his lower lip quivering and his upper lip contorting. His breath came in bursts and chokes. He was alone in the BMW, racing toward I-69, but still he felt the shame. Only two people had ever seen him like this. His mother had held him, rocking gently back and forth, asking, "What is it, Terry?" He couldn't tell her. Couldn't. Sarah, too, had held him as he sobbed and shook, but it was different. Very different. He had wanted to tell her. He had tried. But only a few words came, and he wasn't sure they had made any sense. It was Sarah who had helped him the most.

He should be able to handle it, to accept his fate, to grip courageously if not proudly, the torch passed to him, to stay in the groove carved ahead of him by over a century of Woodwards. Who was he to question it? When he did question, he felt selfish, worldly, unholy. He had tried to talk with God about it, but had always felt it was a one-sided conversation. He believed that the Lord heard him, but he had only heard silence in return. Brother Lawrence said God often leaves us to our own choices. Then we live with the consequences of those choices. It had struck Terry as a lousy way to organize an army.

Sarah's choice had been made as a response to a very clear invitation. He loved to hear her talk about the moment it happened. About the presence of the Lord so heavy upon her that she could hardly breathe, about the scripture verse that sounded in her head, "Come follow me and I will make you fishers of men," about the dazzling white mantle Jesus had taken off and wrapped around her shoulders, about the words of Mary Magdalene rising her soul, "Let it be unto me according to thy will." The invitation and the choice to say yes. There was no doubt about her call to the ministry.

Nothing like that had ever happened to him. All Terry had heard was the stamp of boots marching in step through time. Year after year. Decade upon decade. Fall into line, soldier! Left, right, left right. Stay in formation. Carry on.

As the tires of the BMW chewed through the miles toward the state line, the question plagued him again. Had he received an invitation? He knew no two were alike, but what invitation had he received? And from whom? The Lord? The Church? The family?

And what choice had he made? The choice not to rock the boat? The choice to avoid attracting the ire and rejection of his father and grandfather? The choice to appear to be standing on one side of the fence, but really straddling the top of it? What kind of choice was that?

A coward's choice. Terry flinched and the BMW swerved slightly. The trouble with sitting on this fence was that it was topped with razor wire, and it was cutting him in two. Graduation was in less than a month, ordination in less than two. The closer it got, the more he bled.

The wonderful thing about the Northeast was that it was so compact. The terrible thing about the Northeast was that it was so compact. You could get from one state to another in a couple of hours, an accomplishment inconceivable to Texans or Californians. The trouble was that there were so many people crammed into such small states, that people lived, and drove, almost on top of one another. Terry crossed the first state line at half the speed limit in bumper-to-bumper traffic.

He wondered why Sarah hadn't called. Had she been hurt? Recaptured? Killed? He shook the thoughts from his head, snapping his head with such violence that the sunglasses flew from his face, smacking noisily against the passenger side window.

This was no time for negativity. He would find Sarah and bring her back. Terry knew it was a bigger task than he could handle. Weren't they all. So he prayed. Traffic began to clear and he sped up, still praying. He prayed aloud for Sarah's safety and for peace in her heart and mind. He prayed for wisdom and courage for himself, not only to bring Sarah to safety, but also to talk with her, to be honest - about a lot of things. His voice bounced from the front windshield to the back of the car. He found himself praying again for the men who had assaulted him, and for the people who had taken Sarah hostage. He asked God for justice, but also for mercy. Amen.

The cell phone buzzed in the passenger seat. Terry grabbed it on the second ring and flipped it open to his ear.

"Terry Woodrow."

"Is this the Nearly Reverend Terrance Woodrow?"

"Hi Dad."

"How's it going? You getting excited?" Terry didn't even attempt to answer. He knew his Dad already had the answers he wanted in his own head and would press right through to the reason for calling without even waiting for Terry to respond. "Say Terry, I'm calling because your mother and I would like to buy you your first preaching robe. I've been looking over the catalogues here, and I think I've found one that'll look magnificent on you as you stand before your first flock. Just need the size and we can —"

"Dad, what was it like for you when you were about to be ordained?"

"For me? Oh Terry, my father was so proud. He and my grandfather were part of the group who laid hands on me when the ordination prayers were read. It was a glorious rite of passage."

"Into what?"

"What do you mean?"

"A rite of passage into what?"

"Why, into my ministry of course! The three of us got our picture in the newspaper. Three generations of Woodrow preachers. There we were, all grinning broadly for the cameras."

"Mom said she cried the whole day."

"She never told me that!" he snapped, then seemed to recovered himself. "Probably tears of joy, Terry. She was pregnant with you then. What a joyous time."

"Where'd you live that first year, and the two after that?"

"We lived with my Mom and Dad. It was wonderful, seeing you born in the same house as me so many years before."

"Because the church didn't pay you enough to eat and rent an apartment, so you had to live with your parents."

"Couldn't, Terry. The church couldn't afford it." He paused. "She tell you that too?"

"Yeah, and she said I was the only bright spot in an otherwise dark time." Terry was breathing hard and trying to keep his eyes on the road. "But don't you dare tell her I told you, Dad!" Terry said, more fiercely than he had ever spoken to his father. "For once, don't you say a word." Terry knew he'd crossed the line. "Sorry Dad."

"It's okay. I wouldn't. I won't." He was stammering.

"Who else could she talk to about it, Dad? Church members? And then become the topic of every gossip group? Your parents, who always thought their son walked on water and was destined for ministerial greatness?" Terry felt a sharp pang in his conscience.

"She never complained," his father said softly, almost like he was talking to himself, "but I knew she was angry. It came out in other ways. I always hated not being able to provide a home of our own for you two."

"Why'd you do it, Dad?" Terry could feel the lump rising in his throat again.

"Do what, son?"

"Get ordained."

There was silence on the other end of the phone. Then he spoke again. "There was never any 'why' about it, Terry. It was never a question, so it didn't need to be asked."

"But were you called by God to be a minister?"

"From the cradle," his father said proudly, recovering somewhat. "I was a Woodrow, born to preach, as my Daddy used to say."

"What did Mom have to say about it?"

Another pause. "She didn't say anything."

"Did you ask her?"

"Ask her what?"

"If you were called into the ministry, the two of you together?"

"No."

"Thanks Dad, that helps," Terry said haltingly.

"I can't see how."

"You've been honest with me, Dad. I appreciate that."

"You're welcome, I guess." He heard his father tapping his pen. "You all right, Terry?"

"I could really use your prayers."

"You got 'em."

"How about praying for me right now?"

"Here? You mean, on the phone?"

"Yes," he said softly.

He heard more tapping, then a large exhale. "I pray for you all the time, son. Let's save this one for the next time I see you."

"Okay. Gotta go." Terry closed the cell phone and pulled off the side of the road. The tears came fresh and hot. "Okay," he said again into the empty car, knowing it would never happen. In his entire life, Terry realized, his father had never prayed with him. Not once. The weight of it knocked Terry's head to the steering wheel, and he sobbed. He cried for his Dad. He cried for his Mom. He cried for himself.

Storm clouds gathered overhead and a boom of thunder sounded in the distance. The wind had whipped into an angry gust. Headlights approached the BMW from the other direction. Terry didn't know how long he had been there. He couldn't breathe from his nose. His face felt squishy and his head twice its size. The sickening headache he had lived with for two days was unrelenting. "Gotta get a grip," he said aloud. He started the car and eased himself from the shoulder back into traffic. Around the corner a green sign loomed, announcing the next state line in 102 miles. The cell phone rang and Terry grabbed it. He snorted loudly, trying to clear his nose, then answered it.

"Terry Woodrow."

"It's me," Sarah's whisper voice said.

"Are you all right? It's been almost two hours."

"That long? I'm losing track under here."

"Still under the bed?"

"Yes."

"Good. Stay put as long as you can."

"I'll try. Housekeeping just left. They made the beds, vacuumed, picked the phone up from the floor." Sarah was talking fast. "I had to pull it down again to call you. I thought for sure they were going to lean down and look under the beds. I prayed so hard. When they knocked I about had a heart attack. What am I going to do if they rent the room to somebody? Oh, and they took my shoes with them."

"Slow down, Sarah. Everything's going to be all right."

"I'm trying. Did you get out? Where are you?"

"I'm out and on my way. Be there in forty-five minutes."

"I got lots to tell you!"

"Likewise," Terry said. Neither of them said another word. The silence was deafening. Terry broke it. "I can't wait to see you ... and ... hold you."

There was silence on the other end of the line. Terry panicked. Why had he said it? Terry felt a rush of shame and anxiety. Then he heard it - sniffling. A long breath, a soft cry. Then Sarah's voice. "Call you back."

The line went silent. Terry threw the open cell phone onto the passenger seat and slammed his palm against the steering wheel. "That's great buddy!" he shouted. "Just great. Just because it was true didn't mean you had to say it! Geez Dude, what if you totally freaked her out? Especially because of what she knows about you, what you've done. You knucklehead! Get in reality. It'd be a miracle if she even spoke to you again after you get her back to Ecclesia, and you're saying you want to hold her! Great Woodrow. Make it worse. As if she doesn't have enough to deal with."

He wanted to turn around and race the other way. He wanted to find a rock and crawl beneath it. Anything to keep from having to face her again. "Truth is it's you you're most worried about, Woodrow," he screamed in disgust. "You! As usual. Your embarrassment. Your guilt. Your shame. Avoid it at all costs, right Woodrow? No matter what it costs others." His chest was heaving and both hands were on the steering wheel.

"Well no more," said through clenched teeth. "No more sitting on that fence and letting it rip. No more crawling down whichever side gets me what I want! It's guts time, integrity time." He stepped on the accelerator and raced toward the state line. "I'm going to tell that woman what a jerk

I've been and how much I care about her, and then I'm going to beg her forgiveness, even though I don't deserve it!"

On the other end of the phone line, Sarah barely breathed. She had not hung up the phone.

She heard every word.

Chapter Nineteen

Residence of the Assistant Dean
Ecclesia Seminary

Captain Steele leaned toward the sound, arching his back to look from the Fieldses' master bedroom window. The fire lane was completely obscured from view by the massive green hedges, but the sirens were loud and piercing. They had to be close.

"See what's going on out there," he said to Higgins. "I'll stay with the team." The forensic pathologists were extracting blood samples from the bed cover. Another specialist was lifting fingerprints from one of the broken bed posts. Every few seconds, a flash went off as the photographer captured the crime scene.

It was a lot of blood, Steele thought. He wondered if it all came from one person, or from several. What was he looking at? Evidence of a struggle amongst combatants? A torture? A mutilation? A ritual of some kind? The questions were outpacing the answers, by miles.

He heard rapid, heavy footsteps on the stairs at the end of the hall. A breathless Higgins appeared in the doorway. "Cap, I think you need to see this," he said, motioning him to follow. What now? He followed down the stairs, through the kitchen, to the driveway.

"Thought I sent you to find out what all the sirens were about," he called to Higgins, who was walking quickly to the garage.

"You did, but on the way I found all of this." He spread his hand out before him like he was tossing chicken feed.

"Help me see it."

"Okay, first there is the bullet hole in the garage door."

"You're making it up." It was just an expression. Higgins pointed to a hole in the thin aluminum.

Steele looked across the lawn to the dense stand of trees. "The bullet must have come from over there. We need to find that bullet. Have the men scour the garage and then the woods over there for evidence - a casing, anything."

"And look at this," Higgins walked to the opposite edge of the driveway. He pointed along the edge where the grass met the asphalt. Cubes of glass littered the area. "Safety glass."

"More evidence here than we thought," Steele said.

"Request permission to call Chief Parker for more back-up," Higgins said.

"Speak English, Higgins, for heaven's sake," Captain Steele said wearily. Nevertheless, he knew what Higgins was asking for. "I'll do it." He flipped his cell phone and called the First Precinct, motioning Higgins away with his arm. Higgins walked to the end of the driveway toward the sirens.

"Patch me through to Chief Parker." Finally, he heard a clunking noise followed by a voice.

"Parker here."

"Chief, this is Steele."

"Captain Steele!" Parker said, "There's a coincidence. I was just lifting the receiver to call you."

"Regarding ..."

"Wanted you to see how things were going over there at the seminary."

"I'm here at the Assistant Dean's residence behind the seminary. Your boys just came flying in, sirens screaming and lights flashing. They gave anyone who didn't want to be found enough warning to be long gone before the first officer's foot reached the bottom stair step."

Captain Steele heard Chief Parker curse and something struck a desktop with violence.

"You don't fish do you," Captain Steele said. It wasn't really a question.

"No."

"Didn't think so." Steele sighed. "Spook the fish before you throw your net, and you're going home empty handed." He watched Higgins return, rounding the hedge and shaking his head. "Tell you what Chief," Steele said. "Radio your people to conduct their search and their interviews. Be sure to include the Dean, Rev. Jeremy Tittle, and Woodrow's friend, Sarah Stafford. If they find Terry Woodrow, Reverend George Fields, or Brother Lawrence Stiles, detain them and contact me immediately. Oh, and have them run plates on all vehicles in the seminary parking lots. Check them against seminary registration records. Find out which vehicles belong to the people I just mentioned and whether they are parked in one of the lots. Then have your lead officer report to me at the Fields residence before the team leaves the seminary. I assume you are taking notes. Read my instructions back to me."

Chief Parker recited the instructions nearly verbatim. Captain Steele continued. "And tell your men to quiet down, move quickly, and take perfect notes."

"I'll tell them. Anything else?"

"Tell them the FBI regards the First Precinct as a vital asset to this investigation and thank them from us for helping solve this case."

"Yes sir." Parker's voice brightened.

"Let me give you my cell phone number again."

"I've got it, Captain Steele."

"Stay in touch with me, Chief." Steele closed the phone and grinned wearily at his Lieutenant.

"They're playing cops and robbers over there, Cap," Higgins said.

"So we've heard. And everyone else has heard."

Higgins grinned. "You were young and over-zealous once too."

Captain Steele felt a twinge of embarrassment as images of his first year on the force flicked through his mind. He had run too fast, yelled too loud, pulled his weapon too much, and though he would never admit it aloud, he loved to hear the siren scream and to turn on every flashing light the vehicle had.

He glanced at Higgins. "Lieutenant, we're way behind the perps. We don't even know for sure who's who or where they're hiding. Meanwhile, the victims keep stacking up. We have at least one murder -"

"At least? I only know about James Harnes. You find a body in that bedroom I don't know about?" Higgins pointed toward the second story home beside them.

Steele was grimacing and shaking his head. "Sorry. There hasn't been time to keep you up on every detail. The hospital called about an hour ago. ICU." He paused. "Mother and child are not improving." Both men were silent for a moment.

"But still alive?"

"Yes, but life support's doing most of the work, the doc says. Of course it doesn't help that she's going through cocaine withdrawal. That alone has been known to kill some people."

"Don't like her odds," Higgins scuffed the ground.

"Me neither. But at least she's still with us for the moment. Exactly who did this to her remains a question mark."

"Had to be either Bente or Bontecelli, and my money's on Bente."

"Mine too," Steele said. "But the forensics sweep of the graveyard produced no substantial evidence, other than one bad fingerprint lifted from a headstone near the body and a couple of shallow footprints. Most of the footprints were destroyed by rescue workers."

Higgins jammed his hands into his trouser pockets and studied his feet. "We did a little better at Mrs. Bente's apartment, didn't we?"

Captain Steele nodded. "Lots of finger prints. A real mish mash of them. Forensics is still sorting them out and running them through their database for matches. They matched Harne's prints, which doesn't really help us, Nina Bente's, again no help, Terry Woodrow's, but they weren't relevant to the murder because he was under guard at the hospital."

"Maybe he slipped by the guards more than once, went to Nina's place, and then came back to the hospital," Higgins said.

"One chance in a million. There were two other sets of prints in the apartment, but not surprisingly, whomever they belong to isn't in the database." Captain Steele wanted a cigarette, craved one, even reached unconsciously to the jacket pocket where he had kept them for twenty years. The doctor ordered him to quit last fall, and he finally succeeded as the new year began. Next month would mark six months without a smoke. He still found himself reaching for them. "There are prints aplenty in the Fields residence. It would help if some of them matched the mystery prints from the apartment."

"Woodrow's cleared from this one too, right?" Higgins asked.

"Almost certainly. He was under wraps at the hospital at the time, so he's not really a suspect."

"Is he really a suspect in any of it?"

Steele shook his head and lowered his voice. "Nah. I don't think he knew anything about the smuggled rock. From his reactions, I don't think he even knew Nina was married. He didn't seem to know Bente or Bontecelli. Remember the blank look he gave their pictures. He'd never be able to pick them from a line-up or photo catalogue."

"They knew him, though."

"Most likely from the airport. I'm betting that was the first time they laid eyes on him."

"And he still hasn't seen them," Higgins said. "It was pitch black when Bontecelli knocked him out."

Higgins nodded. "It's not a crime to be screwing somebody else's wife."

"But it's not very bright either, if the wife's last name is Bente."

"We've been over this ground before. He doesn't seem to have known it."

"But ignorance is no excuse," Steele said. "He should have known it. If he didn't even know her well enough to know she was married, let alone a crack addict, he had no business -"

"You're right," Higgins nodded. "If he knew, then he's stupid. If he didn't know, then he's stupid. If he let his balls do most of the thinking for him, as most of us have done at least once, if we're honest, then he was really stupid."

"But stupidity is not a federal offense."

"So he's not really a suspect, although I don't intend to share that with Mr. Woodrow."

"How about his escape? Didn't he break the law there?"

"We read him his rights, but we never formally charged him." Steele glanced again at the woods. "I want him back for his sake, not ours." He turned toward the door leading into the kitchen. "Let's get back up there and break the news to Forensics that we've got a bullet hole, shattered glass, a possible weapon in the woods, and God knows what else down here."

"They're gonna love you for that."

Higgins reached the door first and turned the knob. Neither of them saw or heard the figure appear from behind the hedge and follow them into the house.

Memorial Hospital

"It's called a halter monitor, Mrs. Fields," the doctor said, smiling at Hilary.

"I know what it is," she said, glowering.

"And so you know how it works?"

"I do. I went through this with my mother several years ago," she said with the tone of an expert. "You've got me all wired up and I walk around as normally as any human being can in this nasty hospital. The data from my heart gets stored in this box and you analyze it after a day or so of activity."

"Very good, Mrs. Fields."

"Don't patronize me." She could feel the hate searing from her eyes. Poor doctor would never know it had nothing whatsoever to do with him, that it was free range hate.

"Yes, well, you're free to get up and move around, even walk the halls. Feel free to leave the third floor, but please do not leave the building. We're going to keep you overnight since your echocardiogram is scheduled for tomorrow morning." The doctor walked into the hall and closed the door behind him.

Hilary got up from the bed and dressed quickly. Her blouse and red suit were still damp with perspiration, but she had packed her favorite gray sweat suit. She put it on over the halter monitor, pulled a comb through her short, straight hair, put on slippers, and left the room. In the hallway, she turned right and headed for the elevators. She pushed the up arrow and waited with her arms folded across her chest.

She hated the smell of hospitals. She hated their rules. She hated the ugly clothes they issued patients. She hated being asked the same questions over and over by so many different people. Hadn't anyone heard of information sharing? She hated being told what she could do and what she could not do. And right now, she had to admit, she hated pretty much everything and everyone. She tried to concentrate on the task before her.

Finally the elevator doors parted and Hilary stepped in. She pressed four. The doors seemed to take forever to close. She pushed the fourth floor button again and again, even though it was already glowing bright white. Finally the doors moved. Couldn't they close more quickly, for Christ's sake? At least she was alone in the elevator. The numbers clicked. The chime sounded and the doors inched apart.

Hilary stepped from the elevator, turned left and headed straight for the Intensive Care Unit. She had been here before, when her mother died. Her Mom had entered the ICU talking and smiling. She never saw the other side of the door alive. Her body went straight to the morgue. As

Hilary pressed the button on the wall and the silver metal doors yielded, a different but altogether familiar smell assaulted her. All those years ago, and yet the memory was still fresh. The smell of the ICU hadn't changed. It was the smell of death.

"Can I help you?" A squat woman with short red hair rose slowly from her desk halfway along the inside of the long, arcing counter.

Hilary matched her even gaze. "I'm here to see Nina Bente."

"Your name?"

"Why is that important?" Hilary tried not to show the instant leap in blood pressure and the sudden hammering of her heart.

"Mrs. Bente has restricted visitation. There is a list."

"My name is Fields. The Very Reverend Mrs. George Fields." The words had come cockily from her throat, but as soon as she said them, she almost screamed. She had identified herself! That was not part of the plan. What was she thinking! Hilary battled an overpowering urge to turn and run back through the metal doors. No - that slut must die – and the whore's baby. There was no turning back. She steadied herself against the end of the counter and did not move.

The short-haired woman waddled behind a thick row of monitors. She returned in less than a minute with a clipboard. "Do you have any identification, Mrs. Fields?"

"Yes. No. Is it necessary?"

"Yes."

Hilary hadn't brought anything with her. She patted her sweat pants. What are you doing! Fool! Your sweat pants don't have pockets. Suddenly she saw it. Her wristband, the one they had put on her in the emergency room. She showed her wrist to the nurse.

"Thank you, Mrs. Fields. Your husband was here earlier. Please keep your visit brief."

"I will," Hilary said, still trying to recover her composure. "I just want to pray over her."

"Of course." The nurse led Hilary to Nina's room, and then left.

Hilary moved close to the edge of the bed. The ventilator rose and fell noisily, and the heart monitors blipped in regular beats. The readouts changed numbers every few seconds, flicking slightly higher and then slightly lower. She studied the machines. When her opportunity came, she wanted to be ready.

"Nina, I hope you can hear me," she said in a low, guttural voice. "I'm Hilary Fields, George's wife. I want you to hear me and to hear me good. I'm going to kill you, Bitch. Maybe today. Maybe tonight. Maybe tomorrow. But I promise you this. You won't leave here alive. Know why, Nina? Because you're a dirty little slut, a cheap little prostitute, and that baby inside you is dirt just like you. Dirt! I never could have children, Nina. Did you know that? And then you come along, and lure my husband between your legs. And suddenly there is a baby. A whore's baby you'll use to ruin George and me, won't you bitch! Yes. Of course you will. Unless this machinery here were to malfunction somehow, which it will very soon."

Hilary leaned closer to Nina's ear. "You tried to wreck my life. Now it's going to cost you yours. You tried to ruin George's and my plan. Now I'm going to ruin yours."

Hilary leaned even closer. "I so hope you can hear me, because I want you to sweat. I want you to suffer before you die." Hilary resisted a powerful urge to wad up her fists, raise them over her head, and smash them down on Nina's face. She imagined in her mind doing it again and again. She imagined the blood spurting and the eyes ripping from their sockets. She could feel her mouth twist into a hateful smile.

Hilary's thoughts were interrupted by the sounds of people running behind her, sharp commands being barked back and forth. She turned her head and listened. For an instant, she wondered if she had said something aloud. Had they heard her whispers? Had they seen her smile?

She looked quickly behind her. People ran past Nina's room and around the corner. Then the hospital loud speaker sounded, the voice of a woman's controlled voice echoing in the hall. "Code Blue. ICU. We have a Code Blue. ICU." More people ran by the room. Everyone was rushing to the same room at the other end of the ICU.

Opportunity!

Be ready for your opportunity when it comes, she had told herself over and over for almost two days. Be ready.

Here it was.

Hilary stooped low and crawled underneath the metal bed. She strained her arm toward the ventilator cord plugged into the wall. She inched forward and reached again. There! She had the cord in her hand. She took a deep breath and pulled. Sparks flew from the heavy round wall socket as the cord was disengaged. With a sudden gasp, the ventilator fell silent and motionless. "Die, you little whore!" Hilary whispered venomously and hurried out from the room, back along the curved counter, and quickly toward the wall button. One touch and she was out of there.

Hilary heard the sound of air rushing violently through her nose and mouth, having been knocked from her lungs by someone behind bumping hard into her. She saw herself beginning to fall face first onto the tile floor and a burst of rage went through her. Probably someone running for the Code, clumsy ox! Instinctively, her hands shot out in front of her to break the fall. As she hit the floor, she felt strong hands close around her waist.

The two women skidded together for a fraction of a second, and then the strong hands flipped Hilary onto her back. She was staring into the stern face of a young woman she had never seen before. She had short dark brown hair, and bony shoulders atop a thin, muscular frame. She wore dark purple scrubs. Hilary opened her mouth, but before she could speak, the young woman spoke sharply into her face. "Mrs. Fields, I'm Detective Ryan and you are under arrest. Stay still and you won't get hurt, while I read you your rights." Hilary's eyes wide and wet with fury watched the woman straddle her on the floor like she was a horse and snap a walkie-talkie from its clip on her back. All agents report immediately to ICU." Then she threw the radio down and shouted for a nurse. "Bente's ventilator has been unplugged in Room 14. Hurry!"

Hilary twisted her hips and tried to buck the woman off of her. "Let me go!" Other people surrounded them in the ICU, men and women in scrubs of various colors carrying the same kind of radio Detective Ryan had used. One man, the tallest one, stepped forward. "Mrs. Fields, you have the right to remain silent."

"I will not remain silent, you bastards!" She was kicking and screaming. Saliva was foaming at the corners of her mouth.

"Anything you say can and will be used against you in a court of law…."

"You don't understand! She destroyed my life! She ruined everything! Let … me… go!" Detective Ryan pinned her arms to the floor and Hilary spit up into her face.

"You're going to pay for that, lady." Detective Ryan said and flipped her over onto her stomach. The halter monitor slapped the tile hard and Hilary was pressed on top of it. She screamed and cursed and continued to kick. Her face was purple with fury. The tall officer continued to read her the rest of her Miranda rights, while two others assisted Detective Ryan in bringing Hilary's arms behind her back and applying the handcuffs.

More people ran back and forth along the bank of rooms in the ICU. More orders were barked, some were yelled back and forth down the corridor. Hilary heard it all and screeched with delight.

"Doctor, the ventilator! The plug! … Broken in the socket. Flat line. Code! Code! Code!"

Hilary heard the slap of shoes racing away from her to the other end of the ICU and she laughed. It was an open-mouthed, wicked laugh that belched from her lungs like a scream. "I told you Nina, you whore. Told you I'd kill you and that bastard child," Hilary screamed and laughed again.

"Get her out of here right now!" a strong voice close to her said. The same woman's even voice from the loudspeaker said, "Code Blue. ICU. We have a Code Blue. ICU. All available personnel report to the ICU immediately." Hilary felt herself being pulled to her feet by her arms. She continued to scream-laugh and she was shouting words. Three words, over and over. Her throat burned. Once upright, she let her legs go limp and collapsed to the floor again. She had learned how to do that in the peace marches, Washington D.C., three decades ago. She kicked at someone trying to grab her legs. They would have to drag her out of the ICU. Spit was falling freely from her open mouth.

Hilary heard her own voice screaming the three words over and over at the top of her lungs. She couldn't have stopped the words if she had wanted.

"Die you whore!"

Detective Ryan slapped the button on the wall and the metal doors opened.

"Die you whore!" Hilary screamed louder. The detectives dragged her into the hall. "Die you whore!"

The large metal doors hissed and closed tight, hemming one kind of chaos in, and hemming another out.

Chapter Twenty

Time. We need more time! George rubbed his palms on his pants.

"This car is stolen, and we've got to disappear," Vinnie called from the Mustang's front seat.

But we can't leave without the girl or I'm finished! Beads of sweat burst from George's scalp and stung the cuts on his forehead. Vinnie whipped the Mustang into another turn. No sign of Sarah anywhere along the road for two miles in each direction. She wasn't hiding behind any buildings. Vinnie had pulled behind every one of them.

The local QuickMart up the road a mile hadn't seen anyone. Emil was growling like a jilted lover and vowing to make her pay for this.

Vinnie squeezed his eyes and pointed. "The only place she could be is up in them hills. She'll be mountain lion food by sundown."

"I have to be sure!" George shouted from the back seat.

"You have - to shut up!" Vinnie said over his shoulder. "Next gas station, we fill up and head for Brother Lawrence's place." For the first time in two days, Emil had nothing to say. He stared out the passenger side window.

George squirmed in the back seat. Every movement loosened a fresh smell of urine from his trousers and he cracked open the back window. Think George! You have to silence Sarah. He thought Emil was going to take care of it last night. George glared at the back of Vinnie's gray head. Now he would have to do it. But first he had to get away. Besides, he knew these thugs would find him expendable once the eggs were in hand. George shuddered.

From the swirl of thoughts, a crude plan began to take shape. At the station he would pretend to use the bathroom, but instead run straight into the hills. After Vinnie and Emil gave up looking for him, he would double back and look for Sarah. It's a stupid plan, George! He shook his head. It was all he had. His heart thumped loudly in his ears.

Two miles later, Vinnie pulled the Mustang to an abrupt stop in front of a station with a very old sign and two antiquated pumps.

"I've got to use the bathroom," George said. He knew the lie would attract more nasty comments from Emil. Nothing. Vinnie and Emil opened their doors at the same time.

"I'll watch him," Emil said. George slumped, watching his plan sink like the Titanic. Vinnie nodded, and Emil flipped the passenger seat forward. George crawled out and walked with Emil around the side of the gray painted brick building and pulled the bathroom door handle. It was locked. "I'll get the key," Emil said. *Now George. Now!*

Emil turned back. "Better yet, you get the key." Emil leaned against the dirty brick and propped his left foot behind him on the wall. George dragged himself around the front of the station. Vinnie was holding the gas nozzle into the Mustang's rump and didn't even look up as George passed and entered the station. The owner, a thin, oil-fingered man, stared with his mouth open at George's forehead and then handed him the restroom key.

As George returned, he noticed Emil eyeing him strangely. He slowed as he passed Emil, glancing at him, and then inserted the key and opened the door. Emil's left hand was draped against the heel of his left shoe. George saw a flash from the corner of his eye as he entered the bathroom. Emil followed him in and flicked on the light. A fan motor somewhere above, ground noisily. George's eyes watched in horror as Emil pointed one of George's own kitchen knives at his nose.

"Been saving this for just the right moment," Emil said in an excited whisper. "Recognize this? I stuck it in my sock in your kitchen." George stared at it and shook. He opened his mouth, but Emil stopped him.

"Shut up and listen," Emil said. "We gotta be quick."

George backed into the dirty sink. Emil spun the kitchen knife in his hand and spoke in a hush. "Here's our chance, maybe our last chance, and we've only got a few seconds in here." George searched Emil's eyes. They were fierce and glowing.

"I give you this knife. You stick it in your sock, get back in the Mustang and sit right behind Vinnie. When he pulls out on the road, count to 100 in your head, slowly. I'll be counting too. Then jam this thing through the back of Vinnie's seat as hard as you can. I'll grab the wheel and his gun and finish him. Then we'll get the rock from Lawrence and have us a party."

George's mouth still hung open, but he could feel his head nodding.

"Take it and let's go," Emil said, handing George the knife handle first. George squeezed it hard in his right hand. Emil turned away from him to leave, but his hand stopped short of the door and began to shake. His whole body went rigid. George drove the blade up through Emil's kidney and into his lung, pulled it out and thrust it in again. Then he pulled it out and raked it across Emil's throat. The only sound was the squish of wet flesh and the gurgle of air. Emil dropped to the concrete floor and lay motionless among the dead flies.

George wiped the blade quickly on a paper towel, jammed the knife into his pocket, threw the door open, and ran straight into the bushes behind the station. He heard the door bang noisily. He clawed up the steep incline. His left hand was clenched. He fell, glanced, and saw that he still held the bathroom key. He dropped it like it was a slimy lizard and scrambled to his feet. He clawed into the brush again, further, higher, deeper. The tall weeds towered over his head and parted reluctantly. His legs churned. Keep moving, George! Don't look back!

His lungs ached and his mind burned white with terror. *My God, I killed a man!* His legs pressed through the dense brush. Vines twisted his left leg and he fell. He jerked himself up to a crouch and pressed deeper into the thicket. He heard himself gasping and tried to breathe more quietly. His mind flashed with images of Vinnie's enormous hand grabbing his shoulder and then his throat and he felt a fresh wave of adrenaline. His smooth soled Docksiders slipped and then grabbed the ground again and he crept forward, crawling, climbing.

Below him in the distance he heard noises and for a moment he stopped, trying to listen above the chugging of his chest. He heard shouts, then an engine roaring, gravel spitting, tires squealing. Then the roar of the engine fading. Was it the Mustang? He had to keep moving. George angled left and continued to climb. Nettles and briars tore the skin on his ankles and forearms, but he had no time to feel the pain. Get away! Run, George. Don't stop.

He continued to angle left. The higher he climbed, the less dense the undergrowth became. To his left, George saw a thick stand of pine trees. He made his way to it and slipped in behind one of the larger trunks. He leaned against it for a few seconds and let his chest pump air. Then he flipped onto his stomach and for the first time, he peered behind him. He saw no one. He heard no sounds. Had he really gotten away? Had Vinnie panicked and sped away? Was he alone?

He watched and listened for several minutes. The only sounds came from the black-capped chickadees chattering and rushing from branch to branch in the pines. A wren called loudly from the top of the tree next to George. In the distance, another answered. He listened to them call back and forth and wished they'd shut up. He lay still and listened. His muscles, tensed and hard, began to relax. His back ached from crouching, his thighs from climbing, his fingers from clawing. The torn skin on his ankles and arms began to sting. His mind started to work again.

He could feel the change. Find Sarah. The hunted was becoming the hunter.

Vinnie had finished pumping the gasoline, had paid, and was waiting by the car for Emil and George. He couldn't shake the feeling he'd had ever since they left Connecticut, but couldn't figure what it was either. He had always listened to his gut. It had saved him many times. But now he couldn't hear what it was trying to tell him. He looked at his watch and glanced toward the side of the station. He heard the door slam and expected to see both of them round the corner of the building. No one had come. Was he the only one in a hurry here?

Vinnie got into the car and started the engine. Still no one came. He got out of the car, walked around the side of the building, knocked on the bathroom door.

Then he saw it - blood seeping slowly from under the door. He yanked on the door, but it didn't budge, so he ran to the station owner and shouted for the spare bathroom key. He told the man not to follow him, but he did anyway, shouting that this was his gas station and he could do as he pleased. Vinnie shoved the key in the lock and yanked the door open. Emil was on the floor in a large pool of blood. Vinnie felt the station owner nudge next to him and heard him shout, "Call the cops!"

Vinnie grabbed him by the shirt, "Can't do that, old man." And before he had another thought, he felt the pistol jerking in his hand and saw the back of the station owner's head tear off and smack against the opposite wall of the bathroom. Vinnie shoved the man's body next to Emil's and slammed the door.

He ran back to the Mustang and sped away. He had driven for fifteen minutes before he felt his eyes blink, another thirty before his hands stopped shaking. Stupid, stupid, stupid! "Emil, you stupid fuck. You know who's gonna pay for this. I'm gonna be the one to pay for this."

Vinnie blinked. It had happened so fast - that was not his style. Slow and methodical - that had been Vinnie the Vice's trademark. No sloppiness. No mistakes. He cursed and banged his large fist on the steering wheel. This one was full of mistakes. The biggest one was George. Had he really killed Emil? Seriously? Boss's son offed by a priest? S would never believe it. No, he'd get fingered for it. He'd have the feds and the mob after him! Shit! He crossed the first state line and shook both arms, lifting his hands briefly from the steering wheel.

And where was George anyway? Normally he would have gone back, found him, and taken care of things, tied up loose ends. Slow and methodical. But there was no tying this one up! "I'm a dead man," he said flatly. "I'm still breathing, but I'm a dead man." He looked at the speedometer and slowed to the speed limit. Checked the rear view mirror again. Clear. Vinnie finally pinned the feeling. It had a name. Doom.

He pulled into a rest area lined with fir trees and appointed with large green trash bins and wooden picnic tables. In the center stood two dark buildings. All the sidewalks led to them. He backed into a parking spot halfway between the exit ramp and the buildings. He didn't bother to watch the people coming and going from the restrooms. He didn't even see the people close to his rear bumper walking their dogs. His eyes were fixed on the exit ramp he had just used, and on the road beyond it. He would find out who was following him. He would tie up this loose end. He waited and watched.

A white car approached and passed the exit. A large gray container sat atop the roof and bicycles were strapped onto the rear bumper. Inside Vinnie saw at least four heads, two large in the front, two small in the back seat.

The next car that came used the rest area's exit ramp and Vinnie stared hard. It was navy blue and box-shaped, an SUV. The head of a large Golden Retriever stuck from the rear passenger window. The woman in the front passenger seat appeared to be studying a map. Vinnie grinned at the laughing dog with its huge pink tongue. He waited another five minutes. Nothing.

He let out a big breath and felt the muscles loosen in his back. Maybe he wasn't being followed. Maybe he could get away. Disappear. If he went straight to Brother Lawrence's house, he could grab the rock and be out of the area by sundown. He knew how to vanish - had a lifetime of experience. He smiled, slowly constructing every detail of his plan. It would be his finest hour. Even S wouldn't find him. Vinnie flexed his large shoulders, put the Mustang in gear, and roared back onto the road.

Nearly a quarter of a mile behind the Mustang, a black car with the windows darkened sat idling on the shoulder of the road. The man in the passenger seat spoke without taking his eye from the long monocular resting atop a monopod. "He's rolling again. Call it in."

George rose to his feet and filled his aching lungs. Already his body was calling for a smoke, but it would have to wait. He had to find Sarah and finish this thing. He was glad for the trek back to the motel. He needed time to think, time to formulate a plan to dispose of her body where it would not be found. For now, the mountain lion option seemed best: he would drag her deep into the hills and by morning she would be bones in the cat's teeth.

He also needed to create an airtight story for the Board and the authorities, oh yes and for Hilary, when he returned to Ecclesia. *I was abducted. Yes, that's it. By a cult of Satanists! Look what they did to my forehead! They were going to kill me, but I escaped into the woods and finally found my way to a telephone. Thank God I'm safe!*

George grinned. Not bad for a first draft. He was walking briskly now, weaving through dense pine trees. Every five minutes, he stopped and listened for a long minute.

George saw Sarah's face in his mind, and he suffered a twinge of guilt. *Could he really kill her? Would he, when the moment came?* He hadn't thought he could ever have ... eliminated Emil. But when the moment came, it had been easy. He'd hardly thought about it. But then, Emil was the worst kind of slime, the lowest form of scum. The world wouldn't miss him.

Sarah was different. She was no scum ball. *She's one of your seminarians, for Christ's sake.* Something rose in his body and he felt himself nearly scream aloud. *What kind of monster are you?* His eyes darted quickly. Had he actually shouted it? Or only in his mind?

Buck up man! It's her or you. You know that. You're more important to God's plan. You mustn't let her mess it up! George was walking again, more quickly now. Far in the distance the light was brighter. He was coming to a clearing. He felt the knife in his pocket. At the edge of the woods, George leaned against a tree and surveyed the landscape. The motel was still several hundred yards away. Below, the road stretched right and left in a straight line before a small strip of shops with open field stretching back to the hills on either side.

Traffic was light in both directions. He watched cars and trucks roll past. George wondered why he hadn't heard sirens. Surely when the gas station owner found Emil's body in the bathroom, he would have called the police. George would have heard them rush to the scene. Surely there would have been a great clamor if Sarah, wherever she was, had been able to call the police.

Something wasn't right. Or maybe, maybe something was very right. God was with him. George started across the field, crouching in the tall weeds and moving as silently as possible. His eyes continued to look behind him. They also scanned the road and the shops below, searching, watching for a thin blonde woman with no shoes.

Gas Station

Two matching black cars turned across the opposite lane and rolled to a quiet stop near the gray brick building. A third kept traveling straight on I-69 toward the state line. A man emerged from every door of the two vehicles. Two walked quickly and silently into the gas station. Two more pretended to pump gasoline into the vehicles. Two others hunched over the restroom door. One man opened the trunk of the second car and removed a bottle of bleach, a bucket and mop, and lumps of black plastic. The last man, the one wearing the dark felt hat, watched silently with his head low and both hands in the pockets of his dark wool overcoat. Not a word was spoken.

The two men who had gone into the gas station returned. One went to assist the men who were opening the restroom door. The other rolled out the two black plastic bags. A large black zipper ran the length of each bag down the center. He unzipped them. Two men returned from the restroom carrying the station owner's body, while the third held the door. They placed him in the bag and the man who had unzipped the bags closed it. He turned to see the two men coming with Emil Bente's body. They laid it in the second black bag.

The man in the hat stepped toward the bag and dropped something dark and sparkling into it. A handkerchief emerged with the other hand and dabbed his eyes. Then The Shark nodded and the man zipped it. The bags were lifted into the trunk, and the restroom was bleached, mopped and scrubbed until no trace remained. Even the door was scrubbed on both sides and the sidewalk leading to it picked clean. All eight men returned to their vehicles and rolled slowly to the road. The driver of the lead car glanced at his watch. They had been there eight minutes.

Residence of the Assistant Dean
Ecclesia Seminary

The Dean of Ecclesia followed Captain Steele and Lieutenant Higgins into the Fields' kitchen. He was unshaven, his hair tousled and his khaki pants wrinkled, but it was the radiant smile that Captain Steele noticed first when he turned around.

"Afternoon Detectives," Jeremy Tittle said. "I'm sorry to come barging in like this."

"Not at all Dean Tittle," Captain Steele said. "Please sit down." He motioned toward one of the kitchen chairs.

"Thank you. It's a long walk down here from my home, for an old man like me." Tittle settled stiffly into one of the chairs and mopped his hair with a trembling hand.

"Is there something we can do for you?" Steele said, sitting across the table from him. He motioned Higgins to deliver the message upstairs to the forensics team about the new evidence outside.

"I was going to ask you the same question," Jeremy said. "I heard the sirens and walked down here. Police were heading into Patcher Hall and I saw your lieutenant rushing back and forth in George's driveway." He paused. The smile had faded into a concerned frown. "I know most of your work is confidential -"

"Let me brief you on what I can tell you, Dean Tittle."

"Oh thank you. It's all so troubling."

Captain Steele nodded politely. "Here's the thumbnail sketch...." In bare outline, he told Jeremy about tracking suspects in a cocaine smuggling operation to the Ecclesia campus. Jeremy leaned forward, his eyes squinting as if to brace for each new piece of information. For the moment, Steele gave him no names of the people involved. He told him that one person took the cocaine into the Chapel. It was hidden in thirty-six plastic eggs. Jeremy gasped.

"The eggs!" Jeremy looked like a man who'd just discovered his hair was on fire. "I've seen them."

"I was going to ask you about that," Steele said. "I heard something secondhand from Terry Woodrow, but I want you to tell me personally what you saw."

"George Fields was preaching last Sunday, and in the middle of the sermon, these bags of plastic eggs dropped from beneath the altar. Someone had obviously taped them under there and the tape let loose. Terrible mixing of symbols. I was horrified to-"

"What happened then?" Captain Steele moved him along. He didn't want to sound like the television and say, "Just the facts, man. Just give me the facts."

"Yes, well then Brother Lawrence came from the back of the sanctuary, picked up the three bags of eggs and turned the whole thing into a grand announcement about an Easter egg hunt next Sunday. Made it look staged."

"Like a setup for the announcement?"

"Right. Sometimes these younger preachers will use gimmicks like that. For the shock value, I guess." He paused and ran the back of his fingers along his chin whiskers. "Funny thing was that after the service, I checked the published schedule of Easter events. There was no Easter egg hunt listed. I thought maybe it was a surprise addition. Highly unusual."

"So Brother Lawrence is holding the eggs and making an announcement about an Easter egg hunt. What happened then?"

"He left with the eggs through the Chancel doorway."

"Where does that lead?"

"To the Sacristy."

"I'm sorry. I'm not familiar with the term."

"Think of it as a small supply room," Dean Tittle said.

"Is there more than one door?"

"Yes, there's one at the opposite end of the room. It opens to the hall."

"Does the hall lead to the side exit?"

"Yes, among other things."

"I want you to think carefully," Steele said. "Was Brother Lawrence there after the service?"

"I don't have to think carefully, Captain, because I deliberately went to look for him. He was nowhere to be found. I pulled George aside for an explanation of the incident and he stammered something I don't even remember and suddenly got too busy to talk with me."

"Thank you, Dean Tittle. You've been most helpful." Steele shifted in the kitchen chair. "Now let me fill in a few more gaps for you. You know that two of your students were injured, one critically."

Jeremy Tittle nodded.

"Mrs. Bente's apartment was ransacked and we found the gardener dead in the bathtub."

"How awful!"

Captain Steele nodded. "Especially for the landlady. She went into shock and had to be admitted to Memorial."

"Poor thing. Give me her name, and I'll look in on her."

Captain Steele's sat forward and smiled. "I think she might like that."

Jeremy wrote Nettie Spruill's name on the back of the card Steele handed him.

"I was at the hospital when I learned that Hilary Fields was being admitted with chest pains," Steele said.

"Hilary!" Jeremy's voice was hoarse. "I was expecting her to come through that kitchen door any minute. Is George at the hospital with her?"

"I'm afraid we don't know where George is. His home was ransacked too." He had to be careful now with the details. He paused. "We found evidence of violence in the bedroom. But we haven't found George."

"My Lord," Dean Tittle said, "And how is Hilary?"

"She doesn't appear to be in danger, but with heart matters, one never knows. Last I heard, they were keeping her for tests."

"I'll look in on her too." He wrote her name down. The tremor in his hand made the writing a jerky scrawl. He looked up. "Can you tell me anything else?"

"Actually I was hoping to ask you a few more questions."

"Fire away."

"We've got a few missing persons we'd like to question, if we can find them. Sounds like you don't know where George is. How about Brother Lawrence? Have you seen him today?"

"I haven't. But if we can find George's Ecclesia phone directory, I can get you an address."

"Thanks. We've already got it. How about Terry Woodrow? Have you seen him?"

"He's at Memorial, Room 316, I believe."

"Actually, he's not there anymore," Steele said.

"He was released?"

"Something like that."

Jeremy waited, but didn't press. "I haven't seen him since I visited the hospital yesterday."

"How about Sarah Stafford?"

"Yesterday. At the hospital, in the ICU with you, and then she came to my home for tea." Jeremy paused thoughtfully. "I'm afraid I upset her."

"Oh?" Steele's mind was processing the possibilities.

"She's pretty upset with that boy, Woodrow." He looked up and smiled. "She loves him, I fear."

Steele nodded. "I'd say 'upset' is putting it mildly." The sound of her shrieking and the image of her being carried out of the room by officers filled his head. "So, how'd you upset her?"

"We talked about mercy," he said quietly.

"And let me guess. She wanted blood." Steele had seen hundreds of people who professed faith in God, love of neighbor, forgiveness, all of it ... until they were wronged. Then they became the most vicious and violent perpetrators, exacting their revenge upon those who had wronged them ... wanting blood. The prisons were full of believers.

"She never said what she wanted," Jeremy said evasively, "but she did leave rather abruptly."

"I see."

"I tried to phone her today, but all I got was an answering machine."

"The officers you saw going into Patcher Hall are looking for Sarah and Terry. We'll know soon enough whether anyone has seen them."

Behind them, Steele heard the thunder of feet coming down the stairs. Several people passed through the kitchen door from the living room wearing bright yellow nylon jackets. "Forensics Unit" was emblazoned in large block letters across the back. They wore surgical gloves and carried what looked like large tackle boxes. Others carried evidence in large plastic trash bags and went out the back door.

"Who ransacked these homes?" Jeremy asked. "And why?"

"Good question." Steele decided not to open that discussion. He remembered his instructor at the academy, a large barrel-chested man with a hawk-eyed glare and an enormous handlebar mustache. "Everyone is a suspect," he had barked at the cadets, "everyone. Until the facts prove them otherwise." He had never forgotten it.

"Have you ever been fingerprinted, Dean Tittle?" Captain Steele asked gently.

Jeremy's eyebrows rose dramatically. "Yes, as a matter of fact. It was a requirement of the employment process when I was first appointed to Assistant Dean, part of the criminal background check."

"But you're the Dean, not the Assistant Dean."

"I am now. But first I was appointed Assistant Dean by the Board of Trustees. I became Dean when the former Dean retired, just as George will become the Dean when I hang up the robe." He chuckled without laughing. "If George had his way that would be tomorrow."

Now it was Steele's eyebrows that rose up. "Is Reverend Fields champing at the bit to ascend?" He didn't let on that Higgins had briefed him.

"I've been waiting for him to see it the other way around," Dean Tittle said softly, looking at his hands.

"Other way around?"

Jeremy Tittle nodded. "Not as an ascension to the throne of power, but instead as a descent to the servant's quarters." He spoke so softly that Captain Steele wondered if Dean Tittle was still speaking to him. "The moment I see it in his eyes, I will pass the mantle, and retire." Slowly he pushed away from the table. Steele looked at Tittle's downcast face. He saw deep etching carved all over it. Then Dean Tittle looked up and smiled shyly. "I'm sorry. I-"

"No need," Steele said, holding up his hand. The cell phone in his shirt pocket barked and vibrated. He snapped it to his ear. Jeremy Tittle rose from his chair slowly, stiffly. He looked older than when he had first come in.

"Steele."

Jeremy waved and started to turn toward the door, but Steele's emphatic hand wave stopped him. Neither man moved. Max could feel his eyelids close slowly as the voice on the other end of the phone continued to speak rapidly.

His mouth opened, but what came out was only a deflating sigh. He didn't know how much longer he had listened, or how many seconds ticked by. His mind moved quickly and slowly at the same time, like car tires in a puddle of oil. Thoughts raced, but didn't go anywhere. Connections didn't connect. Pieces of the puzzle popped from their places like popcorn in a pan on the stove. He closed the cell phone without a word and looked up. Jeremy Tittle was watching him intently.

Steele rose from his chair, trying to collect himself. "I'll walk you out." The two men passed through the back kitchen door to the driveway. Yellow coats crowded the driveway and dotted the large lawn. The sun reflected off them with such intensity that both men squinted. He put his arm around Dean Tittle's shoulder and walked him past the forensics team and around the hedge. They walked in silence to the end of the driveway. He released Jeremy's shoulder with two soft pats. "I do hope you'll visit Nettie Spruill at Memorial. I think she needs a friend right now."

"Count on me," Jeremy said. "I'll look in on Hilary too."

Steele held Dean Tittle's gaze. "I'm afraid you won't find her at Memorial."

"Is she all right?"

He wanted to tell the Dean. He just wasn't sure he should. He'd kept his mouth shut the entire length of the driveway. *Need to know basis, Steele!* "We need to find her husband immediately," he said.

"Oh no, she's had a heart attack!"

"Worse." He paused. *Your training, man!* "Hilary Fields is in police custody. She's been charged with attempting to murder Nina Bente, assaulting a police officer, and resisting arrest."

He saw Dean Tittle stagger. He caught the old man by the elbow on his way to the asphalt.

Chapter Twenty-One

Lago-Mar Motel

"Hurry Terry. I really gotta go!" Sarah whispered into the phone.

"I know," he said. The BMW was gobbling the road beneath him. "We've got to get you away from there."

"No, I mean I've got to go. Hurry!"

Terry grinned silently. If he laughed right now, she'd kill him. "I'm only a few miles away. You sure you don't know what room you're in?"

"Wish I did. All I know is it's around the back. I've thought about several ways to get the room number, but they all involve coming out from beneath this bed, and I just can't risk it."

"No, you stay put." Terry paused for a few seconds, thinking.

"Are you hurrying?" Sarah asked.

"I'm hurrying, Sarah. Okay, how about this. I come around the back and park in the middle of the lot. You think you'd recognize your Beemer's horn?

"Yes."

"Okay, I tap the horn once and wait. As soon as you hear it, crawl out and get one of the pillows. I'd tell you to get a towel, but that would involve going near the bathroom.

Open the door just wide enough to drop it outside, then close and lock it again. I'll come to the door and knock once, one hit. You let me in and race for the bathroom."

"How'll I know it's you?"

"No one knocks on a door with only one rap."

"Hadn't thought about that."

"10-15 minutes. Be listening."

"OK," Sarah said.

"I'm hurrying." Terry closed the cell phone. He had tried to sound confident, even lighthearted, for her sake. But he didn't feel confident, and he wasn't lighthearted. His heart felt heavy. He was so disappointed. Disappointed in Terry Woodrow. He knew the Lord had forgiven him. But would he ever forgive himself? He would keep trying but every time he thought about it, a fresh wave of self-hatred flowed through him. Then there was Sarah. Would she forgive him? And even if she did, would she ever trust him again, deep down trust him like she used to?

There wasn't time to think about it. Right now, Sarah's safety was priority one. He wished he had a weapon. Probably better he didn't, since he'd never used one before. But still he wanted one. His father hadn't even allowed him a B-B gun, even though all of his friends had them. He'd never even had a sling shot, come to think of it, or a pocket knife. His mother had nixed the karate lessons - too violent. His dad backed her up - too much Far Eastern religious mumbo-jumbo in that stuff. A memory came and he grinned. His little brother had been grounded for a week for carving his bologna sandwich into the shape of a pistol and pointing it at him.

We were a self-proclaimed nonviolent family. Until the day Dad punched her so hard that Mom fell backward into the Christmas tree and cut up the backs of her arms. Terry had been hiding behind the sofa, instead of in his room asleep, hoping for a sneak peak at the presents he would open in the morning. Worst Christmas we ever had. Mom got four stitches above her eye from the Emergency Room doctor and big white bandages for her arms, while the rest of us sat for hours in the waiting room. Dad never knew I saw him do it. He lied about it to my face, and I pretended to believe him. From that day on, Terry had wanted to trust his father again. He had also wanted a weapon.

And he wanted one now.

He saw the motel sign swelling into view on the right and his pulse quickened. His eyes scanned in every direction. Anything out of the ordinary and he would keep driving and wait for Sarah to call again. The lot in front of the motel was deserted, except for two empty junkers parked backward at the base of the sign. He waited to turn until the last possible moment, and then swung the BMW in a hard right turn along the far end of the motel and headed around back. A white service truck was parked on the far end. A red Cutlass was parked in the middle spot, the one he had wanted. Terry pulled up next to it and peered across the passenger seat into the other car. Real estate brochures and home catalogues were strewn across the passenger seat.

Terry said a quick prayer and honked the horn. Even though he thought he barely touched it, the sound of the horn made him jump. He looked up and down the row of doors. Nothing. What if she hadn't heard it? He thought about beeping again. Take it easy buddy. It's only been a few seconds. His head turned slowly left and then right, his eyes pausing momentarily on each door. Then he saw it. The pillow!

Terry grabbed the keys, leapt from the car, and pushed the button to lock it. He raced for the door and rapped once on it. He heard the dead bolt slide, and the door flew open. He rushed in and slammed it with his back behind him. A thin blonde woman flew crying into his arms, sending the keys noisily to the carpet. She held his neck so hard it hurt, but Terry felt himself smiling. He pulled her into him and straightened his back. He felt her feet leave the carpet. "Thank God," he heard her whisper. "Thank God you're here."

He thought he felt her nuzzle his neck and for a second he wondered if she had kissed him. Probably not. Most definitely not, though he wouldn't have minded. At all. He'd thought about kissing her all the way here, imagined her soft lips against his, her mouth opening to his and their tongues entwining. But he knew it wouldn't happen. It hadn't happened when they were best friends. It definitely wouldn't happen now. Besides, he was sure she hated him. And he deserved it, hated himself for having the thoughts.

"Don't you have to use the bathroom?" he whispered into her neck.

"In a minute," came the soft, muffled reply.

Some seconds later, he felt her arms loose his neck and Sarah slipped down his chest until her bare feet were on the floor. She raced to the bathroom.

Terry sat on the end of the bed. The room smelled like the inside of a fast food restaurant. His empty stomach growled. He leaned his head down to the floor in between the two double beds. The space between the floor and the box springs couldn't have been more than a few inches. He wouldn't have had the nerve to try to fit under there. Under the one closest to the bathroom, he saw a torn bag and wadded paper. Food wrappers? He couldn't wait to hear about this one.

Not here. It wasn't safe. Had to get her out of here, but where to go. If the police and the FBI couldn't be trusted, then they certainly couldn't go back to Ecclesia. Maybe his parents' in California. But he had no money for food or gas or lodging. His mind was still reeling from the day's events. He'd have to talk it over with Sarah. They would think of something.

Sarah emerged from the bathroom and stood outside the door. Her eyes momentarily darted to every corner of the room, then they met Terry's and she looked down. She clasped her hands loosely in front of her, then dropped them to her sides. Her white blouse was untucked and the top two buttons were undone. Terry saw a large red blotch on her chest and remembered her complaining that the box spring had rubbed her raw.

"Come here," he said softly, holding his hand toward her. All his strategic thinking about where they could go, how they could get away, vanished. Now he only wanted to hold her again.

Sarah shook her head slightly, still looking down. Suddenly Terry knew they were going to deal with some painful stuff, right now, no matter how dangerous it was to stay in this room. He didn't want to. But.

Integrity time, Terry told himself. Just be honest, no matter what it costs, no matter how much it hurts you, no matter how bad it makes you look. Just tell her the truth.

"It's time for the truth Sarah," he said slowly, staring at the floor. "You deserve that." He took a deep breath. "You deserved it all along, but I wasn't man enough to be honest, not strong enough to do the right thing." He looked up. A tear rolled down Sarah's cheek. Still looking down, she shuffled to the end of the other double bed, and sat across from him.

"Whooh!" Terry slapped his knee and Sarah jerked. Terry jumped to his feet and was pacing the room. "It's so humiliating!"

It was in his throat. Could he let it out? Could he show himself to Sarah, show her who he really was? It came in a rush.

"Shallow! That's what I am, Sarah. I'm a selfish, lustful, shallow man. That's the ugly truth. I deceived you into thinking maybe I was a godly person, a minister-in-the-making, like you. As long as I kept things from you, you would like me, maybe even respect me. But if you knew the whole truth about me, I would lose you.

"Truth is I was totally magnetized to you from the day we met, thought you were the most beautiful woman I had ever seen. And then I talked with you, and found you were intelligent, hilarious, and so fun to do things with. I even found studying awesome as long as I was sitting next to you. Sometimes it was a little difficult to concentrate because I was so … excited by your body sitting close to mine. I imagined a thousand times leaning over and kissing you. But I never did. You know why?"

Sarah's hair had fallen in front of her face as she continued to look at her hands. Terry saw the hair shake slightly again. She pulled gently at her fingernails. The tears were falling softly onto her crumpled white blouse.

Terry's voice continued softly. "I never kissed you because I knew I wanted more than that, physically, pig that I am, and you had made it clear to everyone at Ecclesia that you were saving yourself for marriage. So I chose to save myself from frustration and be your friend, even though I wanted to be more." He took another, deeper breath. "And then along came Nina." Sarah looked up at him, and then back down quickly, but not before Terry saw the look in her eyes. Saw it, felt it, but couldn't name it. But he sensed this might very well be their last conversation. Still he owed it to her, and to himself, to come clean.

"Nina wasn't anything like you, Sarah. She wasn't funny or particularly interesting to talk with and I never wanted to go places or do things with her. She didn't seem to either. But the first night I met her, she gave me something else I wanted. Wanted bad!"

"Slut. I hate her." The monotone whisper came through the curtain of blonde hair.

"Don't hate her, Sarah. Hate me!" Terry stopped pacing for a moment and leaned toward the top of her head. "I'm the slut. And I hate myself for it." His eyes were moist. "I was the one cashing in a real relationship for easy sex. If anything, she was just a willing victim. I didn't love her. She didn't love me. I wanted her for one thing. Apparently she wanted me for the same thing. Afterward, I felt so guilty. But a few days later, back I'd go for more. A couple times the guilt got to me so bad, I started thinking I needed to marry Nina, to make it all legitimate. But she never seemed the least bit interested in talking about it. Now I know why. Sarah, I had no clue she was married." He was pacing again, not looking at her, speaking quickly, as if rushing the words out would lessen the pain.

"Captain Steele was right. I didn't know her at all. I only knew her well enough to take her clothes off. And you know the sickest part? I felt like a kid taking lollipops from the drug store. I was getting away with it, and nobody knew! I could still be near enough to you, and yet have all the sex I wanted from Nina on the side. See now what an ass I am?" He walked to the corner of the other double bed and sat facing her, their knees almost touching. "I'm the slut." Hot tears burst from his eyes and seared down his cheeks.

His voice cracked. "I am so sorry, Sarah. I'm so ashamed of what I've done. I'm so ashamed of who I really am. I don't deserve to be your friend, or anything more. I've already screwed that up. But ... could you find it in your heart ..." The dam burst and Terry sobbed into his hands. "To forgive me?"

"No." The word was bullet quick from Sarah's mouth, the volume low, the tone firm. She fired again. "No."

Ecclesia Seminary

Steele insisted on driving Jeremy Tittle back to his home on the other side of the seminary, grateful not to have to send another Ecclesia person to Memorial Hospital. Tittle's problem was that he cared, Max thought. He cared about people, and it cost him dearly when people did things to hurt themselves or other people. There's got to be something wrong with letting yourself care that much, he thought. He had often thought that people who let events and other people hurt them had a problem.

But was that really a problem? The alternative was to live with a hard crust, an impenetrable shell. It was great protection, but it also shut everyone out. In the end, you were a walking fortress, but you always walked alone. Max knew it well, had strived years to achieve it, and it had made him a very lonely man. But lately the shell had begun to crack … from the inside.

He felt the cell phone vibrate in his pocket before he heard the ring. He glanced at the number before he answered, but he didn't recognize it.

"Captain Steele."

"Max, this is Maria," Dr. Sanchez said.

"Dr. Sanchez. I was just thinking about you. You're a sound for sore ears."

"I'm not going to tell you how much I've been thinking about you," Maria said. "But I keep the coffee hot and fresh here." She paused. "I assume you've been notified about Hilary Fields."

"Yes, I just got the call. No details, though."

"It's not pretty, Max. I heard two code Blues sound over the hospital intercom within minutes of each other. So I ran with the other doctors to the ICU. Outside the ICU doors, four nurses were standing around Hilary Fields. She was handcuffed on the floor screaming and spitting and cursing at the top of her lungs."

"You serious?" Captain Steele said, then added, "Of course you're serious. Go on."

"I ran past her into ICU. A man in Room Two had suffered a massive heart attack and they had the paddles on him when I got there. I went to Nina Bente's room. Apparently Fields had unplugged the ventilator and they were bagging her while others rushed to get another one."

"Bagging her?"

"Yes, they hook an accordion-like instrument to the tube in her throat and manually pump air into her lungs."

"Why didn't someone just plug it back in?"

"That was the problem. Hilary broke the plug prongs off in the wall socket."

"Is there another one?"

"Another ventilator? I could tell by the panic that no one was sure, but there must be one somewhere in this hospital."

"I was actually asking if there was another plug in the room. I assume it's a specialty plug."

"It is, and there isn't, and that was adding to the panic."

"You mind translating?"

"It is a specialty plug, and there is only one per room in this ICU. They were talking about switching rooms and a couple of other options, but because she was in such severe distress, they didn't want to move her."

"I assume because you are calling me that the situation was resolved and that Bente is stabilized."

"You assume wrong, Captain." Dr. Sanchez's voice was strained, but still as professional as ever, he thought. "I slipped away to call you because they didn't need me. There was nothing I could do. Problem is that there's not much anyone can do. Nina Bente is in real crisis."

"At least they're keeping her breathing manually," Captain Steele said.

"It's not the same, Max. Nowhere near." Dr. Sanchez paused. "I called to fill you in on the details, but also to prepare you."

"Are they losing her?"

"I think so."

"Will you keep me posted?"

"Best I can, Max. I have to go back to the ER, but I'll check on her every chance I get."

"Thanks, Maria." Captain Steele said his good-bye and closed the phone. He had walked to the end of the driveway while he talked. He looked up to see a uniformed officer walking toward him from the back of Ecclesia's administration building. He was a man in his mid-thirties, slight build, and a bright red crew cut.

"Looking for Captain Steele," the officer said.

"You're looking at him, Officer … Neldt." Steele read the nametag on his chest.

"A report for you, sir. No sign of Brother Lawrence. He phoned in early this morning and cancelled all of his appointments. No one has seen or heard from Reverend Fields or his wife. The women on the second floor of Patcher Hall, where Sarah Stafford lives, haven't seen her in a couple of days. Her room looks untouched."

"Good work. Is Stafford's car in the lot?"

"No sir. I was getting to that."

"Didn't think so. You get a description and plates from administration?"

"Right here, Captain Steele. Took the liberty of calling it in to dispatch in case you want a BOLO for it."

Max had to smile. Officer Neldt was so eager. "Good work, Neldt. We need as many eyes on the lookout for that vehicle as possible. Now what about Terry Woodrow?"

"No one has seen or heard from him, sir. His car is in the upper lot, though."

"So we didn't pick up many clues here."

"Maybe one," Officer Neldt said.

"What's that?"

We came across a rental car in the back of the faculty lot. We called it in. Leased to Mrs. Hilary Fields."

"That is interesting." He had looked through Hilary's red Saab parked in the Fields' garage. Why would Hilary need a second vehicle?

He felt Officer Neldt staring at him and he looked up. "We thought – I thought – we could open it up and have a look through it if you wanted."

"Your warrants cover it?"

"Yes sir."

"Then search it, and get back to me."

The officer was gone at a dead run. Steele chuckled and wound his way back up the driveway. As he returned, he found Higgins huddled with a mass of bright yellow jackets.

"What have we got?" he asked.

"A mess," a gray haired man with square, gold-rimmed glasses said. "Looks like there was a party out there." He pointed to the stand of trees they had just searched.

Another man nodded and spoke. "At least three distinct sets of footprints, two shell casings, 30 caliber. Could have been fired by any number of high powered rifles, all the way from a sniper's gun to a stock deer rifle. Weapon appears to be hand held. No tripod marks."

The only woman wearing a yellow jacket spoke. "We recovered both bullets and neither show trace elements of blood. So whoever was shooting didn't hit anyone."

Lieutenant Higgins spoke, looking at his notes. "The team got excellent prints from the bedroom and living room. Someone is running them for comparison with prints at Bente's flat."

"Excellent," Steele said. "What about the blood upstairs?"

The woman spoke again. "Type O-Negative. Appears to have come from a single source. Not enough to suggest a bleed-out."

"Good work team," Steele said. "Get your reports together by tomorrow morning. We are way behind the people who did this, and we need to make up time." He turned to Higgins as the yellow jackets dispersed to the array of vehicles lining the fire lane.

"You're certain there are no eggs in that house?"

"Yes."

"Did you happen to notice the keys to Hilary's Saab?" He pointed to the red vehicle parked in the center of the garage

"They're in the kitchen."

Captain Steele knew that Higgins didn't miss many details. "Why don't you grab them."

When Higgins returned with the keys, Steele sat in the driver's seat, inserted the key in the ignition and turned. Instantly, the engine roared to life.

"Thought so," Steele said. He got out of the car and handed the keys to Higgins. "You can put those back now." He walked out of the garage. Officer Neldt was rounding the hedge with two other officers, each with latex gloves on. He could see the excitement on their faces.

"Find something interesting, gentlemen?"

"In the trunk, Captain." Neldt said. "We found a set of camouflage clothes and another set of dull gray clothes with a dark gray overcoat and a bucket hat. Oh and sunglasses.... But that wasn't the big find."

Captain Steele looked into the young man's wide eyes, and waited.

"We found a rifle with a major league scope on it," Neldt said. "We all agree the scope must have cost more than the rifle."

"Let me guess. The rifle was a 30-0-6."

The officers blinked at each other and then looked back at Steele. "Correct, sir. How'd-"

"And it's been fired very recently." Higgins had returned from putting the Saab keys back in the house and stood two steps away.

"That's correct, sir, but how'd-"

"Excellent detective work, men. Now I want you to do two things. I want you to call the First Precinct and have them turn the forensics unit around and get them back out here. I want them to go over every inch of that car. I want you to stand guard over the vehicle until they get there."

"Count on us, Captain Steele," and they sprinted away.

Steele turned to Higgins.

"I was just going to ask if you wanted me to call Memorial and make sure Hilary Fields doesn't come home for a few days," Higgins said. "This house is still a crime scene and we don't want anything touched."

"No danger of that Lieutenant. Come on. I'll brief you in the car." They walked down the driveway toward the fire lane.

"By the way, Lieutenant," Steele said, "Did you get a good look at those officers from the First Precinct?"

"Yes."

"They look like youngsters, newbies, to you?"

"No. Why?"

Captain Steele shrugged. "Just playing with puzzle pieces." He pointed to their vehicle. "It's past time we paid that visit to Brother Lawrence."

Chapter Twenty-Two

Lago-Mar Motel

"I can't find it in my heart to forgive you." Sarah rose and stood over him. "You've been playing with my life, and with my heart, and I resent it. I'm not good enough for you because I won't spread my legs for you. So you go secretly to some slut and get your pipes drained." She could hear the volume of her voice rise, but she didn't care. "You thought you could have it all, but guess what? You can't. I deserve better than that."

"Yes, you do." The whisper came through Terry's fingers.

"And now look at the mess you've made. There is a life growing inside Nina, and there's a good chance it's yours. That poor child is fighting for its life right now. It lives inside a mother who is addicted to crack and who has been beaten so badly she may not live. That child deserved better, Terry. It didn't deserve to be conceived like that. Who knows? If Nina dies, you might suddenly become a single parent raising that child on your own – if it's yours, and if Nina's husband doesn't kill you first."

"I've thought about that."

"About dying?"

"About raising the child on my own," Terry said. "I'll do it."

"Great. And what do you suppose the Ordination Board is going to say in a couple of months? 'Ah yes, Mr. Woodrow, I see you've been committing adultery for some time now with a woman addicted to crack and married to a crime boss, and that the two of you have produced a child….. Well done, old boy!'"

"Screw them," Terry said through a clogged nose, removing his hands from his face and wiping his eyes.

"Sure Terry. Screw them too. Why not? You've screwed everybody else!"

"That's enough Sarah."

"Oh no it's not. That's not nearly enough. You're a real bastard, Terry, and someone has got to tell you to your face. Your command center is in your crotch. That's what's calling the shots in your life."

"I said, that's enough!"

Sarah shook her head. "Sorry. You've left a lot of pain in your wake, buddy, and you are going to hear me out." She was shouting now, and her face felt hot. Terry looked like a withered bud. No, more like a whipped pup. So pathetic. And so cute. *God, what's wrong with me?*

She shook herself and began to pace. She needed to finish, and he needed to hear it.

"You've lied. You've committed adultery. You've used people to get what you wanted. You've disgraced yourself. You've disgraced the chapel congregation and the seminary. You've disgraced your father's legacy."

"And his father's legacy. Don't forget that," he said hotly. "And his father's father's."

"And now you expect to be ordained."

"No. I'm leaving the ministry."

"How noble," Sarah said sarcastically. "But you weren't talking that way as long as you were getting away with it. It's only because you got caught!"

"I've been thinking about it. I'm not getting ordained."

"Why not?" Sarah's hands were on her hips.

"Because I disqualified myself," he spat out, "for all the reasons you so eloquently slapped across my face." He slumped and his neck sank into his shoulders. He propped his hands on his thighs.

Silence descended upon the room. Neither spoke. Terry swiped angrily at his cheeks as more tears fell. Sarah walked past him between the beds and sat next to him. She looked at the side of his face. It was bent to the floor, his eyes in a fixed stare. She looked at his hair, the way it curled at the back of his thick neck. She studied his broad, muscular shoulders, and the slight arc in his back. She resisted an urge to throw her arms around his shoulders and hold him. Be held by him.

"I forgive you," she whispered and ran her slender fingers down his left arm. She put her hand on top of his.

"What?" Terry's head snapped to face her. "But you said -"

"You asked me if I could find it in my heart," she said softly, "and I told you no because I couldn't really. All I found there was hurt and pain." She pulled his hand into both of hers and looked into his eyes. "But I do forgive you from a much deeper place. My soul. That's where I find forgiveness for you. At the core of my being. That's where God put it when He forgave me."

Terry's mouth was open, and his eyes darted from one of Sarah's eyes to the other. He started to speak, but Sarah quickly, gently, put her index finger to his lips. She noticed that her finger trembled. "I'm not finished," she said softly, dropping her hand onto his again. "There's something you should know." Her eyes fell to the hands and she whispered. "I'm disqualified too." A surge of fear roared through her frame. "I've never told anyone." She felt Terry squeeze her hand gently.

Sarah looked up quickly and held Terry's stare. Her mouth opened and at first nothing came out. Then it did. "I murdered my own child." Sarah could feel her bottom lip tremble. She sucked it into her teeth and held it a few seconds before letting it go. "It was the summer before I came to Ecclesia. I was a counselor at a Christian camp for middle schoolers. He was the camp nurse and part-time youth minister for a huge Baptist church. I went to see him with a fever, but came away seriously hot in a different way." She couldn't look at Terry.

"I wasn't a virgin. Lost that in high school … to the boy who promised to marry me." She could feel her eyes flash and looked up. Terry's eyes had not left her face. "So you see I wasn't saving my purity for marriage.

There was no virginity to save. I made it up to keep men away, to keep it from happening again. I couldn't trust myself."

She sighed and looked down again at Terry's hand in hers. "Anyway, I managed to get sick a lot that summer and made frequent trips to the camp nurse. I thought I loved him, but he never said he loved me. It wasn't his fault. He and I both knew what we wanted. He always wore protection, but still I got pregnant.

"I was beside myself. I couldn't tell my father, the Presbyterian Deacon, or my Mom who had bragged about her daughter, the future minister, to every women's bible study group in the presbytery. I was so scared and so ashamed, and I didn't trust anyone to ask advice. I wanted it all to go away, but I was too chicken to terminate the pregnancy. I prayed and repented and asked for God's forgiveness. I also asked for a way out of the mess I'd made, but I never did see an escape route with His fingerprints on it.

"So I arrived at Ecclesia, the promising young seminary student who was secretly pregnant and terrified that I was beginning to show. I thought about the adoption route, but decided against it because it would mean being exposed for who I really was. I'd be disqualified immediately for ministry in the church.

"At three months, I couldn't hide it anymore with bulky clothes, and I panicked. One Friday I threw some clothes in a paper bag and took the bus across town to the Clinic, the one about a mile south of the railroad tracks."

"I've heard about it," Terry said softly.

Sarah nodded. "The more money you have, the fewer questions they ask. By Wednesday of the next week, I was back in class, pretending to concentrate, pretending to take notes, but instead hearing over and over ...." She fell silent. Murderer. The words stuck in her throat. "It was a girl. The last thing I heard," she choked on the lump in her throat, "was her little heartbeat. Then it stopped." Sarah burst into tears and fell face first onto the floor. "I killed her. I murdered her," she sobbed into the carpet. "Murderer!" The voice coming from her throat was different, deeper. "You killed your baby!" A loud moan erupted from deep within her, a frightening sound coming from a depth beyond the reach of words. Her hands pressed around her abdomen, fingers stretched wide as if to grasp one last time what was no longer there. "Murderer!" She heard another loud, almost inhuman moan erupt from her mouth and felt her knees pull to her chest. Darkness closed upon her. She felt its cold, black talons grip her mind and carry it away.

Sarah's eyes were closed. She heard his voice, distant at first, then becoming clearer. "It's all right, Sarah. You're safe. It's all right, honey." She felt Terry's hand brush her hair, and she reached a hand to her forehead. A damp washcloth was draped across it. Terry was on his knees beside her, gently stroking her hair with the back of his fingers.

"Hi," Sarah said weakly.

"Welcome back," Terry said. "You scared me there for a second."

"How long was I gone?"

"About fifteen minutes."

"Did I have a seizure?"

"More like a meltdown I think," Terry said, stroking her cheek. "But thank God you finally told someone. You'll never again have to carry that burden alone."

"Thank you."

"Thanks for trusting me," Terry said, leaning down and kissing her cheek. He hesitated and whispered, "And thank you for forgiving me."

Sarah wrapped her right arm over his neck and pulled him close. "Thank God. I couldn't do it on my own."

Terry rose to his feet and helped Sarah stand.

"It's not safe," she said, "and we have been playing Russian roulette, staying so long."

"I don't regret it," Terry said, wrapping his arms around her again.

Her mind told her lips to say, "Me neither," but instead they went straight for Terry's lips. It was unlike any kiss she had ever had. She felt her feet leave the ground again, and she wished they'd never land. Their mouths yielded to one another, and their tongues expressed a tenderness beyond words.

After a long time, Terry set her down again and whispered it was time to go. Sarah smiled, stole one last quick kiss, and got on her knees to drag several things from beneath the bed. Terry watched her shove a wad of napkins in her shorts pocket, then inspect several wrapped biscuits. The grease had soaked through the paper.

"Where'd you get those?"

"That's a story for the car. Think we'll eat any of this?" she said wrinkling up her thin nose.

"Might be all the food we can afford."

Sarah shook her head. "I've got some money."

"Then trash 'em, honey," Terry said.

"That's five."

"Hmm?"

"You've called me honey five times since yesterday." She smiled.

"Maybe it's because you're the sweetest woman I've ever known." He leaned down and kissed her softly. "You counting?"

"Mmm-Hmmm."

"You mind?"

"Uh-Uh." She shook her head and smiled. She tossed the breakfast biscuits into the waste basket and they made their way to the door. Terry unbolted the door, and opened it.

It was the last thing they expected.

Sarah flew backward like she'd been struck by a blast of wind.

George Fields stepped over the threshold before Terry could react. His right arm and most of his shirt were covered with dried blood. A wide knife blade reached toward them from his fist. Instinctively, Terry shoved Sarah behind him as the point of the knife pressed against Terry's sternum.

George kicked the door closed behind him and backed Terry and Sarah slowly into the center of the room.

"Sit!" he said, "On the floor." George pulled the vinyl chair from the front corner of the room, shoved it against the door and sat down. His eyes were wide and his chest made a guttural sound. Terry had never seen eyes like that before. It was almost impossible to believe that those eyes sat on the face of his Ecclesia supervisor. And his forehead! Who did that to him? Or did he do it himself? Maybe he'd become a Satanist!

Terry's blood drained cold from his hands and feet. "Reverend Fields, what are you doing? What's happened to you?"

George ignored him. "So Miss Stafford, we meet again." He leaned forward on the front of the chair. His bare legs were covered with scratches and thin lines of dried blood. Sarah noticed that the room was beginning to smell of urine and sweat and blood.

"Your little escape almost worked." George said. "You know I can't let you do that."

"Where is Mr. V?" Sarah said.

"Almost to Brother Lawrence's by now, most likely," George grinned. "He's not here to protect you anymore." A smile curled across on his face.

Terry watched him turn the knife slowly in his hand. "For God's sake, Reverend Fields!" Terry could feel the vein in his neck swelling.

"For God's sake?" George was on his feet, his voice a high roar. "For God's sake, indeed! It is for God's sake that I must protect my position at Ecclesia. It is for God's sake I must become the Dean and defend myself against anyone who would keep me from my holy calling."

"You're crazy," Sarah screamed.

"No. Emil Bente was crazy, crazy to trust me with this." George studied the blood on his hand. "And you." He pointed the blade down at Sarah.

"You are crazy if you think I'm going to let you tell what you know." He swung the blade slowly, mechanically toward Terry.

"You won't kill us," Sarah's voice was strong, defiant, but from the corner of his eye, Terry saw her hands trembling. "You're too much of a coward."

"Tell that to Emil. Of course, he's not hearing much these days. He lost a lot of this," George pointed to the dried blood on his hand, "when I slit his throat." He ran the blade horizontally with great drama.

Terry watched him rock from one foot to the other. He felt strangely calm inside. "There's nothing holy about your calling." Terry tried to keep George focused on him instead of Sarah. "God wouldn't have you murder people to protect it."

"Oh but He would!" The wild look was still there. "The crusades! Thousands of people's throats were slit to protect the Mother Church."

"So now you're a crusader," Terry said, getting up to his knees next to Sarah.

"I will protect the Church! That woman would ruin everything." George said, pointing the knife at Sarah.

"This isn't about the Church." Terry rose to one knee, his right foot on the floor.

"I am God's servant!" George bellowed. "He called me to be the Dean of Ecclesia."

"Would God's servant be called to break the Ten Commandments? What happened to 'Thou shalt not kill?'" Terry stood up.

George's eyes went wide and even wilder. He growled at Terry. "Sit down boy!"

"Can't do that George," Terry said, grabbing a towel that was lying on the bed and stepping in front of Sarah. He wrapped the towel around his left forearm. "Sarah, get in the bathroom and lock the door."

"I'll slit your throat boy," George said. "then I'll carve her to bits."

"In the name of God I suppose?" Terry tried to keep George talking while he looked for an opportunity.

"I am the servant of the Most High God!" George swayed from foot to foot and stabbed at the air with the knife.

"You are Satan's slave!" Terry said with as much disgust as he could inject in his voice.

"You cannot speak to me that way. I am -"

"You bear his mark on your forehead!"

George's left hand slapped to his forehead. "Emil, that bastard. But he paid. I made him pay."

"Emil was a prophet. He knew who you belonged to." Terry forced a laugh, and then braced himself.

George roared and charged. Terry stepped right and swung his toweled forearm as hard as he could into George's right arm. George staggered, cursing loudly, but he managed to hang onto the knife. He charged again. Terry kicked his right leg forward and his foot found its mark between George's legs. At the exact moment of contact, Terry saw a flash in front of him and felt something slash through the muscles of his thigh.

A sickening howl erupted from George's lips. He buckled forward onto the floor. Terry watched him fall in slow motion. Time nearly stood still. Terry felt himself falling backward and caught himself on the end of the double bed. His left knee bent, but his right knee didn't. He looked down. George was throwing up on himself. He was curled into a tight ball, howling and gagging.

Then Terry's eyes found his own thigh. All he could see was the black handle with the stainless steel rivets. The entire blade was in his leg. He felt warm liquid running down the back of his pants leg toward his ankle. The room was growing darker and Terry couldn't focus his eyes. He felt his chest heaving. His leg felt like a foreign object.

"Sarah." Terry wasn't sure whether he had shouted her name, or only whispered it. He felt himself beginning to float. Then he saw her face.

"Oh my God Terry! Stay with me Terry." He heard her voice far away.

"Pull it out," Terry heard himself say from across the room.

"Stay still honey."

"Pull it out. Now. We need it." He felt his back drop onto the bed. He was floating again. Then it came. Pain like he had never felt before. Pain that rushed to his head until he knew it would blow the top off his skull. Pain so sickening that death would be sweet relief. Then he heard a pop in the front of his eyes, and saw a flash of very bright light, growing large and then immediately beginning to shrink until there was nothing.

Sarah stood panting, trying to stop the violent shaking in her arms and legs. She still held the blood-soaked knife in both hands. Blood, Terry's blood, dripped onto his trousers. A puddle of blood grew on the floor around his right foot. He was unconscious.

She heard crashing behind her and a fresh wave of terror gripped her. George! How could she have taken her eyes from him? Sarah raised the knife and whirled around, expecting to see his hands reaching for her throat. Instead, George was next to the door, staggering, bracing against the wall as he tossed the chair away from the door and opened it. He stopped in the doorway and turned his head. The look in his eyes raised hair on her arms.

"I'll be back," he said between gasps of breath. "And when I do, I'll kill you both!" He staggered outside, leaving the door open. Sarah didn't breathe. She felt she was in a block of ice. Then suddenly it shattered and her lungs gulped the air.

Then Sarah heard the engine, then gravel. "My car!" she shouted. She wanted to run to the door and look, but her legs wouldn't work. She watched, paralyzed, as the BMW shot past. The sound of its engine faded. Then there was silence, broken only by a soft dripping sound. She looked over the end of the bed. Blood from the bottom of Terry's tan scrubs continued to drip into the red pool surrounding his shoe. She ran to the door and slammed it, sliding the dead bolt. Then she rushed to the telephone and dialed 9-1-1. She glanced at Terry. He was pale, but his chest was still rising and falling.

She heard a woman's voice in her ear and turned to the phone. "9-1-1 emergency."

"Please hurry. A man's been stabbed in the thigh and he's unconscious."

"Who am I speaking with?"

"This is Sarah Stafford."

"And you say someone has been stabbed?"

"Yes. Terry Woodrow. Please hurry."

"What's the address?"

"Oh God, I don't know!"

"You don't know the address?"

"It's a motel."

"What's the name of the motel?"

"I don't know!" Sarah started to cry.

"Ma'am, try to stay calm. We'll find you. Stay on the line with me while we trace the call."

"Okay." She tried to stop crying, but the sobs continued to choke out.

"Ma'am, you say Mr. Woodrow's been stabbed?"

"Yes," Sarah said. "The Lago-Mar."

"Pardon?"

"The Lago-Mar Motel. That's where I am."

"Okay. Now try to concentrate. Who stabbed Mr. Woodrow?"

"George Fields."

"Is he still there?"

"No."

"Did you see him stab Mr. Woodrow?"

The question stopped Sarah cold. "No. I had locked myself in the bathroom. But I know he did." Sarah looked at the knife. It was still in her hand, and she was covered in blood. Fear gripped her again. What if they accuse her of stabbing Terry? Her fingerprints are all over the knife! "I didn't stab him. You've got to believe me!"

"Ma'am, try to stay calm. You say Mr. Woodrow is unconscious?"

"Yes. Please hurry."

"I want you to place your index finger against his neck and see if you feel a pulse."

Sarah wanted to tell her she was watching Terry breathe, but she did as she was told. "Yes."

"You feel a pulse?"

"Yes."

"Okay, we've located you. Police and the rescue unit have been dispatched. The station's just up the road. Stay on the line with me until they get there."

Sarah sat on the edge of the bed and stared at the knife. She wanted to put it down and wash the blood from her hand. But that might make the police even more suspicious. She thought about wiping the knife handle so her fingerprints wouldn't be on it. But that would make it look even worse!

Oh Terry, please wake up. She imagined being handcuffed and put in the back of the squad car. She imagined sitting in a jail cell filled with dangerous people, waiting for Terry to wake up in his hospital bed. *What if he has amnesia when he wakes and doesn't remember anything, doesn't even recognize me?*

"Stop it!" Sarah shouted aloud.

"Excuse me, ma'am?" the 9-1-1 dispatcher said.

"Nothing. I was talking to myself." *Great Sarah, now they think you're some kind of loony, a multiple personality slasher who talks to the "others" in her head!* She heard noises outside.

"Ma'am. Police and rescue are outside your door. Please let them in."

Sarah hung up the phone, unbolted the door, and opened it. A black uniformed officer looked at Sarah and drew her weapon. The officer behind her did the same. "Do not move unless we tell you to," the first officer said sharply. Sarah blinked.

"Put the weapon on the ground, slowly. Keep your other hand where we can see it."

Weapon? It wasn't her weapon! Sarah bent down slowly and placed the knife onto the threshold of the door.

"Now step back slowly and raise your hands over your head," the officer said. Sarah stepped back and raised her hands. "Back. Back. Stop! Hands over your head. Higher!"

Sarah pushed her hands straight up. Her eyes stared at the end of the pistol pointed at her. Tears streaked down both cheeks. "Higher!" She tried to reach higher, but she couldn't. She felt dizzy and realized she was swaying. *They were never going to believe her about George and Emil. They wouldn't believe any of it.* She watched the first officer step over the knife into the motel room holstering her gun, while the second officer filled the doorway, his gun still trained on Sarah.

The first officer spoke. Her voice was loud and hard. "Turn around!" She felt the officer run her hands up each side of Sarah's rib cage and then pat her shorts' pockets. She felt the officer squeeze something, and then reach into Sarah's right pocket and pull out the wad of napkins. There was a pause and then Sarah heard a soft whistle. She knew without looking that the officer was counting the fifteen one thousand dollar bills tucked in between the napkins. *She's never going to believe me about them, either.*

"Lower your hands and place them behind your back." It was happening. She felt cold steel encircle one wrist, and then the other. She heard the clicking as they tightened. *Oh Jesus, help me! Terry, please wake up!*

The officer sat her on the bed as paramedics rushed past her to Terry on the other bed. The second officer holstered his gun and leaned over the knife in the doorway. The money was on the floor in front of her. The first officer towered over her. Her complexion was very dark.

"I'm Officer Jenkins and this is my partner, Officer Hartwig. What's your name?" she asked.

"Sarah Stafford," she said looking at the gun in the officer's holster.

"Any ID?"

"No."

"Miss Stafford, it is my duty to inform you of your rights before we go any further. You have the right to remain silent. Anything you say…." The officer droned through her Miranda rights, but Sarah barely heard her. *Where are you, Jesus? Why have you forsaken me?*

"Do you understand your rights, Miss Stafford?"

"Yes. Is Terry all right?" She turned to look behind her and toppled over.

The officer sat Sarah back up, but Sarah was still looking behind her. The bed behind her was surrounded with people. She overheard them talking about how impossible it is to stop blood loss from a severed femoral artery. A sudden shot of adrenaline raced through her chest. *Terry might bleed to death!*

When she turned around again, the female officer was squatting down in front of her, smiling. The sharp voice and look were gone. "Want to tell me what happened?"

"Will you believe me, even if it sounds bizarre?"

"Miss Stafford, I believe everyone until I find out that they've lied to me."

"I won't lie to you," Sarah said, wiping tears with her shoulders. "But I suppose everybody says that to you too."

"Not everybody," Officer Jenkins said still smiling. "But I'm pretty good at spotting liars. And I can usually tell when someone is telling the truth. So why don't you explain this mess to me."

Sarah told Officer Jenkins step by step what had happened, from the moment she had knocked on Reverend Fields' door to the moment George sped away in her car. Several times the officer slowed her down, even made her repeat certain details while she took notes.

"And you say the feds are involved?" she asked with eyebrows raised.

Sarah nodded. "Captain Steele. I don't know his first name. Oh, and Lieutenant Higgins, I think. Don't know his first name, either." The paramedics were negotiating a bed on wheels into the room, with an accordion of aluminum tubes supporting it underneath. Sarah stared as it passed, then looked at Officer Jenkins again. "You can call ... wherever it is you call to reach the FBI, and they'll vouch I'm telling you the truth."

"Relax, Miss Stafford. Remember, I'm the one who believes people until they prove to be liars. You're doing fine." Sarah knew it was a ploy, a tactic to keep her talking. Probably Officer Jenkins didn't believe any of it.

"Tell me again about the stabbing," Officer Jenkins said.

"Terry stood up and stepped in front of me. George was holding the knife. Terry told me to lock myself in the bathroom. I did. I heard a lot of noise through the door, and then I heard Terry call my name. I opened the bathroom door and saw George curled up on the floor and Terry on the bed with the knife sunk into his thigh. Terry told me to pull it out. Twice he told me to do it. I didn't want to, but he said we needed it. So I grabbed it with both hands and pulled it out. It was awful. There was blood everywhere. Then I heard George behind me. Somehow he got my keys. He stood in the doorway, and told me he was coming back to kill us both and then he left in my car."

"That's quite a story."

"It's the truth. I called 9-1-1 and here you are."

"So when we arrived, you were holding the knife because you pulled it out of his leg, not because you stabbed him with it."

"Right."

"So how do you explain this?" The officer pointed to the wad of money and napkins on the floor.

Sarah explained about the man in the felt hat, about the first time she had seen him, and about his dropping off food and a rosary, and the money. "Go look underneath the bed. I'm sure there's still a wrapper or two under there. Then check the waste basket. You'll find some greasy biscuits and a torn bag. The man left me enough food for three people."

Officer Jenkins rose and walked between the beds. Officer Hartwig approached Sarah and asked her to stand and turn around. She felt him scraping blood from her hand and wrist. Then he sat her back down on the bed.

Terry had been lifted to the stretcher and was being strapped down. Officer Jenkins leaned down low between the beds, then reached under Terry's bed and grabbed a couple of wrappers. She wadded them quickly in her hand and stuck them behind her back. She returned to Sarah.

"Okay, quiz time: Do you remember what you ate under there?"

"An egg and cheese biscuit and two slabs of hash browns. Oh and a sausage biscuit with cheese."

The officer produced the wrappers. "Perfect score, Miss Stafford. Now, for your sake and for the safety of a lot of other people, let's call the police in Rhode Island and see if they have heard of Captain Steele and …." She scanned her notes, "Lieutenant Higgins." Terry was being wheeled on the stretcher past them, and Sarah sprang to her feet.

"Please may I go with him?" she asked.

"Let's let them do their job and patch that hole. If we can clear a few things up here, I'll drive you to the hospital myself."

The paramedics loaded the stretcher, and were gone in a blaze of lights and a blast of horns.

Officer Jenkins was on the telephone in the room. After some haggling, she got the person she wanted on the line.

"Chief Parker? I'm Officer Thelma Jenkins, New Hampshire PD." she said into her receiver. "Yes, well, I'm sorry to bother you sir, but we have a stabbing up here in New Hampshire and we are trying to corroborate a story." She paused and listened. "Yes sir, I understand that, but these are unusual circumstances. Could you please tell me if you are working with a Captain Steele and a Lieutenant Higgins, FBI, on an investigation down there." She listened again. "You are!" She grinned broadly toward Sarah. "Have you got a number for him? Thank you sir." The officer scribbled on the pad next to the telephone. "Sorry to have bothered you." She hung up the phone and looked at Sarah.

"You win the prize," she said. Sarah stared at her, feeling the exhaustion sink deep in her bones. "I've been told some tall tales in my fifteen years on the force, and there's a phrase we use. 'Tall on tale, short on truth.' But yours is by far the tallest, and it is checking out." She laughed.

"I know this is fun for you, officer, but it's not for me," Sarah said hotly. Officer Jenkins approached her and produced a small key. She inserted it in the handcuffs and they sprang open. Sarah rubbed her wrists and shuddered.

"I'm sorry, Miss Stafford -"

"No you're not," she snapped, "And you don't need to be. I wouldn't have believed me either." She continued to massage the feeling back into her hands. "May I wash up now?"

"Not a good idea. Let's get going. In the meantime I'll call Captain Steele. I'm sure he'll want to be briefed."

"I need a change of clothes. I've got money."

"I'll say you do!" Officer Hartwig said, "But who's going to be able to break a thousand dollar bill?"

Silence rested in the squad car as they rode.

Sarah knew people died from leg wounds when they weren't treated soon enough. She had sat with a family in the ICU last summer. The husband had been shot in the leg deer hunting, and he hadn't been found before he had lost a critical amount of his blood. That was the first time she had heard the term, "bleed-out." It wasn't like he had been shot in the chest or the head, Sarah had reassured the family. But the man died ... from loss of blood. Don't you dare die on me, Terry, not after ... everything.

Part of her was still angry with him. How could he be so shallow? But the finger she pointed showed up, again, in a mirror and it was pointing back at her. She couldn't judge him, unless she herself was willing to be judged. Truth was they were both guilty. How could I have been so shallow? She closed her eyes and let the water soak the top of her head and rush down along thick strands of hair. Neither of them could do the right thing. Neither of them could help themselves. They needed divine help - both of them. It was their bond.

Sarah watched the road fall beneath the front of the police car. Finally she spoke, "Are we getting close to the hospital?"

"Two miles away. You're anxious to see that boy, aren't you."

Sarah looked out the window at nothing.

"I saw the way you looked at him," Officer Jenkins said. "I got a trained eye. I knew early on you'd rather stab your own self than cause that man a moments' pain."

Chapter Twenty-Three

Residence of Brother Lawrence

"Stop here Lieutenant," Steele said. The unmarked sedan rolled to a quiet stop a few yards from the intersection of Route 60 and Bingham, and the agents got out. Steele walked to the intersection and looked down Bingham. It was paved for about 200 yards and then turned to rutted brown dirt. Mailboxes leaned away from the road at different angles every few feet, getting further apart toward the end of the pavement. No two boxes were angled alike, giving the straight section of road a swaying look. After about a hundred yards of hard-pack dirt barely wide enough for one car to pass, the road turned sharply left and disappeared into the middle of thick woods. Fat evergreens mixed with giant oaks and gum trees. The underbrush looked thick and foreboding.

"Well Higgins, doesn't look like there's any way to sneak up on Brother Lawrence. He's going to see us way before we see him."

"Think he's back in those woods?"

"Let's go see." They climbed back into the dark blue Oldsmobile and turned right onto Bingham. The asphalt hadn't been repaired any more regularly than the dirt had been graded. The shocks popped in the ruts, forcing Higgins to slow to a fast crawl. Steele scanned the houses on both sides of the street. Trash and rusted automobiles adorned several lawns. Sun-faded plastic toys littered others. Almost every house had a dusty dog tied up somewhere in the yard. Steele counted seven pit bulls before the car reached the end of the asphalt. Not a good sign.

The closer they got to the woods, the denser it appeared. The car followed the dirt road left at a 45 degree angle. The trees seemed to swallow them. Even the bright late afternoon sun barely penetrated the dense cover above, and the thick brown and green underbrush stretched into the road.

"This is what I call living in the country," Higgins muttered.

"Great place to live if you like to smoke crack," Steele said, his eyes searching the narrowing road ahead. The car lurched in and out of a large rut on the right side of the road. Steele caught himself with a stiff arm to the dash, and shot an irritated glance at his partner.

"I didn't see it," Higgins said.

The road was fast becoming two tire ruts with a weed Mohawk rising between. The high cover of branches seemed to lower, and it felt more and more like jungle than woods. Something brown and square came into view far ahead on the left. It was a sign of some sort. Directly in front of them, Steele saw a wide metal gate.

"Can you read that?" Steele said pointing across Higgins' chest.

"Says 'Park Car Here.'"

"You mean we can't drive to the house?"

Higgins shrugged, put the car in park and they got out. They both stood silent on either side of the car. The stillness was giving Steele the creeps. His instinct told him to unholster his weapon, but he shook it off. *This is not Vietnam, Steele.* Something about this place was loosening the memories again. They came hard and real. He brushed against a low hanging branch. A memory surged. Snake! It had wrapped around his waist in the foxhole while he slept. He wrestled the thick head with both hands. Then the head was free from the body and blood from the severed neck spattered his face. The corpsman next to him sheathed his bayonet and pulled the headless reptile off him.

Steele shuddered and shoved the memory back into the deepest drawer in his mind. He reached to straighten his utility belt. His hands felt the empty air. No utility belt. *This is not the jungle. This is not Vietnam.*

He took a deep breath and started toward the silver metal gate. Higgins followed behind in silence. A crow hollered directly above them and both men jerked toward the sound. Looking into the branches and leaves against the hot, thin shafts of light, Steele saw the outlines of five large birds. Not a good sign, he thought, and then grinned at himself. Easy does it, Steele.

He pulled the latch and the gate gave way to a smooth path covered in dirty rock chips. He looked ahead. No house in sight. The path took a lazy curve to the right, and as they rounded it, a house began to come into view. It was an A-framed log house, jammed into the hillside and propped high atop massive pilings. Steele and Higgins emerged from the path into a tight clearing below the house. An extensive mass of multi-leveled decking surrounded the house on three sides and obscured all but the peak of the A-frame from the path. They had to crane their necks to look at it. Stairs made from railroad ties led up the side of the right deck.

The stillness was screaming DANGER in Steele's ears, but he couldn't sort reality from memory. At the top of the steps, a waist high wooden gate to the deck was ajar. Steele and Higgins stepped through it onto the deck. Almost the entire front wall of the house was glass, from the floor to the roof. An elaborate set of bamboo blinds covered most of the glass. Several large panels at the bottom appeared to be sliding glass doors.

"Any idea where the front door is?" Higgins asked quietly. A squirrel chattered at them from a tree above.

"I'm still trying to figure out which side is the front of the house. Let's try knocking on one of these sliding glass doors." They walked to the one in the center of the glass wall and knocked. There was no sound, no movement. They peered through the glass. Light colored hardwood floors ran the length of a great room. A huge field stone fireplace nestled into the far left corner. To the right was a small kitchen area. The furniture was plain wood with solid brown cushions. Captain Steele knocked again. Nothing. They waited another minute, then turned and walked to the railing of the deck. Below and far to the right, Steele saw a clearing with a dozen or so sheep. He wondered if Brother Lawrence owned this entire area. He looked hard and long in every direction.

"No sign of Brother Lawrence," he said.

"Come to think of it," Higgins said, "I didn't see his car parked by that sign, or anywhere else."

Captain Steele nodded. "We're wasting time here. Let's circle back later." They walked back through the gate and down the railroad ties to the path. It seemed a much shorter walk to the cars. Near it, Steele heard a twig snap to his right. He whirled and stared into the woods, holding his breath and listening.

"You okay Cap?" Higgins said.

Steele realized he was in a crouch. He righted himself and smiled. "A little jumpy I guess." The memories surged. He slammed the drawer again.

The unmarked car made an awkward three point turn in the narrow lane and headed slowly along the dirt ruts around the bend. In the underbrush near the sign, a lump of fallen branches twitched. The darkened eyes in the center of them blinked. The car was gone. A shrill sound came from beneath the leaves, a single call sounding almost exactly like a Carolina Wren. Behind the sign across the lane, a bird answered with two shrill calls. At the bend in the lane, three calls could be heard. High in the tree tops toward the house, four shrill calls sounded. From somewhere along the gravel path came five shrill calls.

All accounted for. Good.

Near the highest point of the hill behind Brother Lawrence's house, a man in full black leathers closed the metal case. He took three quick breaths and folded the camouflage tripod, pushing the legs to their shortest length. He returned them to their hiding place in a hovel of sticks and brush. Then he put a solid black, full-faced helmet on his head and buckled the chin strap. He straddled the seat of his jet black, four wheeled All-Terrain Vehicle and pressed the starter button. With one last glance toward the A-frame below, he turned the vibrating machine around and raced down the back side of the hill toward the meadow.

Time! Toward the base of the hill, he glanced at the speedometer. Sixty-two miles per hour. *Easy does it. You've got to be alive to deliver the message.* He had slowed to fifty-five by the time he leveled out. He skidded to a stop at the gate to the sheep pen, jumped off the ATV, opened the gate, drove through, and closed himself in. He jumped back on and raced through the sheep to the other side. He repeated the process to get out of the sheep pen on the other side. He shot through the clearing on the other side and disappeared into the thickness of the forest.

"Where to, Cap?" Higgins said as the Oldsmobile's tires found asphalt again.

Steele smacked his hand on the front seat. "There's so much we don't know. It's like trying to get your arms around a giant squid. You find one arm and grab it, and four more stretch away from you." He looked at Higgins. "We need more help." Steele opened the cell phone and dialed. After a few seconds, he heard a deep male voice.

"First Precinct, Officer Stendahl."

"This is Captain Max Steele, FBI. Chief Parker please."

"I'm sorry sir but the Chief is not available -"

"Not available!" Steele couldn't contain himself. "He'd better make himself available. Right now."

"Actually, he's not here sir," Officer Stendahl said.

"Where is he?" Captain Steele demanded.

"We don't know, sir. The log shows he signed out this morning. Haven't been able to raise him on the radio or the cell all afternoon."

"That's strange."

"Not so strange for him, sir."

"Tell me, who's the officer in charge when Parker's out?"

"I am, sir," Stendahl said.

"Then let me leave my cell number in case he calls in." Steele recited the information. "In the meantime, there are a few things I need. Can you handle a tough assignment?"

"I hope so, sir."

"Expedite paperwork for a warrant to search the residence of Brother Lawrence Stiles, 321 Bingham."

"Okay. Anything else?"

"Elevate to 'urgent' the status of the search for the vehicles I radioed in earlier. I don't care how you do it, but they must be found. Set up road blocks, check points, whatever it takes. Notify Massachusetts and New Hampshire and request that they do the same thing."

"I'm not sure I have the authority -"

"I'm FBI. I'm giving you the authority!"

"Yes sir."

"One more thing," Steele said. "Check with the forensics lab on finger-prints collected at Nina Bente's apartment and George Fields' house. As soon as you have the results, call me."

He snapped the cell phone closed. "We seem to have lost our Junior FBI agent," he said to Higgins.

"So I gathered, sir. He wasn't much help to us, though. Almost more trouble than-"

"That's what bothers me." Steele crossed his arms over his chest. "This whole thing gets stranger by the minute."

Higgins nodded.

"But some of it's also starting to make sense," Steele said.

"Am I beginning to see a net in your hands?" Higgins said. The two agents exchanged grins. The cell phone vibrated and rang noisily in Steele's coat pocket.

"Steele."

"Captain Steele, this is Officer Jenkins, New Hampshire PD. Sorry to trouble you again, sir."

"No trouble, Officer Jenkins. What you got?"

"I just put Terry Woodrow and Sarah Stafford on a bird headed your way. Woodrow is being taken to Memorial with a severe leg bleed. Severed femoral artery. Too serious to deal with here. A Sarah Stafford says she needs to speak with you urgently."

"Radio a message through the chopper's pilot to Stafford that I'll meet her at Memorial."

"Roger that, Captain."

Steele closed the cell phone and stared at Higgins. "I need to go to the hospital," he said, "and I need you to do some more sleuthing." He grabbed a pad of paper from the back seat and reached into his jacket for a pen.

"Great," Higgins said. "Which foxes will I be trying to pull from their holes this time?"

"I'm making you a list." Steele explained the bare outline of the plan formulating in his head as he wrote. Then he settled in for the long ride into town. His thoughts drifted to Dr. Sanchez. He could sure use a cup of Maria's coffee. "When we get to Memorial, drop me off at the ER," he said.

"This must be an emergency," Higgins said sarcastically and grinned.

"It is." Steele opened his cell phone again and dialed Memorial.

"Dr. Maria Sanchez, ER please," Steele said when the operator answered.

"This is Dr. Sanchez."

"Hello Gorgeous," Steele said smiling.

There was a pause on the other end of the line. Steele watched Higgins wag his head and mimic the words silently with his mouth.

"That's Dr. Gorgeous to you," Dr. Sanchez said drily.

"Any update on Nina Bente?"

"Her status has changed to 'critical,' but I don't have any details. Want me to check?"

"Would you please," Steele said. "Listen, Higgins is dropping me off on your doorstep in about half an hour and I was wondering if you had any of that wonderful coffee." He could feel his cheeks tighten into a broad grin.

"It'll be hot when you get here."

"Which?"

"Bad boy," she whispered.

He laughed. "You're getting a helicopter from New Hampshire soon."

"I just heard. Terry Woodrow."

"Right. Sarah Stafford is with him. Think she and I can reserve the break room for a chat when she gets there?"

"Me first," she said.

"Always," he said. "I'll be there in thirty." He closed the cell phone, still smiling broadly.

"You got it bad Cap," Higgins said, feigning alarm.

"I got it good, Lieutenant, so good." Max could feel the protective shell crack. For the first time in more than ten years, that deep, gnawing loneliness had left him. He straightened in the passenger seat and continued writing the list for Higgins. After a few minutes, he looked over at his partner. "Can't you make this buggy go any faster?"

Higgins smiled. "You want me to break the law?"

"Yes."

"You're desperate, Cap."

"Thirsty." He smiled. "Here's your list." Steele set the pad on the seat between them.

Several minutes of silence later, Higgins pulled the unmarked car around the back of Memorial Hospital and dislodged his smiling passenger. Max had to concentrate to slow his footsteps. He wanted to rush in and scoop

Maria into his arms, but he did his best to walk casually and appear non-chalant. He passed through the ER waiting room and into the back. It didn't appear as chaotic as it had the last time he was there. To his right, he saw a young boy holding a red-blotched washcloth to the side of his head. His anxious mother stroked his arm and spoke softly to him.

Max stopped. Strange things were happening to him. Before, he wouldn't even have noticed the boy. He would have come into the ER seeing nothing but his own goals before his eyes. Something was definitely different now. He was different.

"Sir, are you lost?" The familiar voice behind him whirled him around. He looked into Maria's warm eyes.

"Actually, I think I was," Max Steele said, "but that seems to be changing." He swam in the ocean of her eyes. Maria looked away shyly. Max recovered himself slightly. "Actually doctor, I was looking for something hot." Maria's eyebrows shot toward the top of her head. "To drink," he said quickly. She gave him the 'bad boy' scowl again. "I was looking for the coffee pot." He grinned into her face.

"Right this way sir," Maria said in mock formality. She led him to the break room, but stopped at the doorway and pointed to the fresh coffee waiting on the burner across the room.

"Aren't you coming in?" Max asked.

Maria shook her head. "The last time I did that, you attacked me."

"I'm sorry."

"Don't be," she said, smiling.

"I was going to attack you again," Max said, lifting the pot from the burner and pouring coffee into a Styrofoam cup.

"Try again tonight," she whispered into the room.

"Whatever you say, Maria," he said. "See, I'm practicing my lines."

"I'm feeling lightheaded," Maria laughed.

"I'm feeling crazy about you, Dr. Sanchez."

Maria leaned on the door jamb. "The helicopter landed about ten minutes ago. The surgical team is prepped and ready for Woodrow. Let me go see if I can locate Sarah Stafford." She straightened up.

"Thanks." Steele poured himself into the plastic chair and leaned his elbows on the table. He rubbed his thumb and his middle finger hard along his forehead just above his eyebrows. As long as he kept going, he kept the exhaustion at bay. But when he stopped like this, it rushed him. He felt like he had just finished two hours at the gym. His arms felt heavy, his head like a bowling ball. The cell phone vibrated and chirped, and Steele jumped, spilling a little coffee. The scalding liquid on his fingers woke him fast. He grabbed the phone from his pocket.

"Steele."

"Officer Rick Stendahl from the First Precinct, Captain Steele."

"Yes, Officer Stendahl. What've you got for me?"

"Some moderately good news and some really bad news."

"Give it to me," Steele said wearily.

"Good news first," Officer Stendahl said. "We got lucky on the vehicle search. Within minutes of my call, a Massachusetts patrolman happened to spot the BMW parked at a Walgreen's."

"Man that was fast," Steele said. "They get the driver?"

"No. Only a description. The vehicle was abandoned, but the Walgreen's cashier gave a description: white male, fifties, medium build, brownish hair, holding a napkin to what looked like a nasty wound on his forehead. Said he bought some gauze and a baseball cap, and left."

"Doesn't do us much good," Steele thought aloud.

Officer Stendahl continued. "The warrant to search 321 Bingham is in the works. Should have it in less than an hour." He paused. "The really bad news, sir, is that the lab seems to have lost the fingerprint folder."

"What?" Steele shouted. "Impossible!"

"It's never happened before, Captain Steele. They're scrambling down there. The forensics team handed it off to the specialist. Apparently, he put it in his hand personally. The specialist had it on his desk one minute, and it was gone the next."

"You think it was taken?" Steele's mind was reeling.

"Unlikely sir," Officer Stendahl said. "Security's tight as a drum down there.

"Okay officer, one more assignment for you. I want a list of everyone – everyone – who went in or out of that lab since the forensics unit returned. When you have the list, I want you to call my partner, Agent Bert Higgins. Let me give you the number." Steele gave it to him and closed the flap on the phone. He looked up to see Dr. Sanchez standing next to a pensive looking Sarah Stafford.

He rose from his plastic chair and extended his hand. "Hello again, Miss Stafford. How was your flight?"

Sarah offered her hand and smiled weakly. "I'm terrified of heights."

"Me too," Steele said, offering her the other plastic chair. Dr. Sanchez was already gone. "My first helicopter ride was a nightmare." He watched her shoulders relax.

"Would you like some coffee?" Steele said. "Something from the vending machines?"

"I'd like you to call me Sarah," she said, "and my stomach is too upset to eat. But maybe in a little bit, I might like that apple right there." She pointed into the belly of one of the machines. Poor woman. She's probably starving. He sprang to his feet and fed a dollar bill into the machine. After studying the buttons, he pushed a letter and a number, and the apple fell gently to the bottom tray. He pulled it out and set it in front of her.

"Thank you."

"You're welcome, Sarah. And will you please call me Max?"

Sarah looked up startled. "I'm not sure I can."

"Try. It'd make me feel better." Sarah looked quizzically at him. Steele continued, "How's Terry?"

"He was in and out of consciousness on the flight here, Max," Sarah said the name hesitantly. "They say he's lost a lot of blood and they need to reattach a big artery in his leg."

"And you say Reverend Fields stabbed him?"

She nodded. "But he was after me, said he could never allow me to tell what I know."

"This is unbelievable, Sarah," Steele said.

"I know."

"But I believe you, so don't let any doubt about that add to your stress."

"Thanks," Sarah said. "It was horrible, like living a nightmare, except it was so real."

"So what do you know that Reverend Fields doesn't want you to tell?"

"Reverend Fields isn't what he appears to be. He's a long time crack user... with Mr. B-"

"Emil Bente?"

"Yes, they ordered me to call him Mr. B and the big man Mr. V."

"Vinnie Bontecelli. Go on."

"So, they grabbed me at George's house and we ended up in a motel in New Hampshire. Bente and George were doing crack right in front of me in the motel room, and Bente was threatening to rape and kill me, but Mr. V., Vinnie, kept him away from me."

"Thank God," Steele said, and was immediately surprised that he had said something like that. It was the new Max Steele.

Sarah nodded and continued. "Anyway, Vinnie left in the morning to steal a car while the others were still asleep and I pretended to escape, but really I was under the bed. I called Terry and somehow he got out of the hospital-"

"I'm sorry to interrupt you, Sarah, but for my own curiosity's sake, how did Terry do it?"

"I have no idea. It's one of a thousand things I want to ask him when he wakes up."

"Let me know what he says." He smiled and Sarah returned the smile.

"Anyway, Terry got my car and came to get me, but not before I had a visitor." She paused. "I was under the bed and the door opened and a man with a thick accent came in and talked with me. I still can't figure how he knew where I was. But here's the shocker. He never looked under the bed and I never saw his face. But he dropped his felt hat by mistake on the floor. Max, it was the same guy I saw posing as Reverend Fields in the ICU."

"Whoa!" Max lifted his hands from the table.

"I know! I was blown away," Sarah was speaking quickly and gesturing with her hands. "He spoke so kindly, and he brought me a ton of food from the Burger King, and in the napkins he left me a wad of money."

"Slow down Sarah," Steele said. "I want to make sure I'm getting all of this. Are you certain it was the same man you saw in the ICU?"

"Positive. The reason I know is because of the other thing he left me. Sarah reached in her pocket and withdrew the black pearl rosary. Steele stared at it in silence. His mouth opened, but Sarah continued. "And look what was in the napkins!" Sarah reached into her other pocket and fished out the fifteen one thousand dollar bills. She dropped them on the table and reached for the apple. Steele watched her smell the top of it and then take a big bite.

"The Shark," Steele said softly. But he sure wasn't acting like the man who had earned that title.

"Who?" Sarah said with apple in both cheeks.

"Emil Bente's father," Max said. "It had to be him. But by the way he treated you, it couldn't have been him. Everyone on the street and in the Bureau call him the Shark. He's a killer."

Sarah looked pale. "I can't explain it. All I know is the man who came into that room knew exactly who I was, and where I was, and he was as kind and gentle as could be. His only concern was to make sure I was okay."

"Incredible." Steele whispered. "The gentler side of S."

Sarah was gnawing hungrily on the apple. "He was very kind and left after a few minutes. I never saw him again."

"No one sees the Shark," Steele said, "until it's too late." His mind filled with Bull's face, and the sadness flooded him again.

"Are you okay?" She tossed the apple core into the waste basket behind her and turned back around. Steele saw the concern in her eyes.

"I'm sorry Sarah. Please go on."

"So I stayed under the bed until Terry got there. We opened the door to leave and there was George, covered in blood with a big kitchen knife in his hand. He threatened to kill us both, but like I said earlier, the one he really wanted was me. Terry fought with him and got stabbed in the leg and George left in my BMW." She stopped and looked into Steele's face. "I heard him say he was headed to Brother Lawrence's house. By the way, that's where Mr. V was headed too."

"That's because Brother Lawrence has what they both want," Steele said.

Sarah nodded. "The cocaine."

"Emil Bente too?" Steele asked.

"I was getting to that. George said he killed Emil, stabbed him to death. He pointed to the blood on his arms and said it was Emil's." Sarah shuddered.

"He said he killed Bente," Steele said, hoping it wasn't true. "But you didn't see the body."

"No."

"And from what you know about the Assistant Dean, wouldn't you think his story a little farfetched, a bit of bravado perhaps? Seems a little out of character."

"Until yesterday I would have said so," Sarah said. Steele watched the fear flood her face. "But not now. I looked into his eyes. I watched him move. I heard what he said." The panic was rising in her voice. "Captain Steele, you've got to protect me and Terry. He's still out there, and the last thing he said to me was 'I'll kill you both.' I believe him."

Steele reached deep into his other jacket pocket and extracted a small walkie-talkie. He turned it on, pressed the button and spoke. "Agents Deet and Ryan, report."

The radio squawked. "Deet here," a man's voice said. "Ryan here," a woman's voice said.

Steele pushed the button again, his tone official. "You two stay in ICU. All other agents, report to the ER for re-assignment." He set the radio on the table. "Look at me Sarah," he said. "I promise to keep you and Terry safe. Please try not to worry." Sarah's eyes were moist. He continued softly. "You've been through so much in the last few days." She nodded and he smiled. "And I'll bet you're worrying about missing so many classes." She smiled again.

"I've been so busy trying to stay alive," she said, "that I've hardly had the time or the energy to think about it. But this is crunch time in the semester, and Terry and I are going to be so far behind."

"I'll make sure your professors are contacted and that they know you are on special assignment with the FBI." He smiled. "With a little arm twisting, that might be worth some internship credit."

Sarah laughed and wiped the tears on her cheek. "You think somebody could get my books? I'm not sure I can concentrate, but over the next couple of days I'd like to try. I don't want to lose a whole semester's work."

"We won't let that happen. Try not to worry."

"Thank you, Max. You're being so kind."

"So are you, Sarah. I bet you'd rather stick your finger down your throat than rehearse the nightmare of the last couple of days, but here you are filling in some major information gaps for me. Thank you."

Four people in various colored scrubs appeared in the doorway behind Sarah. Steele introduced her to the agents. "This is the undercover FBI," he said. They don't look so tough in those pajamas, but don't underestimate them." Everyone smiled. Sarah shook their hands. "First, let me clarify for Miss Stafford's sake," Steele said, "Are all of you armed?" Four voices echoed "Yes sir." He turned to Sarah. "You're safe. No more worrying."

"No more worrying," Sarah said.

"Fowler, Terry Woodrow is in surgery," Steele continued. "I want you at the doors to surgery. I want you with that bed every step of the way to recovery. As soon as you get there, call Williams and have her join you there. No one but the docs get to him, and one of you is to be in the room at all times. I'll get the details cleared through administration. Now go." One of the men disappeared.

"Now Williams," Steele said, "I want you to get on the horn to Ecclesia Seminary. I want Sarah Stafford and Terry Woodrow excused from their classes, test, and assignments. Tell Dean Jeremy Tittle to back me up on this. Then I want their books, supplies, and fresh clothes delivered to the hospital. Go." A woman in scrubs disappeared.

"Agents Black and Stake, I want you to find out which room Woodrow is going to after recovery. Make sure it's a private room, and get Miss Stafford set up there with a nice cot. One of you is to be with her at all times. Get her whatever she wants to eat or drink and charge it to my Bureau account. She could probably use a nice cold beer or a glass of wine about now."

"Definitely," Sarah smiled, "Beer. And pizza."

"Pizza and beer it is, Steele said. "I'll keep the radio on. If anything even remotely begins to feel wrong, get on the radio for backup." The agents nodded.

"Thank you so much, Max." Sarah rose and turned with the agents to leave, then turned back, leaned over, and gave him a peck on the cheek.

A moment after Sarah and the agents disappeared through the doorway, Dr. Sanchez's face appeared. She was beaming at him. "I've been outside the door, leaning on the wall, listening," she said. "That's just what that poor girl needed. You are such a sweetheart." She shut the door behind her and walked over to him. She sat on his lap and stroked the side of his face, lowering her lips to his.

After a long and tender kiss, Max came up for air. "That's just what I needed," he said and leaned toward her lips again. The cell phone in his pocket vibrated and rang, and Maria pulled away.

"Don't go," he pleaded. The phone rang again.

"To be continued, later," Maria said, opened the door, and disappeared through it. Max reached for the phone.

"Steele."

"Captain Steele, this is Officer Stendahl again. Have you got a minute?"

"Sure," Steele said, "Any developments?"

"Yes sir. The fingerprint file has been recovered."

"Good! Where was it?"

"The specialist preferred not to say, sir. Too embarrassing. But it's back and he has analyzed the fingerprints from the two houses. The two in question are a perfect match."

"So the same two people trashed both houses."

"It would appear so by the fingerprints, yes."

"Okay, now we're getting somewhere," Steele said. "So when we finger-print our suspects, we'll have 'em where it hurts."

"Yes sir. Oh, and your subpoena is ready to be picked up."

"Good. What about the other vehicle we're looking for?"

"Nothing yet, sir."

"Excellent work, Stendahl. I'll be down there shortly to pick up the sub-poena and to look in on one of your detainees, Hilary Fields." He closed the cell phone and opened it again to call Higgins, but he stopped midway through dialing and closed the phone again. He pulled out his wallet and found a dollar bill. Sarah's apple had looked so good he decided to have one himself. Then he'd call his partner. He fed the dollar into the slot and was inspecting the buttons again, when his ears tuned into the hospital intercom.

"Code Blue, ICU. All available physicians, we have a Code Blue in the ICU." Simultaneously, Steele's jacket pocket squawked. He pulled the radio to his face and pressed the button. "Say again," he said.

"Captain, it's Ryan," the woman's voice said. "You better get up here." Max left his money in the machine and sprinted for the elevators. He smacked the up arrow and it glowed white. He continued to push it while he looked at the two banks of numbers above the two elevator doors. Finally, the elevator on the right opened and he rushed in, pushing four and the button to close the doors.

When they opened again on the fourth floor, Agent Ryan was there to meet him. They walked together to the ICU.

"Nina Bente died," Steele said dejectedly, 'That's what you have to tell me."

"No sir," Agent Ryan said. She hit the red button on the wall, and the stainless steel ICU doors yawned open.

"Wasn't the Code for her?"

"It was, and it wasn't."

"I'm confused," Steele said, following Agent Ryan behind the counter.

Agent Ryan tapped a tall, thin man with a close-cropped beard and round wire-rimmed glasses. "Dr. Glaster, this is Captain Steele. Perhaps you can explain the situation to him." The two men shook hands.

"Nina Bente is in critical condition," Dr. Glaster said.

"I know," Steele said. "My people and Dr. Sanchez have been keeping me informed. What a mess."

Dr. Glaster nodded. "We have a new development. Mrs. Bente is stabilizing a little now that we have her on the new ventilator." His eyes changed.

"But we lost the baby. We tried everything we could think of, but the trauma and the lack of oxygen were too much for the little guy."

"I'm sorry to hear that," Steele said.

"Everyone's sorry. Unfortunately, that's not the last of the bad news. The non-viable fetus -"

"The dead baby?"

"Umm, yes. It poses a dramatic health risk to the mother, but in her condition, so would a surgical procedure such as a D & C. We have a terrible decision to make."

"Who's we?" Steele asked.

Chapter Twenty-Four

George shifted the BMW into fifth gear and raced toward the Massachusetts state line. Once he was in Massachusetts, he hoped to stop and clean himself up, but he couldn't imagine where he could wash blood off without attracting attention. He couldn't walk into a gas station or a fast food place without people seeing the dried blood and calling the police. Same for a rest stop, although in desperation, he had almost pulled into the rest stop 10 miles back. The simplest tasks of life seemed insurmountable challenges today. Something as simple as washing his hands, his face or his clothes, had become nearly impossible.

Then it came to him. His eyes searched both sides of the road for several miles, and there it was – a self-service car wash. He pulled the BMW into the furthest stall. Inside the BMW's center console compartment, he found a plastic container almost full of change. He inserted the quarters and the metal wand jerked in his hand. He pointed the thin wand at his hand, squeezed the trigger and a high pressure stream shot from the end. George shrieked. The water stung like a thousand bees. He needed someone to shoot that thing at him from the other side of the stall, but that wasn't an option. Finally, he chose pain and clean over no bee stings and still dried blood. It would be worth it to see that stuff disappear from his arms and legs.

George turned the metal dial on the wall to soap and sprayed his shirt and shorts. It would have been much less painful if he dared to take them off first, but he couldn't risk it. Soon he was soaking wet and covered with soap. He turned the metal knob to rinse and slowly the soapy water shooting from the end of the wand turned clear and he sprayed himself again, from head to toe. Still dripping wet, he dropped the wand, jumped into the BMW, and sped away.

Now he needed to find a pay phone and call Lawrence. He had to find out if the eggs were safe, and if his secret was safe. He glanced in the rear view mirror. His forehead! He needed a hat. He touched the wounds and winced. A hat was going to hurt.

George pulled into the Walgreen's parking lot and opened the glove box. No tissues, but he did find some leftover napkins. He pressed one of them to his forehead and entered the store, holding it against his head. Ignoring the stares of the salesclerks at his dripping clothes, he grabbed a few rolls of gauze. Then he went in search of a hat. He found a baseball cap with plastic mesh on the sides, an adjustable plastic strap in back, and the words 'Keep on Truckin' on the front. It would have to do.

A few minutes later he was sitting again in the front seat of the BMW, wrapping his head with gauze and easing on the ball cap. After a quick glance in the rear view mirror, George grabbed the container of change and got out. He had seen the outdoor pay phone two doors down at the gas station. A fast food restaurant sat in between the station and Walgreen's. The walk would do him good, and he could pick up some food on the way back.

George stepped gingerly over the curb separating the parking lots, amazed at how sore he was. His clothes were still wet and clung to his body. He wished he'd thought to buy deodorant. He pulled the cap lower on his forehead and winced in pain. He walked slowly around parked cars and across the small patch of grass near the fast food place. He walked around the back of the blue box with the telephone on the side and lifted the receiver. Thank God there was a dial tone. He dialed Lawrence's number. He heard a ring in his ear, and then another, and then a click. Hello?" the familiar voice came through the phone.

Immediately another voice spoke, "Please deposit two dollars and twenty cents." George set the plastic bowl on top of the box and fished in it for quarters and dimes. Don't hang up, Lawrence. He pushed the coins into the slot. The final coins went in with more trouble because his hands were shaking.

"Thank you for using South Intel Systems," the mechanical voice said.

"Lawrence, please tell me you're still there!" George said. He listened. Silence. "Lawrence, it's George." Another few seconds of silence. "Hello?" George shouted.

"I know who it is," Brother Lawrence said evenly. "What do you want?"

"What do I want! What do I want??"

"My, you are so upset," Lawrence said calmly.

"I want to make sure my rock is secure and that our little secret is safe," George said hotly.

"Your rock? It was never your rock, George. It was our rock for a little while, until you and your stupid wife started bringing the heat down around us. I went to Ecclesia this morning and the place was crawling with cops."

"Give me back my rock!"

"Now it's my rock. Now, it's every man for himself."

"Give back the eggs," George said, snarling.

"Can't do that."

"How much did you smoke up?" George could feel his fist clenching and unclenching at his side.

"Some of it. I stashed the rest."

"Give the rest back."

"What are you going to do, George? Call the police?"

"I'm coming to get what's mine."

"You're wasting your time," Brother Lawrence said coldly.

"I'll kill you."

"I don't think so, George. You've got no spine. Why don't you crawl back into that preaching robe and pretend there never were any plastic eggs."

"You don't know who you're messing with," George said. He felt his heart thump in his neck. "Emil didn't either, and now he's dead."

"I wouldn't make threats if I were you." Brother Lawrence paused. "You'd have an awful lot to lose if this ever got out."

"That's low."

"That's life." Lawrence's voice was hard, dispassionate.

"You're about to lose yours." George hissed the word with more violence than he knew was in him. He slammed the receiver down and started back for the BMW. Two steps later, he whirled and began walking toward the gas station again. A Massachusetts patrol car was parked directly behind the BMW and an officer with a broad brimmed hat was peering in the side windows. Another patrol car was pulling slowly into the Walgreen's parking lot.

George walked quickly into the gas station's mini-mart. A middle-aged woman with tired eyes and dyed jet black hair stood behind the counter. She dropped two packs of Kools in front of the young man on the other side of the counter and asked to see ID.

Behind the young man stood a man in his late fifties with greasy work boots and dark blue coveralls, waiting to pay for his quart of beer. George tapped him lightly on the shoulder. "If I pay for that beer, would you be willing to tell me where the bus station is around here and whether I can walk to it?"

The man eyed him warily for a moment, and then said, "You pay for this one and another just like it, and shoot, I'll take you there."

"You're a gentleman and a scholar," George said.

"I don't know nothin' about that now," the man mumbled.

The woman put the Kools back in the cigarette rack as the young man shuffled dejectedly through the door.

"These kids think I was born in a damn bubble," she muttered and rang up the two quarts of beer on the counter. George pulled cash from his wallet, and followed the older man to his truck. Once in the passenger seat, he stole a quick glance at the Walgreen's parking lot. Three squad cars, one with its lights flashing. George sat back in the seat and watched the man behind the wheel chug an entire quart of beer without pausing for a breath. Then he smacked his lips and put the truck in gear.

"You like busses?" the old man beside him asked, pulling out onto the road.

"Not really," George said.

"Well I like beer."

"That's nice." They rode in silence for a minute.

"I like beer a lot," he man said, eyeing George. George leaned against the passenger side door.

"I tell ya what," the old man said. "You keep buyin' the beer, and I'll take you wherever you like." He laughed, and it sent him into a coughing fit that nearly took them into oncoming traffic.

"Even to Rhode Island?"

"How much beer money you got?"

"More than you can drink," George said dryly.

"You ain't never seen me drink."

George smiled. "What's your name?"

"Billy," he said, "What's yers?"

"Buddy," George said. "Okay Billy, I'm in if you're in."

"Let's go, Buddy."

The gods were smiling on him. He would have to think through his story carefully before he faced the Ecclesia Board. Maybe he was abducted by Satanists who drugged him and brainwashed him into thinking he was one of them. In his drug-induced state, he stole a knife and slashed one of them during his escape. That was how he got the blood on him. Still drugged and disoriented, he had made his way back to the only landmark he recognized: the motel. The door to the motel room where he had been held captive opened, and inside he had found two people he didn't recognize. They were trying to hurt him, but he stabbed one of them in the thigh and got away in their car. Eventually, he found his way back to Ecclesia, and as the drugs wore off, his memory began to return. The man behind the wheel interrupted his thoughts.

"You on the run, Buddy?" Billy asked.

"Sort of." George decided to try his story out on the man, see how it played. He went through his story, detail by detail. When he finished, the man was silent for a few moments. Then, not looking at George, he spoke.

"That's the biggest load of horse-hooey I've ever heard!" He roared with laughter. George shook his head and looked at the dusk settling on the landscape. Trees and houses and yards ripped past the truck window.

Back to the drawing board.

The truck slowed and pulled into a truck stop. "Need more beer?" George asked.

"You gonna keep feeding me crap like that last story?"

"Yep."

"Then we need lots more beer," Billy said. "You better have some too, Buddy." He laughed again and coughed over the steering wheel.

"You're probably right." George closed the truck door and entered the truck stop. Two minutes later, he emerged with two large brown sacks and climbed into the truck. "This ought to hold us for fifty miles," he said.

The older man peered into the bags. "Thirty," he said and grabbed a quart.

Residence of Brother Lawrence

Vinnie drove the Mustang past the intersection of Route 60 and Bingham one more time. He craned his neck and studied the landscape. He'd have to stash the vehicle and make his way in on foot. He glanced over at the passenger seat. Crumpled remains of fast food wrappers leeched grease onto the seat. Used napkins lay in wads on the floor. Vinnie took the last two swallows of his coffee and tossed the paper cup onto the floor. He scanned both sides of the road for the next half mile, but saw no gas stations or business parking lots for him to leave the car. He made a U-turn in the middle of Route 60 and headed for the other side of the intersection.

He scratched the gray bristles on his chin. When he glanced in the rear view mirror, his hand stopped on the right side of his cheek. The flashing blue and red lights were close in the rear windshield. Where did that come from?

Vinnie slowed. Relax Vincente. Maybe he's just trying to get around you. Vinnie hit his right turn signal and eased the Mustang onto the shoulder of the road. The patrol car followed. Maybe it was that 180 you did back there. Is that illegal? Vinnie continued to bring the Mustang to a gradual stop. Slowly he reached into his jacket and squeezed the Glock in its holster. He hoped it wouldn't come to that. He glanced again in the rear view mirror as the Mustang came to a complete stop. The colored lights flicked furiously.

Vinnie's eyes darted around the inside of the car. Whoever owns this thing better have the registration in here somewhere. He reached for the glove box, yanked it open, and began throwing papers onto the fast food wrappers in the passenger seat. A loud double rap on the driver's side window startled him and instinctively, he reached for the Glock. Fool! He lowered his right hand and straightened in the seat. Forcing a smile, Vinnie rolled the window down. The police officer's unsmiling face met his. Vinnie was struck by the uniform. It was black, instead of the standard blue or khaki. And his age! The officer was at least as old as Vinnie. But the officer's hand was on his sidearm, so Vinnie wasn't about to start asking questions.

"Just looking for my registration, officer," Vinnie said. Oh Christ, the name on the registration wasn't going to match his license! He hadn't thought of that.

"Just your ID," the officer said.

What a relief! Vinnie worked his license out of his wallet and handed it through the window, the tension draining from his shoulders. The officer glanced at the license, and then flicked it like a Frisbee past Vinnie's nose. It cracked against the passenger side window. "Step out of the car, Mr. Bontecelli!" he barked. The voice was hard and commanding. Vinnie opened the car door slowly. In the three seconds that followed, he considered rolling onto the ground, grabbing his Glock and blowing this antique officer away. But from the corner of his eye, he saw the officer pull his revolver from its holster, and Vinnie's plan vanished in a drop of sweat.

"Face front! Hands where I can see them," the officer called from behind him. Vinnie stood and followed orders. "Now drop your weapons on the ground in front of you, Bontecelli!" Vinnie's eyes shot from the right corner of his lids to the left and back again. How'd this guy know he was armed?

"Now!" Vinnie jerked at the loud sound. Slowly he reached inside his coat for the Glock. "With your thumb and index finger only!" the officer shouted. Vinnie extracted the Glock in his two huge fingers like it was a mouse and dropped it noisily onto the gravel. "Now take your jacket off and throw it on the ground in front of you." Vinnie took off his jacket. His shirt was sticking to his chest. "Now roll your pant legs up to the knee." He did it. A car passed slowly, and for a moment Vinnie considered how ridiculous he must look. He heard the clunk of metal on metal. What was that?

"Back up three steps," the officer in black commanded. Vinnie stepped backward. "Stop! Move to the back of the Mustang and pick up the cuffs." This must be how officers who ride alone do it, Vinnie thought. His mind raced with potential escape plans, but not one of them was going to work with a revolver aimed at the back of his head.

"Cuff your right hand first." With a huge sigh, Vinnie complied. "Now lift your right leg and rest your heel on the back bumper."

"What?" Vinnie cried and glanced at the officer in the black uniform. He saw the barrel of the revolver trained on his head, and decided to stick his right leg out in front of him. He lifted it so his heel was on the bumper. He had to hop twice to steady himself.

"Okay, bend over toward your right knee and put your left arm under your leg," the officer said.

"I can't!"

"You can. You will! Take the other cuff in your right hand and slap it against your left wrist." Vinnie's gut prevented him from bending very far at the waist. After three attempts, Vinnie got his left hand near his right beneath his leg. He slapped the cuffs toward his left wrist until he finally heard the metal slide around it and click.

"Now lower your leg to the ground." When Vinnie's foot slid off the Mustang's bumper, he nearly pitched headlong into the ditch, but he caught himself as his hands slid up the back of his leg. He was bent over like the Hunchback of Notre Dame, and the metal between the two handcuffs was tight against his crotch. Extremely tight. "Now walk to the back door of the squad car." Vinnie tried to rise up and protest, but the metal between the handcuffs pinched him between the legs and he howled.

The officer laughed. "Back door!" The officer opened the rear door. Vinnie hobbled awkwardly to the squad car and got himself turned around for a butt-first entry into the back bench seat. Suddenly he felt knuckles on a strong hand explode against the top of his head and he was hurtling backward into the squad car. His head slammed into the edge of the roof and the cuffs tore at the flesh on both wrists and his crotch. He yelped like a scalded dog and cursed. "This is abuse!" Vinnie screamed.

"Call the cops," the officer smirked and slammed the back door. A minute or so later, the officer threw Vinnie's jacket and gun onto the far side of the driver's seat and dropped behind the wheel. He turned and eyed Vinnie through the full metal cage that ran along the back of the front seat and separated them.

"If this is about that Mustang, I ..." Vinnie began.

"Shut up," the officer said. He started the engine and made a U-turn and sped away on Route 60. The landscape became more and more remote, an occasional house here or there, but mostly woods. Thick trees, packed tightly together, lined the road. The surrounding forest was deep and lush. Soon there were no houses. There was nothing but dense forest and empty road. Vinnie felt the squad car slow. It turned right onto an unmarked dirt road. He craned his neck and looked out the back window. Route 60 disappeared in billows of dust behind the car.

"Where are we going, officer?" Vinnie tried to sound respectful, despite the urge to break the man's neck with his bare hands. The driver didn't answer. Twice more Vinnie broke the silence with the same question. No answer. The dirt road curved left, then right, and then left again. The squad car hurtled into the bowels of the woods. The road narrowed, and tree trunks whipped close by the back windows.

The squad car arced into another wide right curve and then slowed down. Vinnie sat forward again. The doom he had felt before was pressing on his mind and squeezing out rational thought. Then every thought stopped. Fifteen yards ahead he saw two men, one on either side of the road, dressed in black suits and broad-brimmed hats. Each was holding an AK-47. He recognized the men, known them for years. And in that moment he knew for certain that he was a dead man.

"So you work for the man, eh butt face?" he shouted toward the back of the officer's head. "How much he pay you to pick me up?" Silence. Even his taunts weren't getting to the guy. He was hoping either the respectful, or the hateful, approach would get his uniformed chauffeur to do something stupid and give Vinnie one last chance to get away. The squad car lost more speed and Vinnie lost more hope. Four identical black vehicles that Vinnie recognized were parked in front of a small log cabin. Mr. S had always insisted upon identical vehicles, and he always traveled in a pack. That way, anyone who was trying to waste him could never be sure which vehicle he was in.

Vinnie studied the outside of the cabin. It had to be at least twenty-five years old. There were two small stories and four perfectly square windows in front. It looked like a hunting lodge, the place where hunters brought their kills. Like now.

The back doors of the two vehicles directly in front of them opened, and Vinnie recognized the two men who emerged. The officer stopped the squad car and the two men opened the back car door. Vinnie looked into the sunglassed faces. He had known them for many years and considered them family.

"Hello boys," Vinnie said flatly. The black suit on the left called to the officer behind the wheel. "Chief, get those cuffs off him, will ya?"

The officer jumped from the front seat, fumbled with his keys and then leaned into the back seat. He unlocked Vinnie's left wrist and then his right. A half second after his right wrist was freed from the handcuffs, Vinnie landed a vicious fist of knuckles into the center of the officer's face. He hit him so hard that the officer flew from the squad car and landed on his back on the dirt road.

"Vinnie, was that necessary?" one pair of sunglasses said calmly. The other pair rushed to the officer. "Parker, you okay?" Both of Chief Parker's hands were over his face and blood was streaming through his fingers toward his ears.

"He broke my nose!" he howled.

"I'd break your neck off your shoulders if these boys would let me," Vinnie said.

"Easy Vinnie," the first set of sunglasses said.

"And I'd shoot the ass off your frame if Mr. Bente didn't want you alive!" Parker called, still on his back. "Somebody get me a towel. Something!" The second set of sunglasses dropped a handkerchief on his chest.

"Come on Vinnie," the first man said, "S wants to see you." Vinnie stepped over Parker. As he did, he dragged his back foot hard into Parker's ribcage, and the man on the ground howled in pain.

"Somebody kick him in the nuts!" Parker screamed. Vinnie knew it wouldn't happen. These boys hated cops as much as he, maybe more.

The sunglasses flanked Vinnie, and the three men walked in silence toward the cabin. The familiar smell of death was in the air. Often in the past thirty years, Vinnie had wondered when it would be his turn.

There was no porch, just cinder blocks beneath the front door. The roof was a single slant with dark shingles, and it bore a heavy coat of dried pine needles. The sunglasses stopped at the bottom step and Vinnie ascended to the door alone. On the top step, he stopped with his hand on the door. On the other side of the thick wooden door he would see his old friend and look into his steel gray eyes. For the last time. A thin smile curled his lips, but there was no joy in it.

Vinnie opened the door and stepped into the kitchen area. A small Formica topped table sat to his immediate right, surrounded by metal tubed chairs with torn plastic seats. To the left, just in front of the modest fireplace, he saw a large wooden table with a dark felt hat in the center of it. The man with perfectly groomed gray hair sat slightly to the right of the hat with his back to the door. He rose slowly and turned toward Vinnie.

He opened his arms and Vinnie stepped into them, kissing his long-time friend on both cheeks.

"Vincente," the older man held Vinnie gently by both shoulders. He was the only other person besides Vinnie's mother who was allowed to call him by his formal name. He insisted that everyone else call him Vinnie. With Emil Senior, it was different. Now, when he heard Emil speak his name, his eyes filled, and the overflow streaked down his tired cheeks. "Sit down next to me," Emil said, "and tell me what happened."

"You already know Emil," Vinnie said softly. "I've been with you thirty years. You know almost everything."

"That's what has kept me alive in this nasty business." Emil stroked the brim of the hat on the table. "I may know a few things already, but I want you to tell me. Tell me about my son." Vinnie heard his friend's voice crack and his eyes moisten.

"The other day, I was remembering the night he was born," Vinnie said, his eyes filling again.

"I was too," Emil said softly. He stared at the wood in front of him. "What happened, Vincente?"

"I tried my best to look out for him, boss. Honest I did." Vinnie rehearsed, detail by detail, the events since his cell phone call to Emil at the airport. Emil listened quietly and nodded, dabbing his eyes occasionally with a handkerchief. Vinnie wiped his eyes with his fingers and dried them on his pants.

Finally, Vinnie was at the point of telling Emil about the gas station. "I was filling the tank and Reverend Fields was in the bathroom. Emil had offered to go with him to stand guard. I waited and waited, and neither one came back to the car. I walked around the side of the station, saw blood coming from underneath the door, and ran to get the spare bathroom key." The words rushed from Vinnie's mouth. "I told the owner not to follow me, but he cussed me and followed anyway. I opened the door." Vinnie stopped, reliving it again. "And there he was, boss, on the floor. George must have stabbed him. But where he got a knife I'll never know! Anyway, Emil was dead, George was gone and the owner was shouting about calling the cops. And I panicked, boss. I never panic. You know me."

Emil nodded and blinked.

"It happened so fast," Vinnie said. "I shot him. I shot the owner in the back of the head. And then I ran back to the car and sped away. Honest boss, I was in such a mess in my head, I didn't even come to my senses for fifteen miles! By that time, I figured it was too late to go back and clean up methodically like you trained me. I hated leaving Junior's body back there like that. I can't stop thinking about it."

"I cleaned up for you, Vincente," Emil said. "It was a dangerous mess to leave behind."

"I know," Vinnie's shoulders slumped. "I'm so sorry."

"You put the Name at risk. It's not like you."

"I know."

"And. And," Emil's voice was rising, "you didn't even call to tell me."

Vinnie looked at the low ceiling. "I was angry with you." He was dead anyway. Why not tell the truth.

"Angry with me," Emil repeated. "Aren't you a little old for a temper tantrum?"

"Yes," he said quietly, "Please forgive me, Emil." He looked up, but Emil was not looking back at him. Vinnie continued. "But you kept saying I knew what to do. I didn't know what to do. And I didn't want to make a mistake with your son. I - I was so scared!" Vinnie wrung his hands in front of him. Sweat broke from his receding hairline and raced down his gray sideburns. He continued in a whisper. "He was bringing dishonor to the Name. But he was your son, Emil. How was I to know what to do? If it was anyone else, I would have whacked them nice and methodical like, and brought the body back to Connecticut. No mistakes. No trace." He paused. "It was Junior, boss. What was I to do?"

Emil stared in silence at the hat in the center of the table. Vinnie watched his face. He wondered if Emil knew of his plan to snatch the eggs from Brother Lawrence and disappear to the West Coast, and then out of the country. Vinnie's stomach flipped and a wave of nausea hit. He thought he might throw up. Vinnie had always said, always believed, that the

Shark knew everything. That's what made him so powerful, and so dangerous. Many had tried to deceive him. Some had tried to lie to his face. None had survived, and here I am, Vinnie thought, trying to be the first. The silence continued.

"So," Emil said, turning slowly toward Vinnie, "you say Reverend Fields killed my son." The gray eyes were searing, searching. Then his voice softened. "I thought you did it."

"No Emil. I thought you might want me to. Then I thought you'd never want me to. Then I didn't know what to think. In the end, I just ... couldn't."

Emil lowered his eyes thoughtfully. "Our location was bad, the spotter's vision obscured. We saw you pull the gun and fire two shots into the bathroom, and I assumed you had whacked them both. Our men heard two shots." He paused, tapping his fingers on the table. "What didn't make sense when we got there was that Junior had been stabbed, not shot. I couldn't figure why you would slit one man's throat and shoot another, why you hadn't just shot them both or slit both their throats. And the two shots..." Emil's voice trailed off.

"George did it," Vinnie repeated. "Didn't you see him leave the restroom? He must have had the knife. Did you see that?"

"No. We were watching the Mustang and we followed you with the scope when you walked to the restroom." Emil stood and walked to Vinnie. Awkwardly, he knelt until they were at eye level with one another. "I owe you an apology, Vincente."

"No, Emil," Vinnie started, but the older man held up his hand.

"I do. I pride myself on being thorough ... and careful. But I've made two mistakes. One was to withhold my counsel about Junior. I never anticipated the events that followed, so I didn't tell you what to do. I put you in an impossible situation, and I'm sorry old friend." He paused and stared into Vinnie's eyes. "The other mistake I made was to assume that my oldest and closest friend had killed my son. I put two and three together and forced it in my mind to be four. It was five, but I was blinded by anger and grief. He was my only son, Vincente." Emil's eyes filled again. "I'm sorry to have accused you." The two men fell into each other's arms and wept.

Finally Emil broke the embrace and struggled to his feet. "Reverend Fields. Where do you suppose he is now?" he asked Vinnie.

"I've no idea," Vinnie said, "but he was desperate to get the rock back from Brother Lawrence, so I assume he'll end up there."

"I'm counting on that," the Shark said, "I just learned that Hilary, Reverend Fields' wife, killed my grandson and may have killed my daughter-in-law too."

Vinnie gave him a blank look, and his jaw dropped. "Nina was pregnant?"

"Yes. You didn't know?"

"No," Vinnie said, leaning forward. "How did Hilary Fields-"

"She ripped the ventilator plug out of the wall in the ICU. The baby lost oxygen and died." Emil paced the floor along the edge of the table. "Hilary Fields would have been fish food by now if the Feds hadn't caught her in the act."

"How do you know all this?" Vinnie was wide eyed.

"I've people in Memorial Hospital."

"Hmm."

"And on the police force," Emil eyed him.

Vinnie nodded. "I met him, sort of."

"Parker. Chief of Police, First Precinct," Emil said. "A real pig, but he's done a good job slowing down the Feds."

"Sorry boss," Vinnie said, "I think I just broke his nose."

"I'm sure he deserved it. A real prick, Parker, but useful. He's arranging right now for Hilary to have an 'accidental' overdose of one of the medicines they're giving her in the county jail." He and Vinnie exchanged grins.

Vinnie was finally beginning to relax. "I'm so sorry for your losses, Emil. A son. And now a grandson."

Vinnie watched Emil's eyes harden to steel. "It won't go soft for George Fields." He slammed his fist on the table. "Or for his wife."

"What about Brother Lawrence?"

"He's the lamb."

"The what?"

"How do you catch a tiger, Vincente?" Emil's eyes flashed. "With bait! You tie a lamb in the jungle, and then you wait among the vines. When the tiger comes for lunch -wham!" Emil slammed his open hand flat on the table. "Our lamb is waiting in his house."

"With the eggs?" Vinnie asked.

Emil nodded. "Where can he go? And when our tiger arrives, I'll get the signal."

"The Vapor must be here," Vinnie said grinning. The Vapor was an elite team of "invisible" men, the Shark's underworld equivalent to the military's Delta force. Silent. Invisible. Lethal. No one but S knew when they arrived for an operation, or when they left. They would do their work and then evaporate. In all his years Vinnie had never seen them.

"All five." Emil's eyes sparked. Vinnie knew how much he loved the thrill of the hunt. "They don't do radios, so we've got a spotter on the hill receiving their signals and he delivers them personally to me. No radio intercepts. No miscommunications. No mistakes."

"You're the best," Vinnie said. "And the Feds?"

"Chasing their tails at the hospital," Emil said grinning. "We'll be back in Connecticut before their tires roll down Bingham again. All they'll find is an empty house."

"And the lamb?"

"He knows too much, Vincente. He and Parker get wasted on crack every night and share information. Secrets." Emil shook his head. "I'm afraid they'll both be going with us in the trunk of the car."

"We got enough bags?"

"Plenty."

"Can I whack Parker?" Vinnie asked.

"You can have Chief Parker and Brother Lawrence too, if you want him. Otherwise, I'll throw that bone to one of the boys outside."

The gray eyes fixed hard onto Vinnie's. "But the tiger is mine. I want to look in George's eyes as the life drains from them. I want to spit in his lifeless face."

Chapter Twenty-Five

Memorial Hospital
ICU

Captain Steele stared for a long second into Dr. Glaster's eyes. Then he glanced at Agent Ryan. "Could you excuse us for a minute, Dr. Glaster," he said. "I'd like to speak with Agent Ryan."

"Of course."

Steele took Agent Ryan gently by the elbow and steered her out in front of the curved counter. At the wall, he pressed the button and the two steel doors opened. He was silent until they were around the corner and into the hall. He stopped and looked intently into her face. "You smell something, Agent Ryan?"

"I'm feeling very uneasy, if that's what you mean."

"That's what I mean," Steele said. "What business is it of mine to be making decisions about Bente's medical treatment? I'm not next of kin. I've got no jurisdiction over the medical stuff."

"Dr. Glaster seemed so urgent to talk with you, Captain. You were the only one he'd speak with."

"I've got a bad smell in my nose, Ryan. You and Deet need to watch this doc, and anyone else who tries to distract me."

"Roger that, Captain Steele."

"And tell Dr. Glaster that I'm not going to let him take up any more of my time with stuff that doesn't concern me. No, don't tell him that." Steele ran his hand over the bristles on his head. Then he smiled. "Let's see. If he wants to dance, let's make it a slow dance. Let's let him think he, and whoever he's reporting to, has tied us up for hours. Tell him I need a few hours to be alone and think about which medical option is best for Mrs. Bente. After all, her life is hanging in the balance, and I want to give it the full attention it deserves."

Agent Ryan smiled. "I was the lead actress in all our college plays."

Steele extended his arms in front of him and clapped his hands together. "Action." Agent Ryan turned and rounded the corner to the ICU.

Steele pulled his right sleeve up. His watch read 4:46pm. Two more hours of daylight. He opened the cell phone and dialed his partner. The Lieutenant answered on the second ring. "Higgins."

"It's Steele. I smell fish. Meet me at the ER in five minutes."

"It'll take me ten, but I'm on my way," Higgins said. "I have a lot to tell you."

"No time now. I've got a call to make, stat!" He closed the cell phone and opened it again. He walked further down the hall until he was certain to be out of range of listening ears. He dialed headquarters and waited.

"Federal Bureau of Investigation," a man's voice said coldly. "How may I direct your call?"

"This is Captain Max Steele. Patch me through to the Deputy Director, Priority Red."

"Your pass code, Captain?"

"5-6-7-3."

"Give me a minute, sir." Steele paced two steps, turned and paced back two steps. He found himself pacing the same loop over and over - like a target at the shooting range, he thought. Finally, the voice returned in his ear.

"Patching you through to the Deputy Director." Another pause. "This is Charles Tyndale," a thick voice said. "Steele, you all right?"

"Never better, sir," Max said. "But we're advancing on the Bente Cartel and I've got people throwing spikes under my wheels."

"The Shark buys himself lots of help, doesn't he?"

"You wouldn't believe it, sir."

"I think I would," Tyndale said. "Watch your back. Bente's quiet as a mouse, but-"

"But he bites like a shark," Steele said, finishing the Deputy Director's sentence. "I'll be careful, sir. I'm calling because my gut is telling me we're closing in."

"How can I help?" the Deputy Director asked.

"It's a huge request, sir, but I believe I could justify it if I had time to explain. I'm out of time already."

"I trust your gut, Steele. Spill it."

"I need the Blackhawk, radio silence, dispatched right now to the helipad on top of Memorial Hospital in Kingstown. I need it stacked and staffed with specialists in full camo for a surprise visit."

"My God Max," the Deputy breathed. "You know we've only got one Hawk. And besides, that's a little drastic isn't it? How about a Chinook? We've got lots of those."

Steele lowered his voice. "Negative on that, sir. The Blackhawk's our only bird with a heat scope. I know what I need."

"I'm going to have to turn D.C. on its head." Steele heard the Deputy's chair creak in the background. "How soon you need it?"

"Ten minutes."

"Come on."

"ASAP, sir. These fish have slipped our net twice already. It could be our last chance."

"And if your gut's wrong? "

"I'll accept the demotion and the desk job," Steele said.

"My desk might be right next to yours." Tyndale said. Silence hung for several seconds. "I'll scramble the Blackhawk. Priority Red. I may have to go up the ladder for authorization."

"Oh, one more thing, sir."

"What now?"

"I need a squad on the ground to cut off the escape routes. Local police appear to be compromised, so I can't call them in on it." Steele thought for a moment. "Two manned Humvees from Groton ought to do it. Got anybody there who owes us a favor?"

"You lucked out," Tyndale said. "My roommate in college runs the place. Where do you want me to send them?" Steele relayed the area where they could wait for instructions. "I'll need a way to contact them."

"I'll patch them into the Hawk's pilot."

"Thank you, sir."

"Don't thank me yet. I'm not making any promises on the Blackhawk. If I can't get that, none of the rest of it will matter. Give me your cell number again and sit tight."

Steele repeated the cell phone number and closed the phone. He hurried to the elevators and pushed the down arrow. As he waited, he looked at his suit. He was not dressed for this party, and neither was Higgins. The elevator chimed and the doors opened. Max didn't even feel his feet step into the elevator. In his mind, he was already in the helicopter, holding the net, and waiting for the moment.

When the elevator door slid open, Max headed straight for the waiting room. He walked right by Dr. Sanchez without seeing her.

"Hey," Maria said.

Max's head snapped toward the sound, and he felt the muscles in his jaw relax. "Oh hi, Dr. Gorgeous." He smiled.

Maria cocked her head. "You looked like you were concentrating. What's up?"

Max's face went serious. "Maria, I'm in Priority Red."

"What's that?"

"Radio silence. Agent to agent communication only." Max paused. "I can't tell you any more than that."

"Okay," Maria said, "I don't understand, but maybe I don't have to. Sounds important."

"It is," Max said, "But so are you. I can tell you one thing." He leaned into her ear. "I think I'm falling in love with you, Maria Sanchez." He brushed his hand against hers. Maria's eyes sparkled at him. He turned without another word and walked through the Emergency Room doors to find Higgins.

He saw the young partner with the black crew cut standing outside on the walkway.

"Let's go," he said soberly and walked straight for the unmarked car.

Higgins followed. "Where to, Cap?"

"Shopping."

"I hate shopping," Higgins said and received a severe glare from his partner. As soon as both men were inside the vehicle, Higgins pulled the folded list from his inside jacket pocket. "Ready for the answers to your questions?"

"Yep. Let's go over those first, and then I'll brief you on our way to the store. What did you find out?"

"Let's see," Higgins looked at the list. "Question Number One: 'Was the precinct helicopter really in Wayland under repair?' Answer: It was in Wayland, but it was not under repair. It was fully operational ten minutes flight time away."

"Thought so," Steele said.

"Question Number Two: 'Why were the police cars ahead of our agent's vehicles when we threw the net behind Ecclesia Seminary? They were supposed to be backing us up.' Answer: The officers driving those squad cars said that Chief Parker told them, and our guys, that you gave the order for them to go first."

"My, my, isn't that interesting!" Steele said.

"Very. Question Number Three: 'What precisely were Chief Parker's instructions to the two officers who had been guarding Woodrow at Memorial and who were then dispatched to find him?' Answer: He told them to go to Ecclesia with lights and sirens. Said it would spook the rats from their holes."

"Yeah right!" Steele said angrily.

"Question Number Four: 'Did Chief Parker give any instructions to the lab about the fingerprints?' Answer: Parker told the lab to wait until all the evidence was gathered before any comparisons were done. Last one, Captain. Question Number Five: 'Are any vehicles, marked or unmarked, missing from the First Precinct?' Answer: One squad car. Number 19."

"Good sleuthing, partner." Steele shot Higgins an appreciative smile. "Any questions?"

"About Parker?" Higgins said. "No. An awesome piece of detective work, Cap."

"Over the years, I have learned to trust my gut more than my mind," Steele said. "It seems to know more."

Higgins started the engine. "Where to?"

"Army-Navy Surplus."

"You're kidding," Higgins said. "I love that store!"

"Thought you hated to shop."

"That's not shopping," Higgins said smiling. "That's accessorizing."

"That's what my sister said every time she came home from the mall," Steele said. Higgins looked offended. He turned left out of the Emergency Room parking lot and headed for Main Street.

"I had an extremely enlightening conversation with Sarah Stafford," Steele said. He went through a thumbnail sketch of the conversation, and then told Higgins about the Bente baby and the encounter with Dr. Glaston.

"Something the Deputy Director said brought it all together for me," Steele said. "He said, 'the Shark buys himself lots of help.' The hospital's probably littered with Bente employees."

"Same for the First Precinct apparently," Higgins said, "the Chief of Police being first on the list. God knows who else is on the take."

"Precisely why we aren't involving them this time. That's why I told you to be so careful about the way you asked questions of the officers. We don't want the fish to see us coming."

"So we're going for the Shark now?"

"Let's say we're adding him to our list. We know from Stafford that he was in New Hampshire. By now he could be back in Connecticut. But I'm not ruling out the possibility that he's nearby."

"The closer he is, the more dangerous it is for us fishermen," Higgins said, stating the obvious.

"That's why we're … accessorizing." Steele punched him lightly on the shoulder and Higgins smiled. Then Steele laid out the plan for his partner, including the Nighthawk, the Special Forces, the Humvees. By the time he finished, his partner had parked in front of the Army-Navy surplus store, had turned off the engine, and was staring in silence.

"Cap, you're not serious," Higgins said.

"I'm very serious." Steele's cell phone rang. He put it to his ear.

"Steele…. Yes sir. Yes sir. Terrific. Not with him, though. Thank you sir!" He snapped the cell phone closed. "Yes!" he shouted. "We got the Hawk! Higgins, let's pick up some camo and hustle back to the hospital. We're going fishing."

"I could figure most of that conversation," Higgins said, "but what was the 'not with him' comment about?" The two were walking through the entrance to the store.

Steele lowered his voice. "He said if we bag the Shark, it's two weeks in the Bahamas, and I said 'Not with him.' Meaning you."

"I figured that," Higgins said. "Frankly, Captain, I'm much more concerned about surviving until tomorrow than I am about sun bathing." Both men's faces had grown serious.

"I am too, Bert. It's an old trick you learn in the Bureau, though. Distract yourself with the ridiculous to keep yourself from being overtaken by the fear."

"In that case, I'll arm wrestle you for the plane tickets," Higgins said.

"You'll lose."

"That's ridiculous."

"You're catching on," Steele said. "Hurry up and get your stuff. We don't want to miss our ride."

At the rest stop just over the Rhode Island state line, George took the truck keys from Billy's hands as he staggered back from the restroom. Billy cussed loudly, insisting upon driving the rest of the way, but he was in no shape to put up a fight. George helped the old man into the passenger seat, slammed the truck door and ran around to the driver's side.

"First gas station we find, I'll get some more beer," he said to the man in coveralls. That seemed to pacify Billy. He grunted and stared out the window as George shot back onto the highway and hurried for Kingstown.

By the time he saw signs for gas stations at the exit ahead, the old man was snoring loudly beside him. George smiled and adjusted the ball cap carefully. Everything was coming together. He had expected to be dropped off at the intersection of Route 60 and Bingham and to have to walk back to Lawrence's house. Now George could drive right up to the gate, let Billy sleep it off happily by the side of the road, and George would have wheels to get back to Ecclesia with the eggs.

Perfect. Soon he would have Brother Lawrence by the throat, demanding that he give the eggs back, or die. But he'd need a weapon to convince Lawrence he was serious. A gun was out of the question. He'd never even fired one. Besides, people who sold guns asked a lot of questions. He couldn't risk it. He'd have to be more creative.

The miles ticked on the truck's odometer, but George barely noticed. In his mind he was mapping out a plan. The sun had disappeared behind the trees, and the gray dusk was encroaching as the first of the two Kingstown exits came into view. George took it. At the end of the ramp, he turned left. Route 60 was to the right, but the Home Supply was immediately to the left over the ridge. He headed straight for the large orange building.

He parked the truck at the back of the parking lot furthest from the entrance. He turned the engine off, grimacing, hoping it wouldn't wake his sleeping passenger. The snoring from the other side of the cab was rhythmic, and George relaxed. He would be quick, knew exactly where to find what he needed. He got out quietly and hurried across the parking lot.

Once inside he headed straight for the garden tools. He passed the shovels, rakes and sledge hammers. There! He grabbed the double-headed axe by its thick wood handle and hefted it in his hands. Excellent. On the shelf above, he grabbed a hatchet with a metal handle and a leather sheath. These two will chop more than wood. Grinning broadly, he made his way quickly to the checkout. Three minutes later, he had placed his weapons gently in the truck bed, and started the engine. Billy stirred, and George held his breath. But then the snoring began again in earnest, and George aimed the truck for Route 60.

Darkness fell thicker across the landscape. The truck's headlights were dim with age, and George found himself squinting. Thank the stars he knew where he was going. He'd been to Brother Lawrence's hundreds of times at night. He had even made it home from there stoned as a coot. George shifted in his seat. He'd been too long without the cocaine, and his body was complaining loudly. He gritted his teeth toward the windshield. A few miles up the road was more rock cocaine than he'd ever seen in his life, and it was all his! George could feel heat surge into his cheeks, and he pressed the accelerator.

At Bingham he turned right and slowed. The road ruts were deep and harder to see at night. Mailboxes at half-mast came into the headlight beams and then returned just as quickly to the darkness behind him. George wove his way slowly around the ruts. Sleep, old man. One big rut would wake him. He followed the angle of the dirt road into the thick wall of black trees and dense underbrush. The road narrowed and the ruts grew. George stopped. He was almost to the gate and decided to walk the rest of the way. He killed the engine and gently extracted himself from the truck, closing the door most of the way.

He stood by the truck bed, waiting for his eyes to adjust to the night. The air was still and cool, but George's face felt searing hot. He could taste the coke that lay less than two hundred yards ahead. His mind raged. It's mine, Lawrence. Give it back! He reached for the hatchet and tucked it into his belt at the middle of his back. Then he hefted the double-bladed axe from the bed. It was heavy. He ran his fingers carefully along the cold edge on each side. He should have bought gloves.

George listened. The only sound was his breath and his shoes against the hard dirt on the road. His eyes had adjusted enough to see the road ruts stretch in front of him, and George followed them to the metal gate. Far ahead in the distance he heard the faint popping of an engine. He stood still and listened. The engine noise faded, and George swung open the gate. He followed the thin gravel path to the clearing. Above him, Lawrence's A-frame was ablaze with light. Christ, Lawrence must have every light in the house on! The shades were pulled away from the windows, and the wall of glass glowed like a forest fire against the surrounding hillside. George hefted the axe in his right hand and adjusted the hatchet in his belt behind him.

The hatchet handle slapped against his butt as he climbed the railroad ties to the deck. He peered through the window. The kitchen on the right was empty. A fire burned in the fireplace. Then he saw him. Lawrence was hunched over the large oak coffee table that stretched between the couch and the fireplace. A large billow of smoke rose above the back of his round head. George cursed. He pushed through the gate and strode angrily to the center sliding glass door. He didn't bother to knock. He didn't even try to slide the door. With a loud growl, George drew the axe behind him in a wide arc and swung it like a baseball bat into the center of the door. Glass exploded into the house, spraying the length of the hard wood floor.

Brother Lawrence leapt to his feet, lost his balance, and fell onto his back on the couch. White hot embers from his crack pipe flew in the air and landed on his chest. He screamed and beat his flabby chest with both hands. George charged across the hard wood floor to the couch. He raised the axe and brought it down hard into the wood frame running the length of the back of the couch, just below the back cushions. The blade stopped a few inches above Lawrence's hip. Wood chips splintered onto his pants and Lawrence screamed again. George left the axe buried in the backrest of the couch and towered over Lawrence. He reached behind him, pulled the hatchet from his belt, and tore off the leather sheath.

"So Lawrence," he said, panting, "the last time we spoke you were talking pretty tough." George's eyes seared into his. "Not so tough now, are you?" He raised the hatchet over the friar's prone body.

"For God's sake George!" Brother Lawrence said. His voice fell to a whine. "Please don't!"

"Don't what?" George snorted, "Don't castrate you?"

"Put it down George," Brother Lawrence said, his voice a squeak.

"I don't think so," George said.

"We're friends. We can talk about this."

"Were," George said. "Past tense, you fat piece of shit. You're no friend of mine."

"Can I at least get up?"

George motioned with the hatchet, "That chair over there where I can see you." He raised the hatchet threateningly. Brother Lawrence rose slowly, his face twisted, beads of sweat popping from his forehead. He staggered to the brown cushioned chair against the right side of the fireplace and sat.

George followed him with darkened eyes. "You're the worst sort of sewer rat, Lawrence, you know that?"

"Look, I'll give you all the eggs, George. Jesus, just drop that hatchet and calm down."

"You're in no position to negotiate," George said, "or to tell me what to do." His voice rose angrily.

"I'm not telling you what to do," Brother Lawrence said, his tone whiney again. "I'm just asking you to stop threatening me with that." He pointed to the hatchet in George's hand.

"That's funny, Larry. Our last conversation ended with you threatening me. I seem to recall that you threatened to expose certain secrets and ruin me." He paused. "So it's okay for you to threaten me, but I can't threaten you. Is that what you're saying?"

"I'm saying don't hurt me."

"Too late for that, my fat friar," George grinned. "If I let you leave this house alive, you'll just threaten me again. Or worse. Get on the phone to the authorities." George's lips were thin, his eyes wild. "I don't see how I can possibly let you leave here alive."

"You have my word, George," Brother Lawrence said, rising from the chair. "I'll take our secrets to the grave. And here." He reached down the side of the chair and lifted a black backpack. "Here are the eggs. I smoked one of them, but the other thirty-four are in here."

George eyed the backpack hungrily. "Toss them to me."

Brother Lawrence slid the backpack through the glass on the hard wood floor. It slid under the axe handle sticking perpendicular to the back of the couch and stopped at George's feet. George picked up the bag and unzipped it. Brightly colored plastic eggs lay atop the grapefruit sacks in the belly of the backpack. They shone in the blaze of lights on the tall ceiling. George smiled at the precious orbs like they were jewels, and then he zipped the pack closed again. Lawrence was standing in front of the chair, fifteen feet away.

George eyed him. "So you want me to toss this away," he said to the chubby face fifteen feet from his, waggling the hatchet.

"Yes. Please George."

George raised the hatchet over his head and tucked it behind his neck. "Sewer rat!" he spat. He hurled the hatchet directly into Brother Lawrence. The blade split his chest at the breast bone. Brother Lawrence gasped and clutched at the handle. His mouth was open, horror in his eyes. "Oh God," he said. "Oh….." He fell forward. His chest hit the thick wooden coffee table and drove the hatchet head deeper.

"You were lucky, Reverend Fields," a voice behind George said calmly. George whirled to see a man with perfectly groomed gray hair standing on the glassless doorway. His black leather trousers hugged his slim waist and his black turtleneck clung to well-toned chest muscles. "Do you realize how hard it is to throw a hatchet and make it stick blade first into your target?" the man continued. "As a kid, I used to throw one for hours at a tree. I only made it stick a couple of times. Very impressive actually."

"Who are you?" George said, grabbing the axe handle and prying the head free from the back of the couch. His chest heaved like a bull about to charge.

The man in the doorway scratched his large hooked nose and stepped across the glass littered threshold. Seeming to ignore the question, he said, "Before you think about doing anything with that," the man pointed calmly to the axe George held in front of him, "I'd like you to look at your chest."

George glanced, gasped, and the man continued. "I'd like you to notice the three little red dots on your left breast. There are two more red dots on your forehead just above the brim of your hat. I'm certain I don't need to tell you what they are, or how foolish you would be to make any other choice than to drop the axe and sit on the floor."

The crack from the falling axe echoed in the vaults of the ceiling. George sat right in the midst of the glass, seeming not to even notice the shards. His eyes were wide and fixed on the silver haired man.

"You are to be commended for such a wise choice," the man said. "Now slide the axe away from you and push the backpack toward me." George kicked the axe away from him. When he grabbed the backpack, he hesitated. Then he looked down again at the red dots dancing on his chest, and cursed.

"Who are you?" he demanded.

"Your worst nightmare, Reverend Fields." He snapped his fingers loudly. "The backpack."

"They're mine." George shouted, but still tossed it toward the man's black boots. He ripped the ball cap from his head and slapped it on the floor.

The man in black lifted the backpack to his shoulder and walked slowly toward the fireplace. The flaming wood popped and sizzled.

"Do you believe in the Bible, Reverend Fields?" the man said, looking into the fire, his back to George.

"What kind of question is that" George said, watching the red dots.

"The Bible talks about an eye for an eye, a tooth for a tooth."

"That's just the Old Testament, "he said, irritated.

"I like the Old Testament. Don't you?" He turned and seemed to study George sitting on the floor. "I like the New Testament too. It talks about a day of judgment. Do you believe there will come a day when all of us will be judged for our deeds?"

"Not really," George said. He looked angrily toward the fireplace. "What more do you want?" he said. "You've got the eggs."

The man walked aggressively around the left end of the wood framed couch. His voice rose to a shout and trembled with rage. "I want an eye for an eye, Reverend Fields," he said, "and a tooth for a tooth. Your day of reckoning is today!"

"You're not God." George shouted back. "He's my judge."

"I am right now." The man's face was purple with rage. "I'm your judge." He walked to the wall of glass, crossed both arms over his chest and raised three fingers. Moments later, Vinnie appeared in the shattered doorway. His face was expressionless, his eyes hard.

George's head whirled toward the door, and his mouth fell open. "Vinnie! Who is …." He never finished the sentence as the horror of recognition spread across his face.

"Come in, Vincente," the man in black said, a mock smile curling his lips. Vinnie's massive shoulders nearly filled the empty door frame as he stepped through it. George could feel his hands and arms begin to tremble.

The man in black set the backpack on the floor and walked toward George. His black combat boots whacked against the hard wood floor and sounded in the rafters above. "Tell me, Vincente," he said, his Italian accent growing thicker. "Do you recognize this man?"

"Yes sir, Mr. Bente," Vinnie said. The words landed in George's ears like funeral music.

"Mr. Bente," George said, "I can explain-"

"Silence." Emil said, so loudly that the echo seemed to last several seconds.

George could feel his body tremble violently now. He looked around the room wildly. His eyes fixed on the axe.

"I wouldn't recommend it, George," Vinnie said, reading his thoughts.

"Vincente, would you kindly get that black backpack for me?" Emil said. Vinnie lumbered across the room and grabbed the backpack in his large hand. He brought it to Emil. "And now Vincente, would you please go to the kitchen area there and get me the largest bowl you can find." Vinnie returned with an enormous glass punch bowl. "Just put it on the floor in front of Reverend Fields." George's head snapped back and forth between Vinnie and Emil.

Emil dropped the backpack onto the floor next to the bowl. The plastic eggs inside clacked noisily against the shards of glass. He towered over George. "Open it," he said.

"What for?" George squawked. "You already know what's in there."

"Open it!" Emil said. Then more calmly, "Help him understand the importance of obedience, Vincente." In an instant, the back of Vinnie's huge hand landed viciously against the red gauze on George's forehead. George never saw it coming. He fell back onto the hard wood floor, screaming and holding his forehead with both hands.

"Sit up!" Emil said, "and open the backpack."

George forced himself to a sitting position. "You sadistic mother -" He never got the rest of the words from his lips. Vinnie landed another backhand across his forehead with such violence that George smacked the back of his head on the floor. Fresh blood oozed through the gauze on his forehead and also at the back of his head. He was screaming and crying and blubbering incoherently. He sat up, his right hand pulling a piece of glass from the back of his scalp.

Mr. Bente was grinning now. "Let's try again," he said. "Open the backpack, Reverend Fields." Still blubbering, George squinted through the blood running into his eyes and unzipped the backpack. His hands immediately returned to his forehead.

Emil looked at Vinnie and spoke quietly. "Towel."

In a flash, Vinnie returned from the kitchen with two hand towels.

"Reverend Fields," Emil said, "It would appear that tonight you have your own blood on your hands. That's a change of pace for you, isn't it?"

"I don't know what you're talking about." George spat blood as he spoke.

"Oh, but I think you do. But before we talk about that, I want you to count the eggs for me." He dropped the towels in George's lap. "Wipe your hands first please. Then take one plastic egg at a time from the backpack and place it in the bowl. Count them aloud for me."

With one of the towels George wiped the tears and the blood from his eyes. With the other, he wiped the blood from his hands. Then he extended a shaking hand to the backpack and pulled from it a brightly colored plastic egg with clear plastic packing tape around the middle seal. He placed it in the punch bowl. "One," he said.

"Very good," Mr. Bente said as if speaking to a first grader. "Keep going." The blazing lights from the ceiling bounced from the eggs and they appeared to glow. George continued to count the eggs aloud, placing each one noisily in the punch bowl. Soon the bowl was brimming with color. George stacked the last egg on the top of the mound.

"Thirty-four," he said. His hands reached for the towel again, and he wiped more blood from his face and eyes. He looked into the steel gray eyes of the man standing over him.

Emil pointed dramatically to the bowl of eggs in front of George. "Whose eggs are those, Reverend Fields?"

"They're mine," George said weakly, staring at the bowl.

"Wrong." Emil said. "They belong to my son. His wife went to Columbia to get them."

"His wife gave them to me."

"Ahh. I'm told that's not all she gave you." He looked at the hulking man standing next to him. "Help me, Vincente. Don't they call that adultery? Isn't that the word?"

"Yes, Mr. Bente."

"And isn't that forbidden by one of the Ten Commandments?" His tone was mocking, and menacing. "Thou shalt not commit -"

"I know what it says," George said into the towel. Hate raged through every fiber of his being. He'd kill Bente if he got the chance.

"You weren't acting like you knew what it said, Reverend."

"Just take the rock and let me go," George said.

"Reverend Fields, you need to understand something." Emil was leaning over George's shaking frame. "I don't give a fuck about the rock. What I care about is that you took it from my son, and you also took his wife. And then you took his life!"

"I didn't."

"You did." Emil shouted. "Vincente." His face was purple again. "Tell me who killed my son."

"Reverend Fields killed your son," Vinnie said calmly.

George glared up at him. "Rot in hell, Vinnie."

"You first," Vinnie said.

"And how did my son die, Vincente?" Emil was pacing the hard wood floor back and forth in front of George and the eggs.

"Reverend Fields stabbed him."

George began to struggle to his feet but Vinnie pushed him back to the floor, pointing to his left chest and wiggling his fingers. George looked. The red dots were still there.

"Stabbed him to death, you say?"

"Yes, Mr. Bente."

"So, Reverend Fields, what would justice demand?" Emil's eyes were cold steel. "An eye for an eye? Yes. A life for a life." He turned to Vinnie again dramatically. "Stabbed you say?"

"Yes," Vinnie said.

"Tell me, Vincente. Do you still have my son's favorite knife? The switchblade. What did he used to call it?"

"The Bic," Vinnie reached into his black trousers. His enormous hand returned clutching the white pearl handle. He handed the switchblade to Emil.

George gasped. "Please, Mr. Bente. Don't. I'll do anything."

"I heard pleas earlier in this room," Emil said, "from the man with the hatchet in his chest. It's astounding to hear them now from you."

George heard it before he saw it. The blade shot from the switchblade handle and glinted in the bright light.

George squealed and pushed his hands into the glass on the floor trying to back away from the blade.

"Vincente, get me the trash can from the kitchen." Vinnie hurried to the kitchen and returned with a large square can with a black plastic liner.

"Thank you, Vincente," Emil said. "Now Reverend, your friend Vinnie is going to count the eggs back into the backpack. He is going to take them one at a time, and count out loud, just like you did. You see, Reverend Fields, I'm taking them back from you. For my son."

George's face was twisted in terror.

Emil leaned close to his face. Hate looked at hate.

"And for every egg Vincente puts back in the pack," he said slowly, "I'm gonna cut a piece of your flesh and throw it in the trash!"

George's mouth dropped open, but before the scream could come out Emil had plunged the Bic to the hilt into George's left eye. Behind him, Emil heard plastic hit canvas and Vinnie's voice said "One." Vinnie heard George's eye splash against the black plastic lining of the trash can. George was flopping like a fish on a dock.

"This could take a while, Vincente," Emil said. "I've got ten fingers and ten toes to do after I finish with his eyes, ears and tongue. Then I'll still have nine more eggs to go."

"I've got all night, Boss."

Emil glanced back at him. "You said the exact same words to me thirty years ago, remember?"

Vinnie nodded. "The night they killed Mrs. Bente. The night Junior was born." Vinnie heard the splash of the other eye hitting the trash can liner. "You carved near all night."

"We sent their parts to their mommas by U.S. mail, remember?"

"Three," Vinnie counted. He heard another splash. George was still twitching on the floor. "Yeah. Where we gonna send Reverend Fields?"

"To the landfill," Emil was carving savagely on George's head. Vinnie saw him pause from time to time to catch his breath and to plunge the switchblade into George's body. For good measure, Vinnie thought.

Vinnie had just placed the tenth plastic egg in the pack when both men froze and listened. There it was again. The sound of a Carolina Wren called in the darkness. Emil grabbed a towel, pushed himself up from George's lifeless body, and hurried to the glass.

He watched the signals come from the forest. "Danger. Abort," Emil cursed. Vinnie started cramming the rest of the plastic eggs into the backpack.

"Bird," Emil said, still staring out the wall of glass into the night. "Bird?" Just then both of them heard it. Softly at first in the distance and then louder.

"Chopper!"

"Go boss," Vinnie shouted, zipping the backpack.

"The eggs!"

"I'll bring them"

"No. Give me the eggs," Emil said.

Vinnie tossed him the backpack, and watched him disappear into the darkness.

Vinnie grabbed the towel and wiped fingerprints with one hand. With the other, he drew his Glock. He had expected to have more time before the chopper got close, but it was on him within seconds. A strong beam of light flashed directly on him, and then began to throw light into the hillside behind the house and the woods below.

Chapter Twenty-Six

Blackhawk Helicopter

"Is this *the moment*, Cap?" Higgins shouted into his headset.

Steele nodded, his eyes like horizontal straight razors. "This is it! Throw the net."

"Yessir," the Special Forces officer on the heat scope shouted. "Don't y'all love the element of surprise? They're racin' around down there like roaches when the light comes on." Steele didn't know his name, but he had overheard others call him Tex. Now he knew why.

"How many we dealing with?" Steele called to Tex.

"Whole passel of 'em, sir. Still counting."

"Humvees are taking their positions," the Blackhawk pilot said into his headset. Steele adjusted his headset. "Roger that. Any way we can cut off the escape route? Is that meadow big enough to set down in, or can we at least get low enough to offload some personnel?"

"No problem, Captain." The Blackhawk swung away from the A-frame's wall of glass and leaned toward the meadow. It was so quick that Steele was sure he left part of his stomach back on the hillside. He shot a look at the special ops commander seated across from him.

"You've got the ball, Commander," Steele said.

"We got some sci-fi spooks in the sticks below the house, Commander," Tex said, his face in the scope. "We're gonna have to drop right on their saddles or we'll lose 'em on the ground."

"Who's in the mood?" the Commander called into his headset. All eight right hands went up from the men with painted faces seated in the back. Steele and Higgins exchanged puzzled looks. Must be some kind of internal team-speak.

"They've got a spotter on the hill," Tex said. Suddenly a large flash erupted from the hillside.

"Incoming," the co-pilot shouted and everyone braced. An explosion erupted in front of them. The Blackhawk shuddered and continued to hum.

"Low and left." The pilot's voice said calmly. Higgins slumped in relief beside Steele.

"With your permission, sir, let's offload in the meadow first and then engage the hillside."

"Roger that."

"One, two, and five," the Commander spoke calmly into his headsets. "Repel to the meadow. "One, you take your toys to the hill. We'll cover you after we drop the lads into their saddles." Steele saw several black helmets nod. Three men lowered night vision goggles over their eyes and attached their ropes on the spinners next to the open doors of the helicopter.

"Flash from the trees. Small arms fire," the co-pilot said. "The spooks are hostile."

The Commander watched three men disappear from the doors, sliding down their ropes and dropping into the meadow. The Blackhawk rose quickly. "Three, four, six, seven and eight, you're going to be dropping onto their heads. Word is these spooks aren't newbies. If they surrender, strip 'em and strap 'em. Then head for the house." He paused. "If they engage you, take 'em out. We want everybody back for the ride home."

"The Groton boys are in position at the end of both dirt roads," the pilot relayed.

"Remind them that the squad car is not ours," Steele said into his headset. "Don't let it pass."

"I'll tell them," the pilot said. "Commander, you want me at the tree tops in the flat?"

"Roger that," the Commander said.

"What's to keep the spooks on the ground from shooting these guys when they drop on top of them?" Higgins shouted into his headset, looking at Steele. Their matching gray and black camo disappeared into the darkness of the Blackhawk.

The Commander answered him. "Nothing, son. But this ain't their first rodeo, right Tex?"

"Like ropin' slow calves for these lads," Tex said.

"Small arms fire from the deck," the co-pilot called.

"I'm three seconds from tree level, Commander," the pilot said.

"Lock and Load," the Commander said into his headset.

"We're getting strafed!"

"Tex, pull off the heat scope and drop a few cow pies," the Commander said. "I'll light up your targets." Tex leapt to his feet and grabbed a sack filled with dark green grenades. The Commander lunged behind the large spotlight and switched it on again. Light crashed into the forest. Steele was amazed at how quickly Tex could pull the pins and how far he could throw them. Explosions below shook the Blackhawk and both Higgins and Steele grabbed the side bars to steady themselves.

With a loud pop, the spotlight went dark. "Jesus," the Commander said, jumping away from it, "Somebody down there's a good shot!"

"That was eight grenades in 12 seconds!" Higgins said to himself, but his voice was picked up by the headset microphone. His face was a mix of total amazement and fear. Always gathering data, Steele mused. Probably counts his farts.

"Latch and go," the Commander said.

"We're taking metal," the co-pilot said anxiously. "Oh crap, surface to air again from the hillside!"

"Steady," the pilot said, "This bird's got a hard butt." Steele heard a metallic scream nearby and then the hillside to their right flashed and boomed.

"Thank God the guy can't aim that grenade launcher," the pilot breathed.

"Help us retrieve the ropes," The Commander pointed to Higgins and Steele. All three men scrambled to the spinners.

Tex was back on the scope. "Missed every durned one of 'em," he said.

"But you gave them something to think about besides poking holes in the boys dropping on their heads," the Commander said into his headset. The ropes were gathered and the Blackhawk rose quickly and pivoted.

The Commander looked at Steele. "Ball's over to you, Captain Steel. My game's on the ground."

Steele stood and made his way forward. He saw tiny balls of fire spitting from the deck surrounding the A-frame's wall of bright glass.

"I've got a lock on the deck," the pilot said.

"Take it out," he said. A second later, he heard a loud hiss to the left and the right of him as a Hellfire missile from each side of the Blackhawk hissed toward the A-frame. They hit nearly simultaneously, and wood splinters flew into the air. The wall of glass fell in sheets and shattered among the wreckage of the deck. Two large balls of fire rose and thick smoke billowed from the top of them. The bright lights in the ceiling continued to shower thin beams of light through the smoke. Nothing moved on the deck.

Like a giant dragonfly, the Blackhawk pivoted in the air and sliced toward the hillside above the A-frame. "Waiting for orders, sir," the pilot said.

"Send them," Steele said. He heard two more Hellfire missiles hiss from the Blackhawk's sides. They slammed like huge orange snowballs into the crest of the hill.

"I think we poked their eyes out, Captain," the pilot said.

"Nice shot, Simpson," the Commander said.

"Thank you, sir. I got twelve left, if anyone's counting."

"We've got major hand-to-hand on the ground, sir," Tex said.

"How're the lads doing?"

"Hard to tell, sir, but these spooks are no pushovers."

"Let me see," the Commander said, shoving his face into the heat scope. He saw white, ghost-like figures wrestling and striking each other. To the right, he saw one figure stalking another. He scanned back left. Several bodies were no longer moving. He cursed. "If we knew who was who, we could help the lads out."

The commander pulled his face out of the scope and Tex took over again. When he returned to his seat, Steele saw the concern on his face. He looked up and caught Steele staring at him. He managed a smile. "My guys are good," he said into his headset, "very good. Let's check out the sheep."

He looked for approval from Captain Steele. "Roger that. Swing us around, will you Simpson?"

"Swinging, sir," the pilot's voice spoke through the headset. The Blackhawk pivoted like it was on a turnstile.

"Whoa!" Tex said, "We got a fellow on a mini-bike or somethin'. Lookit him go! Whoops, not anymore. Looks like the lads clotheslined him." He grinned. "That had ta hurt."

"Give us a slow 360, Officer Simpson," Steele said. "See any critters on the hillsides, Tex?" The Blackhawk spun slowly in place.

"That's a negative, sir."

"Okay, let's take a quick ride to the other side of the meadow and see if we can cut off the retreat. Then we'll come back and mop up."

"Roger that, Captain Steele," the pilot said. The helicopter shot forward. Within seconds they were over the log cabin.

"Machine gun fire from the cabin," the co-pilot said.

"Simpson, how many vehicles we got in front of the house?"

"Let me slow up and swing around." The Blackhawk banked sharply, and so did Steele's stomach. He wondered if he would be sick.

"I see one unmarked."

"That means there are three unmarked and one squad car on their way to the Humvees at the end of the road. Ask if they want our help."

"Are you serious?" the Commander said.

Steele could feel the embarrassment flush his face. "Guess they probably will, eh Commander?" he said sheepishly. He nodded. The pilot brought the Blackhawk around again and headed toward Route 60. In a matter of seconds, they were upon three unmarked vehicles racing toward Route 60.

"Humvees say help would be great," Simpson said. From the corner of his eye Steele saw the Commander smile.

"Small arms fire from the vehicles, sir," the co-pilot said. "Ahhhh!" All eyes shot toward the front of the helicopter. The co-pilot was holding his face with both gloved hands. Blood was spurting from his neck. The front windshield was peppered with bullet holes. The Commander rushed to the co-pilot. "Easy Frenchie," he heard him say as he applied pressure to the neck wound.

"Engage the vehicles, Simpson!" Steele said angrily. "These pukes are done."

"Roger that, Captain. Fifty caliber strafe?"

"Your call, Simpson."

"Negative, Captain. Yours."

"Sorry. Roger that, Simpson. 50 caliber." No sooner had the words gone into the headset than the Blackhawk shook with the kick from the two 50 millimeter guns mounted on the front. Steele leaned forward and saw the dirt on the road explode in straight rows toward the rear vehicle. Then the bullets hit the back of the car. It exploded into a fireball and struck a tree to the right. The guns never stopped. The straight lines ran up the road to the second vehicle. Another massive orange explosion engulfed the car in flames and it swerved sideways, blocking the road.

The pilot snorted into the headset. "The third car is speeding up. Thinks it's gonna outrun the Blackhawk." The 50 caliber machine guns rattled and the helicopter shook. Seconds later, Steele heard a massive explosion from the ground and saw the third car disintegrate before his eyes.

"Find the squad car," Steele called to the pilot. It didn't take long.

"Stopped on the right," the pilot said.

"Be careful," Tex called, "We got a heat signature crouching by the right front tire. He's pointing something big."

"Parker," Higgins said into his headset.

"Take him out," Steele said.

"Isn't he a cop?"

"Right now, he's a threat, Tex. Take him." The Blackhawk shook again and Steele saw the squad car burst into flames.

"The heat's runnin' up the road. Cowboy's on fire." The Blackhawk adjusted and jerked briefly.

"Eliminated," the pilot said.

"Woulda been burnt toast anyway," Tex said.

"Okay, turn it around and let's send greetings to the nice folks shooting at us from the house." Steele looked at the co-pilot. The Commander was still pressing the wound on his neck, and he was speaking softly to the man he had affectionately called Frenchie. Frenchie's chest was heaving and his eyes were rolling back in his head.

Steele knelt next to the Commander. He hated the mob. He hated every one of those bloodthirsty creeps who thought nothing of killing people to protect their illegal business interests. He wondered if, like his late partner, Frenchie had a wife and kids waiting for him to walk through the front door tonight. He watched the Commander close Frenchie's eyes with two fingers.

The Commander called into the back of the helicopter. "Tex, you okay?"

"Finer than a frog's hair, Commander," he said, but Steele could hear that the enthusiasm had gone out of his voice.

"Keep your face in the heat scope," Steele said. "I don't want anyone slipping this net!"

"Roger that, Captain."

Steele sat down next to Higgins. "You okay partner?"

"Sorry Cap. I lost it."

"Air sick? Or death sick?"

"Both," Higgins said. Steele put his arm around his partner's shoulders. Bert Higgins was so steady and competent, it was easy to forget how young he was.

The Blackhawk clipped through the night air. "Head to the trees in front of the house, Commander?"

"Roger that."

"No stragglers so far, sir," Tex called from the back. The helicopter slowed and passed over the thick trees where so many men had been struggling with each other just minutes before. Tex whooped. "Secure on the ground, Commander. We've got three strapped and prone."

"How many we got standing over them?" the Commander asked into the headset. It felt to Steele that everyone in the helicopter was holding his breath.

"I see three, sir," Tex said quietly.

"Head to the hillside, Simpson."

"On my way."

"No one sir. Hillside's clear. Wait," Tex said. "We got one strapped and prone on what's left of the deck and one standing over him."

"Good. Let's set down in the sheep pen."

"Roger that, sir."

"We got another one strapped and prone by the sheep gate, and two standing over."

Steele did the math in his head. He was sure Higgins had too. Six returning.

"Let's go see which fish we caught," Steele said into his headset.

The Blackhawk was coming to rest gently in the middle of the fenced in area, and terrified sheep were racing for the perimeter.

"Simpson, radio the Humvees to move in and assist us in the mop up and transport," Steele said. "And call fire and rescue and the coroner's office." He looked up. "Got a flashlight in here, Commander?"

"Yes sir Captain." He handed one to Steele and one to Higgins.

They jumped from the side door to the ground. The massive blades were slowing above their heads. Steele walked quickly across the meadow to the gate closest to the house. Two of the special operations personnel he had sat with in the back of the helicopter were there, standing over a man face down on the ground, his hands drawn behind him with a plastic cinch strip.

"How was the fishing, boys?" Steele said soberly. "Heard you clotheslined this one. Tex was pretty excited."

"Tex is always excited," the man on the left said.

"Yanked him clean off that black ATV over there," the man on the right said proudly. Steele's mind was blank, his emotions flat. He couldn't even get excited about flipping the man over. He stood in the darkness, smelling the smoke and watching the flames lick both sides of the A-frame. He flicked on his flashlight.

"Roll him over." The two men took the struggling man by his right arm and tried to flip him onto his back.

"Can't sir," the one on the right said, "He's wearing a backpack." The pack was black and Steele hadn't seen it. The zippers flashed in the beam.

"Get it off him," Steele said. The two soldiers had to undo the strap on each side, but finally managed to slip it off his back. Steele heard a clacking sound inside and his heart began to beat faster. "Let me see that!" He grabbed the backpack and unzipped the top. When he aimed the flashlight beam inside, he shouted. "Yes!"

"What?" Higgins said. Max passed him the backpack. "See for yourself." When Higgins looked up again, his face was beaming. "Eggs!"

"Now flip him over," Steele said. Both his and Higgins' flashlights were trained on the face as it came into view. Steele dropped his flashlight and hugged his partner. Tears shot from his eyes. "It's the Shark, Bert." he whispered. "We got the Shark." The man on the ground growled something in Italian. Steele broke from his partner's arms. "Don't let him out of your sight!" he said to the two special ops men. "Guns trained on his head at all times. And hang on tight to this." He handed the backpack to the soldier on the left.

"Come on," Steele said, dragging his partner up. "There's another one up here." They were both out of breath by the time they reached the special ops soldier guarding the man on the deck. The man on the ground was large, and his leg was bleeding. Steele flipped him over and flashed the beam in his face. He screamed and leapt into the air. It was too good to be true!

"Bontecelli!" Higgins yelled. "It's Vinnie Bontecelli."

"I'll see you assholes dead," Vinnie roared. "Dead!" Steele heard the scream of sirens growing louder in the distance.

"I don't think so, Vinnie," Steele said. He turned away from Vinnie and started back down the steps. Higgins walked silently beside him.

"The Shark," Steele whispered to himself.

"Number One and Number Three in the net, Captain," Higgins said. "The Cartel will crumble without them."

Steele reached the bottom step and flopped down hard. He began to sob. "This one's for you, Bull," he choked, seeing his former partner's face again.

Higgins sat quietly beside him. "These fucks'll never rob another wife and kids of their father," Higgins said. "This is the net they will never wriggle out of."

Steele nodded and wiped his nose on his sleeve. He would call on Bull's widow tomorrow.

"I'm sorry," Higgins said, straightening up and raising his voice slightly, "but I'm just too damn tired to arm wrestle you tonight!" He grinned at his partner.

"That means you forfeit," Steele said, wiping his eyes and smiling into his new partner's face.

Epilogue

Memorial Hospital
Room 316

"When I get back to Ecclesia, I'm going to tell everybody that I've been sleeping with Sarah Stafford for a week," Terry said, grinning from his hospital bed.

Sarah was in the middle of a stretch, having just returned from the bathroom. She adjusted her lime green gym shorts and tucked in the T-shirt she had "borrowed" from Terry's drawer.

"You go right ahead, Mister," she said "There's not a soul in the seminary who'll believe you."

"I won't mention that you've been on the cot over there, and I've been in traction over here." His right leg was elevated and encased in a compression brace.

Sarah leaned over the bed and kissed him on the lips. "I'm going to tell everyone that my knight in shining armor protected me from a murderer." She glanced toward the sink. "I must look a mess."

"Not to me," he said.

Sarah padded to the mirror and ran a brush through her blonde hair. She banded it in a ponytail and returned to the cot, sitting cross-legged on it. "How's the leg?"

"Only hurts when I think about it," he said. "Wonder how they'll take our news."

A knock at the door turned both of their heads. Dean Tittle poked around the door. Sarah noticed immediately that his face was clean shaven and that his thin hair was carefully combed.

"Mind if we come in?" he said.

"Please," Terry motioned to him from the bed. Dean Tittle opened the door wide. His khaki trousers were clean and his white shirt was pressed. "I've brought a friend with me," he said. "Sarah and Terry, I'd like you to meet Nettie Spruill."

"We've met. Hi Mrs. Spruill," Terry said.

"Mrs. Spruill is one of our neighbors," Dean Tittle said. "I looked in on her during her few days in the hospital. We discovered we have a lot in common." He pulled the two vinyl covered chairs to the end of the bed. He and Nettie sat next to each other.

Nettie looked past Sarah out the window. "We both lost someone we loved." She glanced at Jeremy and smiled. "It's nice to have a friend who understands what you're going through." Jeremy returned her smile.

"How's the leg, Terry?" Jeremy asked.

"Doc says I'll be out of this bed in ten days and starting physical therapy in two weeks. By summer, I should be running next to Sarah again."

"It's going to take time," Jeremy said. He looked thoughtfully at his hands. "We're all recovering in one way or another."

Terry's bright smile faded. "How's Nina?"

"We just came from the ICU," Nettie said. She looked at Sarah, "Nina was my tenant." She paused. "She's still in critical condition…. but the baby died." Sarah sucked in her breath and her eyes filled.

Jeremy shook his head sadly. "So much death."

Terry tried to rise up in the bed, winced, and fell back against the angled mattress.

Jeremy continued. "I spoke with Captain Steele early this morning. He said that last night they captured the number one and number three men in the Bente Cartel. They found body parts of the Number One's son in the trunk of a car that was blown up. It's the biggest takedown the Bureau has had in a decade, apparently." Jeremy looked into each person's face. "In the process, they discovered several other dead bodies - George Fields and Brother Lawrence among them."

Silence hung like a pall.

"There's so much to tell you, Dean Tittle," Sarah said softly.

Terry nodded. "About all that's happened and about our news."

"News?"

With considerable effort, Terry sat up in bed. "I'm withdrawing from Ecclesia."

"And so am I," Sarah said.

"But," Dean Tittle said, "if it's about ..."

Terry cut him off. "It's not because of getting assaulted by the Assistant Dean, if that's where you were going. It's really not. Sarah and I have been doing a lot of talking and soul searching. Near death experiences will do that for you."

Terry adjusted himself in the bed. "Truth is that the ordained ministry just isn't for me. There is a disconnect between what would be asked of me, and the authentic me. I'm here because I come from a long line of ministers. But I cannot live someone else's life. I have to live my own. I don't want to be a minister, and I never have.

"Plus, I've seen what the church has done to my father and my uncles. Everyone in the church looks to them and their families to set this impossible standard of a pure life. We have to be perfect. And so from the very start we try to live up to this impossible standard and when we can't, we begin to compromise our integrity. We become what they need us to be. We hide our flaws, become frauds. Ironically, we become the very hypocrites that people can't wait to call us when we're exposed. Then it's easy to be scapegoated and run out of town in disgrace. I've seen it my whole life and I want none of it."

"And my issue, Dean Tittle, is on a systemic level," Sarah said. I'm not saying ministry isn't for me, only that I need a year or so to think things through about how to respond to God's call in a way that fits the real me. There's so much to think through, to pray through." Sarah took a deep breath.

"I know I can be honest with you, and honestly my questions don't negate my call, but they've got me slowing myself down. For instance, what makes me so uncomfortable is that right from the start as an ordained person, the church asks us to teach others as if we have God figured out. We're supposed to know who gets to heaven and how. We know what's good, what's bad, how to get blessed and how to be good. We've got God in a nice, neat package that the church expects us to deliver to the people. But in reality we don't know for sure. We leave seminary with more questions than when we came in. But we have to act like we've got all the answers. Our God is the right God, and you need to buy from us. But what if God is bigger than that? What if God is bigger than one denomination, or even one religion? I cannot go forward with integrity having these kinds of questions."

Dean Tittle was quiet for several moments. Then he rose and moved to the window. When he spoke, it was as if speaking to the world outside. "When I was a young man, I had the courage of my convictions. I was a wild mustang idealist filled with passion. I would reform the church. But then as water laps the edgy rock again and again, year after year, until it's worn smooth, I lost my edge without ever noticing its passing. There were pews to fill, budgets to meet, boards to satisfy and then to chair."

He turned to Terry and Sarah. "How could I not sense it in my spirit that something wasn't right with my Assistant Dean, but not have the character – the guts – to do anything about it, except delay my retirement?"

"It's hard to do the best thing all of the time," Terry said. "As my father always says, 'Thou shalt not should thyself.'"

"Perhaps," he said. "And perhaps it's time for me to submit my own withdrawal letter. See if we can get some edginess back in this seminary."

344

"Maybe you've worked hard enough, long enough," Nettie said.

Terry held up a finger, "But maybe you are God's man to set a new direction, and oversee the hiring process, so that the next chapter in Ecclesia Seminary's life will be an inspiration to all. What if you have been through all of this … in order to rise as the lightbearer. Set it in motion, and then retire and leave it to flourish."

Jeremy stared hard at the young man in the hospital bed, then moved to his side. Taking his hand, he said, "You may not be headed into the ministry, but I know a prophet when I see one. Your words are God's word to me. Thank you."

Nettie smiled at him. "Sounds like an adventure, Jeremy. Perhaps I can help."

She turned to Sarah. "Now Sarah, I was thinking about how much help I'm going to need around the house and in the garden, and I wondered if you would consider coming to live with me. Room and board would be free, and you'll earn two hundred dollars a week."

"You don't look like you're going to need that much help," Sarah said suspiciously.

"Maybe, maybe not," Nettie said evasively. "But you would also be there to look after the house should I … ever care to travel."

"My goodness," Terry said, smiling, "you two have been busy." His eyes jumped from Nettie to Jeremy. Sarah got up, bent over Nettie's chair and put her arms around her. Then she did the same to Jeremy.

"Well, Nettie and I have to scoot," Jeremy said, gathering himself. "Lunch awaits." He approached the bed. "I respect you both, and your decisions. Once you heal, what's next?"

Terry looked at Sarah, then back at Jeremy. "My plan is to grow more spiritual and less religious."

Dean Tittle nodded. "Solid plan. But don't quote me on it."

Room 316 (an hour later)
"You're under arrest."

All heads turned toward the hospital room door where a grinning Max Steele stood in a golf shirt and khakis. Next to him, Maria Sanchez smiled. She wore a yellow sundress and sandals.

"That's not funny," Terry said, grinning.

"I thought it was hilarious," Sarah said, laughing. "This time around."

After the handshakes all around, Dean Tittle said, "Sounds like you dealt a crippling blow to the cocaine industry last night, Captain."

Max shook his head. "Yes and no. It's like a hydra. Cut off its head and several more grow back in its place. That's what's got Vanessa so furious, so stuck in her rage and pain."

"Vanessa?" Nettie asked.

"Bull's wife - my former partner, Nate's wife. Bull was murdered by the Bente Cartel. We just left her to come here. She's hostile and I don't blame her. Said Bull's death didn't count for a thing. My avenging his death didn't either. And in one sense she's right."

"So sad," Terry said.

"Yeah," Max said. "What she doesn't get is that's not why we take these guys down. In the end, we do it because it's who we are. It's what we do."

There was a knock at the door, then it opened and two men in plain suits stepped inside and walked quickly toward Max. At that moment, his cell phone vibrated and began to ring.

"See you outside, sir?" one suit said. "Urgent."

"Of course," Max said, and hurried to the door with them. Once in the hall, he whirled on them, "Don't tell me…. Don't even say it…."

"Sir, Emil Bente has escaped-"

THE END